THE SERIOUS KISS

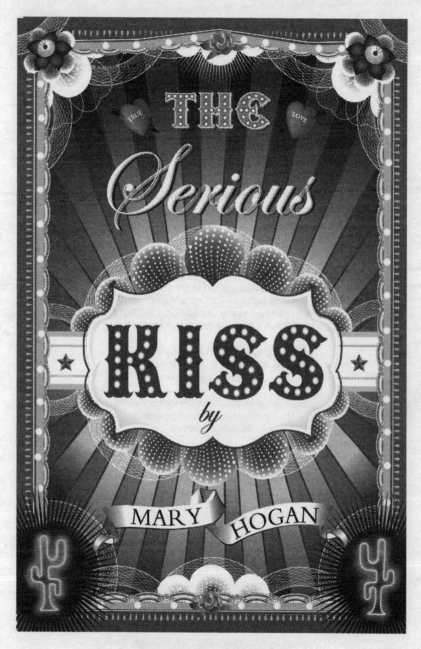

THE Serious KISS

by

MARY HOGAN

SIMON AND SCHUSTER

Acknowledgements:

First, thank you, Mom and Dad, for being
nothing like the parents in this story!
My deepest gratitude also goes to the seriously
talented people who helped create this book:
Venetia Gosling, who taught me how to speak 'English';
Amanda Maciel, for her wit and insight; the agent of any
writer's dreams, Laura Langlie; and Deborah Jacobs from the
Scripps McDonald Centre for Alcoholism and Drug Addiction.
Love and endless thanks . . . etc.

SIMON AND SCHUSTER

First published in Great Britain in 2005
by Simon & Schuster UK Ltd, a Viacom company.
First published in the United States in 2005 by
HarperCollins Children's Books, a division of HarperCollins Publishers

Copyright © 2005 by Mary Hogan
Cover illustration © 2005 Fiona Hewitt
www.maryhogan.com

1 3 5 7 9 10 8 6 4 2

Simon & Schuster UK Ltd
Africa House
64-78 Kingsway
London WC2B 6AH

A CIP catalogue record for this book is available from the British Library.

ISBN: 1 416 90140 X

Typeset by SX Composing DTP, Rayleigh, Essex
Printed and bound in Great Britain by
Cox & Wyman Ltd, Reading, Berkshire

For Bob Hogan,
who makes it possible for
me to do what I love

PART ONE
Chatsworth

ONE

My dad drinks too much and my mom eats too much, which pretty much sums up why I am the way I am: a knotted mass of anxiety, a walking cold sweat. Three weeks ago, when I entered my fourteenth year of existence, I realised the only stable, solid truth in my universe: Being me isn't easy.

"Dinneroo!" Mom yelled down the hall like she always yells down the hall each night as she comes home from work. Her perfume instantly gave me a headache. The slamming of the front door and the jingle of her car keys woke Juan Dog. *Yip. Yip.*

"In a sec!" I yelled back, but I didn't move a muscle. Dinner scares me. In fact, *all* meals and most salty snacks freak me out. They trigger an inner horror movie: *Attack of the Killer Fat Cells.* It's not that I hate food. I *love* it. What's better than hot bread slathered in melted butter? Or, Doritos with an extra blast of nacho flavour? My mouth is watering just thinking of it. But, given my genetics – Mom's size has never even come close to my age and Dad wouldn't need *any* padding to play Santa Claus – I realise that letting my guard down, even once, is an invitation for my fat cells to puff out like blowfish. I'm definitely *pre*-fat. And food is simply too hard to control, too easy to send your

3

whole life careering out of control. So, when Mom called me for dinner, I ignored my growling stomach, lifted the phone back to my ear, wiggled my shoulder blades into the comfy warm groove of my bed, and kept talking to my best friend Nadine.

"So what'd *he* say? Then what'd *you* say? Uh-huh. Then what'd *he* say?"

Through my closed bedroom door I heard one of my brothers playing with his Game Boy. "Get him! Get him! Get him!" I smelled the Mackey D fries Mom had brought home.

"Dirk!" Mom yelled. "Dinnerooney!"

My eleven-year-old brother, Dirk, is three years younger than me, but light-years from maturity. He's not what you'd ever call a high achiever. He's forever stalling for time, saying "Huh?", scratching his nose, and slurping back the pool of drool that builds up behind his hanging lower lip. Juan Dog the chihuahua is almost my age, which, in dog years, means he's like ninety-eight. Juan is what you'd call highly-strung. He yaps so much he levitates his tiny, quivering body all the way off the floor.

"Dirk!" Mom shouted. "Shake your *fannywannydingo*!" Did I mention my mother adds cutesy suffixes to words? She thinks it's youthful and snappy. I happen to know it's too embarrassing for words. One time, about a month ago, she called Juan Dog's business a *poopadilly*. Outside – in front of everybody.

Mom pounded on my bedroom door. "You still on that thing?" Like she hadn't clicked in on the extension twice already. "Dinner's on the table."

4

"I'll be off in a minute!" I said. Then to Nadine: "So what'd *he* say?"

"Rif!" Mom screeched. "Where the heck is Rif?"

That was a no-brainer. Rif, my sixteen-year-old brother, is never around. He hides cigarettes in the tight curls of his ash-blond hair. When no one is in smelling distance, he lights up, takes a long slow drag, then smothers the end with two spit-wet fingers and tucks the cigarette back into his hair.

"Who needs a nicotine patch?" he says. "I got my own method." Whatever that means. One time, about a year ago, the right side of Rif's head started smouldering while he sat in the family room watching MTV. Mom was like, "Call the fire department!" Dad was like, "Isn't there a football game on?" My parents have never seemed like they belong together. And I've never, ever felt like I belong in this family.

"Now, Elizabeth," Mom pounded my door one last time. I groaned.

"I gotta go, Nadine," I said into the phone. "E-mail me later?"

"Yeah. Later."

I hung up, fluffed my flattened hair, and walked down the hall to the kitchen. Rif slithered in behind me, smelling of burned hair gel.

"It's *Libby*, Mom," I said, rolling my eyes.

"Whatever," she said, rolling her eyes right back at me. Mom shoved a stray strand of her cottony overbleached hair back into the cat fight she calls a hairstyle. She tugged on her too-tight orange skirt, applied a new layer of magenta lipstick over the faded old one, removed black eyeliner goop from the corners of her green eyes, and tottered around the kitchen on spiked heels way too high for a woman of her age and heft. I'm not talking stare-at-you-in-the-mall quantities of fat, but my mother definitely hasn't seen her feet, or how sausage-like they look shoved into those strappy high heels, for quite a while. It's hard to believe I came out of this person. My hair is long and brown and shiny. My eyes are blue. I've never worn any make-up, unless you consider Vaseline lip gloss.

My brother Rif once graded my looks a "C."

"Who asked you?" I asked, visibly hurt.

"What's wrong with a 'C'?" he protested. "It's average!"

Which hurt even more. Who wants to be *average*? Mom stepped in for support.

"With a little makeover, honey, I'm sure I could turn you into a 'B'."

Like I said, being me isn't easy. Isn't your own *mother* supposed to think you're an "A" even if you're not? While I'm at it, aren't your parents supposed to set a good example? I'm not saying that my mom and dad are *bad* influences – it's just that they haven't exactly set the family bar very high. I can't remember the last time I saw my mother pick up a book or my father put down the remote control. Mom's idea of the perfect family vacation is Las Vegas, primarily for the cheap all-you-can-eat buffets. Dad dreams of staying home alone with several six-packs while we all go somewhere that has no cell service. Once, he actually said to me, "You know what the worst thing about having kids is? They're always *there*."

Of course, I took it personally. Rif is *never* there and Dirk is still young enough to be ignored. I asked my dad, "Where do you expect me to go?" but he just shrugged and turned up the volume on the TV.

Mostly, it feels like my parents are the kids and we are left to raise ourselves. I mean, they provide food and shelter, but that's about it. Mom and Dad have too many problems of their own to bother with silly stuff like grades, parent-teacher conferences, nutrition, or helping me figure out the difference between maxi and *super* maxi pads and do I need wings?

The other night, as Dad and I watched the Discovery Channel's exploration of the nature-versus-nurture debate, I had a disturbing revelation. My inherited *nature* is filled with the potential for addictions, a butt the size of Texas, chronic self-absorption, word butchering, a fluorescent wardrobe, and truly hideous hair. As for nurturing, well, in my family "nurturing" is mostly edible. Last year, when I was upset that Nadine got into Honours English and I didn't, Mom baked me a tray of brownies and gave me a get well card. She signed it "Luv, Mom," which made me pretty sure she didn't get into Honours Spelling.

That night, it became sickeningly clear that both nature and nurture were conspiring against me. What a rip-off! I have to overcome *Creation* if I want a normal life.

Beside me, on the couch, Dad burped, as if Creation were in total agreement.

I couldn't wait for the programme to end so I could launch a searing discussion about how my dad could become a better role model, but he was already snoring by the final credits, and his undershirt was jacked up revealing a very hairy belly button. Somehow I knew, even if he were awake, he'd snore through my discussion and it would be about as successful as the hundreds of times my mom asked him to stop guzzling beer.

That night, I was forced to face the upsetting fact of my fourteen-year-old life: I'm on my own. It's up to me to create the life I want. I can't leave it up to chance any more than I can eat two slices of Domino's Pepperoni Feast pizza and *hope* my body doesn't notice the five hundred and thirty-four calories and fifty-six grammes of carbs. I must be mistress of my destiny or I'll never even skim the surface of normal. I'll never have a boyfriend or a cool job or a passport with exotic stamps in it. Most of all, I'll never experience the one thing I want most: true love.

I knew exactly what I had to do. And that's when the whole fiasco began.

It was originally Nadine's idea. Maybe it was mine. We're like that, the two of us. Our brains are the right and left hemispheres of one consciousness. She's confident; I fake it. But I can't tell you how many times we've hatched the exact same idea at the exact same time. So, really, it's hard to say who thought of it first. The Serious Kiss popped into existence somewhere in the air between our two heads, right at the beginning of our freshman year.

"You know what I want?" Nadine had asked. We were lying on two blow-up Lilos in the centre of my dirt-flat backyard, tanning our legs. We'd both turned fourteen at the end of the

8

summer, and were evaluating our lives with the wisdom that comes with maturity.

It was the first Saturday after school started. Already I was feeling majorly inadequate. I mean, Carrie Taylor spent a *month* in Greece with her family on some boat (she called it a "yacht") and had the smoothest honey-brown tan I've ever seen. I heard she used olive oil instead of Coppertone, but my mom said, "No way, *daisyfay*," when I tried to sneak ours out of the kitchen.

My own best friend, Nadine, was looking amazing, too. She'd grown taller, slimmer, and blonder over the summer. We've been best friends since she was short, chubby, and bicycled around our neighbourhood with a hacked-up haircut her mother created with the Flowbee she bought on eBay. Now, Nadine's long, straight, much-blonder-than-mine hair is professionally trimmed. When she runs, her hair gently sways side to side like a hula dancer. She's a really good soccer player, too, one of those "natural athlete" types. At school, Nadine wears cream-coloured yoga pants and little tees and always looks effortlessly pulled together. When I attempt a similar outfit, I look as though I forgot to change out of my pyjamas. There's no way you can fake being a "natural" athlete. I've tried. Nadine just laughs.

"Maybe you should stick to basic black," she says, grinning, "to reflect the angst of your soul."

Somehow, Nadine bypassed black angst, along with chin zits and buck teeth and other teen horrors. She's the kind of girl who radiates health and makes you smile just looking at her, like you *know* she's nice. Which she is.

9

Me, I'm forever trying to raise my body-point average past, well, average.

Now and then, I wonder if Nadine and I would be best friends if we hadn't been best friends since we were kids who lived two streets away from one another. Does our connection have more to do with geography than chemistry? All I know for sure is, I don't want to put it to the test.

"You want NASA to invent ice cream that makes you weightless," I said to Nadine, letting humour camouflage my jealousy.

Nadine laughed. "Yeah, that, too." We both reached for our lemonades at the same time and sipped from bendable straws. "But you know what I *really* want?" I knew. Of course I knew. I sighed. "Me, too."

"Wouldn't it be nice?"

"*So* nice."

"What do you think it feels like?"

Leaning back on the rubber pillow of my Lilo, I tried to imagine it. The "it" we were both talking about, of course, was the *big* IT, the IT supreme: Love. I'd pictured true love before. It was full of colour, light. Pink feathers and turquoise ribbons and gold-leaf swirls that flickered in the sun. And it was cool, too, a blanket of satin, air-conditioning that never gave out and wasn't too expensive to run all summer, even at night. Love was soft and smooth and beautiful. Nothing like our cruddy old beige stucco house in Chatsworth, California, that sat smack in the centre of town like a steaming burrito in the hottest part of the hopelessly suburban San Fernando Valley.

Nothing like this yard that had started out as prickly weeds and was now nothing but dry, dusty dirt.

"Why bother planting anything?" Dad had said. "We're the only ones who will see it."

Like we don't matter, and it's only important if other people see it.

No, love was nothing like that. Real love was alive and vivid and out there for everybody to see.

"I think love feels like coming home," I said, adding, "if you actually like where you live."

Nadine laughed again. She always laughed at stuff I said, which made me feel wonderful.

"I think love feels like . . . like . . ." Nadine paused, looked over at me, then we both said the exact same thing at the exact same time: "Love is a serious kiss."

"Yes!" I said. "A *real* kiss. Not some slobber session beneath the bleachers."

"Not some stupid lap-dance kiss in somebody's basement."

"Not a fake kiss just 'cause some guy wants you to think he loves you so you'll do more."

"No, not a liar's kiss."

"No way." I leaned back on my Lilo and said, "True love feels like a deep, soul-melting, passion-bloated kiss."

"A kiss so intense you faint afterwards." Nadine sat up.

"And he revives you with another kiss."

"He lifts your neck with the palm of his hand and kisses you back to life."

"You open your eyes," I said, my eyes drifting shut, "and

11

see him gazing at you with such devotion your heart stops beating."

"Because he is your heart," Nadine said softly.

"And your soul mate."

"And everything in between." We stopped, sipped more lemonade, felt the cool, sweet-and-sour liquid trickle down our throats.

"That's what I want," I told my best friend.

"Me, too," she said.

"That's my goal this year."

"Mine, too."

We both sighed.

Nadine and I had been kissed before. I mean, we weren't lip virgins or anything. But neither kiss had made the earth move . . . or even wiggle. Bert Trout, aka "Fish Boy," kissed Nadine at a junior high football game. He just leaned over and planted one on her.

"It felt like kissing a pincushion," she reported. "His moustache – if you can call it that – was all prickly and painful." It didn't help matters that he missed her mouth entirely. Fish Boy kissed Nadine's upper lip and lower nose, and, truthfully, she couldn't wait for it to end.

My neighbour Greg Minsky kissed me once, but it was way too juicy and it grossed me out. He tried a little tongue action, but no way was I going to gulp Greg Minsky's spit, so I basically shoved his tongue back where it belonged. After that, I pretty much kept my chin down and didn't give him another opportunity. Though he still looks like he might try. Greg rollerblades up and down our street whenever I'm out front and always finds some reason to stop and chat. It's cool. I like him, just not *that* way. He's too skinny, and his butt is a flat inner tube. Unlike me, he eats all the time. But he once made the mistake of telling me that food went straight through his system several times a day. Yuck.

"Yeah, I want a *serious* kiss," I said to Nadine. "A major smooch session. A kiss that means real love. That's my ambition this year."

"Mine, too."

Sitting up, I held up my left hand, placed my right hand over my heart. Nadine did the same. I said, "By our fifteenth birthdays, we, Libby Madrigal and Nadine Tilson, will experience at least one totally real, sincere, meaningful, soulful, poetic, inspiring, knee-buckling, love-filled, journal-worthy, insomnia-producing, appetite-reducing, mind-blowing, life-changing, unforgettable, undeniable, serious *kiss*."

"Just one?" Nadine giggled.

"If executed properly, one is all we need."

"Deal?"

"Deal."

We shook hands, felt excited. The plan was set. All we needed were two amazing, soulful, serious, kissable boys. That, and the nerve to pull it off.

What made me think – given my black angst and glaring deficiencies in the nature/nurture department – that it would be easy?

TWO

My locker wouldn't open. It was one of those days. Fernando High is one of those high schools. Nothing works, not even the kids who go there. Nadine saw me banging the ancient metal door with the heel of my hand. "Kicking works best on mine," she said. Before I could stop her, she gave my locker a Jackie Chan right in the gut.

"Na*dine*." I stamped my foot. "We're going to get in trouble."

"Yeah, like it's our fault their lockers don't work." Nadine kicked it again. The metal bang echoed like a gunshot.

"Let me try that." Out of nowhere this guy named Curtis appeared and practically jammed his entire foot through my locker door. Bang! The noise attracted an instant crowd and a line of students eager to kickbox. Bang! Curtis kicked it again. I sort of knew Curtis from junior high. He'd made a name for himself by refusing to join the basketball team even though he was over six feet tall. The school jocks treated him like he was a traitor. I overheard him say that team sports took too much time away from his band. I think he played guitar, because the fingernails on his right hand were really long.

Shrivelling into the huddle of students, I helplessly watched

14

the dents appear in my locker, praying my locker mate *didn't* appear. Nadine giggled all girly 'cause everyone was gawking, and Curtis, all macho for the same reason, rammed his huge basketball-sized foot against the metal door a third time. Paint chips sprinkled to the cement floor like dandruff. Still, the locker didn't open.

"I don't really need my notebook," I said, my voice about as small and weak as a baby toe.

But Nadine and Curtis had gone too far to stop now. Egged on by the crowd ("Bash it in with the fire extinguisher!") they were both about to fling their whole bodies at my locker when a baritone voice boomed, "That's enough."

Instantly, kids scattered. I froze, frantically composing a plausible explanation for my parents as to why I was expelled in the first month of high school.

Nadine and Curtis tried to run with everyone else, but the principal, Mr Horner, whom everyone called "Mr Horny," clamped one paw on each of their shoulders and said, "Come with me." To me he asked, "Where's your class?"

I almost confessed to not having any class, to being an idiot who let her friend vandalise school property, to often feeling so . . . so . . . *compacted* or something I could explode or, other times, hearing my heart echo in my chest because I'm so empty inside. I nearly admitted to living with a constant vibrating dread humming through my body, which feels as though, at any moment, when I least expect it – like *now* – something awful will swoop down and ruin my already-precarious life. I'll wake up fat or my parents will divorce or

15

my hair will fall out or I'll finally kiss the boy who melts my skin when he kisses me back and he'll wait till prom night to announce to the whole school it was one big joke. Or my best friend will be carted off to the principal's office because of my stupid locker. I almost blurted out how awful it is to feel so uncertain, so out of control – like running on ice or having a rotten hard-boiled egg fermenting in my gut – no solid footing, a constant pre-hurl. I nearly dropped to my knees and begged Mr Horny for forgiveness when he repeated, "Where is your classroom, young lady?"

Oh.

"Building C," I stammered.

"Get on over there, then, before the late bell rings."

"But it was *my* locker," I said. "It was stuck."

"Did you kick it?"

"I hit it with my hand," I said. Nadine and Curtis both looked at me. "My *fist*, I mean. I banged it with my fist. Hard."

"Get to class." Mr Horny turned and led Nadine and Curtis away. I could tell Nadine was mad because her nostrils were stuck in the way open position. Curtis seemed to let it slide. On the way to the principal's office, he low-fived a straggler who, like me, wasn't going to make it to class before the bell.

"See you at lunch, Nadine?" I called after her, but she either didn't hear me or didn't want to.

It was hard enough trying to follow the hieroglyphics of Geometry on the chalkboard, but without a textbook, it was nearly impossible. I mean, we were learning about quadrilaterals in the first month? What was *that* about? "Share with Ostensia," Mr Puente said after he found out my book was still stuck in my locker.

"Uh . . ." Before I could protest, Ostensia was practically sitting on top of me, her desk glued to mine, her garlic breath all over my face. I liked her, had known her since sixth grade, but, man, those home-made concoctions she unwrapped all day at school were aromatic enough to scare vampires away.

"Right here," she pointed, "page twelve. Halfway down, right hand si—"

"Got it," I whispered, then resumed holding my breath.

Truth be told, dividing a quad into triangles didn't interest me in the slightest. And determining the diagonals of a rhombus thrilled me even less, especially when my best friend was in trouble because of me, my locker looked like a car wreck, and the only reason I'd taken Geometry in my freshman year was because Carrie Taylor's boyfriend, Zack Nash, took Geometry with Mr Puente, and he was the boy I'd decided to kiss. Well, not *decided*, actually, unless you consider a pounding heart a decision.

Zack Nash is the boy that I love. There, I've said it. Whew! It has been said. No one knows. Not Nadine or my mom or even the diary I started over the summer that didn't make it past June. I've loved Zack Nash since I first saw him last year. He was walking across the lawn of Mission Junior High with Carrie Taylor, her little finger clasped in his fist. I'm quite sure Zack Nash doesn't even know my name. Still, I've dreamed of his hand reaching for my little finger and his lips calling me home with one velvet kiss.

"Want one?" Ostensia peeled open a foil-wrapped plate of congealed nachos under the desk. The smell rose up like a rotting mushroom cloud. I shook my head and turned away. My stomach let me know I couldn't look at it again. "Later, then," Ostensia whispered. "I have lots."

Out of the corner of my eye I saw Zack Nash wave his hand back and forth in front of his pinched face. He turned around to look at me, his cocoa-coloured eyes staring into my love-struck baby blues. I felt a zap of electricity shoot down my arms. I grinned, tried to look petite. Then, he curled his lip and said, loud enough for the whole class to hear, "Who cut the cheese?"

Of course, everybody exploded in laughter. "Settle down," Mr Puente said, but even he smiled. Ostensia looked all innocent, and I blushed purple. My curse – to look guilty even when I'm not.

"Let's move on," Mr Puente said.

I held my breath, hoping the blood would drain from my face faster.

"Libby? Would you like to come up to the board and draw a parallelogram?"

"Mr Puente, would you like to kiss my . . ."

That's what I wanted to say. But of course I didn't. In fact, I even understood it was Mr Puente's way of saving me from being mortified in front of Zack Nash and God and everybody. But come on! How would standing in front of the whole class *save* me from embarrassment? Hadn't Mr Puente learned anything about teenage humiliation in his years of humiliating us? Not to mention the fact that Geometry had really messed with my head. I'd been a pretty good student before. It always took me about fifteen minutes to figure out what teachers expected of me, then another fifteen to produce it. I was great at that – becoming whatever anybody wanted me to be. But Geometry was my undoing. When I wasn't staring at the smooth creamy skin on Zack Nash's neck, I was gaping at the chalkboard without a clue. Geometry, for me, was how I imagined people who couldn't read saw the world: shapes and squiggles that made no sense whatsoever.

"Libby?"

I forced myself to breathe again.

"No, thank you, Mr Puente," I stammered. Hey, I gave it a shot.

"Come on up here and we'll work it out together." Mr Puente held a stubby piece of chalk in my direction.

Ostensia exhaled and said, "You can do it."

Refusing was useless. Mr Puente could stand there for hours holding that piece of chalk. I'd seen it before. He never gave up. So I stood up. My chair scraped the linoleum floor. The class got really quiet. Tucking my hair behind my ear, I slyly glanced at him. Yeah, he was looking. Zack's head was tilted up and his lips were parted and his beautiful neck swivelled at the same speed I walked. My heart thumped overtime, my cheeks were still aflame, and a dewy coating of sweat veiled my forehead. I could hear my sneakers squeak across the floor. But that's all I heard of the external world. The rest of the noise was deep within my head: buzzing in my ears, blood squeezing through my clenched veins, quick, shallow breaths burning my chest.

"A parallelogram," Mr Puente repeated, handing me the chalk. But I heard it as a deep echo: "Paraaaaaa-llllllelllooooo-graaaam."

Standing with my back to the class, arm raised to the board, chalk perched between my thumb and forefinger, I went numb with panic. I could feel tumbleweeds rolling through my empty skull, hear the dry prairie wind. Once, on late-night cable, I'd seen a psychic hold a pen in her hand over a blank sheet of paper and summon the spirit of James Joyce. I tried it.

"Einstein," I whispered under my breath. "Are you there?"

"What?"

I turned to face Mr Puente. His eyebrows were raised. He asked again, "What did you say, Libby?"

What *could* I say? I was busted. Big-time. He might as well have asked me to draw a road map of Uzbekistan – I didn't have a clue. Sighing, I tossed the chalk on to the ledge beneath the chalkboard.

"I said I could stand here for the rest of my life and not only not know how to draw a parallelogram but eventually lose the ability to draw a straight line, too."

The class laughed. A good, we're-with-you kind of laugh. Mr Puente chuckled, too. I straightened my shoulders.

"An alien apparently abducted my brain over the summer

and sucked out my capacity to understand two-dimensional shapes," I quipped. My face returned to its natural colour.

They laughed again. Harder. I felt their love wash over me, felt empowered, giddy, reckless. Facing the students, my people, I raised my arms in the air, closed my eyes and cried out, "If there's anybody out there who can help me understand the first thing about Geometry, I'll help them with any other subject on earth!"

The class roared. I beamed. Peering through my eyelids, I saw Ostensia raise her nacho-smeared hand. I clamped my eyes shut.

"Anybody! Anybody at all!"

"I'll help you."

It *wasn't* Ostensia. It was male. A boy's voice. *His* voice.

"Maths is easy," said Zack Nash. "I need help with English. Essays."

English? Essays? I love English! I almost made it into *Honours* English. I speak English! Essays are my life! I could not believe that Zack Nash would offer to tutor me in front of the entire class. But there he was, his luscious eyes looking at me without a trace of sarcasm, his blond hair deliciously dishevelled.

"You have two takers, Libby," Mr Puente said. "Pick one, then take your seat so we can get on with class."

Looking out over the bright, full-moon faces of my classmates, I saw Ostensia and Zack Nash, both staring at me, smiling hopefully.

I said, "Zack Nash, I guess. Why not?"

Ostensia's face fell. The walk back to our double desk was long and awkward. She wouldn't look at me. I felt awful. Hideous. Like one of those girls who dumps her friends in the dirt the moment a guy comes along.

It was the happiest day of my life.

THREE

"Dirk, wash your hands for dinner." Mom reached her own hand into the KFC bucket, tore off a piece of Extra Crispy skin, and sucked it into her mouth. Junk food again. My mother'd actually believed Ronald Reagan when he said ketchup was a vegetable.

"I did wash my hands," Dirk said.

"Wash them with soap. Rif, grab the ketchup in the fridgeroo."

"It's on the *table*, Mom."

Yip.

"Juan, get out from under my feet! Who fed the dog?"

"I did," I said. "Can't we *ever* have salad for dinner? Or something you don't order through an intercom?"

"Rif, feed the dog."

"I *fed* him, Mom!"

"Where's Dad?" Dirk, unwashed, was already seated at his place.

"He's on his way," said Mom. Then she sighed. My brothers and I looked at each other. We heard that sigh a lot.

Dinner was yet another psychotic break with reality. Nobody listened to anybody else. Mom threw together a fast-food fat fest before dad got home; Dad's homecoming made us all nervous wrecks. Would he be Jekyll or Hyde? Could we talk to him or would dinner be one tense swallow after another? Eating has never been a pleasurable experience in my house. Unless, of course, I sneak a bag of Pepperidge Farm Milano cookies into my room and eat them alone in bed. Then, it's heavenly, though I have to speed-walk nearly an hour just to burn off three of them.

Mom nervously bit into a bread roll. Mouth full, she mumbled, "Bethy, please pour the milk."

"It's *Libby*, Mom. *Libby!*"

"Oy." She sighed again. "Who can keep track?"

Mom had a point. I *was* into frequent name changes. Hey, was it *my* fault my parents gave me a name with so many variations? What – they expected me to lug "Elizabeth" around for life? Or worse, "Bethy"? I can't tell you how many times people said, "Betsy?" each time I said my name. "No, it's *Bethy*," I'd respond. "As in Elizabeth, Beth, Bethy." "*Ah*," they'd say back, then pretty much refuse to say my name at all after that. Who wants to *th*ound like they have a li*th*p? "Libby" was way more grown-up, anyway. Nadine had suggested it back when she wasn't mad, back when she was my lifelong best friend.

Often, I wished I could trade families with Nadine. Nadine's parents are nothing like my parents. Her family is a pasta sauce commercial. Everybody is always laughing, crammed into the kitchen, encircling a large steaming pot on the stove. Her mom dips a wooden spoon into the vat of spaghetti sauce for a taste, good-naturedly swats her husband away. He hugs her, nuzzles her neck. Her little brother tosses a football with his buddy on the backyard lawn, a golden retriever sweeps the floor with his tail as he eagerly waits for a morsel to drop to the floor. Nadine's older sister carries a giant salad bowl to the large real-wood table, shouts, "Supper in five minutes!" And they call dinner "supper," which is *so* cool.

My parents, on the other hand, are more like the embarrassing relatives. Get this: My dad's name is Lance, but the other salesmen at his work dubbed him "Sir Lancelot" as a joke. You know, the buffed-out knight of the Round Table (yeah right), the hunky guy who had a thing for Guinevere? But after they saw him snarf down a foot-long salami sub all by himself in less than five minutes and slobber beer down the front of his tie, they shortened it to "Lot." Which suits my dad perfectly because he's majorly into excess.

My mom's name is Dorothy, but she's always been known as Dot. So my parents are Lot and Dot. Couldn't you just throw up? People hear their names and assume they're this happy, chirpy couple. Mom wants to keep it that way.

"Nobody needs to know our business," she says all the time. Which really means nobody needs to know the *truth*. If our family had a motto – and of course we don't – it wouldn't be "One for all, all for one" or "Do unto others as you would have them do unto you." It would be "Don't tell anyone." We don't really live in our house on Bonita Drive as much as we hide there. Which probably explains why *Momaroo* has her own language. Shhh! Don't tell.

25

The last time I was invited to Nadine's house for "supper," I sat there and stared at everybody like they were animals in some exotic Family Love zoo. Their ease with one another takes my breath away. Whenever I'm there I try to memorise the way Nadine acts so I can act normal, too.

The front door opened just as I finished filling everyone's milk glass. Dad's rubber-soled shoes squeaked across the linoleum floor. Everybody got real quiet. No one knew if it was going to be a good night or a bad night. We held our collective breath. Except Juan Dog. *Yip. Yip.*

"Perfect timing," Mom said anxiously. "Dinner's on the table."

Yip. Yip. Yip.

"What are we having?" Dad asked from the front door.

"The Colonel."

"Chicken?"

"They had a special. I had a coupon." Mom tore off another chunk of Extra Crispy skin and devoured it.

"Haven't you heard about *hormones*?" Dad's voice was too loud, too slow.

I swallowed air, felt that rotten egg wobble around in my stomach for the second time that day.

"It's KFC," Mom said, swallowing. "Your favourite."

Yippety. Yip.

As soon as my father tottered into the kitchen, I saw that his glasses were hanging off the end of his nose. His mud-coloured hair was sticking up on one side; his belly strained the buttons on his short-sleeved white shirt. My father's nose

26

was several shades of red. As he got closer to the table, I smelled smoky aftershave and mouthwash-covered beer. That's when I knew for sure he'd stopped at a bar on his way home.

"Farmers feed chickens hormones so they have bigger breasts." He scowled. "You tryin' to turn us into *girls?*"

Mom didn't say anything. Dad asked testily, "Well, *are* you?"

"Of course not. It's KFC. They don't do that."

"Anything's possible," he muttered. When he was in one of his moods, he found fault with Halle Berry's navel. I mean, nothing was good enough.

"Honey, why don't you wash your hands and sit down at the table?" Mom said.

"I sell *swimming pools*, for God's sake. How dirty could I be?"

"Okay, then just sit down." She pulled out his chair. Dad landed heavily. Dirk's leg wiggled beneath the table. Rif sat stone-faced, and I crossed my arms and stared at the bubbles dancing on top of my non-fat milk.

Yip. Yip.

"When a man comes home," Dad said, slowly enunciating each word, "he doesn't want *chemicals* for dinner. Understood?"

"Yes."

"A man does not want to be made into a *woman*."

Yip. Yippety. Yip.

"No, of course not."

Yip. Yip.

"A man—"

Yippy. Yip.

"SHUT UP, MUTT!"

We jumped. Juan Dog swallowed his final yip and slithered under my chair.

"Damn dog!" Dad shouted. Nobody moved while we braced for the hurricane. But Dad just sat there staring at his empty plate.

After a while Mom said, "Roll?" waving a red-and-white KFC box under my nose. The smell of steaming buttermilk rolls was almost unbearably delicious.

"No, thanks," I said.

"Pass the rolls to Daddy," she whispered to me. *Daddy?* What?

Rif reached for the chicken bucket. "Want a breast?" he asked Dirk mischievously.

"Huh?" Dirk didn't get it. Mom glared at Rif as she shovelled mashed potato on to her plate. Then she handed the container to me.

"No thanks, Mom. Pass the coleslaw, please."

"Beans?" She stuck a plastic tub of barbecued baked beans in front of my face. My mouth drowning in saliva, I weakened. But the sight of my mother's chin glistening in chicken grease firmed my resolve.

"Thank you, *no*."

"Corn on the cob?"

I just glared. "Did you even *buy* coleslaw?"

Slack jawed, Mom looked around the table. "I thought I did."

Recrossing my arms defiantly, I announced, "There is no way I'm eating one thousand one hundred and ninety calories in one meal!"

"Eat *something*, Libby," Mom responded through gritted teeth.

Indignantly, I reached for the corn, though it might as well have been a roll with all the carbs. Is it too much to ask that my own mother follow our government's nutritional pyramid? Has she ever even *seen* a leafy green? Maintaining my own *hybrid* diet – low cal, low fat, low carb – was impossible in a house where the refrigerator's vegetable keeper had been removed to make room for beer.

Dirk reached across the table to grab the chicken bucket just as the doorbell rang. Mom's head jerked up. We all stopped and blinked. A visitor at our house at dinnertime meant only one thing.

Bill collector.

"Shhhh." Dad sent spit spray all over the table. "Nobody move."

Dirk's arm hovered mid-air. Rif stopped chewing. The doorbell rang again.

"He's not going to leave," Mom whispered.

We'd witnessed this scene before. The first time, about a month ago, Mom innocently got up and answered the door. From the dinner table, we heard her voice morph from a chirpy "Hello!" to a whispered "Leave the bill and I'll pay it tomorrow."

The second and third times, Dad answered the door and

29

gruffly said, "We're in the middle of dinner. Come back tomorrow afternoon."

Of course, no one is at home in our house in the afternoon, so this time, the fourth time, Dad tried a new approach.

"Pretend we're not here," he mouthed.

Dad scraped his chair back, wincing at the sound it made, and shakily stood up. He held his finger to his lips as he teetered on tiptoe to the window beside the front door. At the kitchen table, Rif mumbled, "Our cars are in the driveway. He knows we're here."

Mom glared at him. Dirk's arm, still extended across the table, started to shake. Rif whispered to him, "You move, you die."

"Eat," Mom commanded. "*Quietly.*"

In slow motion, Dirk reached into the chicken bucket and pulled out a thigh, then he gently put it back and fished around for another piece.

"Touch every one of them, why don't you?" Rif snarled.

"Shhh!"

Dad tiptoed back into the kitchen and whispered, "He left."

"Then why are we whispering?" Rif whispered.

"Close call," Mom said, glancing at my father. He sat down hard and reached into the bucket for a piece of chicken.

Yip. Yip. Juan Dog started up again. Dad was just about to drop-kick him into the living room when he suddenly jumped.

"Holy sh—"

"Mr Madrigal?" A man's face peered under the grubby roller-blinds on the window over the kitchen sink.

"Get out of my backyard," Dad screeched.

This time Dad didn't have to tell us not to move. We turned into wide-eyed mannequins all on our own.

Yip. Yip.

"If we could just talk for a few minutes—"

"This is private property," Dad yelled. "I'll call the police."

Yipe. Yip. Yip.

"I have a right to be here, Mr Madrigal. If I could just talk to you for a few minutes."

"I have nothing to say to you."

Yi—

"Shut up, Juan!" Dad's face looked like it was about to pop. Juan shut up, but I could tell he was insulted. I mean, if a dog isn't supposed to bark when a stranger trespasses in his very own yard, when *is* he supposed to bark?

"We can work out a payment plan," said the head in the kitchen window.

Dad sighed. "We're in the middle of dinner." His tone softened.

Mom asked quietly, "Want me to go talk to him this time, Lot?"

Wiping his mouth with the back of his hand, Dad stood. "I'll take care of it," he said, suddenly sounding sober. Then, to the head, "Go back to the front door. I'll give you five minutes."

Dad tucked in his shirt, rubbed the blood and expression back into his face. "Don't stop eating," he commanded.

31

Heads bowed, we ate. I heard my father walk through the family room and open the front door.

"Mr Madrigal . . ." The male voice sounded tentative, scared.

Mom asked us loudly, "So, what did you kids do at school today?"

". . . overdue . . . final notice . . . foreclosure . . ." Scary words floated into the kitchen as we tried to swallow.

Mom sat superstraight. "Dirk?" she asked. "Anything interesting happen at school?"

Dirk nodded. "Mrs McAllister asked me to read my essay on great white sharks aloud to the whole class," he said, grinning.

"The whole class?" Mom echoed. "My goodness." I could tell she was listening with only one ear.

". . . we want to work with you," the man was saying to my father. "We're not the enemy."

"Did you know that more people are killed by elephants than sharks?" Dirk asked.

"Is that so?" Mom crammed forkfuls of baked beans into her mouth.

"More people are even killed by *dogs*."

". . . can't leave without a cheque . . ."

"And a shark's teeth keep on growing back each time he loses one."

". . . I don't want to keep coming out here, either."

"Again and again, no matter how many times he bites something like a seal or a whale."

"Sharks don't bite whales," Rif said. "Any more corn on the cob, or is Libby going to eat all of it?"

I sneered at him. Man, the corn was good.

"They could, maybe," Dirk said, "if they could catch one."

"Whales are the largest mammals on earth, you idiot." Rif reached for a cob. No way was I going to hand one to him.

". . . that would be fine, Mr Madrigal."

"Dot?"

Mom set her fork down, swallowed hard, and turned her head toward the front door. "Yes, dear?"

Dad asked, "Where's the cheque-book?"

A shadow briefly covered Mom's face, but it vanished quickly. She said brightly, "It's in my handbag. I'll get it."

Mom got up and left the kitchen table. Dirk said sullenly, "Sharks are pretty big, too, you know."

When my father returned to the dinner table, his mood had improved considerably. He rubbed his hands together, said, "Pass my favourite chicken." Mom handed him the bucket of KFC, but I noticed she didn't look at him. I'd seen that "not look" before. I knew exactly what it meant.

"Cheques aren't *money*, Lot," she'd screamed at him one night. "There has to be money in the bank."

He hadn't listened then, and he wasn't paying any attention to her "not look" now. I felt sorry for my mom. It must be awful to live in such loud silence – so much to say with no one to listen.

"Is there any slaw?" Dad asked, flipping the pop-top on a fresh can of beer.

33

The first time I noticed my dad had a problem with alcohol, I was about ten or so. Before that, he was just my dad. I was his little girl. He made me laugh and feel special.

"Who's the be*thed* girl in the whole wide world?" he'd ask.

"Bethy!" I'd squeal.

For my eighth birthday, my father organised a swimming party at his office, on a Sunday, when they were closed. One of the perks of being a swimming pool salesman – your own backyard can be a dirt lot because there is a gorgeous outdoor pool at the office.

Mom tied helium balloons to the wrought iron fence around the pool; Dad made a sign for the parking lot that read PRIVATE PARTY. He also turned the office CD player up as high as it would go and pointed the speakers toward the pool. Images from that day are still clear in my mind – the thrill of having a party in a grown-up's space, so close to a busy boulevard, the hysteria of splashing girls in bright bathing suits, Mom's joy, Dad's pride. It was so *normal.*

"Your dad *works* here?" my friend Marjorie had asked, astounded. "Is he a lifeguard?"

"No, silly." I giggled in a superior way, feeling certain that my dad had the coolest job ever. "He sells swimming pools! If you want one, you have to buy it from him!"

I remember Marjorie's wide eyes. I remember Nadine's laughter, too, and playing Marco Polo in the pool, and seeing Dad playfully pat my mother's rear end and kiss Dirk on the top of his little head. That day, Rif was off with his own friends, and I was the *oldest* child, instead of the middle child. I ate cake in my bathing suit without even thinking about it. I invited friends over without worrying what they might see.

But that was a long time ago.

By the time I turned nine, fewer people wanted swimming pools. Dad stopped patting my mother's bottom and began measuring it.

"Is that your second piece of cake?" he asked her at my ninth birthday party in Chatsworth Park.

I remember the way she looked at him, her eyes wet. She didn't talk to him for the rest of the party, and I felt like crying even though it was my birthday.

Little by little, my funny, loving father faded away. His body was there, but *he* wasn't. Some other guy was living inside him. This stranger was sarcastic, unreasonable, short-tempered, and occasionally violent. He never hit us or my mother. Instead, he took his anger out on the walls. Behind several oddly-placed framed prints around the house, fist-sized holes gape. And the knuckles on my dad's right hand are bigger than they are on his left because they never get the chance to heal right.

"Happy fat day to you!" Dad sang to Mom that day in Chatsworth Park. Marjorie heard him. Her eyes went wide again. This time, I saw fear and embarrassment in them. She knew something was wrong with my dad. And, worse, she acted like it was contagious. She went home early, and eventually she stopped wanting to play at my house. After a while, I stopped inviting anyone over. I didn't want them to see my dad passed out on the couch or smell his brutal breath when his mouth hung open. Nadine was the only friend who kept coming anyway. She saw what was going on, but we never talked about it. I didn't bring it up, and she didn't, either.

It took me a while to totally understand what was happening to my family. It wasn't until one night, four years ago, that I was absolutely sure.

Like I said, I was about ten years old. My parents were having a dinner party, the only one I ever remember them having. Mom had been cooking for hours. The house smelled all garlicky and yeasty like hot bread. Mom's cheeks were flushed and her voice was an octave higher than usual. She let us eat Wendy's hamburgers on trays in front of the TV. "Clean up your own mess," she trilled. "Then go to your rooms and stay there."

Dad was dressed in one of his ironed white work shirts and pressed khaki pants. He wore loafers with little tassels. I remember watching those tassels bounce back and forth as he scuffed across the family room floor. I offered him one of my onion rings, he said, "No thanks," then plopped down in an easy chair and popped the top of a beer.

"Ah, Lot." Mom sighed when she saw him. Then she disappeared into the kitchen and we scampered off to our rooms.

Rif was sleeping over at his friend's house that night, but Dirk and I decided to eavesdrop on my parents' party through the heat vent in my room. It was easy enough to listen just by sitting in the hall, but lying on our bellies pressed up to the heat vent seemed more fun at the time.

". . . and he drove off and was gone for an hour and a *half*!" bellowed my dad's work friend who was one of the guests. (Dad was moonlighting as a car salesman then.) Everybody laughed. I heard Mom echo, "An hour and a *half*?"

"I thought I'd have to pay for that car out of my commissions for the rest of my life!"

They all laughed again. Then Dad said, "Yeah, like you'd ever make enough to buy that car." There were a few twitters, but the laughter noticeably dimmed.

Mom, her voice still unnaturally high, said, "More bruschetta, Sam?"

"Sure."

"More wine?" Dad asked.

"If you're pouring."

"He's *always* pouring," Mom chirped. I could tell it was a joke, but nobody laughed.

The dinner party got louder as the hour got later, and Dirk fell asleep on my bedroom floor. I left him there and lay down on my bed listening through my open door. Dad's voice changed entirely. It was louder than everybody else's, slower. And he said mean things.

"Never met a dessert you didn't like, right, Dot?"

I remember feeling queasy, ashamed for him. I was humiliated for my mom, too, because I heard someone say, "We really should get going," and my dad, all slurry, shouted, "Going? Was it something my wife said?"

After the guests left, which was shortly after that, my mom started to cry and my dad started to yell. "Just once, Lot," Mom sobbed. "You couldn't stay sober *once*?"

"It was a *party*! People *drink* at parties! I noticed that my drinking didn't disturb your appetite."

"If you could hear yourself," Mom cried.

"If you could only *see* yourself or I should say, your*selves*."

That night, the word "alcoholic" first crept into my head. I knew better than to say it out loud. I didn't want Dad's wrath aimed at me. I also didn't want to listen to my parents fight any more. Even then, I knew there were some conversations a kid shouldn't overhear. Because once you hear it, how can you ever forget?

The next day, my parents pretended to be fine around us, but I knew. They wouldn't look at each other. Mom's jaw was set tight. Dad watched a lot of TV. After that night, I understood what I'd been witnessing for years. Alcohol stole my father from me. It replaced him with a man who was mean to my mother and made our whole family feel like hiding.

At first, I felt sad that my funny, loving daddy was gone. Then I got mad. He wasn't *kidnapped*; he took himself away each time he opened a can of beer. Why couldn't he bring himself back? And why did my mom let him go? Why didn't she make him go to rehab? How could a mother let her kids grow up with such bad role models? And who has only *dirt* in their backyard?!

When I wasn't angry at my father, I was terrified of becoming my mother. Without proper nurturing, wouldn't nature run rampant? Was it my destiny to endure whatever life dished out?

Just thinking about it made my mouth go dry.

"I'm sorry." That's what I wrote on the subject line of my e-mail to Nadine that night after I finished my KFC corn-on-the-cob dinner. I'd tried to see her at school, but she stiffed me at lunch, and she had marching band practice after last period. I'd waited in front of the music room until some other band student told me they were practising on the football field that day. No way was I walking clear across the campus to have Nadine snub me in front of the whole marching band and the entire football team, too.

"Please don't be mad at me, Nadine," I wrote. Then I stopped. As I sat in front of my computer, hands perched on the keys, I couldn't figure out what else to say. Yeah, I felt awful that my best friend was carted away because she was trying to help me. But did I tell her to kick the smithereens out of my locker? Didn't I say that I didn't need my notebook, and she kept kicking anyway? Doesn't anybody ever listen to me?

Suddenly I was furious. How dare she pummel my locker! And who let that jerk Curtis and his size thirteen feet mangle the door? Not me! What, she expected me to lie to Mr Horny and say that I did it? Ostenchia breathed her bad breath on me all during Geometry. Did she care? I spent the whole day without my books, I'm going to get an incomplete on my homework assignments, not to mention the fact that my locker mate was like *raving* mad when she couldn't get her lunch out of our locker. Did Nadine care? Did she? Plus, the greatest moment in my whole entire life happened that day and I didn't have anyone to tell! What, she thinks Zack Nash wants to be tutored by just *anyone*? What, she thinks it's no big deal that I'm finally ready to admit he's the boy of my dreams after a *year* of silently obsessing over him?

The phone rang. I ignored it. Let my brothers get it. My hands were flying across the computer keys. Exclamation points and bold face capital letters littered the text. It's about time my so-called best friend got a piece of my mind.

". . . time to take RESPONSIBILITY –"

"Libby. It's for you." Mom called from the family room.

I ignored her. Continued my rant.

"– for YOUR own actions!!!!"

"Libby! Phone!"

I signed it, "Elizabeth Madrigal, *true* friend." Then, I hit the Send button, yelled "Okay" to my mom and reached across my bed for the extension.

"Hello?"

"Libby?"

It was Nadine.

"What do *you* want?"

"I'm in love!"

FOUR

Doesn't that just take the cake?

I know, I sound like an old lady, but doesn't it? Nadine ruins my locker, spends lunch period in detention with Big Foot Curtis, and ends up with a date to go to the movies with him Friday after school.

"He's so amazing," Nadine said to me the next day in the cafeteria, completely forgetting about our little tiff and not even mentioning my angry e-mail.

"Yeah, you told me."

"He plays acoustic guitar and bass. Can you believe it?"

"No. And I couldn't believe it when you told me on the phone last night."

"Mr Horny made us sit in *total* silence for an *entire* hour, so we were *forced* to pass notes."

"Uh-huh."

"You cannot believe how well you can get to know someone without saying one single, solitary word."

"You want Pizza Hut or Taco Bell?" We were holding up the line. Fernando High's cafeteria was a miniature version of my own home. In fact, it could have been catered by my mom. Every year local fast-food hangouts bid for the privilege of delivering junk food to Chatsworth's future leaders. In an attempt to teach us democracy, the student body was allowed to vote. Apparently, my pencilled-in request for a salad bar was disregarded entirely.

"Who can eat?" Nadine squealed.

I picked up a chicken taco and diet soda and headed for the cashier. Nadine, twittering non-stop in my ear, made a humming-bird look relaxed.

"Two whole pages, front and back, of *stuff*. Amazing, real stuff. He's a poet, you know, not just a musician. I'm going to save those notes to show our kids."

Oh, brother.

"You know what the best part is?" she asked.

"He'll fix my locker?" That flew right over her head. Nadine bulldozed on.

"The best part is, if everything works out the way I think it will, the way I hope and *pray* it will, Curtis will turn out to be the boy who delivers the big one."

I swung my leg over the cafeteria bench and plopped down. Nadine sat beside me, facing out in case (yeah, you guessed it) Curtis walked by.

"You know," I said, "one hour of detention can't really tell you anything about a person." I was tempted to confess I'd spent over a year silently studying Zack Nash and barely knew him at all. But Nadine's mind was on her possibly very real love life, not my imaginary one.

"Sometimes one hour is all you need," she said softly, petting the back of my head in a superior know-it-all way that really frosted me.

"And sometimes it isn't," I shot back, yanking my head away.

Nadine just sighed. "You'll see, Libby Madrigal. Before the year's out, *way* before, Curtis and I will have a serious kiss. You'll see. I know in my heart it's going to happen. In my *heart*."

I believed her, which was the worst part. It's not that we were in competition or anything. It's just that I wanted my serious kiss to be first. Or at least at the same time as hers. This way, I was just learning to walk, and she was about to win an Olympic gold medal in track and field. How had this happened? My best friend, my very best friend, had zoomed so far ahead of me she was a tiny speck on my horizon.

"Hey."

"Hey!" Nadine leaped to her feet.

Curtis and his friend Ray – or Roy – or some other one-syllable "R" – walked up to our table. Curtis asked me, "How's your locker?"

"Still concave," I said. Then, in response to Ray/Roy's dumbfounded look, I added, "As dented as it was yesterday."

Nadine said, "We heard that whole bank of lockers is going to be replaced."

We did?

"Curtis and I overheard Horny's secretary talking to the handyman over the phone yesterday."

Oh. *That* "we." Nadine and I weren't even a "we" any more. I wanted everyone to leave so I could swallow my taco in one bite.

"At least Libby got her books out of there this morning," Nadine reported. Her voice wasn't usually so singsongy. I wanted to barf. "Horny had the handyman open it with a crowbar. They gave Libby and her locker mate a brand-new locker."

"On the far end of campus," I mumbled.

"Cool," Ray/Roy said. Then he wiped his nose with the back of his hand.

Curtis turned to Nadine. "A bunch of us are heading out to the Boulevard for a bite. Wanna come?"

"Yes! I mean, yeah, that would be great. I'm starving."

I just looked at her. Nostrils flared. The way she looked at me the day before when Mr Horny hauled her off to the best detention of her life.

"Can Libby come, too?" she asked. Nice try, I thought.

"Yeah. Whatever." Curtis began to look impatient.

"You guys go ahead," I said, flipping my hair casually. "I'm tutoring Zack Nash and I have to find him anyway.

Nothing. Zippo. Not one word of recognition. Not, "Zack Nash? That cute guy?" Not, "Wow. I didn't know you knew Zack Nash." Nada. Zilch*arooney*. Nadine shrugged, spun on her heel, said, "Okay," and then left. Just like that. I watched her disappear across the school's front lawn. With Ray/Roy and Curtis, the boy she was going to seriously kiss.

Doesn't that just take the cake?

FIVE

Dad was trying to pop the neighbour's dog with an air-gun when I got home from school. He lay flat on his belly up against the chain-link fence in our dirt backyard, his face ruddy and his sweaty arms covered in earth.

"Mangy mutt!" I heard him scream.

My father's battle with Winnie, the white Maltese next door, was psychotic. He went nuts every time the dog barked, and the dog barked every time her owners weren't home. Obviously her owners weren't home right now. Apparently my dad *was* home, in the middle of a workday, which wasn't a comforting sign.

"Hold *still*, you wimpy floor mop!"

"Here we go again," Rif said, joining me at the sliding glass door. "Canine versus asinine."

Winnie is as neurotic as dogs can get. Not that I blame her with a gun-toting maniac next door. I swear my dad loves to hear the sound of our neighbour's car backing down the driveway. He gets very still, waiting. Then, the moment Winnie makes a peep, he's flying across the room to the closet where his old air-gun and extra box of pellets are stashed – off-limits to us, of course. A few weeks ago, Dad woke us all up in

45

the middle of the night because the sliver of paper he balanced between the air-gun and its shelf had fluttered to the floor.

"Who took it?" he spat at us in a rage. "Was it you? You? You?"

Dad wasn't drunk. He was hungover, which was way worse.

"Nobody touched your air-gun, Lot," Mom said wearily, holding her robe closed at the neck. "The kids know better than that."

"I know better," Dad yelled. "I always put that gun on a tiny piece of paper so I'll know if someone used it. And that paper was on the floor."

"Maybe it blew down when we were in the closet getting something else," Mom suggested.

"And maybe Christmas will be in July this year," Dad snapped back at her.

Dirk tried to warm his bare feet on the back of his pyjama legs. Rif stood stone-faced. I simply yawned and waited for Dad's steam to run out. I knew he didn't think I'd taken his stupid air-gun. I hated guns. It was me who tried to stop Dad from shooting Winnie until Dad threatened to plant a pellet in *my* behind.

"Let's go to bed, Lot," Mom said.

"Not until I get a confession. Who took it? You? You? You?"

After each accusatory "you," my brothers and I shook our heads. For once I actually looked innocent, being too tired to blush or sweat. Finally Mom said, "That's enough, Lot. The kids have school tomorrow."

Dad cleared his throat, seemed to abruptly see the ridiculousness of his midnight interrogation. He's like that, my dad. His sanity occasionally catches up with his insanity and takes him by surprise. It's as if he suddenly remembers the way he used to be, before beer muddled his brain. At those moments, I can almost pretend things are the way they once were.

"Here she is," Dad would sing on Saturday mornings when I came to the breakfast table in my pyjamas, "Miss Chats-a-worth!"

To be honest, glimpses of my old dad just upset me. When I'm sure he's lost for good, he shows up and gets me missing him again. I don't want to miss my father when he's right in front of me. Too many other things stress me out.

"All right," he said that night. "Go to bed. But we all know an air-gun is not a toy, right?"

"Right."

"It's a dangerous weapon."

"Dangerous weapon," we repeated in exhausted unison.

"That piece of paper must have blown down," he mumbled as we padded off to bed. Dirk said, "Goodnight" at the door of the bedroom he shared with Rif, then fell face first into bed.

Rif excitedly whispered to me, "Now I know about the paper. Next time I can just put it back!"

So, that day after school, Rif and I stood in the family room watching the man who created us aim his precious air-gun at a ten-pound ball of barking white fluff. The muzzle of the rifle poked through the fence. Winnie was hoarse from barking. Juan Dog, peering through the glass door with us, swallowed dry dog spit in terror.

"Who's top dog now!" Dad bellowed maniacally. Then we heard a pop and a loud *ping!* Dad never hit Winnie, which added to his frustration, but he often pinged the neighbour's swing set, completely confounding the family who lived there. We'd see Mr Halpern examining his pock-marked slide while scratching his head. Lucky for Winnie, Dad was a bad shot. Unlucky for us, he was a huge embarrassment (not to mention a horrible role model). How do you admire a parent who not only wages war with a little dog but always loses, too?

The worst was the time Winnie was in heat and Dad had shoved Juan Dog under a gap in the fence. "That'll mess with their heads," he'd snarled.

But Juan had just stood there, hunched up, shivering. Winnie's barking scared him. His ears drooped like two wet Kleenexes. He looked pathetically back at my dad, tried to shimmy backward under the fence into the safety of his own yard.

"What, are you, *gay?*" Dad had growled at him, blocking his re-entry with the butt of his air-gun. It wasn't until my mom walked outside and shrieked, "Have you finally lost every last one of your brain cells?" that Dad abandoned his attempt at genetic sabotage.

With so much going on outside, I didn't notice what had happened inside. In fact, it wasn't until Mr Halpern's car drove up and Dad scurried back into the house, that I noticed our living room couch was gone. That's also when I noticed my dad was still in his slippers.

"What happened to the sofa?" I asked.

"Nothing," Dad answered, then he peered out the window to watch Mr Halpern examine his swing set. "Loser," he said, smirking.

Rif reached into his hair and left the room.

"Dad, the couch that used to be in the living room is gone. Did you know that?"

"Of course I *know*," he scoffed. Then he asked, "What time does your mother usually get home?"

"In a couple of hours," I said.

"Good," said Dad, then he slapped his slippers over to the fridge, opened it, and pulled a six-pack out of the space where vegetables are supposed to be. I sighed. He said, "Not you, too, Libby. Not today."

I sighed again and went to my room.

My ears buzzed as I walked down the hall, past the gaping space in the living room, past Juan Dog who was cowering beneath an easy chair.

"Bethy is me*thy*." Dirk threw a used wadded-up Kleenex at me as I passed his open bedroom door.

"Dirk is a jerk," I replied, slamming my own door.

Inside, I lay down on my bed and stared up at the ceiling. It felt like I had a dictionary sitting on my chest. The Oxford English, unabridged. I took a deep breath, tried to relax, but my whole life felt like too-tight jeans. My own home was suffocating me.

How had I been born into this circus? How could I escape?

Reaching my hand up to my face, I felt the bump on the

ridge of my nose, ran my fingertip across my straight teeth, traced my cheekbones. Picking up the ends of my long straight hair, I checked for split ends. Finally, I came to the conclusion I always came to eventually: I'd been adopted. No matter how many times my parents denied it, I just couldn't believe that the people I lived with were connected to me via blood and DNA.

The screaming woke me up. At first I didn't know where I was, but the smell of pepperoni pizza jolted my memory. It was dinnertime at the Madrigal house. Mom had just come home with our dinner on the passenger seat.

". . . just made the decision . . . without consulting . . ."

She was yelling at Dad.

". . . count on your support. Just *once* . . ."

Dad was yelling at her. They were both yelling right outside my bedroom door.

"Support?" Mom shouted. "Any other woman would have dumped you years ago!"

Dad shouted back, "I don't see anyone blocking the door!" To emphasise his point, Dad slammed his fist against my door.

Here we go again.

Heart pounding, my first reaction was to throw open my bedroom door, leap between my parents, and scream at the top of my lungs until they stopped screaming at each other. I'd done that before, *exploded* in front of them. Face purple, pulling out my hair, I'd shrieked, "Shut up! Shut up! Shut up!"

Amazingly, they had shut up. They'd stopped insulting

each other long enough to tell me to go to my room. Which I did. Through my closed bedroom door, I heard them stomp down the hall.

"See what you've done to your daughter?" Mom had barked, not far enough away for me not to hear.

"Me? What about you? You're her mother!"

"And *you* are her drunken father."

After that, I learned to leave them alone. They had enough to fight about without fighting about *me*.

Like now, for instance.

"Bash up the whole house while you're at it!" my mother was screeching.

Dad sounded as though he were doing exactly that. So, I leaped up from my bed and wedged the back of my desk chair under the doorknob the way I'd seen them do on TV. No way was my raging lunatic of a father barging in to create an instant window in one of *my* walls.

Slapping on my headphones, I turned my CD player up high, tried to calm my thudding heart. Suddenly I remembered reading a magazine article about meditation. It said you could tune out the world by sitting still and breathing. Weren't you supposed to hum, too?

"This was *my* house and I'll bash it if I want to!" Dad's fist hit the wall again.

Was?

Cross-legged on my bed, eyes closed, I hummed. I tried not to hear the plaster chunks falling to the floor or Juan Dog's hysterical bark.

Humm. Hummm.

"Happy now?" Mom growled. "Maybe you broke your hand this time!"

Yip! Yip!

Hummm.

The phone rang, disrupting my quest for inner peace. I quickly untangled my legs, yanked off my headphones, and lunged for the extension in my room before either parent could get annoyed with the sound of the ring and yank the cord from the wall.

"Hello?"

"Libby?"

Blam! Dad hit the wall again.

Dirk shot out of his bedroom yelling, "Stop it! Stop it!"

Yip! Yip! Yip!

"Who is this?" I could barely hear the voice on the phone. All I wanted was to get rid of whomever it was so I could pull Dirk into my room and we could hum together.

"Dirk, get back to your room!" Then to my father, Mom sneered, "You think you're Mr Tough Gu—!"

Bam! She screamed as Dad's fist hit the wall again.

"It's Zack. Zack Nash."

Yip! Yip!

"Lay a hand on me and you're dead. I swear it!" Mom shrieked.

"Zack?" My heart leaped into my ears.

Bam! "Are you *threatening* me? Do you *dare* threa—"

Yip!

"Hi, Zack! Hi!" Panic instantly fried my brain. I couldn't think of a single intelligent thing to say. Instead, I giggled hysterically into the phone. "How *are* you?"

I took the cordless as far into my closet as it would go without losing reception. I curled up and tried to hold the phone in the soundproofing of my armpit.

"Big bad man in his bedroom slippers!" Mom mocked my father. She was out of control. Was this about the missing couch? What did he mean it *was* his house? I'd never heard my mother stand up to my dad like this before. It was as thrilling as it was terrifying.

"I'm cool," Zack said. "I was wondering if—"

Crash! Either my mother or my father (God, I hope it wasn't Dirk) had picked up something and thrown it. I heard a grunt, a thud, and a huge crash. Juan yelped and darted down the hall.

"What's going on there?" Zack asked.

"On? What do you mean *on*? On?" I bit my lip, suddenly realising that I, too, was on the verge of losing control.

"Uncle Randall's chair?! How *dare* you!" Mom went ballistic. Apparently, the "thing" that had been thrown was the old chair she'd inherited from her uncle. It was the only thing she had of value, she often said. I thought it was ugly. The tapestry seat was all threadbare and the curvy wooden legs were all scuffed. But Mom called it an "heirloom" and dusted it more than she ever dusted any of our other cruddy furniture. It sounded as though Uncle Randall's chair had been busted to bits.

"You've crossed the line, Lot," Mom wailed, part crying, part bellowing in a crazy voice I'd never heard before.

"That noise? Are you outside?" Zack asked.

Squeezing further into my closet and my armpit, I desperately tried to sound breezy as I said, "Oh *that*. Uh, that's construction. We're, uh, adding a room. A new kitchen."

"Oh." Zack didn't sound convinced.

"You want to end it? You want to end it right now?" Mom was sobbing now.

"Stop it! Stop it!" Dirk was wailing, too.

"I was wondering if we could meet tomorrow after school?" Zack said. "You know, to help me with my essay? I have a paper due the next day."

"Walk out that door and you are *never* coming back. *Never*. I'll take the house, the cars. You'll be on the streets."

Yip! Yip! Juan had returned.

Dad wasn't crying. I noticed, too, that he hadn't volunteered to take the dog or us.

"Sure," I said to Zack, my voice too high. "That'd be great. Great. Tomorrow."

"Cool. So . . ."

I could hear Dad shouting, Mom screaming, Dirk crying, and Juan Dog barking. The only thing I *didn't* hear was what Zack Nash said to me next. All I knew was that it was a question, and, in panic, I answered, "Absolutely!" He said, "Bye," and I hung up without knowing what on earth was happening with my family or what I'd just agreed to do with the boy I was now one microscopic step closer to seriously kissing.

SIX

Nadine highlighted her hair. Without even telling me. She'd stopped by the chemist on her way home from school, bought "Born Blonde" hair colour, and locked herself in the bathroom after dinner to streak platinum peroxide through her long, already blondish, hair. Without even telling me.

"Your mom let you do this?" I asked, incredulous.

"Not exactly," she said, smoothing her stripes down at the back. Then she looked at her watch, said, "Geez, the bell's about to ring," and took off for her class. I took off after her.

"What do you mean, 'Not exactly'?" I asked.

"She didn't exactly know I was going to do it. I mean, she didn't know until she saw it already done."

My jaw dropped. Is this what a potential boyfriend does to you? Turns you into a juvenile delinquent? "You did it anyway? What did she say?" I asked, breathless.

Nadine turned to me and frowned. "She said I'm grounded till my roots grow back one inch. Can you believe it? One whole inch!"

The late bell rang. We both sprinted to class. On the way Nadine said, "No phone, no TV, no e-mail until my hair grows an inch! My mom is such a beast." Then, just before peeling off into her third period classroom, she stopped and asked me, "Do you think an inch will grow out by Halloween? I'm hoping Curtis asks me to the Fright Dance."

"Uh. I dunno." That's all I could manage to say. It was the end of September. Halloween was a month of hair growth away. Fright Dance? Doesn't that just take the cake?

I barely made it to American History. Mr Redfield was just shutting the door when I zoomed in.

"Glad you could join us, Miss Madrigal," he said.

Sitting down, catching my breath, I tried to focus on his lecture, but all I kept thinking about, over and over, were Nadine's blonde stripes. How could she? It was so unfair. She already almost had a date to the Fright Dance? What's up with that? I'd heard all about Fernando's freshman Fright Dance. It was supposedly more fun than the prom. Part haunted house, part masquerade party, part dance – how could it *not* be totally great? But only the coolest girls went to Fright Dance with guys. The rest of us dressed up with our friends and went in a group. Fright Dance is one of the few times going with a group of girls is okay. I mean, the school year starts in September, Fright Dance is at the end of October – who could possibly have a boyfriend by then? I wanted to cry. How had this happened? How had I lost her so fast? What kind of best friend bleaches her hair without even telling you or plans to go to Fright Dance with a boy instead of you?

The walk to my new locker in Siberia felt endless. Thank heaven it was the mid-morning break. Otherwise, I'd never make it to my next class on time. My locker was at the farthest edge of campus, over by the new bungalows, along a million open-air corridors that were about as dusty as our backyard. I could barely put one foot in front of the other without sweating in the uncomfortable heat. And the last thing I wanted on my favourite, brand-new, embroidered blouse that cost one month's worth of allowance plus three weekends of babysitting was a sweat stain. Not when I was tutoring Zack Nash after school and he was tutoring me.

Fernando High School, shoved up against the foothills of the Santa Susana mountains, compensated for its lack of beauty with enormous size. All the buildings were either brown, beige, or a sort of crusty yellow. And they were spaced far apart from one another. We called it "campus" instead of "school" because, yeah, it sounded grown-up and college-like, but also because a campus is really the grounds of a school, and Fernando High certainly covered a lot of ground. Getting from one end of campus to the other could take, like, fifteen minutes in platform sandals, ten minutes in tennis shoes. Kids with money brought fibreglass skateboards to school and showed off their zigzag moves in front of everybody. Greg Minsky never brought his skateboard.

"It'll just get ripped off," he said. But I suspected it was because he had a hard time balancing with a heavy, full backpack on his back. The guys who rode skateboards at Fernando High appeared to have more money than homework.

My mom told me the area around Fernando High is full of history. Like Fernando itself is the name of some Spanish king who sent missionaries to California to tame the natives and turn them into Christians. Which explains the ancient San Fernando Mission a couple of miles away. It looks totally cool from the outside, but I've never been inside because my parents keep saying, "We should go to the mission one of these days," but "one of these days" never comes. All I remember learning about the missions in junior high was that the Spaniards thought they were all holy and stuff, saving the Indians, but they actually brought lots of diseases with them that killed thousands of native Californians. Just goes to show you – forcing people to be who you want them to be is a real killer.

There is one cool thing about our little corner of the San Fernando Valley, though. It's actually a way off campus, but the kids at Fernando High have adopted it as our own: Oakwood Cemetery. Fred Astaire and Ginger Rogers are both buried there, not next to each other, but I bet they dance together in the afterlife. If there is an afterlife. Visiting the cemetery after dark is a ghoulish pastime around here. Especially after Fright Dance on Halloween. Which makes me feel upset all over again. If Nadine and Curtis cruise the cemetery after Fright Night, I'll just die.

Anyway.

My locker was a gazillion miles away, but I was feeling surprisingly confident in spite of my best friend vaporising before my eyes. I knew my new blouse looked good, and I was wearing my favourite Levi's shorts, washed just enough times to be comfy. Last night I went all out and borrowed Mom's nail polish to paint my toenails *Vroooom!* (Translation: bright red.) Believe it or not, it looked very cool. And I blew my hair dry that morning, even though it's already straight, so it would be *super* straight. How could Zack Nash resist?

It wasn't until I was almost at my locker that my confidence disintegrated into tiny, shrivelled pieces.

"Hi, Bethy."

Carrie Taylor leaned against my locker twirling her impossibly long, perfectly blonde, naturally super-straight hair around one, olive-oil tanned finger.

"I'm Libby now," I said, sounding retarded even to me.

Carrie just chuckled.

"I've been waiting for you . . . Libby."

"Me?"

"Yes, *you*. Why else would I walk this far? Man, is this locker a punishment or what?"

"My other locker—"

"Yeah, I heard." Carrie sounded bored as she stepped back to let me try to remember the combination to my lock. She had that effect on me. I lost my mind around her. I felt like a wart. Everything about Carrie Taylor was smooth. She didn't have a single freckle on her face – not even one bump – just skin that looked like coffee with extra cream. Her lips were naturally mauve coloured. Her eyelashes were blonde, and she didn't even wear mascara. And her khaki shorts, rolled up to obscenity, revealed tanned legs so satiny I swear she shaved them every *hour*.

"Zack told me you're helping him with his essay after school," Carrie said.

"Yeah, well, if I can. I mean, I'll do my best." Why did I sound so guilty? Could Carrie Taylor see that I wanted to seriously kiss her boyfriend?

"That's really cool, Bethy."

I let the name thing go. "Thanks," I said, though I wasn't sure what I was thanking her for.

"I mean, you're so smart and everything."

"Thanks," I said again, though my voice sounded a bit weaker. Why was she here?

Carrie toyed with a tiny gold heart on a gold chain around her neck. Had Zack given that to her?

"I guess I'm grateful in a way," she said. "If I was smart like you, Zack would never be my boyfriend. You know how guys like him hate brainy girls."

I started to say "thanks" again, but I stopped myself. I'd just been insulted. Some brain. I couldn't even tell when I'd been slapped in the face. And hadn't Carrie Taylor just insulted herself? Why did it sound so good when Carrie called herself a moron?

"Well . . ." It's all I could think of to say. My locker finally opened and I had to concentrate real hard to figure out why I was there at all. Oh yeah. My Geometry book. Next class. Zack Nash and utter confusion. "Gotta go."

"Me too," Carrie said. "Cheerleading practice. Can you imagine them making us practise on a hot day like this?"

"How hideous."

"Listen to me, complaining already. I should be thankful they let me on the Varsity squad at all! It's, like, *unheard* of that a freshman makes varsity cheerleader. God, I am such an ingrate."

"Ingrate? That's a mighty big word for a dunce."

That's what I wanted to say. But I didn't have the nerve, not when Carrie Taylor's toe ring was just so perfectly situated on her flat, lovely, tanned middle toe. Carrie didn't need *Vroooom!* Her toenails and her fingernails were naturally pink, with natural white half moons edging each digit.

Instead, I said too brightly, "Well, I'm off to class." Horrified, I noticed I almost said, "classaroo." My shorts were sort of bunched up inside my thighs. I tried to dislodge them as I walked away, but they just bunched up even more.

"Oh, Bethy, I almost forgot," Carrie called after me.

I turned to face her.

"I have a message for you from Zack," she said.

Just hearing his name in connection with mine made the hairs on my freckly arm stand up. "For me?" I stammered.

"Zack is absent today, but he said to tell you he still wants to meet you after school. In the library."

"Oh. Okay. Cool."

Then Carrie nearly blinded me with her superwhite teeth, and I was left to navigate Geometry all on my own.

It felt like two hours, but it was actually only half an hour. Still, I knew in my gut that Zack Nash wasn't going to show.

"Did you miss the bus, dear?" Mrs Kingsley, the librarian asked me.

61

"No. I'm meeting someone. Or I was *supposed* to meet someone."

There were only about two other students in the library with me. There was no way I could have missed Zack, even though I checked each cubicle like five times. Eventually Mrs Kingsley started looking at me with pity in her eyes. That's when I decided to leave.

"If a student named Zack Nash comes in," I said to her, "could you please tell him I had other plans and couldn't wait?" It was a last-ditch attempt to salvage some dignity.

Mrs Kingsley nodded and smiled that pity smile again. I could tell in her eyes she knew what I knew – Zack Nash had stood me up.

All the way home, I was on the verge of tears. I felt so . . . so . . . *God*, I don't even *know* how I felt. It was just this lumpy pain in my stomach, like I was a terminal loser. What was I thinking? Yeah, like Zack Nash would ever seriously (or otherwise) kiss me or even treat me like a human being.

The closer I got to home, the worse I felt. Our house had become a combat zone. My parents weren't speaking to each other. The house was full of land-mines. One wrong move, one mistaken word, and our whole lives would blow. Dad had stormed out the night before, hadn't come home until it was becoming the next day. His stumble over the footstool in the family room, and subsequent slurred, curse-filled rant, woke everybody up. Though nobody moved. As ever, we braced ourselves for the hurricane, for the gale-force wind that would tear the roof off our lives at any moment.

"Libby, is that you?" Dad's voice greeted me from the living room as soon as I walked in the front door. He wasn't blotto, not yet, but I could tell he'd had a few. I sighed.

"Yeah, it's me," I said, making my way to my room.

"C'mon in here, Lib. Your friend is here."

Friend? My heart stopped. Please, oh please, if I've ever done anything good in my life, let that friend be Nadine.

"Where have you been?"

The voice was familiar. Wretchedly, sickeningly, barfingly familiar. Like looking at an awful car accident, I knew I should run the other way, but I couldn't resist. Turning, I walked towards the living room, unable to breathe. And then I saw him. An image I'd carry with me for life burned on to my eyes. There, sitting on a kitchen chair, next to my half-drunk dad, who was still in his bathrobe, slumped in a shabby, fake-leather recliner, beside Uncle Randall's busted heirloom chair and the dusty, hair-balled space where the old couch used to be, in the middle of our cruddy living room and pathetic, secret life, was the boy I'd now never, ever, kiss. Now Zack Nash knew everything. There was nowhere left to hide.

SEVEN

It was a miscommunication (yeah, right), an honest mistake (uh-huh), a case of me not hearing right (oh, *puhleeese*). Carrie Taylor insisted she'd told me Zack Nash would meet me at my *house* after school.

"If I said 'library' it was a pure boo-boo," she cooed when I saw her again. "I'm so sorry if I messed you up."

I would come to believe there was nothing pure about Carrie Taylor. Nothing at all.

It was awful.

It was mortifying.

It was very nearly obscene.

Seeing Zack Nash sitting in my dumpy house with my slobbery, half-sloshed dad was the worst moment of my life.

"What do you mean where have I been? Where have *you* been?" I demanded when I walked into my house and saw him there, panic disintegrating my manners.

"I've been right here," Zack said. "Waiting for you."

Juan Dog stood quaking at his feet, barking. *Yip! Yip!*

"How have you *both* been?" Dad asked, too slowly, completely missing the gist of the conversation. His robe fell

64

open. He caught it just before we all saw something we'd *never* forget.

Yip! Yip!

"You've got to get out of here, Zack," I practically shrieked. "I mean, we've got to get out of here. I mean, do you still have time to work on that essay? It's not too late, is it? Is it?"

Zack looked at me slack-jawed. I was obviously on the brink of hysteria. Terror, shame, guilt, humiliation all ricocheted through my head like a pinball gone berserk. My whole body went on tilt. No matter how many times I screamed Shut up! Shut up! Shut up! in my head, I was utterly unable to stop babbling.

"We should work in the kitchen. No! The family room. No! My bedroom. *No!* God, no. The backyard. No! Uh, want a soda? A soft drink of some kind?"

"Okay, sweetheart," Dad mumbled. "Do we have any Orangina?" One slipper dangled from his bare big toe. "With ice?"

Juan kept barking. *Yip! Yip!*

Suddenly Rif burst through the front door, slamming it hard. His hair was uncombed, his shoes untied. He grumbled something about global warming, then clomped heavily down the hall to his room and slammed that door, too.

Zack showed no signs of getting up. Though I couldn't blame him. I'm sure he thought my head would soon spin all the way around and I'd hurl pea soup. He looked terrorised when I lunged forward and grabbed his arm.

"C'mon!"

Yip! Yip!

"Quiet, Juan!" I screamed. Mercifully, Juan shut up. He toddled after us.

"Nice to meet you, Mr Madrigal," Zack stammered, tripping over his feet as I dragged him into the kitchen.

"Any time, lad," said my father.

Lad? Would the humiliation ever end? Dad was now a *leprechaun*?

As I rushed Zack from the living room, Dad called after me, "Don't forget my Orangina, Bethy."

"Betsy?" Zack asked. "Is that your real name?"

Yip! Yip!

Oh God, please take me now, I silently prayed.

Mom stored the case of Orangina she bought at Costco in the garage underneath the forty-pound bag of dog food she bought for our two-pound Chihuahua and the jumbo pack of toilet paper she bought for us.

"I'll be right back," I said to Zack, sitting him at the kitchen table. "Don't move. I mean, please just sit right there and I'll be right back. I just said that, right? I mean, hang out in the kitchen, if you would, while I get my dad's Orangina in the garage."

"Hey, what happened to the construction?" Zack asked innocently. "When my parents renovated our kitchen it took, like, months."

"Construction?"

Yip?

"The kitchen renovation you mentioned over the phone," Zack said. "All that banging."

"Ah yes, the renovation." I stalled for time. My lower lip hung like Dirk's, my brain locked in a panic freeze. I could feel circles of sweat expanding in my armpits. True, few rooms in the world needed renovation more than the Madrigal kitchen. Mom had wallpapered the eating area with Friendly's wallpaper. Not a smiley, happy wallpaper, but the *actual wallpaper* from the Friendly's restaurant chain, complete with the Friendly's name and logo. No, I am *not* kidding. The construction company she worked for had built a Friendly's in the valley and there was a roll of wallpaper left over.

"Can I take that?" Mom had asked her boss.

"To the dump?"

"No. I want to take it home."

"Why?"

"So I can wallpaper my kitchen with it."

He laughed, thinking she was joking. That's what Mom told us when she brought the large industrial roll of wallpaper home. We laughed, figured she was joking, too. A week later, we were eating every family meal in a Friendly's restaurant dining room. Mom's explanation: "Diners make me feel happy." Then she added, "Besides, nobody will see it but us."

Who would have thought Zack Nash would be sitting on one of our vinyl chairs at our faux-wood table in our Friendly's dining nook? It was simply too hideous to imagine.

"We're actually just starting construction," I explained, a trickle of sweat slowly making its way through my hair. "That's what you heard. The *beginning* of renovation. The *banging* part of it. Yeah, the, uh, constructionists won't start up here for, God, like two weeks or something. That's what they told us, anyway."

Constructinists? Ah, geez.

Zack just stared.

"Libby! My Orangina!" Dad called from the living room. At that moment, I loved him more than I could express.

"Right away, Dad!" I called out. Then I excused myself to the garage to wrestle with the Costco tower.

Only in the dark, cool dampness of the garage could I begin to breathe again. I shut my eyes, leaned against the door, inhaled deeply, and blew it out. I started to feel calmer, more human. Everything's going to be okay, I said to myself. Zack probably didn't even notice that Dad was blotto. Dressed in his robe at four in the afternoon? That could be considered artistic.

As good luck would have it, I didn't need to dismantle the Costco tower after all. I was able to wriggle my hand underneath all the piled-up stuff and pull out three Oranginas. Then, to be on the safe side, I pulled out two more just in case my dad or Zack wanted seconds. My heart was actually returning to its normal beat when I pushed through the door and made my way back into the kitchen.

Pwoosh! The pop top on the beer can sent a fine beer spray into the air. I saw my father's Adam's apple bob up and down and heard his swallow as he gulped a mouthful of brew. "Never mind about the soda, Lib."

I nearly dropped all five Orangina bottles right there in our Friendly's kitchen.

"What are you *doing* in here, Dad?"

He responded with a deep, belly burp.

"We have to study! Zack has been here too long already. We need the table. He has an essay due tomorrow." I so frantically rattled off all the reasons why my dad had to leave, I didn't notice he'd begun to cry.

"I'm gonna miss this dump," he said, sniffing.

Zack seemed unfazed by the horror unfolding before our eyes. "My mom felt the same way," he said, gently, "before our kitchen renovation."

"Zack, we have to leave," I blurted out. "Now. Right now."

"Good times . . . so many good times . . ." Dad slapped the palm of his hand on the table so hard Zack, Juan, and I all jumped. "Right here at this very dinner table."

"Zack, you're going to get an 'F' in that essay!" I was practically screaming at him. Juan Dog got scared. *Yip. Yip.*

"Chill out." Zack stood up and slung his backpack over his shoulder. My dad tightened the terry cloth belt on his robe, stood up, too, then fell back in his chair.

"You're good people, Jackie," he slurred as his ruddy, flushed face squeezed up into another outbreak of tears.

Ah, *geez.*

Just take me now, God. A single thunderbolt to the head.

"Where are we going?" Zack asked as I shoved him out the front door.

"How about Chatsworth Park?" I suggested, my dry mouth smacking.

"Chatsworth Park? Isn't that a little far?"

"Why don't we just walk for a few minutes," I said quickly. "We can walk and talk . . . about your essay."

"Okay," Zack said dubiously.

Grateful beyond belief, I exhaled. My heart was still racing, but outside the house I felt considerably calmer. Like the stillness after a tornado twists through a trailer park, I felt strangely peaceful though wrecked. Six inches away from the boy that I loved, my emotions were too spent to freak me out.

"Good, good," I said. "Let's walk."

So we walked. We passed a 7-Eleven mini mart and a bunch of kids in baggy pants hanging out by the ice machine. We passed a doughnut shop that smelled like vanilla and baked sugar, a dry cleaner's that reeked of chemicals. It was hot out, but I wasn't sweating any more. The warmth actually felt good for a change. I exhaled.

"Writing an essay is like having an argument you win," I said after we'd walked in silence awhile. "You start off stating how you feel about something or what you want to prove, then you prove it. At the end, you say, 'See? I told you I was right.'"

Zack chuckled. I loved it when he chuckled.

"What is your essay supposed to be about?" I asked.

"Passion," he answered, and a spark of electricity shot through my entire body. "We're supposed to write an essay about something we feel passionate about."

Please God, don't let his essay be about Carrie Taylor.

"I want to write about pitching," he said, "but I don't know where to begin."

"Pitching? Like in baseball?"

"Yeah, like being a pitcher and standing on the mound and knowing the entire game is in your hands. To me, that's passion."

I knew all about that. I saw Zack pitch a game once, last year. Nadine made me go to the inter-school game because she had a crush on the third baseman. I barely noticed any of the players; my eyes were locked on the mound. Zack Nash stood there, in his snug uniform, twirling the baseball in his fingers, hoofing the ground with his cleats, adjusting the bill of his cap, slyly glancing over his shoulder at the base runner. Then he reached high over his head, brought his hands back down to his heart, and catapulted the ball across home plate. It was mesmerising. Yeah, I knew all about the passion of pitching.

"The pitcher's mound is the centre of the universe," he said quietly. "It's the top of Mount Everest. When you're up there, there's an eerie kind of silence. I mean, you can hear the crowd, but they're sort of background noise, like rain falling or something. What you really hear is the catcher, speaking to you with his hands, his eyes. He knows you, everything about you. He's *concentrated* on your every move. He can tell if you're upset just by the way you grip the ball. He knows how to calm you down. He knows what you're going to do even before you do it. It's totally close, that relationship, like best friends. I mean, the way we communicate, the way we know each other, it's almost like *love*."

I was speechless. I wanted to be a catcher, *his* catcher. I longed to communicate silently with him, with my hands and

71

my eyes. I wanted to drown out all the background noise and concentrate on his every move.

"My girlfriend thinks I'm crazy," Zack said, laughing. "She says baseball is just a dumb game."

"That's because she's just a dumb blonde."

That's what I *wanted* to say. But of course I didn't. The mere mention of his "girlfriend" totally ruined the spiritual moment I was sure Zack and I had just shared. Instead I blurted out, "You don't need me, Zack." Then, frantically editing myself I added, "I mean, you don't need me to help you with your essay. You've got it all right there."

"Right where?"

"That stuff you just told me, that's poetry. That's passion. That's writing. Just write it down."

He thought for a moment. "Thanks," he said finally. "I'll do that."

"You're welcome."

I waited for more, for him to say, "I never noticed how beautiful you are and how smart. How could I have missed it?" Instead he said, "I've gotta go."

"Go?"

"I have an essay to write."

I burst into laughter — way too loud for the joke. Zack had that perplexed look on his face again.

"Thanks again, Betsy," he said.

I didn't correct him. When Zack Nash called me "Betsy" it sounded like poetry.

EIGHT

October was the month from hell at the Madrigal house.

It was the longest stretch of silence I can remember. It scared everybody. Even Juan Dog didn't dare interrupt the tension in our home with a bark or a whimper. It was that bad.

"Libby, please pass the McNuggets," Mom would say.

"Libby, when your mother is finished selecting her McNuggets, could you please pass them back to me?" Dad would say.

"Libby, when your father is finished with the honey-mustard sauce, could you please pass it to this end of the table?"

"Libby, if your mother isn't using the barbecue sauce, could you please hand it to me?"

My arm would reach right and left across the table, and I'd watch my parents not look at me or each other. My mother deliberately chewed her food as if each bite were packed with explosives. Dad washed chunks of food down his throat with mouthfuls of beer. I don't think he chewed at all. Rif kept his head down and was the last to arrive and the first to leave. This went on for days, almost two weeks, in fact. One night, overcome by the stress of witnessing the disintegration of our parents' marriage, Dirk burst into tears.

73

"My best friend is joining the Boy Scouts and I can't even go with him," he wailed. "You need a parent's permission slip!"

Mom said, "I'll give you a permission slip, honey."

Dad said, "Libby, if your mother is finished taking her pizza, could you please hand me another slice?"

Early Saturday morning, I was awakened by the unmistakable sound of a buzz saw coming from the garage. I know what that sound means; I watch crime TV. Petrified, I lay rigid in my bed, my heart thumping out of my chest. My God, he's done it, I thought. I listened for screams, imagined the worst. I couldn't even cry for my mom, not yet. The shock was too fresh.

Rif peered out his bedroom door just as I did. We both looked terrified. Dirk wasn't there. Had my father taken him, too? Were we next? The blood drained from my face and pooled somewhere in the lower part of my stomach. Rif whispered, "Follow me." I swallowed, followed, too scared to be left alone. We tiptoed down the hall, toward the hideous, high-pitched whine of the buzz saw. Rif held up his hand to stop me before we reached the door to the garage. Then he asked, "Ready?"

I nodded, but I wasn't ready at all. Paralysed by the thought of seeing what I was about to see, I clamped my eyes shut as Rif blasted open the door.

"Good morning, kids."

Whistling and clear-eyed, Dad was cutting segments of chair spindle. Uncle Randall's chair was upside down on his workbench, porcupined with clamps.

"Hand me that wood glue, would ya, son?" he asked Dirk.

Stunning us both, Mom appeared with a steaming cup in her hand. "Coffee, Lot?" she asked.

"Ah." He sighed, reaching to hug her. "My angel of mercy." Clearly, they'd worked things out.

I remember every second of that day, every millisecond. My family seemed to glow around the edges. My dad was my dad again. He was funny, charming, silly. We couldn't stop smiling. Mom made lemonade, and ham-and-cheese sandwiches from scratch.

"Just a little *snackywacky* to keep body and soul together," she chirped. She served them on a tray in the garage where Dirk was helping Dad fix Uncle Randall's chair so he could earn a Boy Scout merit badge.

I brought our old radio out and plugged it into the socket over the workbench. Mom turned to an oldies station and danced with my father when "My Sharona" came on. Even Rif tapped his foot. I felt so happy, I wanted to cry, just burst into tears the way I sometimes do when *Oprah* does a story on a woman who digs herself up from the depths of despair and finds true love in a soup kitchen. I wanted to kiss every member of my family and hug them hard with my full body the way Oprah hugs her inspirational guests.

That night, Mom cooked dinner. And I helped.

"Could you please plug in the George Foreman, Libby?" she asked. I lit up. My brothers and I had pitched in to buy Mom a Lean Mean Grilling Machine a couple of Christmases ago, but she had only used it once. "If only I could throw it in the dishwasher," she said, by way of lame explanation. "Who has time to hand wash a grill?"

Happily, I plugged George in and ripped up a head of lettuce for a salad. *Romaine*, not iceberg. I even made a vinaigrette from scratch. Mom marinated five chicken breasts and told me to pour five glasses of milk.

"Five?"

"Daddy's drinking milk with us tonight," she said. This time, when she said, "Daddy," it sounded perfectly right.

Everything was perfectly right. Mom asked, "Need any help with your Fright Dance costume?"

I couldn't believe she even knew about it. Stunned, I stammered, "No," and Mom walked over to me and encircled me with her arms. She stood on her tiptoes and kissed the top of my head.

"Everything's going to be okay, sweetie. You'll see."

In my mother's fleshy arms, smelling her smell, I felt like a kid again. I remembered a time she took me to a mother-daughter fashion show at a fancy department store in Encino. I wore white gloves and black patent leather shoes. She wore a pink dress that made me think of bubble gum. We ate little sandwiches that had no crusts and watched women parade by us in the most beautiful clothes I'd ever seen. Mom was beautiful, too. As I gazed up at her, I thought, When I grow up, I want to be just like my mom.

That was when we were two girls in a family of guys. We read *Family Circle* magazine together and clipped recipes. We went shopping at the mall and ate ice cream cones. That was when Dad drank only one cocktail after work, and Mom ate salads. I was young and things were simple.

It felt like we were back there again.

With the grilled chicken breasts and homemade romaine salad on the table, my family held hands in a circle and said grace. Well, Rif, Dirk and I *mumbled* grace because we'd forgotten the words. At the end, before "Amen," Dad bowed his head and said, quietly, "Thank you for my family, this food, and the strength to be a better dad."

I nearly burst into tears.

After so long, it felt so . . . so . . . *normal.*

Then, the police came to the door.

At first, Mom was actually *relieved* it wasn't a bill collector.

"Does a Richard Madrigal live here?" the uniformed officer asked my parents. Mom's face abruptly fell to the floor.

"We call him Rif. My son, my younger son, my other son, couldn't pronounce 'Rich' when he was a baby, and, well, the nickname . . ." Mom was babbling.

"Are you Richard's parents?"

"What has he done?" Dad asked.

Rif leaped up from the dinner table and dashed to his room. I didn't move a muscle. I wanted to hear everything the cops were saying.

"Your son has been identified on a surveillance tape in a shoplifting incident."

"Shoplifting?"

"Apparently he took several cartons of cigarettes."

"Cigarettes?" Mom's mouth fell open. "My son doesn't smoke."

Upon hearing that, I stood up and bounded down the hall to get Rif in his room, but he'd already escaped out his bedroom window. I saw sneaker footprints in the dirt of our backyard.

Winnie, the neighbour's dog, was barking her guts out.

Deflated, I plopped down on Rif's unmade bed. Couldn't we ever have a family dinner that wasn't a freak of nature?

The Chatsworth Police Station looks more like a library than a police station. The low, beige brick buildings are lined up neatly with one another. Law and *order*, I thought when my dad drove up with all of us in the car.

"Libby and Dirk, you stay home," Mom had said earlier that evening after Rif came home and confessed. Well, he didn't officially confess until Dad swatted him on the head and a cigarette butt shot out like a popped kernel of corn.

"No way am I staying home," I'd said.

"Me, either." Dirk was scared of going to a real-live police precinct, I could tell. But he was more scared of missing a family outing. They were so rare in our family.

So, it was about eight that night when the Madrigal family piled into the car and drove to the edge of the San Fernando Valley to the police station to turn Rif in. On the way, of course, we stopped for fast food. No one had been able to eat Mom's home-cooked meal with Rif's impending arrest stressing everybody out.

"You never know what kind of crud they're going to feed

you in jail," Mom said testily to Rif. Then, to the intercom at the drive-through window, she shouted, "Four Whoppers, four large orders of fries, a chicken sandwich, no bun, four regular Cokes, and one Diet Coke."

Some things never change, even when your big brother is a perp.

In the lobby of the precinct, Dirk and I sat on a bench while my parents disappeared with Rif and a detective. They were gone for about an hour. I have to tell you, it wasn't as exciting being there as I'd imagined. I spent the first fifteen minutes examining the colour head shots of past and present police chiefs. I bought Dirk another Coke from the vending machine. The rest of the time, I pretty much watched him swing his legs back and forth under the bench. Dirk said, "I sure hope I never get arrested."

I shot back, "People don't just get arrested, you numbskull. They commit a crime and they get *caught*. If you don't want to do the time, don't do the crime."

Instantly, I regretted my tone. It wasn't very sisterly, to say the least. I'd always tried to protect my sensitive little brother from my insensitive family. And here it was *me* being mean. I reached over and put my arm around Dirk's shoulder as he hung his head, still swinging his feet.

"Everything is going to be okay, you know."

He nodded unconvincingly.

"It is," I said. "I swear."

Please God, I silently prayed, Let what I just said be true.

Finally, my parents emerged from the interesting section of

the police station, walking behind Rif. "Community service," he grumbled, "and counselling."

"Which I've requested for the whole family," Mom said proudly.

"All of us?" I asked, incredulous. "What did *I* do?"

"A problem with one family member is a problem with the whole family," Mom said, obviously quoting Dr Phil. Then she marched out of the door to the car.

"No it *isn't*!" I screeched, racing after her. "Rif is the thief, not me!"

Rif said, "They get you hooked on nicotine, then they won't let you buy cigarettes! It's a conspiracy to get the parks cleaned up for free."

Apparently, his community service included a trash bag and a broom in Chatsworth Park. In the car, Dad turned the ignition and pulled out of the parking lot. Mom said, "You got off light, Rif. You could have gone to jail."

"But we got off heavy!" I whined, repeating, "What did I ever do to deserve counselling?"

Dad suddenly piped up, "She's right, Dot. This isn't fair."

Mom glared at him. Buoyed by my father's resistance, I followed suit. "No. It *isn't* fair."

"In fact," said my dad, "I'm not going to do it."

"Me, either," I said. "I'm not going."

"Me, either," Dirk said, then inexplicably began to cry.

"We're all going," Mom said.

"No, we're not." Rif had jumped on the bandwagon. He crossed his arms in front of his chest.

"*You* are *definitely* going, Rif," Mom said. "It's a court order."

"Court schmort," Rif said. "The judge was on the *phone*."

"What difference does that make?" Dad asked, getting annoyed.

"If I'd been allowed to go before the judge, I could have pleaded not guilty on the grounds of conspiracy."

"Conspiracy! You were caught on tape shoving three cartons of cigarettes down your cargo pants!"

"Which I *would* have paid for, if I was *allowed* to!"

Dirk cried louder. Mom said, "This family needs help, and now is our chance."

"I'm not going," I said over and over.

"We're *all* going," Mom said firmly, "and that's an order."

"An order? An *order*?" The car suddenly got very quiet. Dirk's periodic sniffs were the only sound other than the hissing of steam shooting out of my father's ears. "The day I take order from you, Dot, is the day you fit into a size two."

"Big bad man," my mother said mockingly to my dad.

"Not as big as your ass, my dear," he shot back.

Ah, geez.

My parents were off and running again, essentially picking up where they'd left off a few weeks earlier when Dad busted up Uncle Randall's chair. Our brief intermission of family harmony was over. The long-running Madrigal main feature – *Scream* – was playing again. Dirk, Rif, and I tried to get real small in the backseat. Well, that's not exactly right. I tried to disappear altogether. By the time we pulled into our brown driveway in front of our beige house, both my parents were seeing red. Mom leaped out of the car before it was totally stopped, slammed the door, and refused to speak to my father at all after that.

Like I said, October was the month from hell. The only bright spot – and I mean the *only* one – was Zack Nash.

NINE

We were casual hi-bye buddies at first.

"Hi, Zack," I'd say when I saw him standing by the drinking fountain.

"Bye, Libby," he'd say, when I was behind him as we left Geometry class.

He never said anything about my dad or his robe or his slobbery tears. I don't think he even noticed our missing couch or dirt backyard. And, after I summoned the nerve to tell him my name wasn't Betsy, he never called me it again. All of which made me love him even more.

"I got a 'B' on my essay!"

Breathless, Zack came bounding up to my Siberian locker.

"I've been looking all over campus for you," he said.

Of course, I couldn't think of anything to say back. A sappy smile was pasted on my face and I couldn't stop hearing five unbelievable words over and over in my head. Looking. All. Over. For. You. He looked all over campus for me? For *me*?

"Thank you so much, Libby," he said. His lips were the colour of raspberries. Had his teeth always been so white? I wanted to tilt my head back, lower my eyelids, part my lips, and let him thank me properly. *Seriously.*

"I owe you a Geometry session," he said.

"Forget Geometry. Just kiss me. Now. Before your moronic girlfriend shows up and asks if buffalo wings are really made from tiny, flying bison."

That's what I *wanted* to say.

"Yeah," is what I said.

"Next week, okay? After school."

"Perfect."

I was looking at his eyelashes. They were curled and long and perfect. The eyelashes of a seriously kissable boy.

We met in the school library. At my insistence.

"Hi, Mrs Kingsley," I said, steering Zack past the librarian's desk before we went to a back cubicle to study. "I found him. Zack Nash. He was at my *house* the other day. A misunderstanding."

Mrs Kingsley blinked slowly. I could see her trying to remember who I was. Zack clearly wondered why I was telling her this, too. His thick eyebrows were pressed down into his luscious lashes.

"We'll start studying now," I said, smiling smugly.

Zack was already halfway to a table near the back of the room. I scurried after him, popping a piece of sugarless gum in my mouth to make sure my breath was minty fresh.

"Geometry is about sizes and shapes instead of numbers." Zack dived right in. "You have to sort of *see* it more than *think* about it."

He opened his textbook. I sat next to him and opened

84

mine. Not only was he gorgeous, he smelled of fabric softener.

"Remember the five postulates?"

"Some of the guys in da Vinci's *Last Supper*?"

"Ha-ha, Libby."

I laughed, he laughed. Amazingly, I wasn't too nervous to make a joke – dumb though it was. In fact, I felt completely calm only inches away from the boy that I loved. Had the intense stress of seeing Zack Nash in my house with my dad in his robe zapped all the fear out of me? Was this some sort of post-traumatic *relaxation* syndrome?

"The next quiz is on circumference and congruent triangles."

I groaned.

"Don't worry. You can do this."

When Zack Nash said it, I actually believed it.

We worked together in the library for about an hour. Miraculously, Geometry began to make sense.

"That's a ninety-degree angle! And so is *that* one!"

"Right." Zack beamed and I felt beautiful.

Two days later, as Mr Puente handed out the quizzes in class, Zack flashed me a thumbs-up. For the first time since the semester began, I felt eager to take a maths quiz. At least, I didn't feel like the class dunce any more. Not when it came to congruent triangles.

After the bell rang, as we shuffled out of class, it was all I could do to keep from flinging my arms around my hero, Zack Nash.

"I got it!" I squealed. "I saw it! You're awesome."

"I told you," Zack said, as proud as I was.

After the triumph of the Geometry quiz, our hi-byes had more depth.

"Hey," Zack said, as he passed me in the hall. This time, he nodded, too. He may have even raised his eyebrows and everyone knows what *that* means.

"See ya," I said, on my way to the bus, trying to sound as sexy as an unnurtured, genetically-challenged, angst-filled, hopelessly gaga girl can.

By freshman Fright Dance, Zack Nash and I were extremely close to actually being friends. All I needed was a little time. Luckily, I had four high school years to make him mine. *Seriously* mine.

TEN

It's hard to tell which was more pathetic: Nadine chasing after Curtis at Fright Dance or Carrie chasing after Zack.

"Who are you supposed to be exactly?" I asked Zack, the one moment Carrie wasn't plastered to his side. Whoever he was, he was *gorgeous*. My heart pounded with the beat of the dance band on the gymnasium stage. Or was it being so close to him?

"I'm Ga—"

Carrie, spotting Ack about to utter a word without her, dived to his side. She tucked her hand into his, nestled up to his side, and shouted, "What are you two talking about? Algebra?"

"It's *Geometry*, you idiot."

That's what I wanted to say. I also wanted to mention that I'd gotten an "A" in Pre-Algebra, and would probably get another "A" in Algebra next year, but that would have sounded as desperate as she did. Ever since Carrie tried to sabotage my tutoring session with her boyfriend, I'd seen her in an entirely different light. Not a flattering pink glow, either. More like a deep, envious green. She'd started waiting for Zack outside Geometry class, and if she'd see me happen to walk out with him, she'd make some cheesy remark like, "You *still* need help with your homework, Bethy?" No matter how many times I told her my name was Libby, she never got it right. I could tell Zack was embarrassed. I could also tell Carrie was totally jealous, which was pretty laughable. I mean, she had him body and soul; I had him for quadrilaterals. She could seriously kiss him whenever she wanted to. I had to make do with wishing, hoping, praying, and pleading with the universe that Zack Nash would one day dump Carrie Taylor, then turn to me and say, "You're *it*. You're the only girl I want." Yeah, right.

"I was just asking Zack who he was supposed to be tonight," I said to Carrie at Fright Dance.

"*We* are Gwen Stefani and Gavin Rossdale!" she chirped. Zack rolled his eyes. So *that's* why Zack had his hair slicked back.

"I couldn't think of anything," he mumbled apologetically.

"That's why you have me," Carrie said, kissing his neck and nibbling his earlobe. Now I rolled my eyes. Zack looked about as comfortable as a boy buying his first condom.

"And who are you supposed to be?" Carrie asked me as soon as Zack's earlobe was out of her mouth. "Einstein?" She giggled.

"I'm Betty. Betty Rubble. Nadine is Wilma Flintstone."

Zack chuckled. God, I love it when he chuckles. Carrie said, "*Très* Stone Age."

"Thanks," I said. "We wanted costumes that really rock."

Zack laughed out loud. Man, I love it when he laughs out loud. Oddly, I felt calm again. Seeing Zack without losing my power of speech, going to my first freshman dance, wearing a gigantic blue bow in my hair – it all felt incredibly *normal.* Was it possible that my statement to Dirk in the police station really was true? Everything really *was* going to be okay?

"Let's dance!" Carrie tugged Zack on to the dance floor, and I watched him self-consciously sway back and forth while she wiggled obscenely all over him. Oh, brother. She's such a show-off. When being beautiful is just about all you have to offer the world, I guess it feels mighty insecure. I felt sorry for her. (Okay, I *tried* to feel sorry, but all I really felt was mad that she was such a conniving back-stabbing you know what.)

Fright Dance *was* totally cool. I had to hand it to the decorating committee. Before you could get into the gym, you had to pass through the Haunted Corridor. It was completely dark except for the black lights that flashed each time thunder roared. Somebody had the majorly ingenious idea of hanging a million pieces of string from the ceiling, just long enough to tickle the top of your head and freak you out. They played lines from scary movies, like the one where Hannibal "the Cannibal" Lecter purrs, "I'm having someone over for dinner tonight."

But what almost made me run home screaming was the "Guts" initiation at the end of the Haunted Corridor. If you had the guts to blindly put your bare hand into three dark buckets, you were allowed into the dance. Each bucket was covered in a black sheet with a hand-sized slit in it. The first was labelled EYEBALLS. Every girl before me who stuck her hand in screamed. The guys acted tough, but I could tell they wanted to scream, too.

"You go first." Nadine, a huge raw-hide bone twisted into her hair, dug her fingernails into my arm. My heart was pounding so loudly. I had my own internal thunder. Taking a deep breath, I shoved my hand into the blackness and nearly gagged. Inside, I could feel gooey, slimy, round balls – lots of them. I pulled my hand out as quickly as I put it in.

Nadine did the same, only adding a bloodcurdling shriek.

The second bucket, INTESTINES, was just as slimy and gooey. By the time I reached the third, PUS, I couldn't wait to yank my hand out and run to the restroom to wash all the "guts" off.

"Peeled grapes, spaghetti, and cream of wheat."

That was the consensus in the bathroom. Still, everybody scrubbed the "guts" off their hands and felt queasy until the shimmying and sweating of the first big dance of the year made us all forget.

"Have you seen Curtis?" a breathless Nadine, aka Wilma Flintstone, asked me as she rushed off the dance floor. The bone in her still-striped hair was flopped over to one side. She tugged at the top of her leopard-print tube dress.

"How could I see Curtis? Can anyone see Curtis?"

"Ha-ha, Libby." Curtis had arrived at Fright Dance as the Invisible Man. Which meant he wrapped a gauze bandage around his head, with two eye slits and a mouth slit, and he wore one of his dad's old hats. Each time I *did* see Curtis, he was unravelling more and more.

"I haven't seen him lately," I said to Nadine.

She groaned. "My mom is picking us up in an hour!"

Nadine's hair hadn't grown out an inch before the big Halloween Fright Dance at Fernando High. But it was almost there, so her mom relented and let her go to the dance . . . with *me*. Mrs Tilson drove us to the gym, and planned to pick us up at eleven-thirty sharp. Which completely messed up Nadine's plan to seriously kiss Curtis at midnight.

"You're not Cinderella," I told her. "You could kiss him at eleven."

Exasperated, Nadine whined, "You don't understand."

She said that a lot lately, which really ticked me off. Just because one friend almost has a boyfriend doesn't mean the other can't understand what it's like. If explained properly, that is.

"Try me," I said testily.

"A group of us planned to go to Oakwood Cemetery after the dance."

Oh. "A group?" I asked.

"You're invited, of course. I mean, if you won't feel left out."

As I glared at my best friend, I made a mental note: *I, Libby Madrigal, do solemnly swear never to make my girlfriend feel bad about not having a boyfriend.*

"It doesn't matter anyway, Nadine," I yelled over the music that had just started up again. "Your mom is picking us up at eleven-thirty, so neither one of us can go." Then I added, "I'm going to find someone to dance with before the night is over."

And I left. Hoping to find Greg Minsky or some other guy who felt like dancing with a prehistoric girl who wore a chunky choker made of giant Styrofoam beads that were painted to look like rocks.

"Wanna dance?" Greg Minsky, Old Faithful, held out his hand. He was dressed as Bill Gates, which pretty much meant that he looked like he always did.

"Yeah," I said. "Let's dance."

Greg asked, "Want to go to Oakwood Cemetery with me at midnight?"

Nadine sulked all the way home in her mother's car. For some reason she was annoyed with me because her mom refused to let her go to the cemetery with Curtis. Like I could've convinced her mom to let her stay out past eleven-thirty if only I'd tried.

I didn't let it bother me. I knew Nadine would be fine in the morning. So I leaned my head against the window, thought about how kind Greg Minsky is, how fun Fright Dance was, how cute Zack Nash will always be and how my life was finally, finally starting to feel sort of okay.

"Thank you, Mrs Tilson," I said as she pulled up in front of our house and tossed me an air kiss like she always does.

"Goodnight, sweetheart," she said.

"Goodnight, Nadine," I called into the back seat. Nadine just grunted.

The lights were all on inside our house. It looked rather cosy, lit up like that. I felt happy, actually glad my parents were still up so I could tell them about the Haunted Corridor.

92

"Elizabeth?"

Mom called me from the living room as I walked through the front door. I was just about to tell her for like the millionth time that it's Libby when I walked into the living room and noticed the whole family was there. Dirk, Rif, my parents, and Juan.

"What's wrong?" I asked, my stomach plummeting to the floor.

That's when Dad dropped the bomb.

ELEVEN

Dad was stone-cold sober on a Friday night, which should have been my first clue that our lives were about to change forever. Rif was home before midnight on Halloween, which should have been my second.

Dad took a deep breath, then said, "We're moving."

No one said a word. Not a peep. Had we heard him right?

"Moving?" I asked.

Dirk said, "Huh?"

Rif said, "We're moving? A new house? For real?"

"Moving?" I repeated. The knot in my stomach tightened.

"Yes. Moving."

Stunned, nobody moved at all. Mom looked down at her hands and quietly petted her Press-On nails.

"For *real*?" Rif repeated.

"For real," Dad said.

"Cool!"

"That's incredible!"

"My own room!"

"We're finally leaving this dump!"

Dirk and Rif whooped and hollered. Rif held up his hand

94

and Dirk slapped a high five. I looked at my mother, who was now slowly rotating her wedding band around and around her finger. Instinctively, I reached down and gripped the seat of the kitchen chair Mom had brought into the living room for me to sit on.

"To Barstow," Dad said abruptly. Then he plopped down on his recliner with a loud *thunk*.

"Where?" Dirk's lower lip glistened.

Mom fixed her stare on the dustballs that were still huddled together where the couch once was. Rif just sat there and stared into space. I suddenly gasped, realising only then that I'd been holding my breath.

"What?" I burst out. "Why?!"

"This is a grown-up decision that your father and I had to make," Mom said. "I'm sorry that your lives will be disrupted, but there's no other choice. We'll pack up the house this weekend and move early Monday morning."

Early Monday morning. Those three words echoed in my head. Early. Monday. Morning. I wouldn't have the chance to say goodbye to anybody at school?! What about Nadine? What about Zack? What about congruent triangles? How could this be happening?

"No way," I said.

Dirk asked, "Is Barstow a street near us?"

"I'm not going." I crossed my arms firmly in front of my chest.

"Barstow is a city, you idiot," Rif snapped at Dirk. "It's about halfway between here and Las Vegas."

My mother glared at him. How did he know that?

"I don't care where it is," I said. "I'm not moving. I'll live with Nadine."

"If Libby lives with Nadine, can I have her room?" Dirk asked.

Now I glared at Dirk. Is that all I meant to my little brother? I felt like shoving a dustball up his nose. But I was too upset to do anything.

Disrupted? Had my mother apologised for *disrupting* our lives? Wouldn't *ruining* our lives be more accurate? Why Barstow? And why *now*, just as Zack Nash and I were on the road to becoming the friends that would eventually lead to becoming the serious kissers?

"What's going on?" I asked, near tears. "You can't just dump this on us!"

"Hey, I'll be sprung from community service," Rif said, grinning. "Cool."

"Sometimes adults have to make difficult, adult decisions," Mom said. Dad memorised his slippers.

My eyes nearly popped out of my head. They pick *now* to act like adults? What about last month when I needed a ride to the library and Dad suggested I hitchhike? Or the time I asked Mom the difference between a French kiss and an American kiss and she totally bailed on the truth by telling me that the French only kiss *cheeks*?

"I don't understand what's going on!" I repeated, my voice becoming desperate and whiny.

"There's nothing to understand. We're moving on Monday

and that's that." Dad sighed and stood up. "It's late. We should all get some sleep."

Nadine spent the weekend at my house sobbing. "It can't be true! Tell me it's not true!"

"It's true."

"It *can't* be true!"

"It is." I was numb. I moved like a robot around my room, throwing stuff into cartons without caring if it broke or not. My life was over. Why should I care if I busted a CD player?

"How could you do this to me?" Nadine wailed. "What about our serious kisses?"

That's when I started to cry. "You'll have to have yours without me."

"It won't mean as much if I can't tell you about it."

"Call me. If phones work in the armpit of the world." I sniffed hard and threw my reading lamp into the box.

By Sunday evening, the only things left to pack were the sheets on my bed and my toothbrush. Like zombies, Nadine and I left the Chatsworth house and wandered the streets of our neighbourhood in an emotional daze.

"I need you to do something for me, Nadine," I said, as it began to get dark.

"Anything. You name it."

Stopping on the sidewalk, I faced my best friend and took a deep breath. "Will you please tell Zack I said goodbye?"

"Zack *Nash*? The maths guy?"

"Yeah. Tell him what happened, okay? Tell him I won't ever forget hi—"

Greg Minsky suddenly appeared behind me on the sidewalk. He clamped his hands over my eyes, which he always did, which always annoyed me. His palms were clammy. He held on way too long, after I shouted, "Greg! Let go!" a million times. Pressing his body to my back, he wriggled with me. I could smell his Right Guard deodorant.

"Greg! Let *go*!" Really, I was in no mood.

"Let go of her, Greg. *God.*" Nadine gave him a little shove. Releasing me, he asked, "Is it true?"

I ran my thumb under my bottom lashes, adjusted my dishevelled shirt. "I hate it when you do that."

"*I hate it when you do that.*" Greg mimicked me in a sappy, singsong voice. Boys are so immature. "Libby, is it true?"

"Yeah. It's true," I said.

His face fell. "Man," he said.

"I know. It sucks."

"*Man!*" For a second I thought Greg Minsky was going to cry. Hanging his head, he jammed the toe of his sneaker into a crumbling crack in the concrete. I felt awful. I liked him, but he liked me *that* way. Story of my love life. I mean, Greg's a nice guy, but I can't get past the zit clusters on either side of his chin and his unibrow. Not that I'm Miss America. It's just that I've never been able to drum up an attraction to him. I knew I'd never want to seriously kiss Greg Minsky. Never.

"Here," he said, crowding Nadine out and shoving a letter at me. I felt queasy, didn't know what Greg Minsky had to say

– in a letter, no less. So I just stood there. If I didn't touch it, I didn't have to read it, right?

"Take it," he said. Sighing, I reached out and took it.

"Read it," he commanded.

"You want me to read it now? Like, in front of you?"

"Yeah." That serious action was going on in his face again. Like the time he'd planted the slobbery kiss on me. Nadine stepped back, sniffed. I felt like I'd swallowed a shovelful of mud. Obviously he wasn't going to budge. So I opened it. Right there in front of him.

Greg Minsky had written me a poem.

Once a Life
Two souls floating, searching,
passing in the dark night.
One soul turning, seeing.
Who's there?
Is it you?
No answer.
Hello?
Silence.
The room is empty.
It's cold and colourless.
The walls are bare.
The only sound is the hollow echo of a beating heart.

Instantly, I felt like I always feel when I read a poem – panic. Am I getting its *true* meaning? Was he saying that we were two souls passing in the night? Was his heart hollow, or mine? And, what, he expected me to concentrate on deciphering poetry with him staring at me like that?

"Get it?" he asked.

"Of course," I lied. "It's beautiful."

"It's a going-away present," he said. "For you."

"It's beautiful." I racked my brain for something else to say, but what else could I say?

The three of us stood there in awkward silence until Nadine sniffed again and said, "I'm so sorry, Lib. I've gotta go. Curtis is supposed to call."

"I should go, too," Greg said. "I have homework."

My two friends hugged me hard. Nadine kissed my cheek and told me she loved me; Greg, thankfully, didn't do either.

"Call me as soon as you can!" Nadine said. Then she added, "I can't deal with saying goodbye."

"Me, either," I said.

Both of my friends promised to visit as soon as they could drive. Then suddenly, just like that, they left. I watched them grow smaller and smaller on the sidewalk, looking back only once.

PART TWO
Barstow

TWELVE

At first, I wept dramatically in the back seat of the Corolla, clutching a wadded-up Kleenex to my red, runny nose. But each time I wailed, Juan Dog lifted his little head and wailed with me.

"Mom, how could you dooooo this!" I bellowed.

Ahhhooooooo! Juan imitated me. *Oooh, oooh.*

Juan's howl made Mom, Dirk, and Rif laugh, which really made me mad. So, eventually, I let the tears flow soundlessly down my cheeks. I suffered in the loudest silence I could muster.

I'd seen the outskirts of Barstow before. On TV, when the new rovers landed on Mars and dune-buggied around and sent those orange pictures back to us. That's what Interstate Fifteen to Barstow looked like. *Mars.* Only without the orange colour. As far as the eye could see was dirt and sand and scruffy scrub dotting the planetary landscape. As we drove further into oblivion, I felt so low I could walk under a snake with a beehive hairdo. There wasn't even a Burger King. I mean, you could *die* out there.

"You've *got* to be kidding." It was all I could say between bursts of tears. Over and over, "You have *got* to be kidding me."

"It's a *desert*, honey," Mom said by way of explanation.

"No way."

"Really, it's the Mojave Desert."

"I *know* it's a desert! No way am I living in the middle of a desert. What's going on? Why are we here?"

Mom ignored my questions, just as she'd done for the past hour. After fourteen years of watching her *not* tell us the truth about all kinds of stuff, I knew she could easily *not* tell us why we were moving to Barstow for the entire car ride there. Which is exactly what she did (and didn't) do. Stubbornly, she stared through the windshield, following Dad in the U-Move truck, with Rif, Dirk, Juan Dog, and I squished into her car. No one wanted to drive with Dad because the U-Move wasn't air-conditioned. Even in November, even before noon, it was hotter than baked asphalt.

We drove forever on the freeway. At first, it was bumper-to-bumper traffic, one driver per car, cell phone in one hand, coffee mug in the other – the typical southern California commute. Angelenos would rather spend hours in traffic than be caught dead riding a bus. Mom didn't seem to care, settled her *fannywannydingo* into the car seat, and propped her elbow on the windowsill. I leaned my head against the window and let Juan lick the tears off my face.

By the time we reached Pasadena, the traffic had thinned out and the U-Move became a small square ahead of us. At the junction to Interstate Fifteen, Dad was hardly visible, he was so far ahead.

"Do you think he's trying to ditch us?" Rif asked, joking.

Mom barely smiled. She said, "Apparently we'll have to make it there on our own."

Briefly lifting my head from the window, I blew my nose.

By the time the landscape became lunar, we'd driven about two hours. I was cried out, exhausted by despair. Fernando High, Nadine, Zack Nash – they all seemed a gazillion miles away. Juan Dog was softly snoring on my lap. Dirk opened the back window and pelted us all with sand and heat.

"Shut the window, you moron," Rif snapped. The sweltering, overhead sun made Chatsworth seem balmy. The dry, hot wind made everyone squint. Quitting smoking hadn't been easy on Rif or us. He was in a perpetual foul mood, and he dragged everybody down with him.

"*Plants* don't even live here," I moaned, looking at the desolation stretching out in every direction.

"*You're* the moron," Dirk said to Rif, rolling the window back up.

"We stay on this road, right?" Mom asked Rif. Dad was long gone.

After gazing through the windshield, Rif concluded, "There's no *other* road."

So we drove. Eventually we saw a flicker of white, then neon, then what looked like a mall up ahead. "It's a *mirage*, right?" I asked haughtily.

"Outlets!" Mom's face lit up. "In-N-Out Burger! Kids, look! Del Taco! Shall I pull off?"

"No," said Rif. "Turn around."

My sentiments exactly. Mom said, "We'll scope out the outlets another time. We're almost there!"

"Almost *no*where," I said. Mom merrily continued to ignore us. She pulled off the freeway, followed the signs to Barstow. Which I noticed wasn't necessary. Rif was right – Barstow was the middle of absolutely nowhere. It's an old, medium-sized town surrounded by endless, flat Californian desert. The only way you'd miss it is if a humongous tumbleweed blew into town and got stuck on one of the ugly brown stucco buildings.

Mom saw it differently. Turning onto Main Street she chirped, "Oooh, look down there at the old railroad station! Look at the quaint shops!"

I said, "Oooh, look at the tattoo parlour."

"And look, Mom, body piercing!" said Rif.

"Military surplus."

"Knives, new and used!"

Mom's *look* was a knife, a dagger, actually, catapulted into the back seat. We shut up, suffered in silence. Juan, shaking, looked up at me, then out the window as Mom drove through the dreariest downtown I'd ever seen. The women looked like truck drivers, the men looked like Hell's Angels. The whole dirt-brown town seemed like time had forgotten it entirely. Butch Cassidy and the Sundance Kid could have been hiding out there for fifty years and no one would have bothered to look.

"Can't you feel the history here?" Mom squealed. "This used to be part of old Route Sixty-six!"

"Where's the new house?" Even Dirk was getting impatient.

"Look at the cute McDonald's! It's built into railroad cars!"

We all groaned at that one. Even the McDonald's looked old.

"Are we almost there?" I asked, dejected. I couldn't wait to lie facedown on my bed until college.

"We have to make one quick stop first," Mom said.

Now, we groaned even louder.

Mom consulted a crumpled piece of paper she pulled from her handbag, kept driving her one-woman tour. "It's not nowhere, Libby! Wal-Mart! Did you kids see the Wal-Mart we just passed?"

"A trailer park!" said Rif sarcastically. "Did you kids see the trailer park up ahead!"

With that, Mom flipped on her blinker and turned into the trailer park's front entrance, underneath the arched sign that read WELCOME TO SUNSET PARK.

"Ha-ha, Mom," I said.

"Har-de-har-har," said Rif. "We get the joke. You don't have to continue the white trash tour."

Mom disregarded the howls of her young. She drove down the little streets of the trailer park, past white rock lawns, brown rock lawns, beige rock lawns, green Astro Turf, metal awnings, "patio" tables made of cinder blocks, ceramic guard dogs, and row after row of large rectangular metal trailers.

"Are we even *allowed* in here?" Dirk asked. Mom said nothing, just kept driving. The paved streets were covered in desert sand.

"There's a communal pool," she said. "A rec room. Look! A tree!"

Rif and I peeked at each other and instantly knew the score. Mom had gone mad. She'd seat-belted herself in an old Toyota and chosen Barstow, of all places, to lose her marbles.

"Feel like an ice cream *coney-woney*, Mom?" I asked gingerly.

Suddenly, the car stopped with a lurch. "Eureka." Mom sighed. Stunned, we watched her release her seat belt, unlock the car door, and reach for her handbag. Rif and I simultaneously turned our heads to stare out of the window. The abrupt stop had engulfed us in a dust cloud. It took a few moments to settle down, but out of the grit emerged the figure of a woman, floating toward us, dressed in a flapping orange kaftan, weighted down with a thick turquoise necklace.

"Nana!" Mom cried out.

Who?!

Nobody moved. We sat there, flabbergasted. Except Mom, who heaved herself out of the Toyota and ran in small baby steps across the gravel road to *kiss, kiss* the wrinkly old woman with her arms extended. My brothers and I just stared at the two of them.

Yip.

"Kids, come meet your grandmother."

No one stirred. As far as I knew, all my grandparents were dead.

Yip. Yip!

"Come on, gang!"

Yip! Yip.

"You keep sitting in that car you're going to turn into three fried eggs!"

Yip! Yip! Yiiip!

If Juan Dog wasn't licking his lips in the way that let me know he had to go to the bathroom real bad, I never would have left the car. I would have refused to budge until my mom got back in the car, deserted the old lady, and drove us home to Chatsworth where we belonged. I'd learned from studying the Civil Rights movement in school how powerful passive resistance could be. Dead weight in the back of a two-door sports coupe would be near impossible to dislodge.

Yiiiip! Yiiippppppp!

"All right, you little runt," I snapped at Juan. Rif opened the passenger door and Juan leaped out. Slowly, the three of us unfolded out of the car.

"You must be Richard," the woman said to Rif, shaking his hand.

"We call him Rif," Mom said.

"And you must be Dirk," she said to Dirk. Dirk shyly hung his head and smirked. "Yeah." He giggled. Rif disappeared behind the trailer.

"And you . . ." She wafted toward me like a giant orange manta ray. "You must be Elizabeth."

"Bethy," said Mom.

"*Libby!*" I shot my mother an incredulous look.

"Bethy Libby," said Nana. "How unique!"

"It's *Libby*. Period."

"Libby Period? Is that like Cher?"

Oh, brother. I just looked at her. Mom stepped in. "Nana, our Elizabeth prefers to be called Libby. For now."

"Of course!" said Nana. "Libby suits you perfectly. Libby Period is so . . . *cumbersome.*"

The elderly woman cupped my face in her hands and stared at me. Her eyes were watery but an intense contact-lens blue. In the blinding sun, her short, spiky hair was so red it was almost violet. Each finger on her bony, speckled hands was ringed with blobs of silver and coral. Her fingers clacked when she moved them.

"Absolutely magnificent," she said as she hugged me. I tensed.

"I don't mean to be rude," I said into her shoulder, "but who are you?"

Pulling back, the woman teared up and bit her lower lip. "Your parents never spoke of me? Never showed you any photographs?"

I shook my head. Mom looked down at her chubby toes.

"I'm your father's mother, Libby. I'm your *grandmother.*"

I just stared. Clearly, this was some kind of trap. Even the worst parents in the world wouldn't deny their kids a nana. *Would* they?

"By the way," my, uh, grandmother said, sniffing, "where's my son?"

"He'll be here soon," Mom answered without looking up. "He had a few, um, errands to run."

The old woman's face fell. "Oh, well." She sighed. "I've waited twenty years to see him. What's twenty minutes

110

more?" Then she turned to us and said, "No sense waiting for him in the heat. Come inside, my darlings. I've waited a whole lifetime to meet you."

Rif rejoined us in front of the trailer, popping a Smint into his mouth. As he passed me, I could smell that he hadn't quit smoking after all. He followed "Nana" and Dirk through the metal door of her trailer. Mom stood in the street looking for Dad's U-Move. I didn't budge. I mean, the woman was a complete stranger. My grandmother? Living in the same *state* all these years? If it was true, my parents were either heartless or psychotic. I didn't know whether to feel furious or turn myself in to Social Services.

"Come on in, Libby!" the old lady said at her trailer door. "I won't bite."

I just stared at her.

"I swear. No biting whatsoever."

I had to believe her. What other choice did I have?

THIRTEEN

"Let me get this straight. My grandmother *isn't* dead?"

Mom and I were alone in the searing heat outside my newly discovered nana's trailer. No way was I going inside until I knew the truth.

"Not exactly," Mom said, her yellow patent leather handbag dangling on her forearm.

"Not *exactly*? Is she a clone? A robot? A mirage?"

The hotter it got outside, the more heated I felt inside. A line of sweat made its way down my flushed cheek, stopping at my gritted teeth. Glaring at my mother, I added, "Is the lady in that trailer Nana's long-lost *twin*?"

"Shhh! She'll hear you."

"Hear what? That you were just *kidding* when you told us she died before I was born?"

Mom draped one fleshy arm around my shoulder and led me down Nana's dusty street. Each passing second made me madder and hotter.

"The truth is," Mom said in a low voice, "your father and his mother never got along."

Wriggling out from under her sweaty arm, I snapped, "So?"

"So, it was easier for him to pretend that his mother had passed away."

"Easier?"

"You know, because he didn't want to talk to her."

Stunned into silence, I felt the trickle of sweat drip off my chin.

Seriously, I could not believe what I was hearing. Though I *should* have. It was so . . . so *typical*. How many years had we lived with my dad's bad behaviour? How often had we all pretended he wasn't drunk when we knew he was? Of course my parents would rather deprive us of a grandparent than deal with reality! Avoiding the truth is what they do best. Our family is one big fake out. Even our last name: Madrigal. A madrigal is a musical love poem. Get *out*. Our family is *so* not a musical love poem. We're more like a CD that was left out on the pavement in a Barstow summer.

"When your grandfather died," Mom continued, "your dad had sort of, um, a big fight with his mom."

Hands on my hips, I asked, "What kind of a fight?"

"A *family* sort of fight."

"What does *that* mean? The silent treatment for twenty years."

"Exactly my point! Your father didn't want the anger to simmer for years, so he decided it was better for the whole family if he pretended his mom had passed on."

I gaped at her. "Better for who?"

"Whom," Mom corrected me.

"Better for *whom*?" The word "whom" hurtled out of my

113

mouth like an angry dust storm. "Better for us to grow up without a grandmother? Wouldn't it have been *better* for Dad to get over it? Apologise? Do what he had to do to bring the family *together*? Isn't that what parents are supposed to do?"

Mom resumed looking for Dad's rental truck.

Images of childhood birthday parties, Christmas mornings, Thanksgiving dinners – all the times it would have been cool having a grandmother – flashed through my mind. Was she someone I could have talked to without violating the family's shhh-don't-tell policy?

The trailer door opened with a loud creak and my grandmother – not a twin nor a clone but the real deal – poked her head out and chirped, "Lunch is almost ready!" Then she popped back in and shut the metal door.

Emotionally overloaded, my head felt like a wasps' nest. I could almost feel the synapses in my brain misfiring. I wanted to either scream or crumple into a heap. I wanted to go home. I missed Nadine and staring at the back of Zack Nash's creamy neck in class. I even missed Ostensia and her stinky nachos. What was going on? Why me? Just as my life had finally begun to feel normal, I'm kidnapped to a hot, sandy street in the middle of nowhere, about to eat Spam or Primula or whatever else they call "food" in a trailer park with a woman I've never met, who gave birth to my father and just may have made my life easier if I'd been allowed to know she existed.

Life more than sucks.

Suddenly, a new image flashed through my brain. Panic radiated from the centre of my chest, down my arms, and out my fingertips. I wheeled around to face my mother, grabbed both of her flabby upper arms, and gasped, "We're not moving into Nana's *trailer*, are we, Mom?"

Mom laughed out loud. "Don't be silly. Do you think we would do that to you?"

Without waiting for an answer, Mom waddled toward my grandmother's trailer, saying, "Let's go in. I'm starved."

Entering my new nana's trailer was an out-of-body experience. It was like passing through the flames of hell into air-conditioned heaven. It was *gorgeous*. I couldn't believe my eyes.

"Isn't this the biggest trailer you've ever seen?!" Dirk rushed toward us as Mom and I walked through Nana's front door.

"We call them *mobile homes*," Nana said. "Though the only thing that's *mobile* around here is the garden gnome in my front yard, and technically, he just fell over."

Dirk was right. It *was* huge. My family stood in the centre of a modern, sleek, stainless steel kitchen. Polished copper pots hung from the ceiling; a huge butcher's-block island sat beneath them.

"Is that one of those Sub-Zero refrigerators?" Mom sputtered.

"Yes! Food *never* goes bad!"

I didn't have a clue what a Sub-Zero was, but Nana was beaming. My brothers and I clung to one another like a chain gang. We gaped open-mouthed at my grandmother like she was an archaeological find. Which, of course, she kind of was.

The smell was unbelievable – garlic, roasted meat, melted butter. My stomach erupted in gurgles and growls. Mouth-watering concoctions were simmering on the eight-burner stove. Nothing even *close* to Spam and Primula. In the centre of the surprisingly large, open space, an oval pine table was set with gold-rimmed porcelain and glistening crystal glasses. I'd never seen anything as classy before. The kitchen belonged in a magazine. The rest of the trailer must be awesome. Already, it was much nicer than our crummy Chatsworth house.

"My goodness," Mom said, as flabbergasted as I was. "Can we have the grand tour?" Her bag still dangled on her arm.

"Absolutely." Drying off her hands, Nana turned away from the sink to face her four relatives. Standing still, she swept her arms through the air. "Voilà! This is *it*."

"This is it?" Rif asked.

"Lovely!" Mom swallowed.

"You live in a *kitchen*?"

"Rif!" Mom pinched the back of his arm. "It's *lovely*!"

It was lovely, but it was also true. Nana's trailer was one big, gleaming, air-conditioned kitchen.

"I've always wanted a gourmet kitchen," she explained, "so I gave myself one. I tore down the walls and said what the heck! You only live once. Why not live near the refrigerator?"

Nobody said a word. Was she joking?

"You sleep in the *dishwasher*?" Rif asked, chuckling. Mom smacked the back of his head, and we all gasped when a cigarette butt shot out.

"Rif!" Mom snapped, snatching the butt off the floor and shooting him an angry look.

"It's quite all right," Nana said, oblivious to the fact that my

116

brother had just been busted for smoking. "My bed is over here." She led our huddle around the wall-mounted TV/VCR to a large oak armoire behind the dining room table. Opening the doors, she showed us her pull-down bed, tucked neatly inside, flat up against the wall.

"Cool," said Dirk.

"The bed is on springs. It comes right down when I'm ready to go to bed, and pops back up in the morning."

"You never have to make it?" Dirk asked.

"Never."

"Awesome."

"And I can lie in bed and eat off the dining room table if I want to!"

"Lovely," Mom said again. Her handbag slid down her arm. "Is there a . . . uh, restroom?"

"I use the sink."

We froze in horror. "Just kidding," Nana said. She flung her head back and howled. "That always scares 'em. The bathroom is over there." Nana walked over to another oak armoire across the room and opened the door. Inside was a tiny shower stall, a toilet, and a small basin. "It was featured in *Trailer Life*! A friend of mind designed this for me. Isn't it fabulous?"

"Just lovel—" Mom's handbag hit the floor with a *thunk*. She left it there while she stuffed herself into the armoire and closed the door.

Suddenly, we heard a scratching sound at the front door.

"Juan!" I screeched.

"The neighbour's grandson? Invite him in," said Nana.

Diving for the door, I swung it open and saw Juan Dog looking up at me pathetically, trembling on the welcome mat, his huge eyes misty.

"Oh, baby, I'm so sorry I forgot you!" A trio of poops sat a few feet away like three big Hershey's Kisses. I scooped Juan into my arms and kissed his head. "Nana, do you have a plastic bag?"

Nana spotted Juan. "My, what do we have here?" she asked, stroking his elephantine ears.

"This is our chihuahua, Juan Dog," I said.

"He's adorable! But you don't have to keep him in a plastic bag, Libby. I have a vacuum cleaner."

I gaped at her. Then, I sighed. Of course my grandmother was a nut job! Why would it be any other way?

Suddenly, I envisioned the "big fight" my dad had with his mom:

Dad: "I don't wanna sleep in a kitchen!"

Nana: "Then sleep in an armoire!"

Dad: "Why can't we be normal?"

Nana: "We are normal! Now, put the dog back in the bag!"

Swallowing hard, I held Juan and tore off a sheet of paper towel.

"I'll be right back."

Outside Nana's trailer – mobile *schmobile*, no matter how beautiful it was, it was still a *trailer* – I cleaned up after Juan, threw it in the nearest trash can, and decided to skip lunch. Food smelling that good was too dangerous. It had an obese aroma. Better to not know what I was missing. Even if it was only one lunch, I couldn't risk it. Especially now that I had the genetic threat of becoming a woman who *lived* in a kitchen!

I decided to walk off my hunger. After all, we were moving into a new house that night. Which, of course, meant only one thing in our family – extra large, extra cheese, pepperoni *pizza*.

The Barstow heat was almost unbearable. It fried the inside of my nostrils each time I inhaled. The asphalt was squishy beneath my feet. Juan lay draped over my arm, either dead asleep or passed out. Briefly, I wondered if my family even noticed I was gone. Probably not.

The whole trailer park looked like a bizarre metal cult. Lined up next to one another, on the diagonal, each trailer was pretty much a copy of its rectangular neighbour. They were separated by bulbous septic tanks and boxy air-conditioning units. I could hear television sets blaring and the unmistakable violins of daytime TV. Someone peeked at me from behind a lace curtain, but snapped it shut as soon as I peeked back.

Except for the curtain peeker, Nana's street, Paradise Way, was deserted. The lack of life was eerie, like I really was on Mars. Apparently, all the kids were still in school.

Just as I was about to give up and run back to Nana's air conditioner, something amazing happened. My body began to feel light. My stomach stopped growling. The scalding air felt *good*, like a cedar-lined sauna. Purification via perspiration. It baked my insides and quieted the anxiety hum in my brain. I felt relaxed, released. Oddly, the hideous turn my life

119

had taken was now a fuzzy *ping* in the back of my brain instead of a throbbing ping*pong* from the left side of my head to the right. My lungs acclimated to the desert heat and felt soothed instead of scorched. I inhaled deeply and enjoyed the crackle of my nose hairs as they fried. In spite of myself, I began to feel lighthearted. Hopeful, even. Miraculously, I found myself thinking, Maybe everything *will* be okay.

"Probably sunstroke," I joked to myself. Then I stopped, took a deep breath, and felt my chest expand with warmth. Yeah, I could handle visiting my grandmother here once or twice a year. It wouldn't be *so* bad. Even if she was bonkers.

In the distance, I heard voices and splashing in the pool. Hey, there *was* life on Mars!

"Myrna looks like a Siamese cat."

As I snuck up to the chain-link fence surrounding the pool area, I heard female voices and the *blap, blap* of gentle swimming.

"Her ears wiggle when she blinks, he pulled so tight."

Juan Dog and I crouched behind a prickly, dry bush. The voices woke him. His ears were sticking straight up.

"She told me she wanted to look younger than her ex's new wife."

An old lady on a sagging Lilo in the shallow end of the pool had a thatched hut on top of her head. I'd never seen such a huge hat. Her geriatric friend was painting her toenails under an umbrella near the diving board. They shouted sentences at each other across the pool.

"Her mouth looks like the joker in that movie. What was it? *Batman?*"

Both women wore brightly flowered, skirted swimsuits. Their legs resembled blue cheese, and it was obvious they had to bend way over to pour their pendulous breasts into their suits' pointed double-D cups.

"Myrna's eyebrows are over her ears! Little earmuffs!" One of the antique bathing beauties laughed so hard she erupted in a coughing fit.

Yip! Yip!

"Shhh," I whispered into Juan's big ear.

Licking his tiny lips, he leaped out of my arms and wiggled his little body through the gate. Apparently, Juan now associated old women with delicious food.

Yip! Yip!

"Juan! Get over here!"

"What on earth?" The lady with the red toenails hoisted herself out of the chaise longue and waddled over to the fence on her heels.

"Juan Dog! Come!" I said through gritted teeth, still huddled behind the bush.

Yippy. Yip.

"What a darling puppy!" The woman with the toenails bent down to pick Juan Dog up. "Look, Charlotte," she called to the old lady on the raft, "remember the Taco Bell puppy!"

Juan hated being called a puppy, *especially* the Taco Bell puppy. I emerged from behind the bush and entered through the gate. "You little rascal," I said reprimandingly, reaching up to save him. But the lady held on.

"He doesn't like strangers," I said. Mocking me, Juan

gently licked the lady's cheek and tucked his little head into her triple chins.

"There, there," she cooed. "I'm not a stranger."

"I'm just visiting," I stammered. "I should get back."

Charlotte and the old lady exchanged a look. "Oh, we know who you are."

"You know me?" I blinked.

"We've been expecting you! Elizabeth's granddaughter, right?"

Elizabeth? Was it possible I was named after my grandmother and no one bothered to mention it?

"You're one of the Madrigal kids, right?"

Of course it was possible. Anything was possible with my family's don't-ask-don't-tell policy. Geez, I'd only learned my very own grandmother was alive and kicking an hour ago.

"Um, right," I said.

Charlotte, the Lilo lady, shouted, "Do you have a swimsuit on under those shorts, hon?"

Charlotte slid off her raft and plopped on to the pool stairs. Clutching the railing, she heaved herself up, padding along the hot cement to fetch her towel. Her feet looked like dried starfish. Suddenly, the ping-pong game in my head resumed. I wanted to go home. I longed for Geometry class and our dirt backyard. What was Nadine doing now? Had she forgotten me already?

Annoyed at my parents all over again for ruining my life, I reached for Juan. The old woman held him closer.

"Could you please give me my dog back?"

"He's so comfy!" The woman holding Juan turned and lowered herself on to her chaise with Juan still lost in the folds of her skin. The other one hobbled closer to me, leaned forward almost touching my nose with her nose. "Yep. I see the resemblance," she said. "You've got a lot of Elizabeth in you. Let me get you a bathing suit. I have an extra one in my locker."

Still dripping, she turned and hobbled off.

"I can't stay," I called after her. "As soon as I get my dog, I'm leaving."

Scoffing, she said over her shoulder, "Don't worry. I just had the bathing suit cleaned." Then she added, "By the way, I'm Charlotte and Dr Doolittle over there is Mim."

Mim was busy tickling Juan under the chin. I'd never seen him so happy.

"Nice to meet you both," I said stiffly. "But, uh, my family is probably looking for me."

Mim said, "Leave the Taco Bell puppy with us. He's falling asleep."

Juan Dog's eyes were droopy and I could swear I saw his lips curved upward in a sappy grin. Traitor.

"I can't. We're moving into a new house and—"

"It's okay. I'll bring him over later, when he wakes up." Mim was now rocking Juan back and forth. Was that *snoring* I heard?

"We're neighbours," Mim added. "I live on Eden Way and Charlotte's on Nirvana." She kissed the top of Juan's head. "You're on Valhalla Drive, right?"

"No. My grandmother lives on Paradise Way."

"I mean *your* trailer is on Valhalla Drive."

"We don't have a trailer," I said.

"It's not ready yet?" asked Charlotte. "Your granny has been driving the construction workers crazy."

I started to feel sick. Please, God, let heatstroke distort your hearing. And, if it does, please, God, let me have heatstroke.

"*Mobile home*, Charlotte," Mim said. "You don't want this sweet young girl thinking she's moving into a trailer."

Now, I began to feel faint. Juan continued to snore blissfully.

Mim asked me, "Did your grandmother tell you about the big party?"

My inner ping-pong game was suddenly an Olympic event in my head with slam serves and killer volleys.

"The whole trailer park is invited to your trailer warming. Mim is bringing her famous baked beans, I'm making cake—"

In a blur of sound waves, I lurched forward and snatched Juan Dog from the folds of Mim's neck. Startled, he woke up and shook his head. Together, we bolted for the gate, Juan's huge ears flapping.

"No running around the pool!" Charlotte shouted. "Sunset Park rules!"

FOURTEEN

"How could you?!" I burst through Nana's trailer door.

Mom's head snapped up, a half-eaten noodle whipping her face.

"There you are!" Nana said. "Your lunch is still warm, Libby. Would you like milk? A soda of some kind?"

"Were you ever going to tell us? Did you think we wouldn't notice?" I practically spat the question at my mother.

"Libby, Nana made wild pig spaghetti! From *scratch*." Elated, Dirk dragged a piece of warm garlic bread through the sauce at the bottom of his pasta bowl.

"Wild *boar* fettuccini," Nana corrected him, "with truffle oil."

"You're not going to want to eat when I tell you what's going on," I said to my brothers. "We're moving *here*. Into this trailer park! Not a house. A *trailer*."

"Mobile home," Dirk said, then he gazed lovingly at his grandmother. Nana smiled and stroked his head. Then she glanced at Mom, but Mom just stared at her fork and licked wild boar off her lips.

"You're wrong, Libby," Rif said calmly.

"I'm not wrong!" I exploded. "Am I, Mom?"

125

My mother gulped. Juan Dog bounded out of my arms and sat, shaking, at my mother's feet, hoping for a spill.

"Not all mobile homes are big kitchens, you know," Nana said gently.

"I can't live in a trailer park!" I cried. "Only losers live in trailer parks! Our house in Chatsworth was bad enough! Who ever dreamed we could sink lower than that?"

It was hurtful to my grandmother, I knew. But I was too upset to care. Did she care that my parents had ruined my life?

"No," said Rif. "You're wrong about me not wanting to eat. This food rocks. No matter where we live."

All I could do was stare. What was *wrong* with these people? Was *everyone* in my family completely around the bend?

Mom finally chose to speak. "Eat something, Libby. You'll feel better."

My body nearly levitated off the floor, I was so angry. "*That's* your solution to the end of my life? Eat a wild pig?"

"Boar," Mom said quietly.

What could I say? I was, literally, speechless. I felt like howling. How could this be happening? I'd never have a boyfriend now! My serious kiss was seriously gone – lost among the septic tanks and Astro Turf lawns.

Too upset to formulate actual words, I stamped my foot, crossed my arms in front of my chest, tried to mentally block the amazing aroma from entering my nose, and shot Mom a death stare.

"I have a fabulous idea!" Nana clapped her hands together. Her rings sounded like a pocket full of change. "Let's not wait for Lance. Let's look at your new home right now."

Dirk squealed. "Will I have my own room?"

"Absolutely! You each have your own room."

Good, I thought. I can't wait to lock myself in mine.

"Come." Nana held her hand out to me. Dirk reached up and slipped his grubby hand into hers.

"I like it here," he said, beaming up at her.

"You'll all love it here, just as I do. Follow me."

Love living in a trailer park? Never. No way. Not *ever*. No matter how much I was dying to taste wild boar.

Everybody scraped their chairs back and stood. But instead of leaving out the front door, Nana led us to the back of her trailer. We wound around her dining room table and snaked past her toilet armoire.

Lagging behind the others, Rif said to me, "Don't you know that it doesn't matter where you live? Life sucks everywhere."

Finally, someone in my family made sense.

Just beyond Nana's back door, there was a tiny backyard, with one chair and a round red Weber barbecue. The heat instantly calmed me. I felt less like exploding, more like pulling a sheet over my head and willing myself into a coma.

"This is where I sunbathe," Nana said.

What a hideous view for her poor neighbours, I thought.

It was still dead quiet except for the humming air conditioners. A low, chain-link fence with a tiny, swinging gate separated two trailer lots. Nana held the gate open for us and shuffled us through.

"Should we be trespassing through someone else's backyard?" Mom asked.

"You're not trespassing, Dot," Nana said. "You're *home*."

"Home?"

"Home?"

"*Home?!*" An echo passed through our family. Dirk's jaw hung open as he grinned; Juan stepped aside to avoid the inevitable splat of drool. I felt my whole body melt into the ground. My mother looked dumbfounded. Clearly, she was shocked to hear that we would be living right *behind* my father's mother. I mean, if you shouted out the rear window of Nana's mobile home, you'd hear it clear as day at our place. Nana's suntanning sessions would now be *our* scenery. Suddenly, I found my voice.

"Eat something, Mom," I said sarcastically. "You'll feel better."

Mom didn't even snarl at me; she was too dazed.

"C'mon inside!" Nana was positively glowing. "I've been running the air-conditioner!"

Inside, Nana swept her arms open like she was Vanna White. "This is the living room," she sang. "Over there is the bathroom. Full size! A tub, even. The master bedroom is in the back, and, just as I said, you each have your *own* rooms!" Nana's eyes were bright white elevator buttons, her smile psychotic.

"Where's the kitchen?" Mom asked innocently.

128

"At my place!" My grandmother exploded in glee. "That's the beauty of it! I gutted the whole trailer and redid it for you! I figured you needed bedrooms more than a kitchen so I got rid of all the appliances. Of course, I bought you a hot plate . . ." She pointed to the corner of the living room. "You know, in case you want a cup of tea in the middle of the night. Isn't it fabulous!? I've already called my editor friend at *Trailer Life* and he's sending over a photographer as soon as you get settled in. Isn't it just the most fabulous thing?!"

Again, nobody moved. Beads of sweat appeared on Mom's upper lip even though the air-conditioner was on full blast. Her face was flushed. Now I felt scared. As soon as Dad finished running his *errands* (yeah, right), he'd stumble into this new home and discover it had no heart. Not only that, but the woman he'd rather mourn than talk to was only smelling distance away. Dad was going to freak out. Could you bash a hole in a metal wall?

"See, honey?" Nana said to me, wrapping both arms around my shoulders. "Everything's going to be just fine."

Her hug smelled of garlic. I stood as stiff as a garden gnome.

"That's what you think, because you don't have a clue."

That's what I *wanted* to say. Instead, I said nothing. My stomach was doing cartwheels; the ping-pong match in my head was into overtime. All I kept thinking was, How unfair is it that my life is over when it was just starting to begin?

At that moment, we heard the squeak of Dad's U-Move brakes as he pulled up to the front door of our brand-new kitchenless mobile home.

"Is that Lance?" Nana asked excitedly, letting go of me.

My heart started doing cartwheels, too. Rif disappeared down the hall and Dirk's face got all pinched like he was about to cry.

"You'd better go," Mom said quickly to Nana. "I mean" – she softened her tone – "we should get settled in."

The truck door slammed as Mom gently prodded Nana toward the back door before Dad came in through the front.

"I haven't seen my son in so long I don't even know if I'll recognise him," Nana said.

Now Mom draped her arm around Nana's shoulder. "We need to give him a few minutes to relax before the big family reunion. You know how it is after a long drive."

Nana obviously didn't know how it was, but she was too smart to question it. Either that or the fact that my mother was practically shoving her out the back door was enough of a hint. She dutifully made her exit, waved at Dirk and me, and sailed off in a flapping triangle of material, announcing over her shoulder, "Dinner's at seven sharp. I'm making mulligatawny!"

Mom greeted Dad at the door like she was Donna Reed on speed. "Hi, honey!" she sang. "You made it! Come in! Come in! Come *in!*"

My brother and I cowered in the corner of our new empty living room. Dad growled, "I got lost." The moment he'd entered our new pad, we knew he hadn't been lost at all. His breath smelled sour and yeasty. His glasses were about to fall off his nose completely.

"So this is it?" he asked.

"It certainly is! Look how spacious!" Mom was whacked out. Her hands fluttered midair like they were trying to escape her wrists. I watched them flop, left then right, like some ghoulish tennis match.

"Where's the woman?" Dad asked.

"She's invited us for dinner!" Mom squealed. Dad groaned. Now my mother's hands clapped insanely together. "Don't worry, we have plenty of time to unpack."

With that, Mom turned to us and flapped her hands toward the door. I took it to mean that she wanted the caravan from the U-Move to the trailer to begin. It was too surreal to question. Still upset, I yelled down the hall for Rif. He appeared, reeking of smoke, and walked outside to the open U-Move truck. Reluctantly, I followed.

"Libby, grab the other end of the coffee table, would you?"

"Rif, kiss my ass, would you?"

My parents got us into this mess, they could move us into it, too. No way was I lifting a thing. I just stood there, arms crossed in front of my chest.

"Libby!" Mom appeared, looking frantic. Dad was inside. "Forget the table," she whispered. "Find the coffee and the coffeepot as soon as you can. We've got to sober your father up before dinner."

It took my father about twenty minutes to realise there was no kitchen. The coffeepot percolated in a corner of the living room floor. Mom snatched all the boxes labelled "dishes" or "pots and pans" and quietly stacked them near the hot plate.

131

My brothers and I walked back and forth from the U-Move like robots, waiting for the fuse to blow. It wasn't until Dad and Rif rolled the refrigerator through the trailer door on a dolly that the fireworks began.

"I'll take it from here, Dad," Rif said once they were inside. I admired the effort and wondered where Rif planned to stow the fridge.

Dad said, "You can't handle this baby yourself." Then he yanked his baggy old work jeans up at the waist, tilted the dolly unsteadily back, and began to roll. Dirk, my mother, and I just stood there and stared, openmouthed, like three Pez dispensers. Dad stopped, scrunched his eyebrows together, and said, "Hey, wait a minute."

That's when Mom decided she had to go to the bathroom. *Chicken.*

Dad turned to me and asked, "Where the hell is the kitchen?"

"Interesting you should ask," I said, stalling, waiting for the toilet to flush and Mom to reappear. But the only sound was the *fwonk!* of the refrigerator as Dad set it back on the ground.

"What the . . . Dot! Get out here."

Now I heard the toilet flush.

"Coffee, Dad? I made it fresh." I pointed to the coffeemaker on the floor, but that just made him madder.

"*Now*, Dot."

My mother reappeared in the living room with fresh lipstick and a pained expression. She said, "Yes?" all innocent, like she didn't know what was about to go down.

"I was wondering, dear, if you could lead the way into the

132

kitchen. It's so hard to see from behind the refrigerator." Dad didn't seem drunk at all now. In fact, he seemed more than sober.

"We all have our own rooms," Dirk said, extremely close to tears.

Mom took a deep breath. "Don't get mad, Lot," she began.

"Mad? Why should I be mad? Has someone *stolen* our kitchen? Did someone sell it? You were in charge of arranging this whole move. Surely you wouldn't forget to make sure we had a kitchen, would you? Not when the kitchen is your favourite room in the house."

Here we go.

Mom bit her lip, tears began to rise in her eyes. "Your mother—" she started.

"My mother? What about my mother? Didn't I tell you that I would only agree to this move if my mother was a minimal part of our lives? If I rarely had to see her or talk to her or even hear about her? Didn't I?"

"Yes," Mom said softly.

"So why am I hearing her name before I've even moved into my house?"

Uh-oh. I glanced at the back window. His mother was probably hearing this entire conversation.

"Your mother had the trailer redone," Mom said quietly.

"Redone?"

"Without a kitchen."

"What?!"

"Dad, we all have our own rooms!" Dirk burst into tears.

This time Dad shouted, "Then why don't you all *go* to your own rooms!"

Like fighter pilots at an air show, we peeled off in unison. Snatching Juan Dog, I chose the bedroom at the far end of the trailer, Dirk ran into the room next to mine, and Rif shut the door of the third bedroom, lit a cigarette, and blew the smoke out his small, slide window. I could smell it right away. If Dirk was doing what I was doing, we both had our ears pressed to the door.

"You *trusted* that woman?!" My father shrieked. "It's bad enough we had to lower ourselves to move into a trailer my mother bought—"

"Mobile home."

"Look around, Dot! Do you see any *wheels* on this thing? They only call them mobile homes so you can fool yourself into thinking you haven't sunk this low permanently!"

"Keep your voice down, Lot. She'll hear you."

"Hear me? Where is she? Hiding in the closet with her broom?"

"Shhhh, Lot. She's next door."

"Next door?" My father sounded like his head was about to pop. "My mother is next *door*? What kind of dumb-assed, pea-brained, simple-minded, stupid—"

"STOP!" Mom erupted in a bloodcurdling scream.

Even Juan stopped fidgeting. I think the whole trailer park must have halted, perched in mid-sentence waiting to hear what would happen next. My heart pounded out of my chest. I couldn't move, couldn't breathe.

"Stop it! Stop it! Stop it! Stop it!"

Mom screamed again, then she got deathly quiet, and Dad didn't say anything more. The silence in the mobile home was as thick as tapioca.

"You've come to the end of the line, Lot." My mother's voice scared me. It was as sharp and ragged as a hangnail. "With me, your children, your life as you've been living it. The end of the line."

Dad mumbled something I couldn't hear. Something indignant. Mom barrelled on through.

"It's not *my* fault we're in this mess. You should be grateful your mother took us in."

"Grateful? The woman hasn't spoken to her only son in twenty years!"

"Give me a break! You haven't spoken to *her*."

"Why should I? Where does she get off telling me I can't have a beer?"

Now it sounded as though my *mother's* head would pop.

"Can't have a beer? Can you even hear yourself? Your father drank himself to death and your mother had every right to refuse to watch the same thing happen to her son. All she said was she'd talk to you when you stopped drinking. *You* let twenty years pass!"

Oh my God. So *that* was the big "family" sort of fight! At first, I couldn't believe my ears. My father kept a grandmother out of our lives because he'd rather have a beer? He preferred to pretend his own mother was *dead* than give up the brew? Then I realised it was *exactly* like my dad. Hadn't he once forgotten to pick me up at school when I was sick because he went to El Torita for lunch and had three tequila shots? Didn't I spend four hours doubled over on the nurse's cot watching her feel sorry for me?

Yeah, I could imagine my dad being so selfish. I mean, we were living in a trailer! What further evidence did I need?

When Mom continued, her voice was slow and icy. "You put me in charge, and I *took* charge, Lot. Are you ready for this?"

Dad didn't say a word. I still couldn't breathe, couldn't move. My mom didn't sound like my mom at all when she said, "I made a deal with your mother. We can live here as long as you don't drink. Your mother has given us a roof over our heads and a chance to start over. Fall off the wagon and we're out of here. *Homeless.* Your family, Lot, will be out on the street because of you. Your drinking cost you your job, your home, your friends. Keep it up and it will cost you your family, too. You've said a million times you can stop drinking whenever you want to. Now's the time to prove it. You say you're not an alcoholic; fine, it shouldn't be a problem. If it is, get help. We have no money and nowhere else to go. It's up to you now. *Only* you."

The mobile home suddenly vibrated with the *thump, thump, thump* of my mother's footsteps down the hall. I nearly jumped through the ceiling when she knocked on my door.

"Let's go, kids," she said, pounding on all three of our bedroom doors. "Time to get you registered for school."

That's when the doorbell rang.

"Get lost!" Dad shouted.

A tiny voice on the other side of our new metal front door squeaked, "I'm from *Trailer Life*. I'm here to photograph your mobile home."

FIFTEEN

Desert Valley High School was a disaster area. Cracked asphalt, peeling paint, tired old cinder-block buildings that looked more like bunkers than classrooms. Everything was litter-box grey or dirt brown, even the grass, the trees, and the distant Calico Mountains.

Getting there was even worse.

"There's just so much I can take," Mom muttered to herself, the car leaping forward at green lights, jerking to a stop at reds. "He thinks he can ruin my life? I don't *thinkywink* so."

An open bag of Doritos sat between my mom's legs. Her fingers were stained orange. We'd been driving around in circles for half an hour, past the same tiny taco stand, exhaust repair shop, dentist's office, insurance storefront. Nobody said a word. Except Mom, of course, who talked mostly to herself in angry, guttural grunts.

"I'm at the end of my rope. It's about time he was at the end of his."

Finally, she looked right and left out the windshield and sighed. "Rif, will you please get the map out of the glove box? That school is *somewhere* around here."

While Rif rummaged around, Mom kept circling. Past the

tiny taco stand, the exhaust repair shop, dentist's office, insurance storefront. Sitting in the backseat, with Juan Dog on my lap, I watched Barstow pass by the window yet again. It never looked any better. I felt sad, scared, angry, upset – so many emotions; it was impossible to fully wallow in just one. Well, there was one feeling that rose above all the rest: confusion. Complete mind-numbing confusion. A mere week ago, I was struggling with Geometry, memorising the back of Zack Nash's neck. Now my life was spun around and plopped on its head, totally disoriented. It took all the strength I had just to keep my eyes open and focused so I could see the bad news coming and dodge it before it hit me, *splat*, right in the face.

"This is a map of *California*, Mom," Rif said. "I can get you to San Diego or Sacramento."

"How hard could it be to find a high school?" Mom circled Barstow one more time. Suddenly, Dirk leaned forward from the backseat and blurted out, "Is Dad an alcoholic?"

I held my breath. Juan did, too. We leaned forward with Dirk, listened to the hum of the engine and the soft blowing of the air conditioner. My brothers and I looked like an exhibit in the wax museum, waiting, locked in anticipation. I felt thrilled and terrified at the same time. The palms of my hands tingled. I'd been waiting for this moment all my life. A moment of *truth*. No more hiding. No more secrets. The other shoe could finally drop. My family would finally face what we'd secretly known for so long. Mom took a deep breath, licked her fingers clean. We braced ourselves.

"There it is!" she cried. "Desert Valley High. I should have stayed on the road I was on before!"

I groaned. Story of my life.

I felt tears well up again, felt my chest pinch. Desert Valley High made Fernado High look like a Hawaiian postcard. WISH YOU WERE HERE. Wish I was *there*.

Mom parked right in front of the front steps. Wouldn't you know it, we got there exactly at three o'clock, just as the metal double doors were spitting out students. She stopped too suddenly and the car lurched and screeched, causing *everybody* to look at us.

"Oops," she said. "My heel caught."

"Don't stop here!" I shrieked, sinking low in the seat, pulling my sunglasses out of my pack and slipping them on my red, puffy face. Now my main emotion was complete and utter mortification.

"Mom! There's a parking lot!"

Ignoring me, she said, "I'll only be a few minutes." Then she heaved herself out of the car, tugged at her too-tight lime green dress, and took the car keys with her. I wanted to shrivel up and tuck myself into my own crumpled Kleenex. Better still, I wanted to disappear altogether.

"Nice car, man." Some students walked past us, looked at Rif, and laughed. Rif reached into his hair for a cigarette.

"Do you think they have a pool?" Dirk asked. Rif and I both rolled our eyes. A pool? This high school looked like it didn't even have a cafeteria. While Fernando High was all spread out, my new school seemed like it had fallen into a trash compactor. There were a lot of kids, but they were squished among the tired old buildings.

My heart sank. How could this happen? How could life keep getting *worse*? My spirit felt like a marble in a fishbowl, sinking quickly and permanently to the bottom. Peeking out the car window, I observed my future classmates in their natural habitat. Most looked like thugs to me. Tough no-smilers. Girls with thick black hair and even thicker black eyeliner. Boys with buzz cuts and tattoos and way-too-baggy pants. Very scary. What terrified me most, though, was the incredible amount of *skin*. Yeah, it was hot out, but man! The girls wore short shorts with platform sandals and spaghetti-strap T-shirts with no bra. They clipped their long hair up in messy twists and laughed and chatted as if there wasn't less than a skimpy yard of fabric between their naked bodies and the whole wide world. Two different couples were all knotted up, making out right there on the front steps. In front of *everybody*. As I sat there, the car getting hotter and hotter, it felt like I was stalled on the railroad track – nothing to do but hope the white puff of smoke in the distance isn't the locomotive.

"Look, Libby, I found Wally." Dirk pointed to some nerd in a red-and-white-striped T-shirt sitting on a retaining wall, reading a book called *Calculus and You*.

"Now maybe you'll finally have a boyfriend." Snorting as he laughed, Dirk sounded just like a wild boar.

"Wally" didn't look half bad. At least he didn't scare me to death.

By now, tons of students had swarmed around the car, checking us out. Some pointed through the window, others indicated there was fresh meat in their midst by flicking their heads in our direction. It was so hot, sweat marks were expanding in my armpits. My sunglasses slid down the damp bridge of my nose.

Through a clenched jaw I declared, "I'm not going here. I'll live with Nadine. I'll join the circus."

It got harder and harder to breathe inside the car. We didn't dare roll down the windows, clinging to last bit of air-conditioned air. Just as I was on the verge of hyperventilating, Rif startled me out of my impending panic attack by opening the car door and stepping out. Dirk, wiping his nose on his sleeve, followed them.

"Where are you going?!" I screeched. Neither one of them paid any attention to me. Typical! They got out of the car and let the crowd swallow them up. Calm as you please. Rif glanced right and left and lit up. Can you believe it? Just like that. Rif was Rif no matter where he was or who happened to be with him. And Dirk, well Dirk basically imitated every-thing his older brother did without thinking too much about it. Which left me, the emotional psycho.

Soon it was clear I'd suffocate if I stayed in the airless car much longer. No way was I going to sit there and fry alone. I swung open the door and squirmed out of the back seat. "Stay," I commanded Juan Dog. But it was so hot and he hung his head so pathetically I relented.

"Oh, all right." I picked him up, slammed the car door shut, and scrambled after Rif and Dirk across the school parking lot to the edge of a brown football field. Breathless, I commanded, "Rif, get back in the car." But even as I said it, I knew he'd scoff at me. Which he did. Dirk, the idiot, stuck his tongue out and shoved his hands deep into his pockets, trying to look cool.

"Rif . . ." I said again. This time I tapped my foot. That ought to do it.

"Get lost," Rif said to me. Then he walked away and merged into a nearby group of lowlifes. Dirk joined him.

"You new?" one of the guys asked Rif.

"Will be," said Rif, taking another deep puff before stamping out his cigarette.

"Cool, man."

"Hope so."

"What year?"

"Junior."

"Whoa, dude."

Their Neanderthal sentences drove me crazy. I spun on my heels and loudly stomped back to the car.

"Your girlfriend?" I heard one of them ask.

"My *sister*."

"Oh, man."

"No kidding."

Mom still hadn't returned. Right back? Yeah, right! Juan was panting and I was sweating so much my hair was plastered to my forehead. Everyone was looking at me, talking behind their hands. I hurried to the car, got in, and sat there like a blob of bread dough in the oven.

"The girl and the mutt are two hot tamales," I heard somebody say. Then I heard lots of somebodies laugh. Totally red-faced, I rolled down the window, but it was no use. The air was so stifling, Juan and I had to get out of the car before we both passed out.

"Oooo, how *cute*."

I froze.

"Look, Sylvana, the Taco Bell dog!"

Oh, God.

Before I could turn around, a swarm was upon me. There must have been only three or four girls, but it felt like *hundreds*. Juan Dog and I were instantly swallowed up in CK cologne, lip gloss, squeals, and skin. Lots of skin.

"He's so *cute*."

"Look at the darling puppy!"

"Can I hold him?"

"Number *one*, he's *not* a puppy. He hates being called a puppy. It's not his fault that he's so small. Do you call short people little babies? No? I didn't think so. Number *two*, we bought him *years* before that stupid Taco Bell commercial. He's *not* the Taco Bell dog. He's *Juan Dog*, a beautiful canine in his own right. Number *three*, my mother will be here any moment and we have to get going, back to our very complete lives, away from this dust bowl dump. So in answer to your question, no, you *can't* hold him. He's mine and he hates girls named Sylvana who have long, straight hair and tanned legs and flat belly buttons with gold hoops sticking out of them."

That's what I *wanted* to say.

144

Instead I said, "Yeah. Okay." Then I just stood there. Like a dope. I let them pass Juan from one set of pastel-painted fingernails to another like he was some kind of hairy, shivering football or something. That's what I did, feeling as small and ashamed as I'm sure Juan did.

"Can I let him run around a little?" one of the Sylvanas asked.

"Well . . ."

She set his tiny paws on a patch of hot, prickly, dead grass and he hopped around pitifully.

"How *cute!*"

Before I could bend down to save him, Juan hunched up his back, brought his hind legs up close to his front legs, and squeezed one off. In front of God and the Sylvanas and all of D.V. High, Juan Dog *pooped.*

"Oh," one of the girls covered her white teeth and tittered.

"Eeewwww," said another.

Beet-faced, I lamely asked, "Anyone have a plastic bag?"

They looked confused, like I wanted to take it home or something. "Or a tissue, scrap of paper, gum wrapper, anything?" My voice was growing weak.

Nobody said a word. They stared at me as if I'd ruined the party. Juan beamed. Yeah, *he* was feeling fine.

"This your car, ma'am?"

Wheeling around, I saw a police officer standing at the front of our car. In his mirrored sunglasses I could see my tiny purple-red face.

"Uh . . . no . . . it's . . . uh, my mom's." The flashing lights on top of his squad car had attracted the attention of the

145

whole school. What, he was going to arrest me? Wasn't the Robo-Cop routine a tad over the top? I wanted to die.

"You can't park here," he said. "The school buses pull in here."

"Oh. Well . . . my mom . . ."

"Let's go," Sylvana said to her friends. The other Sylvanas nodded and stepped over Juan's poop, away from me as fast as possible.

"You going to clean that up?" the officer asked me, pointing to the little Tootsie Roll Juan had left on the grass. We were now encircled by a growing crowd of silent, gaping students. I looked up and saw Wally with his calculus book under one arm and a superior smirk on his face.

Lord, please take me now.

"Bethy?"

Her voice pierced the crowd, panicked and shrill. "Bethy?!" The students receded like low tide and made way for my mom. Fingers splayed, her tight green dress wrinkled, her baby toe poking out of her high-heeled sandals, Mom rushed forward, her face flushed with worry. "What happened?"

"Nothing, Mom, we—" Before I could say more, she took one more fatal step and landed smack dab on the centre of Juan Dog's *poopadilly.*

"Eeewwww." The crowd groaned in unison. Turning my head away, I silently prayed for a quick, massive heart attack to put me out of my misery.

"What on earth?" Mom looked down. "Oh, Bethy!"

"Oh, Bethy!" Someone in the crowd loudly mimicked her. It was Rif.

*Not the type of coronary from which you can be revived, please,
but instant, permanent, chest-clutching death.*

"Move along, kids. Party's over." The cop sidestepped the
poop pancake and dispersed the crowd. Someone joked, "Ah,
don't be a party pooper!" and everyone howled. Mom slipped
her shoe off and scraped it on the kerb while Juan toddled up
the hill with the group.

"Juan! Get back here, you little runt!" Juan, looking scared,
ignored my mom and quickened his pace. "Bethy, go get
him."

"Rif, go get him!" I said.

"Dirk, go get the dog."

Dirk, low man on the Madrigal totem pole, skulked up the
hill to get Juan, who had stuck his head inside somebody's
lunch bag.

"Where are your keys, Mom?" All I wanted to do was crawl
into the back seat, turn on the air-conditioner, and stay there
till college.

"Will you at least give me a Kleenex?" Her smelly sandal
dangled from one chubby finger.

"Here." Rif appeared out of nowhere with a fresh tissue in
his hand. Prince Charming.

"Thank you," Mom said to Rif, sneering at me.

What did I do?

"Your *keys*, Mom?"

"Your dog, miss?" An unfamiliar voice spoke behind me.
Turning, I was suddenly face-to-face with the most gorgeous
creature I'd ever seen. Okay, scratch that. He wasn't Brad or

Leo or Zack Nash. He wasn't drop-dead dazzling in a traditional Hollywood hunk way. This guy was *deep,* soulful. I could tell. He wore glasses, though they were the way cool kind. His T-shirt was untucked, his baggy shorts well-pressed, his deck shoes brand-new. This guy had blond hair and pearly-white fingernails and firm ancillary veins that snaked all the way up his naturally muscled arms.

This was a guy I could definitely seriously kiss.

"Miss?"

"Eliza*beth.*" Mom's impatient voice felt like a toothpick in my ear.

"What?"

"Take the *dog.*"

Oh. I suddenly became aware that the guy was holding Juan Dog out to me. Juan's little legs were wiggling frantically, his neck strained. He looked like a cockroach flipped on its back.

"Oh! Sorry." I came to, blushing instantly, grabbing my dog. "This is Juan." *Great, Libby, introduce your dog!*

"I found him in my lunch sack," the guy said. "Apparently Juan likes leftover meat loaf sandwiches more than I do."

I laughed way too loud and long for the joke.

"Elizabeth, take the damn dog, get your brothers, and get in the car."

Mortified, I stammered an awkward "thank you" and glared at my mother as I struggled to slither gracefully under the seat belt strap, into the back seat of our crappy old car. Let *her* get my brothers, I thought. What, I'm their babysitter?

As soon as I was settled in, I looked out the window to

watch the boy who just replaced Zack Nash in my dreams, a serious candidate for my serious kiss. But he was already gone. I sighed. Juan sighed, too, curled up on my lap, and licked his lips. To my utter amazement, I found myself thinking maybe Barstow wasn't going to be so bad after all.

SIXTEEN

"Lance!"

Dressed in a fresh kaftan, this one a blinding chartreuse, Nana completely encircled my father in fabric. Tears streamed down her wrinkled brown cheeks.

"My baby boy, Lance!"

I held my breath, braced for another explosion.

Dad simply said, "Mother." Then he busted free from her embrace.

"Let me look at you," Nana squealed, fluttering after him.

Mom, pale with panic, lunged for the table in the centre of Nana's trailer kitchen. "Something smells scrumptious! Shall we sit anywhere?"

"You look tired," Nana said to my dad. "It's been rough, hasn't it?"

"Rif, you sit there. Libby, sit there . . ."

Nobody moved. We stared slack jawed at my dad and his mom. Nana kept pawing him; he kept inching backward. Dad was nearly pressed against the toilet armoire when Nana said, "I'm so proud of you, son. How long have you been sober?"

"How 'bout I sit *here* and, Dirk, you sit *there*?" Mom's

voice screeched like a long skid. She flashed us a black look that said Sit. Down. *Now.*

We sat.

Dad said nothing, skirted past his mother, and took a seat at the far end of the large table.

"All that matters is we're here now, right, Lance? The whole family." Nana smeared the last of her tears across her face with the back of her hand.

"Lot," Dad muttered, reaching for one of the steaming, aromatic tureens in the centre of the table.

"Yes." Nana sniffed. "There's plenty for everyone."

"My name is *Lot* now," said Dad. "Lance died twenty years ago."

Dinner that night was so tense it nearly snapped. My parents weren't speaking to each other, we didn't dare say a word, and my grandmother was oblivious to the fact that her newfound family was on the verge of a meltdown.

"Everybody unpacked?" she chirped.

Dad guzzled colas all dinner. He flung his head back, opened his mouth, and poured the carbonated sugar directly down his throat.

"That *can't* be good for you, Lance," his mother said.

Dad responded with a deep, round, gaseous belch.

"It doesn't matter," Nana said. Then she repeated, for like the *millionth* time, "I'm just so happy to finally have you home." Puppy-eyed, she stood and reached across the table to squeeze his hand. He snatched it away.

151

My emotional Richter scale had already registered a mega-quake and several aftershocks that day. By dinner-time, I was wiped out. I didn't feel much of anything. Except hunger.

Gastronomically, my grandmother was awesome. Her food danced down my tongue, exciting each bud on its way to my throat. The first bite was a burst of intense flavour, then subtle layers of smoke, spice, sweet, and salt erupted like tiny fire-works. It terrified me. I was dying to pile my plate high with curried aubergine, grilled lamb shanks, and fresh spinach bread with herb butter. Not to mention mulligatawny soup. The rich colours on her table were as luscious as the rich smells. Every meal here? I was never going to make it. It was one thing to eat a Grilled Chicken Salad at McDonald's when my family was devouring Double Quarter Pounders with Cheese. I could handle refusing to eat seven hundred and sixty calories and forty-eight fat grammes of fast food. But *gourmet* food? Controlling my portion sises was going to be next to impossible.

"More mulligatawny, Libby?' Nana asked.

I swallowed hard. "No, thanks."

"It's one of Emeril's recipes," she said. I stared blankly, as did my whole family. "'Bam? Crank it up a notch'?"

Nothing. Nana glanced up at the heavens, made a praying gesture with her hands. "Thank you, God, for bringing my family to me so I can teach them about *life!*" Looking at the rest of my family, she asked, "Who's ready for more soup?"

Mom and Rif held their bowls up; Dad gulped another cola. Dirk said, "I've never eaten yellow soup before. It's so good I don't want to know what's in it!"

Nana glanced at God once more.

"Can I please have more yellow rice, too?" Dirk asked.

While Nana served us, she asked, "Who knows why saffron is the most expensive spice in the world?"

Yip!

"Anyone?"

Juan, sitting beneath the table at my feet, was impatient for me to drop another chunk of lamb.

"Because," she said, "the orange stigmas of the saffron plant have to be picked by *hand*."

No one responded. Juan Dog licked the Italian tile floor.

"Can you imagine? By *hand!*"

Mom smiled a crack and nodded her head. Dad took another gulp. I noticed his hands were shaking and his forehead was damp.

"Who knows what *poha* means?"

Dirk erupted in giggles.

"Dirk? You've studied Indian cooking?"

Still laughing Dirk said, "No, but Juan *pohaed* in your backyard earlier!"

Peeved, I scowled at him. He wasn't supposed to tell! I didn't have a plastic bag with me and it was still sitting there. Oblivious, Nana barrelled on through.

"*Poha* is rice!" she said. "*Aloo* is a potato, *kishmish* are raisins, *podina* is mint. These are all common ingredients in the Indian kitchen."

Mom mumbled something about the food being delicious no matter what was in it. Dad kept his head down and chewed.

153

"It takes a while to familiarise yourself with all the terms." Nana seemed so unaware of the tension around her table it occurred to me she might be senile. Either that or the woman was as thick as a sack of *poha*.

"So tell me," she said, "all moved in? Are your rooms big enough? Is the air-conditioner working well? Barstow is hot by day, cool by night. Be sure to shut it off."

We bobbed our heads up and down, raised our eyebrows. Rif even gave her the thumbs-up sign. We didn't tell our grandmother that her son had installed the refrigerator in the living room, right next to the couch, and announced, "Anyone moves this, I'll cut off his or her arm." We didn't tell her where he told the *Trailer Life* photographer to shove his camera, either.

As the spectacle of our first family dinner played out in front of me, I found myself stealing glances at the old lady with the bright red hair. She had the same nose as my dad's, same cowlick in the left front of her hairline. I imagined her holding my father in her arms when he was a baby, singing lullabies to him. Had she made his favourite meals for his birthday? Did she kiss his boo-boos when he fell off his bike? Did he bury his head in her chest and weep when his father died? Did my father grow up in a trailer park?

I also found myself searching Nana's face for similarities to my own face. Would I look like her when I was old?

Suddenly, I felt mad all over again. Having a weird grand-mother was better than having no grandmother at all! I've been robbed! Isn't it some form of child abuse to tell your kids their nana is dead, then spring her on them fourteen years later?

Dad interrupted my thoughts with another loud burp.

"My goodness, Lance, where are your table manners?" his mother asked.

"My name is Lot," Dad said. "Don't call me Lance again."

Nana looked hurt. Mom looked annoyed. And everyone pretty much resumed chewing and not talking to one another after that.

The only bright side to my family's insanity was the fact that it was a great distraction. With my parents feuding, I didn't have time to dwell on my own dismal life. I didn't have time to miss Nadine or Fernando High or Mr Puente's lame jokes about geometric theorems. I didn't have the energy to worry about turning into white trash or being hated by everybody at the new school I was starting in the morning whether I liked it or not.

"Save room for dessert," Nana said, finally. "I made tiramisu."

I stifled a groan. Why me? That's what I thought over and over. Why, of all the kids in the world, did everything awful happen to *me*?

SEVENTEEN

The *tap, tap, tap* of Mom's Press-On nails against my bedroom door woke me early the next morning. It was just light out, already hot. Mom held a wrapped box in her hands. She sat on the edge of my bed.

"I know this is hard on you, honey," she said quietly. "It's hard on all of us."

At first I thought I was dreaming. I didn't say anything, just kept my head on the pillow waiting to see where this dream would go. When Mom reached up and brushed the hair out of my eyes, I marvelled at how real it felt.

"I have a present for you," she said. And I smiled, expecting the package to unwrap itself and reveal its contents to me.

"Don't you want it?" Mom asked.

Oh, yes, I thought. What is it, Mommy?

"Libby?" Mom shook my shoulder. "Are you awake?"

Startled, I looked at my mother. "Mom?" I asked. "Is that really you?"

She laughed. "Yes, silly. Who did you think it was? Santa?" She handed me the box. "For the first day of the rest of your life," she said.

Sitting up in bed, I was now fully awake. Reality came

crashing down on my head – I was living in Barstow, in a trailer, about to start my first day at the worst school ever. Even the thought of seeing the gorgeous guy with the incredible hazel eyes didn't lift my spirits. Carefully, I unwrapped the gift (we always saved wrapping paper in our house) and opened the box. My mother beamed.

"Breakfast is at Nana's in fifteen minutes," she said, getting up from my bed. "I can't wait to see you in your new outfit." Then she kissed me on the forehead and left me alone in my new metal room.

Rest of my life, here I come.

Nana insisted on waiting for the school bus with us, even though the stop was directly in front of the entrance to the trailer park.

"We're old enough to stand alone," Rif attempted. We both knew there was no budging her. Nana had proudly pulled major strings to get the bus to pick us up right at the front gate of the trailer park. Dirk's school was across the street, lucky for him. She didn't know how embarrassing it was.

"No grandchild of mine is going to walk a million blocks to the school bus. I pay taxes."

"Really, Nana. You don't have to—"

"Yes, I *do*."

So she did. We were the only kids picked up at that spot. Apparently the other kids who lived in Sunset Park drove to school or walked. But Nana would have none of that. She stood between my brother and me, one arm around each shoulder. I wore the tacky new pastel-green frilly outfit Mom bought me from Wal-Mart. And brand-new matching pastel-green canvas shoes. Yeah, I know. My heart sank when I lifted the ensemble out of the box. Hadn't she ever even *looked* at her daughter? What gave her the idea I'd *ever* wear such a hokey outfit? No way was I going to make my first impression in a new school in *pastels*!

Still, I couldn't erase her face from my mind. That eager, hopeful, apologetic, loving, desperate look she'd given me as she sat on my bed, gift in hand. Her face reminded me that her life was ruined, too. We were *all* stuck in Barstow. I couldn't stomach hurting my mom's feelings by showing up at the breakfast table in jeans and a rumpled black T-shirt pulled out of the bottom of my suitcase.

So I wore it.

I looked like the nerd of the century.

And I brought my real clothes with me in my backpack so I could change the moment I got to school.

"Finally!" Nana took her hands off our shoulders and clapped them together.

Just over the crest of the hill, the familiar orange-yellow colour rose like a hideous sunrise. We watched the bus driver put on his blinkers and flashers, practically taking out a billboard announcing he was pulling over to pick up the losers who lived in Sunset Park. Nana stood like a peacock, a huge turquoise medallion hanging around her neck. My heart raced. I felt dizzy. Nana sealed our fate by loudly asking the bus driver, "When was your last drug test?"

158

The whole school bus erupted in laughter. My face burned so red it felt like sunburn. Rif didn't care. He high-fived everyone as he pimp-walked down the aisle to the back of the bus. Me, I simply tried not to barf as I kept my head down and searched for the first empty seat out of the corner of my eye.

"Who's *that?*" I heard some guy ask.

"Nobody," another guy answered.

Recognising the voice, I glanced up. It was *him.* The soulful blond boy who'd given Juan Dog back to me the day before. The boy I thought I might one day seriously kiss. When he caught me looking at him he said, "Keep moving. You're not sitting with me."

I wanted to cry. I wanted to explain how this had happened, how my life had veered wildly off course and careered into Barstow. I wanted to pull my clothes out of my pack and show everyone who I really was. I longed to turn the clock back to last year, when I was happy and didn't even know it. Instead, I watched my grandmother waving at me out of the back window as she shrunk to a tiny turquoise dot in the bus's exhaust. Then I grabbed an empty seat in the back and stared at my fingernails.

"Nobody wants to sit with me, either." A girl's voice in front of me jolted me back to reality. I looked up. She said, "I'm Barbara Carver. It's okay. *I'll* be your friend."

Ah, geez.

Every high school has a Barbara Carver. She's a five-time loser: overweight, acne, braces, glasses, and bad hair. No, make that *awful* hair. Barbara gathered a tuft of hair on top of her head into an old rubber band; it shot straight into the air like Old Faithful. Her fingernails were chewed so ferociously they were ten bloody half-moons.

I gulped. "Thanks. I'm Libby Madrigal." Then I settled into the bus seat and imagined how nice it would feel if the vinyl seat opened up and swallowed me whole.

Barbara stood, swung around, plopped down beside me and chatted all the way to school.

". . . so if you want to join a club, you pretty much have to organise it yourself."

"Uh-huh."

"And sports, there's like football and stuff. But if you want a really cool sport, like chess, you have to organise that yourself, too."

"Uh-huh."

As Barbara Carver filled me in on the limitations of Desert Valley High, I felt more and more woozy. My head was doing loop de loops. Each time I took in a breath, I felt dizzy when I exhaled. Hang on, girl, I repeated over and over in my head. Hang *on*. Everything's going to be okay.

We rode past Wal-Mart, through downtown, hung a right after the police station. My ears were hissing. By the time we passed the same tired old taco stand I'd passed several times the day before, I could barely hear Barbara at all. My ears were filled with the sound of the ocean. My upper lip was damp with sweat.

". . . so you want to stay away from them. I mean, like they are totally bad news."

160

Barbara continued her monologue, but all I heard was *whoosh!* All I felt was dizziness and a growing sense of panic.

The bus lurched to a stop, the door swung open. "Careful getting off, kids," the driver said. "No pushing."

Standing shakily, I let the crowd sweep me along in its current. My vision was blurred, I saw twinkling white lights. In the next horrible instant I felt like throwing up. Saliva flooded my mouth. The more I swallowed, the more liquid came rushing in. My stomach churned.

"Are you okay?" Barbara asked behind me. But her voice sounded so small and far-away I didn't think she was talking to me. My heart raced as my stomach lurched closer to up-chucking the egg-white omelette Nana'd made for breakfast. I grabbed for my backpack. Lunch, and my non-nerdy clothes, were the only things inside it. I figured I could barf on Nana's smoked turkey wrap and suffer the additional humiliation of wearing my pastel ensemble all day. If I stuck my head far enough inside my pack, I could hurl and no one would even know. Dizzy, nauseous, and nearly off the deep end in terror, I fumbled with the clasp.

"Move your butt," someone yelled to me. It sounded like Rif.

"Shut up," Barbara snapped back.

"I wasn't talking to you, crater face."

"Good one, Shakespeare. Got any more original lines?"

Somehow I made it to the door. The bus steps were blurry. The crashing waves in my ears were now deafening. My hand clutched my stomach. Inch by inch, I managed to crawl down

161

the bus steps. My knees didn't give way until I stepped on to the sidewalk. There, I folded like an accordion right into the gutter.

"Step over her!"

That's the last thing I heard before my head smacked the pavement.

"It looks worse than it is, Mrs Madrigal," I heard the nurse tell my mom over the phone. That's when I reached up to feel my head. An enormous bandage covered the right half of my forehead, almost into my eye. It felt like a bath sponge.

"A nasty scrape," the nurse said to me, hanging up the phone. "You fainted. You'll be fine."

"Did I throw up?" I asked, wondering if I not only had to drop out of school in disgrace but move out of California, too.

"No. You just passed out."

I nearly fainted again when the nurse helped me into a sitting position, and I saw my reflection in the mirror across the room. "Can I have a Band-Aid instead of this . . . this . . . *maxi pad* on my forehead?"

"It's a *bandage*, and you'll need it if you start bleeding again," she said efficiently. "Do you have a headache?"

"No."

"Good. Any dizziness?"

"No."

"Nausea? Blurred vision?"

"No. I'm okay now." Even my heart had returned to its normal beat. "I think it was just a slight panic attack."

"Fine," the nurse said. "Then you can go to class."

That's not what I expected to hear. Suddenly I remembered, yeah, I did have a headache. "Can't I go home?" I asked. "Now that you mention it, my head does feel a little achy."

"Your mom said you should go to class if you could," said the nurse. "And I think you can."

My mom?! What did she know about my body? My mortification? The fact that my life was truly over if I started the first day of my new high school dressed like a lime-green mathlete with a *pillow* taped to my forehead!

"Here," said the nurse. "Let me help you to your feet."

Gripping my arm, the nurse supported me while I stood up. "If you bleed beyond the bandage, or feel sick at all today, come back in," she said.

Before I could protest, the nurse patted my shoulder and released me into the wilds of Desert Valley High.

Mr Tilden asked the class, "Who knows the difference between a metaphor and a simile?"

I knew his name because it was written on the class schedule I held in my trembling hand. I heard his question because I was standing, frozen, outside the closed door of my second period English class. The doorknob was inches away from my hand, but I couldn't bring myself to reach out and turn it. My heart pounded wildly. Trickles of sweat dribbled down into the cotton bandage on my forehead. As I took one tiny step forward, my too-new green canvas shoes squeaked on the exterior cement sidewalk. My backpack sagged against my rear end. Considering waiting it out, I looked at my watch. Then I looked at my schedule. There were still twenty minutes left before the end of class. No way could I wait it out just standing there. Or could I? Maybe now would be a good time to go to the bathroom and change my clothes?

"Door locked?"

My head jerked up. A handyman with a million keys hanging from his belt walked purposefully for the door.

"Well, I . . ."

Before I could say more, he tested the knob and the door opened easily. Annoyed, he said, "You've got to actually *turn* the knob, missy."

"I'm new," I stammered. Then I reached up to touch my bandage as some sort of explanation.

He softened, led me into the classroom. "Knobs turn to the *right*," he said slowly. The eruption of class laughter made me wish I could hide my whole body beneath that bandage. The handyman patted my shoulder just as the nurse had done and left.

"Can I help you, young lady?" Mr Tilden asked.

"I'm in your class," I said. But my voice was so dinky I barely heard it.

"Pardon?"

Gulping, I took two steps further into the class. The moment I was in full view, no one said a word. It was the silence of curiosity, of alarm, of contempt. The walk to Mr Tilden's desk felt longer than the trip to Bartow, and twice as hideous. If my legs were working properly, I would have turned around and run . . . all the way back to Chatsworth.

"Are you in my class?" Mr Tilden asked.

I nodded. Handed him my note from the nurse. He read it, nodded himself, then looked at me with pity. To make matters worse, Mr Tilden gently put his arm on my back and led me to a desk like I was an invalid. To make matters the worst they could possibly be, he said, "Brian, could you please get up and give Elizabeth your desk?"

"It's Libby," I squeaked. But I'm sure no one heard because Brian, some grubby-looking guy in the front row, groaned and said, "I thought gimps go in the back."

EIGHTEEN

Nana walked Rif to the front gate of Sunset Park the next morning. I stayed home. I blinked a lot and told Mom I had a horrific headache, blurred vision, and dizziness. None of it was true, of course. But, man, I deserved a day off. Maybe the whole semester. Enduring the first day at my new high school dressed like a suburban mom with a giant white turban on her forehead was more than any fourteen-year-old should be required to bear.

My first day had been one humiliation after another. Barbara Carver was the only person who said a word to me all day. And, like some demented sports announcer, she ran the instant replay reel over and over.

". . . and there you were, splat, in the gutter! You passed out! Splat!"

I felt like a virus spreading through campus. As I moved towards groups of giggling kids, they clammed up, looked away, melted off. No one wanted to get near me. Like they might *catch* me or something.

". . . and there was blood on the sidewalk and everything!" squealed Barbara. "*Spalat!*"

"I'll make chicken soup," Nana declared, once she heard I was staying home from school.

"Hmm?" Mom wasn't paying attention because she had a job interview at Wal-Mart, and Dad, bizarrely, decided to spend his day on the couch watching soap operas in Spanish.

"Ella tiene una problema con su espina."

"¡No!"

"Si. No tiene sensibilidad en sus piernas."

"¡No!"

"Si."

Just when you think your family can't get any weirder.

So Nana scuttled off to her kitchen, Mom waddled to the bathroom to varnish her hair with hair spray, and Dad reached his arm up from the couch to open the refrigerator and pull out a six-pack of cola.

"I'm feeling a little less dizzy," I said, though no one even came close to caring.

Since I knew Nana's chicken soup would begin with an actual *chicken*, I figured I had a least half an hour before anyone noticed whether I was dead or alive. I decided to take a walk, work off a few extra calories so I could eat a noodle or two. All the kids would be at school; I wouldn't "infect" anyone.

Reading my mind, Juan Dog stared hopefully in my direction, licking his tiny lips.

"Okay, you can come."

Thrilled, Juan Dog leaped off Dad's lap and ran to my feet.

"I'm taking Juan for a walk, Dad."

"Bueno." His eyes never left the tube.

Stifling hot air swallowed me up the moment I stepped into the glaring Barstow sun. I lowered Juan Dog to the pavement and watched him sniff and hop around, his tiny feet scorched by the scalding cement.

"You asked for it," I said.

My forehead was already sweating into my bandage. My lungs even felt hot. But soon, as before, the dry heat felt good. It calmed me, in spite of myself.

"Get your *head* wet, Gracie!"

A female voice floated on the air as Juan and I passed Eden Way on the way to the pool.

"The water isn't going to bite you, Gracie!"

The same two old women I'd seen the last time were there. Charlotte was wearing her signature straw hat; Mim's skin still rippled like cake batter. They were both standing at the edge of the pool shouting to another old woman who doggy-paddled her way through the deep end, the rubber flowers on her bathing cap flapping with each pawing stroke. "Stick your head in and swim, for heaven's sake!"

Gracie continued bobbing; Charlotte and Mim kept yelling at her. "Your head! Dunk it!" As I quietly circled around the fence to the other end of the pool area, I saw an old man in a wheelchair parked near the shallow-end steps, clapping his hands together and grinning. His smile was all gums.

Yip!

"Shhh, Juan."

Yip, yip! Excited by the action, Juan Dog barked again. *Yip!*

Charlotte jerked her head up and shrieked. "It's the grandchild and the puppy!" She trudged over, swung open the gate, and flagged me in.

168

"Got your suit on?" she asked.

"No, I was just taking a walk," I said.

"Nonsense! Get in here."

"What's that on your forehead?" Gracie shouted from the side of the pool.

I shouted back, "A bandage. I fell."

"Concussion?" she asked.

"No," I said. Gracie shrugged and resumed doggy-paddling.

Mim called from the far end of the pool. "Did you *bring* your swimsuit?"

"Um, no."

"That's okay. I have an extra in my locker." She turned and lumbered into the rec room.

"No . . . thanks . . . really . . ."

Charlotte said, "I'll mind the little one while you swim." Then she snatched Juan right out of my arms. Startled, I warned again, "He doesn't like strangers." But just as he'd done with Mim before, Juan nestled his little head into the drape of flesh beneath Charlotte's chin and went right to sleep.

"Well, he sure likes me," she sniffed. I felt betrayed. The little runt.

"Here it is!" Mim sang, returning poolside dangling a turquoise-and-orange flowered one-piece that was obviously several sizes too big for me, not to mention too hideous to wear.

"I don't really swim," I said lamely.

"Nonsense!" said Charlotte.

"There's nothing to it," Gracie called from the pool. To prove it, she pushed off from the edge and took a full ten minutes to reach the other side. The old man in the wheelchair clapped and made weird smacking noises with his gums.

"It oughta fit you just fine." Mim held the bathing suit up and squinted. Apparently she was blind, or in major denial about her size. "You're welcome to borrow it."

"And the pool's just been cleaned," Charlotte added, stroking Juan's head and murmuring, "there, there." Juan was softly snoring like a little sewing machine. *Rat, tat, tat.*

"Thanks, but I was just exploring."

"Why not explore the deep end?" Gracie shoved off again and doggy-paddled across. The old man clapped again.

"As soon as school lets out, I was hoping to find some kids my age."

Charlotte, Mim, and Gracie glanced at each other then exploded in laughter. "Kids her age!" The man in the wheelchair erupted in a silent, toothless laugh.

"Or college age," I mumbled, trying to sound mature. That made them laugh even harder.

"Hon, this is a *retirement* home," said Charlotte.

Despite the heat, my insides froze. Strangely, the lapping of the water became louder than Charlotte's voice. Still, I heard her repeat "A *retirement* home." It echoed in deep slow motion: *Re . . . ti . . . er . . . ment . . . hooommme.*

Gracie offered helpfully, "Irene what's-her-name on Paradise Way is only sixty-two."

"A *retirement* home?"

"Didn't your grandmother tell you?"

"A retir—"

"The only reason they let you live here is because your grandma built this rec centre."

Suddenly, it was hard to breathe.

"She invested almost all of your grandpa's life insurance money right here in Sunset Park!"

"Last year, we added a DVD theatre!" Gracie yelled from the pool.

Charlotte said, "Your grandmother helped make Sunset Park one of the most desirable mobile retirement homes in the area. There's a waiting list a mile long."

"Some of us simply refuse to expire." Gracie giggled.

"They squeezed your family in at the head of the line."

Stunned, I tried to move but couldn't.

Charlotte said, "Why not take a dip, hon? Like I said, the pool's just been cleaned."

"This suit oughta fit you just fine," Mim repeated, shoving it into my hands.

In a surge of desperate energy, I crammed the bathing suit under my arm, yanked Juan Dog from Charlotte's chins, and bolted for the gate.

Gracie yelled after me. "Look! I can dunk my head!"

The gate slammed shut behind me. The last thing I heard was Charlotte shouting, "No running around the pool!"

ELEVEN

I staged a hunger strike. It was the only way I could protest forcefully enough. Slowly, I'd waste away. Nourishment would pass these lips only when my parents restored the life they stole from me. I'd stop the secrets and lies right here, right now.

On the outside of my slammed bedroom door, I posted a sign that read NO FOOD. NO WATER. NO VISITORS. To my astonishment, everyone obeyed. I lay there for *hours*. It was the first time my family ever did what I asked them to do. Nana didn't even attempt to deliver her promised chicken soup.

Just before noon, Mom poked her head in. About time, I thought.

"Guess what?" she said.

"What?" I asked indignantly.

"I got a job! I start tomorrow! The jewellery counter. Can you believe it? It's the best department in Wal-Mart. They have a new shipment of cubic zirconia coming in. Guess who is in charge of arranging the display case."

"Congratulations," I said, my voice dripping with sarcasm.

"Thanks, sweetie. You sure you don't want anything to eat or drink?"

Defiantly I stated, "Yes. I'm absolutely sure. No way am I eating a single solitary bite or drinking a sip."

"Okay, then. I'm off to get a manicure. I want my nails to look *perfect* when I show customers our new line."

Mom left and I fell back on my bed. What was *wrong* with these people? What good is a hunger strike if no one notices?

Feeling utterly powerless, I did the only thing I could do under the circumstances: I waited until I heard the screen door close behind my mother's rear end, and I snuck in the living room to find the cell phone Dad had hidden. Our regular phone wasn't installed yet, and, in retaliation for his forced sobriety, Dad had forbidden us from using his cell.

"We're a family," he'd said. "We'll suffer together."

Finding his phone was a piece of cake. Spanish soap operas blared on the television. Dad was asleep and snoring on the couch, an empty cola can rising and falling atop his rounded gut. I tiptoed into my parents' bedroom and searched through Dad's dresser. Bingo. I found his phone in five minutes flat.

"Nadine?" The moment I knew school was out and her cell was on, I dialled my best friend's number.

"Libby!" she screamed. "How *are* you?"

"Life sucks," I said, borrowing a phrase from my brother.

As I was taking a breath to fill Nadine in on all the hideous details of my hideous new life, she said, "I miss you so much! I've been dying to talk to you! Thank God you have a phone. What's your new number?"

Before I could take a breath, she was off and babbling again. "Curtis and his older brother and I went to Zuma Beach

Monday after school and it was so cool. The sun was hot and Curtis looked even hotter in his wetsuit. I so wish you were there. He surfs! Did you know that?"

"No, uh—"

"School is a nightmare without you. My whole day is dismal. How's your new school? Fernando High is exactly the same old drag."

"You think *Fernando* is a drag," I began.

"Just a minute!" I heard Nadine shout to someone, then to me she said, "I can't believe this! I have to go. My ride is here. Paige's mom is dropping us off at the mall."

"Paige?" My heart fell to the floor.

"You remember Paige Dalton? She's great. You'd like her."

Paige Dalton was a *cheerleader*. Paige was friends with Carrie Taylor. How had *my* best friend become friends with Paige Dalton in less than a week?

"Paige is friends with Curtis. That's how we met."

Ah.

"Can I call you later?" Nadine asked, obviously impatient to get off the phone. "What's your new number?"

"We don't have a phone yet. I'll call you."

"Oh, Libby. I miss you *so* much."

"I miss you too, Na—"

"I'm *coming*!" Nadine hollered to the gaggle of girls I could hear in the background.

"I have to go, too," I said loudly. "My friend Barbara Carver is showing me around Barstow tonight."

There. That'll get her.

"Awesome," Nadine said sincerely. "When we get our driver's licences, we can all hang out."

I tried not to feel the sting. I could hear Nadine climbing into Paige Dalton's mother's car. Digging my fingernails into the hard plastic of the phone, I said, "Our new house is amazing. There are lots of cool kids around here, too. They hang out at this old landmark McDonald's in a bunch of railroad cars. You *have* to see it. It's awesome. And my school, well, there's so much going on I don't know when I'll have the time to do homework."

"Wow, Libby. I thought you said your life sucks."

"Yeah, well, that was just an expression. Kids say that around here . . . when they think something is, um, good." I winced.

"Ah." I didn't fool Nadine for a second. Which made me feel even more humiliated. I wanted to delete the past five minutes, start over.

"Call me?" Nadine asked sweetly.

I swallowed. "Sure."

"Luv ya."

"I love you, too," I said, trying not to sound as desperate as I felt. The silence pierced straight through to my heart. Nadine was gone, off with her cheerleading, mall-shopping friends. Soon to experience a serious kiss. Aware that her former best friend was a liar. Falling back on my bed, tears flowed like the tide at Zuma Beach.

*

175

The next morning, I refused to get out of bed. I lay there beneath my covers, the air-conditioner blowing full-blast, Juan Dog curled up at my feet like a hairy, big-eared snail.

Mom knocked. "You okay, Libbydoodle?"

"Yeah, *right*."

"How's your head?"

"My *head* is fine," I growled.

"Good. I'm off to work!"

I said nothing. No way was I going to reply, "Have a good day!" Not when my parents had moved me into a *retirement* home, for heaven's sake. Not when my own mother didn't notice that I was starving to death and refusing to go to school. What kind of parents did I have? I could lapse into coma! What did they care? As I lay beneath the covers, my stomach rumbling, I considered never talking to anybody again. What was the point? My life was over.

"Wish me luck!" Mom sang. Then she vanished without waiting for me to wish her anything. Not that I would wish her anything good. Not in a million years.

Shortly after I heard the front door slam three times, I heard the refrigerator door open and a *pffit* sound as Dad plopped down on the couch and popped open a soda can. Then I heard voices.

"So you claim he promised to pay for the damage?"

"I never promised to pay!"

Apparently, Dad had shifted from watching Spanish soaps to watching Judge Judy.

"I have him on tape!"

Feeling majorly depressed, I sank into the mattress, determined never to get up again. To pass the time, I slathered lotion on my arms and smeared some on Juan's head, making his little hairs stick straight up in spikes.

"Anybody home?" Someone was on the other side of the door, tapping softly.

"Go away," I grumbled.

"Okay." It was Nana. I heard her footsteps walking away.

"What do you want?" I called, loud. The footsteps returned.

"I brought you a little something."

"What is it?"

"Can I come in?"

I sighed. "All right."

Nana opened the door, entered, and shut the door behind her. She held a plate in her hand, covered by one of those metal warmers they use for room service in fancy hotels. "Thought you might be hungry," she said. Did I smell butter and garlic? Something green . . . basil, maybe?

"I'm not," I lied. The aroma of whatever lay beneath the metal cover was unbelievably alluring. My mouth drowned my tongue in saliva.

"My mistake." Nana quietly turned to leave with my food in her hands. Man, she was good.

"My life is *over*," I declared.

Nana turned back and sat next to me on the bed. "How much longer do you have?"

Groaning, I asked, "Why won't anyone take me seriously?"

"I'm sorry, Libby. Do you want to talk about it?"

"No."

"I'm sorry about that, too." She made another motion to leave. What was *wrong* with this family? Didn't anyone care that I was wasting away to dust?

"If you change your mind, I'll be in my kitchen making grilled scallops over frisée for lunch," Nana said, placing the plate on my desk and reaching for the doorknob.

"How *could* they?" I blurted out.

"How could who?"

"How could my parents move us into a *retirement* home?!"

"Ah." Nana returned and settled herself on the edge of my bed. "I was wondering when you'd notice all the wrinkles around here."

"How *could* they?"

"Do your brothers know?"

"I don't think so." Though Rif *had* noticed that the speed limit inside the trailer park was fifteen miles per hour, and most drivers drove ten.

"What were they thinking? I mean, my parents might as well have moved us into a convent!"

"Is it that bad?"

"It's just so . . . so . . ." I stopped. How could I tell my grandmother how I *really* felt? This was her home, after all. How could I tell her I didn't want to live with a bunch of old farts? In a trailer? The humiliation of it! Would Nana ever understand how much my family embarrassed me, how I begged God, "Please, don't let me become my mother?" Or how my own father – her son – made me feel so confused and unsafe? It's awful to watch my dad disappear into alcohol, to have to tiptoe around him, making sure no one says out loud what we're all thinking. My family hides, so no one will see *him*. We feel ashamed of ourselves because we're so ashamed of him.

How do you tell your newfound grandmother you feel *damaged*? There are no words to express how much it hurts to see my dad all melted and drooling and baggy eyed. Why would a father let his daughter see him lose his manhood every day, fade into the couch and stop caring about his kids, and treat their mother like she's an intruder in his own private blurry world? Doesn't he realise I'll carry that image with me all my life? How am I *ever* supposed to have a boyfriend or a fiancé or a husband if my image of men is so warped?

The most unsettling thing of all, of course, is that my dad stopped drinking since we moved to Barstow (as far as I could tell), and he's as weird as ever.

My mouth hung open, but nothing came out. How could I tell an old woman what it's like to have your parents one day just *decide* to destroy your life? Without even *asking*. To *ruin* your whole entire life without even saying sorry! My best friend has already traded me in for a better model. All the boys I've ever liked like somebody else. Greg Minsky freaks me out, and Zack Nash looks at me like I'm his little sister. Like I'm invisible! And now I'll never get the one thing I really want: a serious kiss. It's too late. I'm branded a loser for *life*.

How could I express how terrified I was to start over in a new school? My whole life is one giant hold button – *blinking,*

blinking, blinking – waiting for whatever dreadful thing is going to happen next.

Nana reached her veiny, ring-encrusted hand up to tuck a strand of hair behind my ear. She sighed. "Sometimes there's so much to say it's hard to find even one word."

I nodded.

She said, "It's a funny thing, though. Teens and old people have a lot in common."

Staring at her, I struggled not to roll my eyes and grunt.

"Old age scares people," she said softly, "so they don't like to see it. They herd all of us into retirement homes, pretend not to hear us when we talk. Younger people treat older people like children. We feel powerless much of the time, our bodies are giving out, doing bizarre things they never did before. Betraying us. But you can only share what's happening with other old people – who else wants to hear about constipation and arthritis and bunions? Certainly, no one wants to hear about bladder control. It's a joke on Jay Leno! That's how society feels about us – people are so scared of becoming us, they can only mention us in jest. Really, society barely *tolerates* old folks. Sound familiar?"

I nodded, blinked. Of all people, I thought my grandmother would be the *last* to understand.

"It's lonely being old," Nana continued. "You're invisible. Men are not attracted to you; women cling too tightly. And there's that cloud that follows you around night and day: Will this year be my last? Have I done enough with my life? Will I be missed?"

180

Nana stared off into space for a moment. Suddenly, in her face, I could see the woman she once was. The fiery widow who declared, "To hell with what others think of me, I'm living in a *kitchen!*"

"It's true," I said quietly, "society barely tolerates *both* of us."

Smiling, Nana took my hand and squeezed it. "I tell you one thing, my love," she said. "It's a secret that's taken me seventy-five years to discover."

"What?" Straining, I lifted my head off the pillow.

"*No one* has any control."

"Nobody?" I let my head fall back down.

"Nope. Control is only an illusion. Striving for it is a waste of time. Life itself has a plan for you that's playing out right now, on its own, without your intervention. No matter what you do, life is going to win. You cannot control it. It's foolish to try. You've got to *let go*. Let life's flow carry you along in its current. Don't resist. Sit back and enjoy the ride. Watch where life takes you. Stop trying to steer it. Life will always win, my darling. Give it up. Let go."

Nana stroked my cheek, then leaned over to kiss me on the only patch of my forehead that wasn't covered by a now-filthy white gauze. In my ear she whispered, "In the meantime, you might want a little snack."

My grandmother left me with a wicked frittata and a big surprise: I wasn't so alone after all.

TWENTY

I awoke the next morning with a new resolve. To let go.

"Whatcha making?" Mom asked me as I stood at Nana's stove, dots of flour on my old T-shirt, my forehead bandage gone. No doubt left atop my unmade bed.

"Pancakes."

"Pancakes?"

"Want a stack?"

Mom looked alarmed, not sure what to say.

I slid the spatula beneath the bubbling batter and flipped one of the cakes. Mom sat at the table and asked, "Are you okay?"

"Never better. Butter?"

The enormous pancake stack slanted and wiggled as I carried it to the table. Nana and my brothers had already eaten; in fact, they were already gone. Off somewhere living their lives, going to school. Me, I was letting life carry me in its current.

"Syrup, Mom?"

"You seem well enough to go to school, Libby," she said.

"We'll see."

Life wanted me to stay home for the rest of the week.

"Libby—"

"You're going to be late for work, Mom."

My mother glanced up at the clock, said, "Oh, dear," and rushed back to our trailer. I settled in for the most delicious pancake breakfast I'd ever eaten. Juan whined beneath the table, but I pushed him aside with my foot. Cutting little pancake triangles with my fork, I shoved several layers into my mouth at a time. Letting go never tasted so good.

After breakfast, I decided to forgo a shower. I let go of bathing, too. Why bother? Who cared if I was dirty or clean? My head was fine. A brown scab covered pink, tender skin. It didn't hurt, just itched a little. Sliding my bare feet into flip-flops, I wore the same boxer shorts I'd slept in, scooped up Juan Dog, and left.

It didn't take long to make my way to the pool. As I approached, I could hear the same chatter and lazy slapping of the water. Charlotte wasn't there yet, but Mim and the clapper in the wheelchair were, plus a new old lady who was totally bald. She swam slow, deliberate strokes back and forth across the pool. In my new frame of mind, they all looked stunning.

"Beautiful day!" I called out breezily as I walked through the gate.

"Good morning," Mim said, then she asked gently, "How are you, dear?"

"Never better. Happy as a clam. Snug as a bug in a rug. And you? How are your bunions?"

Mim looked startled. With Juan Dog in tow, I dropped myself into an empty chaise and closed my eyes. The sun was already blistering hot and it was just past nine.

"Sunscreen, dear?" Mim asked. "The desert sun is treacherous." Eyes still closed, I shook my head no, stretched out. Listening to the gentle ripples in the pool, I imagined I was floating down a river on my back, destination unknown – letting go, letting life sweep me along in its current. What did I have to worry about any more?

When we were little, Mom used to call Rif, Dirk and me her three dwarfs: Breezy, Dopey, and Warty (me), as in worrywart. Then, who could blame me? I mean, who *wouldn't* worry, when life was always one big question mark? The way I figured it, I was the only one in my family who recognised how bad things can be, how many perils there are to life. The way I saw it, I was the only one who worried *appropriately*. But not any more. From now on, Mom would call me her dwarf Bright Side. Or *Floaty*. Yeah, from now on I'd be Floaty, the girl who goes with the flow.

My sunburn was just surfacing when I returned to Nana's for lunch.

"Yikes," she said, taking one look at me. Then she reached past the sink to snap off a frond of aloe from her window box herb garden. Dirk, home for lunch, kept poking my arm to see his white fingerprint. Dad didn't even see me; he was staring at something imaginary crawling up the wall. "Will ya look at that," he said over and over. When Mom came in she winced and asked, "Want some *Noxemawema* for that?"

Shrugging everybody off, I sat down to eat. "What smells so good?"

184

"Grilled chicken and avocado wrap with pecorino romano and garlic mayonnaise," Nana said, quietly rubbing aloe juice on my hot red arms and angry red forehead.

My eyes teared up with joy.

By evening, my eyelids were practically swollen shut. My lips were huge chorizo sausages and my thighs were blistered. Mom came into my bedroom and placed a cool, wet cloth over my face. She kissed my head.

"Poor little red riding face," she said.

I tried to smile beneath the face cloth, but my skin felt prickly and stiff. Soon I noticed it didn't hurt as much when I didn't move, when I lay flat on top of my bed in the blast of the air-conditioner. Which is exactly what I did. All night. And the weekend, too. The only time I got up was to go to the bathroom.

Oddly, it felt as if I was *watching* myself instead of being myself. I didn't feel the sunburn as much as notice it. Briefly, I wondered why life had decided to singe my skin – particularly my lips, when I really needed them to taste Nana's food – but then I chalked it up to the Master Plan. How can you question a Master Plan? Besides, my old life was over anyway. Clearly, the new one included pain.

Mom appeared periodically with fresh face cloths, Nana with fresh food (cold, of course). Grateful, I tried to say "thank you" but my huge lips could only say "Fwank eh," so I chose to be silent. Until mealtimes, when Nana checked on me and I managed to lift my head and whisper, "Is there any honey-baked ham weft?"

My world shrunk to the size of my bedroom ceiling. I stared at it so long, it began to look like the white sands of Zuma Beach where Nadine romped in the waves without me.

TWENTY-ONE

My face looked much less scary Monday morning.

"You going to school?" Mom asked.

"I doubt it." At Nana's breakfast table, I was devouring Cajun sausages and poached eggs.

"Let me rephrase that," Mom said. "You're going to school."

I looked up from my plate. "How can I let life flow in the confines of high school?"

Mom's face knotted itself into a mixture of exasperation and bewilderment. She said, "All I know is, you're going to flow your duff right on to that bus today. And you have twenty minutes to get ready."

Life told me I ought to listen to my mother or else.

Desert Valley High looked completely different to me. It was still ugly, but I didn't care. The low concrete buildings resembled bunkers huddled in the desert. Beyond the rusty chain-link fence, the Mojave spread out flat and wide over a mile to the foot of the dirt-brown mountains.

As I walked through campus in my green Wal-Mart shoes (what did I care?), I noticed that the biggest difference between Fernando and Desert Valley was the *atmosphere*.

D.V. High was much more retro than my old school. The cafeteria (yes, there was one, but it was old and disgusting) served meat loaf sandwiches instead of Big Macs. Many of the male teachers had scruffy beards and wrinkled ties. Most of the women wore Birkenstocks. Teacher-wise, it's *that* kind of place: A school that time forgot. Student-wise, it was more like *Boyz N the Hood*, that old movie about South Central L.A. Lots of macho strutting and angling for position, the girls both scoffing at and standing by their *boyz*. I'm not saying it felt like there might be a drive-by or something. There weren't metal detectors or roving video cams. But there was a lot of posturing – guys and girls who stood around and sneered at everybody and thought they were more than cool. To me, with my new perspective, Desert Valley High School seemed like a decrepit old pit bull – more bark than bite, hopelessly past its prime but unwilling to admit it. I mean, nobody even rode skateboards. It's like they don't know what's going on in the outside world.

"Welcome back." Barbara Carver met me at my locker. It was so dented it looked like my old locker at Fernando.

"Thanks." I smiled at her, stashed the roasted red pepper and mozzarella sandwich Nana had made me, and headed for class.

"Meet me here at lunch, okay?"

"Okay," I said. What did I care? Barbara was as good a friend as any. At least she wouldn't dump me for a *cheerleader* in less than a week.

My pastel canvas shoes squeaked on the cement as I walked

away. Across the quad, a guy with eyes as black as his hair was staring at me. I smiled, but he just nodded. His gaze made me feel like a walking X-ray, as if he could see my rib cage expand with each breath. There was something about his intensity that made my face flush instantly. There was also something about him that made me feel good. His eyes weren't judging me, they were simply taking me in. Later that day, I found myself scanning the desks in all my classes, disappointed that he wasn't there.

Academically, I quickly discovered I could graduate from D.V. High in my sleep. Geometry? Forget about it. Who needed to know what a trapezoid was if Zack Nash wasn't the reward? I chose, instead, to take courses I knew I could ace and wear my "loser" label with straight-A pride.

Rif embraced our new high school like they were old war buddies or something. With Rif, it was easy. He simply fell into the group of bad boys. Rebels know how to spot one another instantly. Everywhere he went, guys in baggy army surplus clothes opened their ranks to include him. Everywhere I went, girls in tight tank tops tightened their circles to keep me out.

Except, of course, one girl.

"Follow me," Barbara Carver said at lunch.

"Where?" Not that I really cared. I just wanted to make sure I had enough time to eat. Nana had baked white chocolate brownies.

"Out," Barbara said.

Shrugging, I grabbed my lunch, slammed my locker, and plodded along beside her in the direction of the fence.

As we walked off campus, one student puffed his cheeks with air while his friend shouted, "Make room! It's an elephant and her roasted peanut!" Another yelled, "Nerds of a feather stick together."

That started a chain reaction.

"The Losers' Club!"

"Tubby and Cher!"

"*Lez* be friends!"

I was mortified. I'd never been taunted like that before. My resolve to let life flow *dissolved* into a desire to shove Barbara away and explain to the gathering crowd, "I'm not who you think I am. I'm in a slump, that's all. Haven't you ever had your life ripped out from under you? Haven't you ever felt like nobody understood you? Haven't you ever wanted to belong, but nobody would let you in?"

That's what I wanted to yell, so they would take a second look, stop judging me as the lame-o who fainted on her first day of school, wore a couch cushion on her head, and Wal-Mart canvas slip-ons on her feet because her family couldn't afford real sneakers. I longed to clarify the fact that *Barbara* befriended *me*. I was just going with the flow, you know?

"You talkin' to me?" Barbara yelled at one of the guys who made fun of us.

"Yeah, I'm talkin' to you, lard ass," the skinny boy yelled back.

"Ignore him, Barbara," I said, blushing for her. She ignored me instead.

"You talkin' to *me*?" she said again to the boy.

"If the ass fits, wear it," he said, doubling over with laughter.

Barbara dropped her backpack and hulked across the dead grass. The boy looked stricken but stood his ground. His friends were all around him. No way was he gonna run from a fat girl.

"Do you have any idea how lardy my ass really is?" Barbara asked him. "Do you have any notion how heavy I really am?"

I swallowed. Or tried to.

Stunned, the boy said, "Like, it's so obvious. You're, like, *huge.*"

"Huge, huge," she repeated, her fingers rubbing her chin. "So hard to define exactly what the word 'huge' really means." Then her face lit up. "I know! I'm going to show you. I'm going to let you feel how huge I really am. So you'll know, you'll know forever."

In one surprisingly agile wrestling move, she sat on him. Barbara pinned the guy on the dry grass in the middle of the quad. Red-faced, he wriggled beneath her girth. It was the most hilarious thing I'd ever seen. His friends were hysterical with laughter. A bigger crowd gathered. I glanced around for the boy I'd seen earlier, but he wasn't there. Barbara sang at the top of her voice, "Can you feel it?" as she pressed her lard ass on top of him.

"Get off me!"

"Say *please.*"

"Move your butt, you tub of lard!"

"I didn't hear the magic word." Barbara didn't budge. The

skinny kid looked like he might suffocate. The rest of the kids were actually cheering for Barbara now.

"Flatten him, lard ass!" one of the Sylvanas squealed.

"Get *off*!" The boy screeched. Then, in a breathless, butt-squished voice he added, "Please!"

Barbara got up, dusted her hands off, and said, "I just had a baby-sitting job."

Everybody roared, Barbara bowed. And I felt a feeling I hadn't even come close to feeling since we arrived in Barstow: pride. As unexpected as snow atop a cactus, I felt proud that Barbara Carver was my friend.

"The best part of Barstow is on the wrong side of the tracks."

Barbara took me on a tour. "Hurry up," she said. "We only have an hour."

Practically running, I followed Barbara Carver down a side street gritty with sand. The midday sun was blistering. I'd decided to help life give me a break and slathered sunscreen all over my face while we hurried across Main Street.

"This side is where all the hideous fast-food places are, the tourist motels, the Wal-Mart."

"My mother works at Wal-Mart," I said, ashamed.

"Everyone's mother works at Wal-Mart!"

I beamed. "Yours, too?"

Barbara kept walking fast. "No. My *step*mother works at Wal-Mart. My real mother lives in New York with her boyfriend."

"Oh." I didn't know what else to say, which was okay when I was with Barbara Carver, because she always did.

"I'm hoping to follow in my mother's footsteps and find a boyfriend who moves me to New York, too. I'd even accept Victorville or Palmdale. Just as long as it's not here. And as long as he's a real boyfriend, not one of those serial killers who pretends to be in love with you so you'll get in his car. I mean, how low can you sink? Your first ever boyfriend is a *serial killer*?"

I just looked at her. What do you say to *that*?

"The wrong side of the tracks is the real Barstow." Barbara blathered on. "If you hurry, we can have lunch at my favourite spot."

"I brought lunch," I said.

"Not like this," she replied.

We continued downhill until we passed an old, long brick building.

"That's the Mother Road Museum," Barbara said. "Boring, unless you like railroad stuff and Route Sixty-six memorabilia."

"What's the big whoop about Route Sixty-six anyway?" I asked.

"It's like one long road almost all the way across the country. They call it 'the Main Street of America.' I guess it was pretty cool when they didn't have freeways. Now, it's just a way to get tourists to drive through small, crappy towns."

I nodded and wiped the sweat off my forehead with the back of my hand.

"That's what I call Big Moe," Barbara said, pointing to a huge, lumpy rock in the dry Mojave River bed across from the museum. "Little Moe is over there."

"You name rocks?"

"What else is there to do around here?"

I laughed.

Barbara chugged over an old iron bridge across a non-existent river. I couldn't help but think she was incredibly fast for a chubette. I struggled to keep up. Along the way, she announced points of interest.

"Rainbow Basin, down there, has lots of fossils.

"Calico Ghost Town is an old miner's town. Kind of hokey but interesting for newbies.

"Ancient Aborigines once lived in that valley."

Amazingly, Barbara Carver made Barstow sound sort of interesting.

When we finally got over the bridge, past the railroad tracks, Barstow changed completely. It felt like we were in a giant sandbox dotted with dried-up weeds. Where the other side of Barstow had seemed dead, this side seemed dead and *buried.* The houses looked more like sheds. There wasn't a flame-broiled burger in sight. Instead, Barbara led me into a tiny shack with a hand-painted sign that read AQUI.

"We're here," Barbara said. "Literally."

I knew enough Spanish to get the joke. Barbara knew enough to order, *"Lo mismo. Para dos."* She explained that she eats there several times a week, always the same, always *lo mismo.*

"What did you order?" I asked.

"You'll see," she said.

The smell of cilantro and onions made my mouth water. I

forgot all about Nana's sandwich, let life flow me to the only table inside. Outside, dusty construction workers sat at picnic tables in the sun or in their trucks, eating burritos and drinking *cervezas*.

"I'm buying today," Barbara said. "Next time lunch is on you."

I didn't argue. Especially after I bit into the burrito she handed me. My mouth exploded with flavour. It was smoky and spicy, with grilled steak, melted cheese, fresh salsa, avocado, and lime. It tasted so good, I wanted to bury my face in the warm flour tortilla.

"Welcome to my Barstow," Barbara said, grinning while she chewed.

TWENTY-TWO

My family settled in pretty quickly. Which got me thinking about life in general. You sleep, eat, do homework, go to school, hang out, watch TV, go to bed. The *details* are the only difference. Which, of course, makes all the difference in the world.

That night, I slipped into feeling sorry for myself again. I missed Nadine, Zack Nash, and even Greg Minsky. Barbara made me laugh, but she wasn't my *best* friend. Best friends know all your secrets and love you anyway. I still felt too embarrassed to even invite Barbara over. I still had tons of secrets to keep.

The big secret, of course – the whopper that no one in my family dared reveal – was the fact that my dad wasn't much different now that he was sober. He guzzled colas instead of beers. He sat slumped in his chair all day, eyes bleary from watching non-stop TV. He grumbled at my mother, ignored us, told Juan Dog to shut up, burped. The father I once knew – funny, loving, *there* – was still gone. It began to look like he was gone for good.

That night, I lay flat on my bed, face down, and – even though I tried not to – cried myself to sleep.

*

Each week, I spent part of my allowance at Aqui. Unbelievably, I didn't get fat. The explosion of blubber I feared, once I let myself actually *eat*, never materialised. My stomach stopped growling – that was the biggest change in my body. Pretty soon, it dawned on me that food wasn't the enemy after all. *Over*eating was. I could actually have breakfast, lunch, and dinner and not turn into my mom! Unless, of course, I ate like a lumberjack or a fast-food fiend, and I was neither. Feeling healthy actually felt good.

Getting to know Barbara Carver felt good, too.

"Popularity in high school doesn't mean squat," she said one day on our way to Aqui. "Just ask Johnny Depp. They used to call him Johnny *Dip*."

Barbara didn't care what anyone thought of her. She told me, "It's a choice you have to make. Are you going to give some dumb teenagers power over your self-esteem? Or are you going to empower *yourself* and become whomever you want to become?"

When she wasn't cracking me up, she was saying deep stuff like that. And using cool words like "empower" and "whomever." I'd never met anyone who had so many things to feel insecure about but felt totally secure anyway. Just hanging out with her made me start to see things differently. Like, my happiness just might be in my very own hands. Even when bad things happened, I didn't have to be depressed *forever*.

Incredibly, life's Master Plan was flowing me into a less

stressed-out space. Though Nadine was a hundred and forty miles away, my serious kiss was light-years away, and my former self was a quickly fading memory, I had Barbara and burritos and air-conditioning and Nana's cooking and Juan Dog's huge, silky ears.

TWENTY-THREE

You'd think I would have been thrilled to get out of school for the day; you'd think I would have been honoured to make Desert Valley High's Most Promising Students list so quickly. But the truth was, my new high school was filled with so many dunces, I could get straight A's with my brain tied behind my back. And the field trip they gave the thirty of us on the list seemed like homework to me. A geology walk? Through a humongous rock formation called Devil's Punchbowl? Right next to the San Andreas Fault? Why couldn't they reward our brain power with a bus trip in the other direction – to Las Vegas?

"Wear hiking boots and layered clothing," Mr Rhinehart, the Earth Sciences teacher and leader of our expedition, said. "It's a six-mile hike, one thousand feet up, and you may be cold as we climb but hot as we chug along."

Six miles of chugging? Near one of the biggest earthquake faults in the world? I was *not* looking forward to it. Even though Barbara was also one of the Promising Students, I'd rather contemplate my bright future at the Tanger outlet mall.

"Everybody on the bus!" Mr Rhinehart wore shorts and thick socks and heavy boots. His legs were tanned and muscled, very hikey looking. The first-aid kit he strapped to his backpack didn't make me feel any happier about hiking through desert rocks. He wasn't going to suck snake venom out of my thigh, was he? He wouldn't have to make a splint out of an old tree limb for my broken arm, would he?

"Let's sit in the front!" Barbara was excited about the adventure. Her backpack was weighted down with two fat burritos from Aqui.

Sitting next to Barbara, smelling the burritos already, I watched the other smarties board the bus. They weren't just freshmen. Which is a real clue about my school – out of four grades, only thirty kids were considered "promising." Almost all of them were too nerdy for words.

Except him. *Him.* The guy I'd seen across the quad watching me with his black eyes. My heart lurched as he got on the bus.

He wore a heavy green army surplus jacket over baggy camouflage pants. His hair was thick, tar black, and in an overgrown buzz cut. His skin was smooth milk chocolate. A silver cross dangled from his right earlobe. Everything about him was exotic, scary. He even had a black tattoo circling his upper arm. I'd seen it before when I spotted him at school hanging with his Latino homeboys.

As he passed me on the bus, I felt his stare burn through my skin. His eyes were dark caves. You couldn't look in them very long without falling in and flailing around for air.

"On the way, we're going to play Geology Jeopardy!" Mr Rhinehart said. Barbara and I groaned, but several kids behind us clapped and squealed.

"I'll give you a geologic answer," Mr Rhinehart continued, "and you raise your hand if you know the question. Be sure to phrase it in the form of a question."

The Guy sat at the back of the bus. I found myself wishing we'd sat at the back, too.

"It divides time into eons, eras, periods, and epochs," Mr Rhinehart began, as the bus left dusty Barstow for our destination an hour and a half away.

"What is the geologic time scale?" someone shouted.

"Raise your hand, please. But that's correct!"

I swivelled around to see who got the answer right, but ended up locking gazes with The Guy. He didn't smile, didn't nod or wave. He just stared at me with his bottomless black eyes, and my whole body went numb.

"It uses decay to determine the numerical ages of rocks."

By the time we reached Pearblossom, California, and the Devil's Punchbowl Visitor's Centre, I practically had a graduate degree in geology.

"What is radiometric dating?" someone in the middle of the bus shouted.

Barbara was asleep next to me. I gently tapped her shoulder.

"We're *aqui*," I said, knowing she'd wake up faster if I used the Spanish form of "here" and the name of her favourite restaurant.

"*¿Aqui?!*"

I was right. Barbara woke up instantly and said, "I'm starving."

"Everybody out of the bus and in a line," said Mr Rhinehart. "Five-minute bathroom break, then we're hitting the trail."

I looked around. I didn't see anything that resembled a punchbowl, satanic or otherwise. All I saw were rocky hills and tufts of scrub. And a long, uphill trail. The Guy stepped off the bus and walked toward me. A zap of electricity suddenly shot down my arms. It seemed as though he was about to say something, but Barbara tugged my sleeve and said, "C'mon. If we don't go now, we'll have to use the devil's *toilet* bowl."

By the time Barbara and I started up the hill, The Guy was way ahead.

"Look! The devil's pebble! The devil's dead branch!"

Barbara cracked jokes the whole way. As usual, she walked superfast.

"Isn't that the devil's dirt clod?"

As I raced to keep up, the cool air and Barbara's dumb jokes lifted my spirits. I guess some emotions are like menstrual cramps. When they first appear, they make you feel like curling up in a ball. But if you gut it out, they fade enough for you to ignore them and get on with it.

"Stay on the trail, kids," Mr Rhinehart yelled over his shoulder at us. "You don't want to disturb any snakes."

"Snakes?" I gulped, staring at the ground.

Barbara chugged on up the trail.

"Rattlesnakes?" I asked.

"And others," she shouted over her shoulder.

"Others?" I hurried to catch up.

"Copperheads, sand boas, corals, kraits, mambas, vipers, probably. That kind of thing."

Two of the other Promising Students looked like they wanted to run back to the bus. Like me, they were hoping their promise wasn't about to end in a place where the devil served punch.

"Don't worry," Barbara said, panting, "Snakes are more afraid of you than you are of them."

"Chickens."

I jerked my head up. The Guy stood a few feet ahead, standing on a small boulder jutting out from the side of the trail. He said, "Snakes prefer chickens over humans."

Barbara groaned. "Yeah, like there are chickens roaming free all over Pearblossom."

He didn't blink. He just stared down at me and said, "Or rats, rabbits, mice, prairie dogs – anything they can eat in one gulp."

Jumping down from the boulder, he stood so close to me I could smell his skin. It not only *looked* like milk chocolate, it smelled like it, too.

"Unless it's a python," he said, not moving one inch away from me. "They can swallow a deer . . . or you. If you see a python, run."

"There aren't any pythons around here, Warren," Barbara said, exasperated. "Are you going to get out of her way or what?"

"Or what," said Warren, flashing his black eyes at me.

My heart thumped so hard I was sure it would hammer his chest. Barbara *knew* him.

"Who's your friend?" Warren asked Barbara without taking his eyes off me.

"She's not a mute," Barbara scoffed. "Ask her yourself."

A jolt of electricity now shot through my entire body. I could feel the hairs on my arms stand up. I thought my heart would leap out of my chest and bounce down the trail.

"Who are you?" he asked me, grinning.

"Libby," I squeaked, suddenly aware that the trail was on a cliff. Just then, in a flash, I realised how far I could fall if I let myself.

"Hello, Libby. I'm Warren Villegranja. My friends call me Warrenville."

PART THREE

Warrenville

TWENTY-FOUR

I couldn't sleep. My bedroom window was wide open; the cool night desert air chilled the room, made me snuggle beneath my blankets. Juan Dog softly snored at my feet. The whole trailer park was asleep. But I just stared out the window, at the blue sliver of moon, and thought about *him.*

"Pocahontas," Warrenville had said to me at school, the day after our field trip, suddenly appearing behind me at my locker. "Did you read about Pocahontas yet?"

I muttered, "I don't think so."

"The movie version is full of crap."

"Oh." Not knowing what else to say, I focused on shoving books into my pack. Not that I needed them, but my hands were trembling and my knees felt like Silly Putty.

"The truth is, she was only *nine* years old when she was kidnapped by the Jamestown colonists. She didn't look anything like the babe Disney created."

"Uh-huh."

"And her name wasn't even Pocahontas. That was her *nick*name. Like P. Diddy or something. Her real name was Matoaka."

"Uh-huh."

"Why does everyone have to *lie*? That's what I want to know."

I froze. Did he expect an answer? Had he caught me in a lie? Had he heard about my dad?

"Adults say they want you to tell the truth, but even that's a lie," he went on. "*No one* wants to hear what's *really* going through a kid's head. They would freak out. Freak *out*." Then he asked me, "Wanna get something to eat?"

I'd never met anyone like Warrenville before. He was fifteen, a sophomore, but he seemed more like twenty. His mom was dead, he told me. His dad worked for the state, sixty miles away in San Bernardino.

"You like tacos?" he asked.

"Yeah, I like tacos."

"Follow me."

Truth be told, I would have followed Warrenville *anywhere*. In silence, we crossed the iron bridge to the "bad" side of town. I figured we were going to Aqui, but Warren led me into an even smaller shack with no sign on it at all. A bell on the door announced our entrance. An old lady with kinky grey hair emerged from the back and burst into a smile the moment she saw Warren. He hugged her. They spoke Spanish. When I asked if she was his grandmother, he said, "She's *everybody's* grandmother."

Warren ordered goat tacos.

"Goat?" I asked.

"Trust me," he said. Then he sat down at the only table in the place. Too nervous to eat anyway, I shrugged and sat across from him.

"Let me guess," he said, narrowing his eyes at me, "you think tacos taste like the food you eat at Taco Bell."

"Well, um, yeah." I mean, it's called *Taco* Bell.

"Today, you eat a real taco."

At that moment, the grey-haired lady trudged over and set two plates in front of us. Steam rose up to kiss my face. It smelled like lamb and cilantro.

"Try one," Warren said.

I swallowed. Then I picked up the warm, soft corn tortilla, folded it over the hot meat, and took a bite. The fresh lime juice intensified the flavour of the roasted goat. The tortilla tasted like flat cornbread. It was fantastic.

Warren smiled. I smiled, too. Together, we ate six goat tacos, drank mango juice, and said almost nothing. Which, bizarrely, felt exactly right.

When I got home from school that afternoon, the refrigerator was gone; our living room looked like a living room. Dad had left a note that read, "I'm off to find a job." Rif was in his bedroom doing homework. But all that wasn't the most extraordinary part of the day. *Barbara was with me.* I was feeling so happy about Warren, I decided to swallow my embarrassment and let Barbara see where I lived. I wanted to practice opening up instead of closing down. So I held my breath, bit the inside of my cheek, and led my friend into the asylum.

"You have a pool!" Barbara squealed, as we hopped off the bus and walked under the arch that read WELCOME TO SUNSET PARK.

Mim waved from her chaise longue as we walked by. "Come for a swim," she shouted.

"No, thanks," I said. Then, Barbara stunned me by asking, "Why not?"

"Yeah," Mim yelled, "why not!? You still have my suit?"

"Maybe later," I called out as I tugged on Barbara's sleeve.

"It's so clean in here," she said. "All the little front yards are so neat!"

As I pulled Barbara further into Sunset Park, I noticed, for the first time, what she was talking about. We passed a trailer with a bonsai garden in the front. A tiny bridge spanned smooth, black rocks. A white Buddha meditated beneath a miniature tree. Another trailer had a winter theme, with small white rocks as snow and a fake deer with his nose painted bright red. They were actually kind of cute. I'd passed them every day and never noticed before.

"My grandmother lives here," I said, leading Barbara into Nana's kitchen and introducing them to each other.

"Wow!" Barbara said over and over inside Nana's home. "Wow! This rocks!"

"Would you girls like a little kiwi fruit salad?" Nana asked.

"Yes! Wow!"

We ate our after-school snack, then I braced myself for the moment of truth.

"Our trailer is this way," I said, swallowing, motioning toward the back door. Barbara followed me outside.

"Trailer? No way. I've seen trailers. This is no trailer!"

"Well, technically, they call them mobile homes, but—"

"It's so cool in here!"

A blast of air-conditioning hit our faces the moment we walked through the door.

"My house is so hot, you sweat in the shower!" said Barbara. "It's like iced tea in here. Refreshing!"

Refreshing? Living in a trailer? In Barstow? With a bunch of old people?

That's when I noticed that the refrigerator was gone and Dad had acted like a normal dad by getting off the couch and looking for a job. With the huge, white elephant missing, our living room looked incredibly normal. I could hear Rif's CD player down the hall. Barbara said, "Show me your room!"

I showed her my room. It had four walls and a window and a bed that was perpetually unmade. It had a white desk and a wicker chair and a bookshelf stuffed with stuff. My closet was filled with my same old clothes, and my pyjamas were hanging on a hook on the back of my door, where I'd left them that morning. Standing there, in the middle of my room, seeing it through Barbara's eyes, was a revelation. It looked oddly *normal.* Maybe living in a mobile retirement home wasn't so weird after all.

Refreshing!

TWENTY-FIVE

Nana had been planning it for weeks – all year probably – and the whole trailer park was grateful. Thanksgiving dinner in the rec room was the event of the year. Nana was in charge, everyone was invited, and each year had a different theme.

"This year, it's Chinese!" Nana announced at a meeting she held to elect the decorating committee. "Szechuan turkey!"

"We can string lanterns around the pool," Charlotte suggested.

"Or one of those paper dragons!" squealed Mim.

Frieda, a widow who lived on Heavenly Way and had a stroke the year before, shouted, *"Fawaahs!"* but nobody understood her because one side of her face was all droopy. Nobody but Gracie, that is.

"Fireworks," she translated.

"Fabulous!"

That year, Nana had decided to combine Thanksgiving with our trailer-warming party. Mim was asked to make sesame noodles instead of her famous baked beans; Charlotte made a cake with a layer of green tea ice cream. Everyone was excited about the big event. Everyone but me.

"Should I invite him?" I asked Barbara.

"Yes."

"Then he'll know I really like him."

"So don't invite him."

"He already told me his dad wants him to spend Thanksgiving at his aunt's house in Riverside, and he doesn't want to go. I would be doing him a favour."

"Then invite him."

"How can I invite someone I barely know to meet my whole family? And the whole trailer park!"

"Then don't invite him," Barbara groaned.

Barbara was beyond tired of talking about Warrenville. She rolled her eyes every time I mentioned his name. Barbara was spending Thanksgiving weekend with us. Her dad and stepmom were taking her step-siblings to Disney World in Florida. An experience she'd had before.

"I needed another vacation after spending my vacation with the brats," she told me. So I'd asked Mom if Barbara could spend the night in our trailer and join us for Thanksgiving dinner. She'd told me to ask Nana, who, of course, said *yes*. "Invite the brats, too! The more the merrier."

"I'm not going to invite him," I said to Barbara, suddenly remembering the promise I made to myself when Nadine made me feel like a loser for not having a boyfriend. "It'll be just us."

"And the whole trailer park," Barbara said.

"You're right. Should I invite him?"

She sighed. "He's pretty strange, you know," she said.

"And you're normal?" I asked.

"He doesn't even like Aqui!"

"I know. But I like him. What can I say?"

What could I say? The *click* I heard in my brain was loud and distinct. Warren and I *fitted* together. I just knew it. We were both outsiders. It felt right being on the outside with him.

A few days ago, at school, Warren appeared behind me and asked, "Ever sing a polyphonic secular song?"

"Huh?" I said.

"You should, because you're a Madrigal."

Another time, he cupped his hands over my eyes, the way Greg Minsky used to do, and stood there behind me, silent, until I said, "I know it's you, Warren." I always knew when Warren was near me. His whole being radiated heat. Unlike Greg Minsky, I didn't care if Warrenville stood so close to me I could feel the muscles in his body.

Since I met Warrenville, everything looked different. Desert sunsets were the most spectacular things I'd ever seen. Purple wild heliotropes were awesome. Sand swirls and scrub and tacos and centipedes were incredibly beautiful. Even watching Dirk watch the TV was wonderful because of the angelic look on his face. Seeing my mom all flushed from a great day at Wal-Mart filled me with joy. Nana's fingers, covered in wonton dough, were suddenly rays of sunlight that made me happy just looking at them.

Was it the beginning of love? I didn't know. Was he the guy I wanted to seriously kiss? Definitely.

"I should invite him," I said. "Unless you think I shouldn't."

Barbara groaned even louder and walked away.

Mr Belfore wore a satin robe as a kimono and sweat socks with his flip-flops. He lived on Nirvana Street and was considered eccentric by everyone at Sunset Park. Which is saying a lot, considering Nana's toilet armoire and the tiki hut Charlotte wore as a hat. Mr Belfore arrived at Thanksgiving dinner with a chopstick behind each ear.

"I wanted to wear them in my hair," he explained, "but I don't have any hair."

Barbara found an old Chairman Mao-type jacket in a thrift store on Main Street, and wore navy blue trousers with black canvas Chinese shoes. Mim carried a Chinese fan. Unable to find anything better, I wore a long black skirt and a red satin shirt. To complete the look, I painted my fingernails in Mom's *Vroooom!* red nail polish, and had her buy me the reddest lipstick Wal-Mart had. Honestly, I didn't look bad.

Amazingly, even my mom and dad got into the Thanksgiving spirit. Dad bought a box of fortune cookies and handed them out to everyone; Mom made a small handbag out of an empty Chinese take-out carton with glued-on sequins and everything. My parents actually seemed happy. Dad, after a month of TV Zombie Detox, was slowly coming back to life. After the long holiday weekend, he had a job interview at a car dealership in San Bernardino. Mom, tired of having aching feet, bought larger, more comfortable shoes, and joined Weight Watchers.

"I've lost two and a quarter pounds!" she said at breakfast. "Only twenty more to go!"

215

I waited for Dad to say, "Twenty? Don't you mean fifty?" But he just grinned and said, "Way to go, Dot."

Rif and I looked at each other like our parents were aliens. Dirk burst into tears and said, "I feel so glad!"

After breakfast, Barbara came over and we helped Nana stuff the Szechuan turkey with water chestnut and peanut stuffing. Later, we filled the pool with small, flickering, floating lanterns. Mim wanted to buy carp to swim in the pool but Gracie told her they'd die in the chlorine. Incredibly, Mom found battery-operated fish in the toy department at work. They "swam" around the pool, and everything.

Mr Belfore helped us arrange rectangular tables all around the edges of the pool, so everybody was facing one another with the twinkling water in the centre. When it was all set up, Frieda said, "It's *bufa!*"

Nobody needed Gracie's translation to know what she said. "It certainly is beautiful, Frieda," Mim said.

While Barbara checked on Nana's ginger-spiced yams, I slipped into our trailer to make a phone call.

"Nadine?"

"Libby! Happy Thanksgiving!"

"You, too. That's why I'm calling."

"How are you?" she asked.

"I'm good. We're about to have dinner down by the pool. Everyone will be there soon. You?"

"Curtis is coming over. My family is here."

"Have you—?"

"Not yet. Have you?"

"No." We both knew what we were talking about. A serious kiss.

Nadine said, "I'm hoping mine will happen tonight."

"I hope so, too. For you."

"Thanks."

Neither one of us said anything for a few long seconds. We used to wrap ourselves in each other's silences like old flannel blankets. They were comfortable, familiar. Now, our silences were awkward, filled with stuff no one wanted to say.

"So—"

"So, say hi to your family for me."

"You, too."

"Okay, then."

"Okay."

She sounded relieved. I felt sad. I knew my friendship with Nadine was over. Well, not *over*, just never the same again. A month earlier, I would have thought it was impossible. But there it was – in less than three weeks, we both had begun to move on.

"Listen up, everyone!" Nana stood near the diving board, a large glass bowl in her hands. "For those who are new, we welcome you."

The grey-haired crowd and their families burst into applause. My parents grinned. Mom adjusted her sparkly handbag on her arm. Mr Belfore tapped his chopstick against his wineglass.

Nana continued. "We have a Thanksgiving tradition here at Sunset Park. Gratitude Prayers. There's a piece of paper and a pen next to each plate. Your fee for the feast we are about to partake of is to write down one thing for which you are grateful. Something in the past year."

"And if it was the worst year of your life?" someone joked.

"Even in the worst of times, there's always something to be thankful for."

I was beginning to see that she just might be right.

"I'm going to pass this bowl around the tables. Put your Gratitude Prayer in the bowl, and we'll complete the ceremony as soon as everyone is done."

Rif scoffed. "How long is this going to take? I'm starving."

I shrugged, reached for my pen. All I could think of writing was Warren, Warren, Warren, over and over. I was so grateful that Warrenville had entered my life. Even though I'd decided *not* to invite him, out of respect for Barbara, he was on my mind and in my heart all day.

"What did you write?" Barbara asked me after I dropped my Gratitude Prayer in the bowl and passed it on.

"Something," I said, smiling. Then I added, "I'm glad it's just you and me tonight." Without Barbara, I would have had no one.

The sun was beginning to turn the sky orange as Nana took the bowl of Gratitude Prayers to the barbecue she'd set up in the corner. Small flames flickered above the rim. She set the bowl down, plunged one hand into the sea of papers, and began to read aloud.

"I'm thankful for another year of life."

"For the raise in Social Security."

"AARP discounts."

After she read each one, she tossed it into the fire and we watched it sizzle up to heaven.

"Lipitor."

"Fosamax."

"Viagra."

Everyone twittered at the litany of prescription drugs. Nana continued reading.

"I'm thankful for my parents' health."

"For a roof over our heads . . . even though it's a metal roof." The group laughed again. Nana looked at Mom and smiled.

"For new friends." Barbara looked at me and grinned.

"Dark sunglasses." (Rif's, of course.)

"Roasted sesame oil." Everyone knew that was Nana's. "And family dinners."

"Orthopaedic shoes."

"Grandchildren."

"Sundays."

"For learning how to let go."

Yeah, that was mine. It was embarrassing to hear it out loud. Still, I was glad I wrote it. Even though I wasn't sure I knew how it felt to let it *all* go, I was incredibly grateful that I was starting to learn. A month ago, my life was over. Now, it felt as though a new life was beginning. I felt sad for losing what I had, but – amazingly – I was feeling excited about the future. It's weird how everything can suddenly look up when your whole world is down the drain.

Nana kept reading the Gratitude Prayers.

"Laser eye surgery."

"Plastic surgery."

The group snickered again. Nana finally burned the last of the prayers. She held her hands together, tilted her head back, and said, "God, please accept our thanks. We all hope to talk to you next year." Then she hollered, "Let's eat!"

With that, several of the older grandchildren paraded in with plates of steaming food. The air smelled of ginger and scallions. Juan yipped under the table. Nana passed me and kissed the top of my head.

"Goat tacos!"

A familiar voice bellowed from outside the pool's gate.

Yip. Yip.

The group stopped passing food and stared. My heart fluttered.

"I'm grateful for goat tacos and chipotle chilis."

Warren opened the gate and walked in.

I stood up. "What are you—? How did you—?"

The group resumed chattering, reaching, scooping, and eating. I heard Mr Belfore say, "I'm grateful for this pork bao."

"Barbara invited me," Warren said, as she scooted over to make room for him.

I gaped at her. She quietly asked, "A person can have a boyfriend *and* a best friend, can't she?"

Best friend? Boyfriend? I was too happy to let either label weird me out. Not that night, when everything felt so right. Flinging my arms around Barbara, I couldn't stop grinning. Nana walked up to us.

"Sorry I'm late," said Warren, extending his hand shyly. "I'm Libby's friend, Warren Villegranja."

Nana shook his hand warmly. "Anyone who's thankful for goat tacos and smoked jalapeño peppers will always be welcome in my home."

TWENTY-SIX

I suspected that somewhere, out there, there were Thanks-giving dinners like this. We laughed, savoured the food, and enjoyed one another's company without tension as thick as lumpy gravy.

Mom was on the other side of the pool, and Dad had wandered off somewhere. Rif nodded his head, saying hi. He'd seen Warrenville at school. Dirk giggled and blushed.

"Scallion pancake?" Barbara asked Warren.

"Why not?"

I started to explain my nutty grandmother and her traditions, but Warren didn't seem to care. He piled his plate high and ate heartily. He reached under the table and squeezed my knee. My whole insides were flooded with light. I felt warm and astonishingly calm. Warren fitted in so easily and naturally, I forgot to be ashamed of the trailer park and my elderly neighbours. I even hugged Mim and let Juan nestle into her chins. I ate seconds of everything without once worrying that my satin shirt might pull at its Chinese buttons. Thanksgiving came only once a year, after all.

As candles flickered atop the pool, paper lanterns swayed in the desert breeze, and garlic and ginger infused the air, I felt happier than I'd ever felt in my life. It wasn't Warren or Barbara or Thanksgiving. It was more than that. Suddenly, without warning bells or bugles trumpeting, I felt totally, completely, absolutely *normal*.

"Elizabeth Madrigal?"

A man in a policeman's uniform stood behind me. Instantly, I panicked. I flashed back to Chatsworth and Rif's arrest and bill collectors at the door.

"Yes?" I said, weakly, I'm Elizabeth Madrigal."

He looked confused, said, "Is there another Elizabeth Madrigal? An older lady?"

"Oh! Yes! My grandmother." Heart pounding, I stood up and led the officer around the pool to Nana. Her face darkened as he got closer.

"What happened?" she asked abruptly.

Quietly, he answered, "There's been an accident. Your son. He's okay, but he's in the hospital."

"My son?"

Nana and I both spun around to look for my dad. Mom sat alone by the diving board next to Frieda. Another surge of panic rushed through my body. Where was my father?

"He must be in the bathroom," I blurted out.

The police officer placed his hand gently on my shoulder. "I'm sorry," he said.

Nana swung into action. "Libby, get your mom and brothers and meet me at the gate."

In a daze, I did what I was told. I never said a word to Barbara or Warren, just followed my family to the front gate

223

of Sunset Park where we silently waited for a taxi. Our old Toyota, the only car our family had, was gone.

Nobody could speak. We were too stunned, too hurt, to form any words at all.

"I didn't want anyone smelling beer on my breath," Dad explained drunkenly, from his bed at Barstow General. "I was going to order extra onions."

My father had left Thanksgiving dinner to drive to the only open liquor store in town and buy a case of beer. He'd sat there, in the liquor store parking lot, chugging one can after the other. Then, to cover his tracks, he'd headed for the landmark McDonald's to order a burger, extra onions. Only he was too drunk to drive. My father's right fender rammed the corner of McDonald's converted railroad car, knocking it off its foundation. Thankfully, McDonald's was closed for the holiday. No one was hurt but my father. Dad broke his nose. The fire chief told us they found him passed out at the wheel.

"Why, Lot?" Mom asked him in the hospital. "Why?"

It was a question we all wanted answered. He'd been doing so well! But Dad didn't say anything. He hung his head and sat there, like a zombie, his glasses falling off his bandaged nose. I couldn't look at him anymore. I felt so disappointed I wanted to bury my head in a pillow and sob.

So much for gratitude.

So much for beginning to feel normal.

TWENTY-SEVEN

Dad's accident made the local news that night and the front page of the paper the next morning. The newspaper photograph was too mortifying for words. My father was handcuffed and dazed, his nose bloody. Two uniformed police officers stood on either side of him. The caption read:

FRIES WITH THAT?
Drunk Barstow Man Slams into
Landmark McDonald's Restaurant

My dad: Drunk Barstow Man. It was too humiliating for words. I felt like someone had let all the air out of my life. I felt flat, deflated. And the worst part of all? I didn't hear a word from Warrenville. Not one word over the entire Thanksgiving break.

If you ask me, we *all* got busted. Mom made us stand behind Dad, as a family, in front of the Barstow judge. His gavel hit the wood with a loud *clack*.

"Your driver's licence is suspended for six months," he said. "You'll pay restitution to McDonald's, perform one hundred and eighty hours of community service, and go straight into the rehab centre."

Mom raised her hand.

"Yes?" the judge asked, looking annoyed.

"I was wondering, your honour, if you could order the whole family into counselling?"

Rif gasped. I stamped my foot and Dirk started to cry. Nana, standing erect and proud next to us added, "I'll second that motion."

The judge rolled his eyes. "I can't force your whole family into anything, Mrs Madrigal. But I will strongly suggest it to your husband's rehab counsellor."

Rif exploded. "Mistrial!"

The judge narrowed his eyes at Rif and asked, "Are you Richard Madrigal?"

Rif swallowed. Dad said, "Yes, your honour, he's my son."

Peering through half-frame glasses, the judge flipped through a folder on his desk. "Have you completed *your* community service?" he asked Rif.

Rif stared straight ahead, speechless.

The judge said, "The computer spat out your name. Just because you move doesn't mean you're free from paying your debt to society."

"I didn't mean it about a mistrial. Really, sir." Rif blinked and tried to look innocent.

"Richard, your community service starts this weekend. You'll remove the graffiti from the boulders in the Mojave River bed. That *is* an order."

Big and Little Moe? I wondered. The judge added, "You'll be given the supplies. Be sure to wear sunscreen."

"But—" Rif started.

"Next case." The judge's gavel came down hard.

On the way home, Mom came down hard, too. "This family is going to pull itself together if it kills us." Then she asked, "Who's hungry for a low-cal *snackywacky?*"

TWENTY-EIGHT

There we were. All of us. In *therapy*. Ugh. Dad's rehab was in Victorville, so the rest of us drove down there for family sessions with him.

"Why are you here?" the therapist asked us in the first session. His name was Josh, and since he didn't ask us to call him Dr Josh, I assumed he never quite made it to med school.

Josh went around the circle. "Rif? Why are you here?"

"It's a family outing," he said sarcastically.

"Lot?"

"The court made me."

"Libby?"

"My mother made me."

"Dirk?"

"I dunno."

"Elizabeth?"

"I'm here for my son."

"Dot?"

"I don't know what else to do."

Josh – Just Josh – nodded his head. "Is anyone here because they need help?"

We sat stiff and silent, like five trees in the Madrigal petrified forest.

"Okay," Josh said, adjusting his frameless glasses with his slender, girly fingers. "Over the next few weeks, you may feel differently about why you're here. In this group, we'll cry, yell, laugh, feel awful, feel great, feel awful again. You name it, we're going there. The point is to fully explore what it means to grow up in an alcoholic family, what it means to be an alcoholic, what happens to the spouse of an alcoholic, and how some kids act out and act *up* under the stress of it all."

"I'm not an alcoholic," Dad mumbled.

Rif and I side-glanced at one another.

"That's the perfect place to begin," Josh said. "*Definitions.* Everybody ready to dive in?"

Nobody said a word. So our skinny therapist, with his bushy brown hair and wrinkly white shirt, who looked like he was still in high school, dived in by himself.

"Alcoholism is a chronic disease that often gets worse over time and can kill you if not treated."

Dad sighed. Nana nodded. Mom fished around in her purse for a Kleenex. The only window in the therapy room was covered in vertical blinds. Not that there was anything to look at. But staring at a dreary parking lot was better than sitting in a circle and "sharing my feelings" with Just Josh and my family.

"Basically, if using alcohol is causing *any* continuous disruption in an individual's personal, social, spiritual, or economic life – and the individual doesn't stop using alcohol

– that would be *harmful* dependence. Often, denial and rationalisation become a way of life. Does any of this sound familiar?"

Mom looked at her hands. Dad said, "I'm not in denial. I'm just not an alcoholic."

Rif laughed out loud. Dad shot him a look.

Josh asked, "Rif, do you have something to say?"

"Yeah," said Rif. "Three words: Barstow trailer park."

The rest of us stopped breathing. No one had ever stood up to my father like that. In *public*, too. I looked at the window again. If it was open, I would have leaped out.

"What do you mean by that?" Josh asked.

Boldly, Rif looked directly at Dad. "If you're not an alcoholic, Dad, why did you lose your job and our house? Why did we have to move into a trailer bought by your mother?"

"Yes, Lot," Mom piped up. "Why?"

Now I considered jumping through the glass. Anything to get out of that room. Dad apparently had the same idea. He got red in the face. His nostrils flared when he stood up and said, "I don't have to put up with this crap." Kicking his chair, Dad headed for the door.

"Actually, Mr Madrigal," Josh said, "you do. This is part of your court-mandated rehab."

Dad stopped. But he didn't sit down.

Josh added softly, "Would you rather go to jail?"

His question hung in the air. The tension in the room felt like a saddle on my back. Suddenly I wanted to scream and pound the walls with my fists. I wanted to rip the scarlet letter off my chest, stop being the daughter of the "Drunk Barstow Man." I wanted *answers*! Why did Dad start drinking after he stopped? How could Nadine move on so fast? Why won't Warren call me or even look at me at school? When I saw him on campus, I swear he saw me, but he looked away fast and stayed in the tight circle of his friends. Why did everything always go wrong at the precise moment it seemed like it might – for once – go right?

Barbara had said, "Boys are jerks." But I knew that wasn't true. Not Warren. It was me. Something was wrong with *me*.

"Please take a seat, Mr Madrigal," Josh said.

Dad sat. He crossed his arms in front of his chest and slouched so low in the chair he nearly disappeared.

For a few long moments, Josh didn't say anything. Nobody said anything. It was the loudest silence I've ever heard. Finally, Josh cleared his throat and looked each of us in the eye.

"I'd like to try something a little unconventional. Is everyone up for it?"

Still, nobody said a word.

"Here's what I'd like you to do," he said. "For our next session, I'd like each of you to write a letter to Lot about how his drinking has affected you *personally*. The letters should be specific and completely honest. Spill your guts. Tell him how you really feel. We'll read them at the next session. Are you all willing?"

Mom nodded her head energetically. The rest of us shrugged.

Dad asked, "What am I supposed to do?"

Josh answered, "Listen."

231

TWENTY-NINE

Writing my dad that letter was one of the hardest things I've ever done. I held a pen in my hand for almost an hour before the words began to flow. After *not* saying stuff for so many years, it felt like I was stabbing him in the back. I mean my *dad*. How could I tell him the honest-to-God truth?

But I did. I spilled my guts in a letter. Next, I needed to find the guts to read it out loud to him.

Nana drove us to Victorville the following week. On the way, my family talked about school, sand, Thai food, carbs — anything but the letters we all carried. I was a basket case. Would my father hate me after I read him my letter? Would he refuse to come home? Was this the beginning of the end of my family?

Josh greeted us all with handshakes. Dad was already in the therapy room. He kissed Mom, hugged his mother and us. He seemed relaxed. Which made me feel even worse. How could I hurt him when he'd been living next door in the rehab centre working hard on getting better?

"Let's get started," Josh said. We all sat down and he said, "First, I want to acknowledge how hard it was for everyone to write their letters. I also want to recognise how difficult it will be for Lot to hear what his family has to say. But you have to feel the hurt before you can heal. And healing is what we're all about here. Who wants to read his or her letter first?"

Dirk raised his hand.

"Go ahead, Dirk," Josh said.

Dirk opened his letter and burst into tears.

"It's okay to cry," Josh said, softly. "It's okay to feel whatever you feel."

Is it okay to feel like leaping through the window? I wondered, my pulse racing.

Sniffing, Dirk read his letter.

"Dear Daddy,

"When you get drunk, you make me scared. You yell at Mom and Juan, and sometimes me. It makes me want to cry. And once, I saw Mom crying in the laundry room, when she didn't know I saw her. But I knew she was crying because of you. Please stop drinking.

"Love, Dirk"

Dirk sniffed again, and wiped his nose on his sleeve.

"Very good, Dirk, thank you," said Josh. Dad started to speak, but Josh held up his hand and said, "I'd like you to wait until all the letters are read before you comment. Would you be willing to do that?"

Dad nodded.

"Good. Rif? Would you like to go next?"

"Our dog ate my letter," Rif said, smirking.

Josh didn't react. Instead, he turned to me and said, "Libby? Ready?"

Instantly, my heart pumped blood into my ears. My palms got sweaty and I felt light-headed.

Josh said, "It's okay. Take a deep breath."

I took a deep breath, shakily opened my letter, stared at it, and read.

"Dear Dad,

"My heart is pounding as I write this letter. Now that it's finally time to tell you how I feel, I'm nervous. I don't want you to hate me. But I do want you to know how it feels to be the daughter of a dad who disappears little by little every day, right before my eyes. It's scary. One day, will you be gone forever? I miss the funny, smart dad I used to have. Drunk Dad is mean. He's embarrassing. He makes me mad. It's like you'd rather ruin our lives than stop drinking, which seems really selfish. And you've made me feel ashamed of you, when I used to think I had the coolest dad in the world. How could you do that?

"Remember that camping trip we took to Big Bear Lake? You and Mom rented a camper van. Rif and I played crazy eights in the back. Dirk was just a baby, so he slept the whole way. I keep thinking about that first night, around the fire pit, eating toasted marshmallows and

*making up ghost stories. It was all of us. Together. It
wasn't anything special, but I think, maybe, it was the
happiest night of my life. Because our family was just like
every other family. We were normal.*

*"I don't know if I can explain this right, but your
drinking makes me feel empty. In the same way that night
at Big Bear Lake made me feel full. Your drinking makes
me feel lost, like I don't belong anywhere.*

*"Mostly, Dad, I feel like something is wrong with me.
Something is missing. I don't know what it is, or if I can
blame you for me feeling so . . . unnormal. Maybe this is
what kids feel like when their parent dies. Because, it's
kind of like you did die. The real you. The dad who's only
in my memory now.*

"Love, Libby"

Too scared to look up, I didn't. I waited for Josh to say
something, but he didn't, either. Instead, Dad's voice was the
first sound I heard.

"I'm so sorry, baby," he said, almost whispering. Josh didn't
cut him off. "You're right. I have been selfish. I'm so, so sorry."

"Thank you, Libby," Josh said. "And you, Lot. We have a
long way to go, but we've taken a huge first step."

Mom and Nana went after me. They both cried all the way
through their letters, both said how hard it was to see Dad
destroy himself. But I could barely hear them through the
loud thumping of my heart.

THIRTY

Barbara's stepmother decorated their whole house with stuffed animals. I swear, there were fake furry things in every room. Except Barbara's.

"She knows better than to set foot in here," Barbara said. A sign on her purple-painted bedroom door read, BEWARE: HAZARDOUS MATERIALS INSIDE. I think it was actually true. I found an Oreo under her bed with green hair growing on it.

Since I'd begun family counselling, Barbara was full of questions.

"Have you cried yet?"

"Has your dad cried?"

"Is Just Josh anything like Dr Phil?"

Me, I just had one question: "Why is Warren avoiding me?"

Barbara groaned. "Who knows?"

"Why do you *think*?"

"Why don't you ask him?"

"Yeah, like I'm going to ask him why he dumped me when we weren't even together!"

Barbara sighed. "Want a Fudgsicle?"

"No."

At that moment, I made a decision. Josh had explained that an alcoholic's family members often "walk on eggshells" around the user, trying not to rock the boat. They stuff their own feelings and feel isolated because they don't want to face what's really going on. I'd done that hundreds of times before. But no more.

Standing up, I marched to Barbara's bedroom door.

"I want *answers*. Are you with me?"

"Where are we going?" Barbara asked, excited.

"You'll see. Follow me."

We marched across the old iron bridge, over broken beer bottles, past Aqui, almost to the base of the Calico Mountains. We walked and walked and walked. Since it was December, it was warm instead of hot. But the wind whipped sand into our faces and up our noses. By the time we got where we were going my green canvas shoes were white with dust and my lungs were full of dirt.

"The old drive-in?" Barbara asked.

"Rif told me this is where all the guys hang out."

Barstow's Skyview Drive-In was a huge, empty dirt lot, surrounded by a chain-link fence. The large movie screen was still there, as was the old Snack Shack, but all the speakers were gone. Clearly, no one had seen a movie there in years. Barbara and I snuck through a hole in the fence. The noise was deafening. I could hear engines revving and guys yelling, "I'm next!" A thick dust cloud swallowed up the action in the middle of the lot. As soon as it cleared, I saw Rif.

"His time is up!" he shouted. "I'm next!"

Barbara and I hung back and watched my brother hand some guy five dollars, and hop on a dune buggy. He gunned the engine, then hurtled forward yelping, "Wahoo!"

It looked incredibly dangerous and incredibly fun. Rif rode the dune buggy in a circle, like it was a bucking bronco. The wheels kicked up so much dust it was hard to see anything. Was this even legal? Probably not, since the only adult there was the guy taking all the kids' cash.

"A buck a minute," the cash guy yelled. "Two-minute minimum."

After five minutes, a bull-horn blared and Rif slowed down. As the dust fell back to the earth, I scanned the crowd. It didn't take long to see him. His black hair was grey with dirt, and his brown skin was ashen. Still, my heart lurched. I tried to will his dark eyes to turn and look at me, but Warrenville was in line to ride the dune buggy next. He handed over five bucks and hopped on as soon as Rif hopped off.

Instead of riding in a circle, Warren revved the engine and drove straight for the far fence. I panicked. It looked as though he'd ram right into it. But he swerved just in time and careered over a huge dirt pile, flying through the air and landing on all four wheels. The crowd went wild.

"Did you see that?" I asked Barbara, excited.

She scoffed. "Macho man."

As soon as the dust settled, Warrenville and I locked gazes. In the middle of shaking the dirt out of his hair, he caught sight of me, and my heart kicked up its disco beat. Barbara and

I were the only girls at the drive-in. In fact, I heard someone ask, "Who let *them* in?"

But I didn't care. I was there for one reason and one reason alone.

"Can I talk to you for a second?" I said, walking straight up to Warren even though my legs wobbled like rubber bands. Barbara waited for me near the Snack Shack.

"Oooo. Warrenville gets busted!"

"Mommy wants you home."

The boys in line made fun, but I didn't care. "It'll only take a second," I said.

Warren nodded. He led me over to the far fence, away from the action, and said, "Yeah?"

There he was, inches from my face, his caterpillar eyebrows up, waiting. My heart hammered my rib cage. My tongue felt like a piece of cardboard.

"You know that Santa-Claus-down-the-chimney thing?" I said. "It's a *crock*. Totally made up! A fat guy could never slide down a chimney. Why do people lie? That's what I want to know."

Warren smiled softly. He remembered his rant about Pocahontas.

"I was wondering," I said, biting my lower lip, "is everything okay? I haven't seen you much at school."

Warren stopped smiling, looked away. "Yeah," he said. "Everything's fine. I've been around."

I waited for him to say something more, but the next thing he said felt like an ice pick to the chest.

"I've gotta go. My friends are waiting."

Warren sauntered away and I nearly crumpled to the dusty ground. If Barbara hadn't appeared, I probably would have stayed there, in a heap, until the dry wind blew me away.

That night, as I was getting ready for bed, our phone rang. I got it by the third ring.

"Hello?"

"I did it," Nadine squealed.

"Did what?"

"Had a serious kiss!"

Oh.

How could I tell the girl I used to tell *everything* to that I didn't want to hear about the happiest moment in her life? How could I tell her I was feeling too upset and confused to even care? When I'd got home, I'd taken a shower, washed the dirt from Skyview Drive-In down the drain. I couldn't wait to crawl under the covers and pull a blanket over my life.

"Great! What was it like?" I asked, forcing my voice to sound cheery.

"Awesome! Incredible! It was everything we imagined it would be that day in your backyard. My knees got weak and my heart pounded and I thought fireworks would shoot off the top of my head. Curtis is a *great* kisser. Very dramatic. He sort of bent me over backward like we were in an old movie or something. Kissing him felt like the whole world was on fire!"

"Wow." It's all I could think of to say. Then I added, "I'm

really happy for you, Nadine." And I was. At least one of us would know love.

"You'll get your kiss, too," she said. "One day. You'll see."

In my head, I figured she was probably right. But in my heart, a serious kiss – true love – felt as far away as the distant look in Warrenville's eyes.

THIRTY-ONE

By mid-December, Barstow store owners had trotted out their tired holiday decorations and the weather cooled to a comfy sixty degrees. Each day, I got up, got dressed, caught the bus, and went to school. When we weren't at Aqui, Barbara and I hung out at her place or mine. Rif scrubbed graffiti off Big and Little Moe, Mom had manicures during her lunch breaks at Wal-Mart, Dad got better in Victorville, Dirk played video games, and Nana made Ethiopian food with chickpeas.

"Not many people know that the Ethiopian Christmas holiday is celebrated on January seventh," she said. "Part of the traditional holiday meal is a sourdough pancake called *injera* that acts as an edible plate!"

Things were back to normal at the Madrigal mobile homes – well, as normal as life can get when your dad is in rehab and the boy you thought was "the one" barely nods his head when he sees you at school.

"Guys are jerks," Barbara said again. But it didn't make me feel any better.

The one bright spot in that dismal month was – believe it or not – our therapy sessions with Just Josh and Dad. I learned a lot.

"An alcoholic parent is like having a 'king baby' in the

family," Josh said during one session. "Instead of being mature and responsible and taking care of the kids, like a well-functioning parent does, the king baby is grown but still immature. He requires a lot of attention, the way babies do. In fact, he becomes the centre of attention. The whole family is always watching him, watching out for him, covering for him."

Mom leaned forward, listening intently.

"When there's a king baby in a family," Josh continued, "the children are forced to grow up before they are really ready to. They have to *parent* the king baby in a sense, because he's not up to the job of parenting them. It's very scary for kids. It feels unsafe, which creates a tremendous amount of anxiety. Because, you see, the child knows deep down that he or she is really faking it, *pretending* to be able to handle it all. But, of course, she can't, can she? After all, she's just a kid. Does this sound familiar?"

"Yes!" Rif and I said in unison. Dirk looked scared.

Another time, Josh explained how family members can become so entangled in the life of the alcoholic, they forget to have a life of their own.

"It's important to detach, with love. No one is responsible for Lot's behaviour but Lot himself. You all have to let go."

Nana nodded and smiled at me.

Maybe because we were all there ready to listen, or maybe because he was ready to talk, my father slowly began to open up.

"Just like you, Libby," he said, barely above a whisper, "I watched my father disappear. He sold insurance in San Bernardino. We had a house, a normal life, the three of us. Until his drinking took over. Just before I graduated high school, we lost the house. My parents moved to Nana's trailer in Barstow. It wasn't a nice retirement home then, it was a dump. I lived with my friend's family in San Bernardino until I graduated. I was so ashamed of my dad, I told everyone he got a job as a dealer in Vegas."

Glancing around the room, I noticed my brothers looked the same way I did – *agog*. We'd never heard any of this before. The mere mention of my grandfather was taboo in our house. *Shhh! Don't tell.* For the first time in my fourteen years, I understood why.

"My father was the man I most wanted *not* to be," Dad said, "and here I am, *exactly* like him."

Josh said, "That's why we're here. To break the pattern."

After that session, Dad took Mom's hand and led her into the hallway outside the therapy room. My brothers and I followed until Nana said, "Let's give them a few minutes alone, okay?"

We nodded and hung back. Still, I could hear my dad ask my mom, "Why have you and the kids stuck by me all these years?"

Mom didn't hesitate. "Because we're a *family*," she said. "And that's what families do."

At that moment – for the first time since I can remember – I felt like I really did belong in my family. We belonged *together*. For better or worse.

On the last day before Christmas vacation, I felt a hand tap my shoulder as I organised my locker.

"Hang on, Barbara," I said, without turning around. "I'm almost done."

"Libby."

The voice was male, familiar. I wheeled around, and there he was.

"Hey," Warren said.

I just stared at him, my heart thudding, unable to think of a word to say.

"I've been a jerk," he said.

Even more speechless, my mouth hung open.

"Can you come with me?" he asked. "I want to show you something."

I nodded. Truth was, after everything, I'd still follow Warrenville anywhere.

We left campus, walked down the hill, and continued across the iron bridge.

"Insects breathe through tiny pores in their bellies," Warren mentioned, as we crossed the dry riverbed. "And dragonflies have the best eyesight of almost all insects."

I grinned. Warren was always full of so many obscure facts.

"Did you know that the average male has up to twenty-five thousand hairs on his face?"

"No, I didn't know that."

"Now you do," he said, grinning back at me.

Eventually, my heart stopped racing, and a blanket of calm engulfed me. Maybe I'd been through too much to feel tense anymore, or maybe it was something else. Something about Warrenville that relaxed me. I let him take me where he wanted me to go. I let life flow.

We turned left after Big Moe and walked up a dusty road. There weren't many houses around, just dried fields and scrub. Until we came to a clearing. A small, metal arch marked the entrance to a cemetery. The wrought-iron gate was open. It was tiny, nothing like Oakwood Cemetery in Chatsworth, and old. Some of the gravestones were so wind-whipped you couldn't read who was buried there. Others were brand-new. Warren took my hand. A surge of electricity shot through my whole arm.

He said, "I want you to meet my mom."

Warren led me to a small headstone at the far end of the cemetery. It read, HERE LIES CECILIA VILLEGRANJA, BELOVED WIFE AND MOTHER.

Squeezing my hand, Warren said, "My mother was killed by a drunk driver. Right out there." He pointed up the road.

I looked up the dusty, deserted road. When I turned back, Warren was facing me.

"I freaked out about your dad. I'm sorry. I know it's not your fault. I'm pissed off at all drunk drivers. How could someone drive when he's high? When someone's mom could be on the road walking home from work? How could anyone do that?"

"I don't know," I said, quietly.

"I shouldn't have cut you out. I'm sorry. I went a little crazy."

"It's okay, Warren. I went a little crazy, too."

Bending down to shake the dust off the dried flowers decorating his mother's grave, Warren said, "Mom didn't like fresh flowers. She hated to watch things die."

THIRTY-TWO

The desert behind Warrenville's house goes on forever. He lives in the middle of nowhere, beyond the outskirts of Barstow. It took us half an hour just to get there. His house was a patchwork of plaster patches and wooden supports.

"Each week something new falls apart," he said. "Each week my dad and I patch it back up. Dad calls it our quilt house."

I thought about my house in Chatsworth and our Barstow trailer, how ashamed I was of them. Now, looking at Warrenville's funky mended house, and his obvious love for it, my cheeks got hot. Why have I wasted so much time worrying about what other people think? How stupid is that?

The sun was still high in the sky as Warren and I shared a soda in his backyard.

"It's so dead around here," I said.

"Dead?"

"The desert, I mean," I added quickly.

"Girl, there's *nothing* dead about a desert." Standing, Warren took my hand and led me far into the flat, dirt-brown field beyond his house. "When I was growing up, my mother showed me all the *life* here. There's a heliotrope there, over

247

there a yellow linanthus." He pointed to wildflowers popping through the dry desert soil.

"That's a brown-eyed evening primrose." He kicked a stone off into the emptiness. A low, dry bush rustled. "If we stood here silently, and didn't move until dark, we could watch the desert wake up before our eyes. Coyotes, owls, iguana, prairie dogs, jackrabbits, rattlesnakes . . ."

I winced. "Maybe we should move."

"Why?"

"I hate snakes."

"How can you hate snakes? That's like saying you hate *nature*. Without snakes, the eagle might die of starvation, the desert would be overrun with rats. Snakes are as beautiful as bats, as beautiful as scorpions, as beautiful as . . ."

He went on. I just stared at him, smiled inside. In truth, there was nothing as beautiful as he was. His cheeks were aflame in the sunlight, his black eyes even blacker and more intense against the powder blue desert sky.

". . . as beautiful as vultures and tarantulas . . ." Warren continued his list. I longed to touch his face, his hair. I wanted to reach under his jacket sleeve and trace my fingertips all the way around his tattoo.

". . . as a wild donkey," Warren went on. "As beautiful as a black widow spider, as a fish . . ."

"Hey, wait a minute," I interrupted. "There aren't any *fish* in the desert."

"That's what you think," he said. "Pupfish live in mineral hot springs throughout the desert. Like I told you, there's life and beauty everywhere. You just have to know where to look."

I knew exactly where to look. Straight into Warrenville's eyes.

"You're right," I said softly, my voice suddenly buried deep within my chest.

"I know," he said, just as softly, right back at me.

Suddenly, Warren took a step closer to me and reached for my hand. He lifted it up to is chest, held it against his beating heart. "This is *my* life," he whispered. My heart thumped, too.

I stood absolutely still. Afraid to breathe, afraid to move. The rhythm of our two hearts seemed to shake the whole earth. Suddenly, Warren's face was against my face, and his lips were against my lips. They felt velvety. He smelled like fresh cilantro; he smelled like spring. I pressed my lips harder against his and he parted his mouth, wrapped one arm around me, flattened my hand against his pounding heart. We kissed. Our kiss lasted a lifetime. I could hear the flutter of desert life awakening around me. Or was it me? Was it *my* life awakening around me?

All I knew for sure was that Nadine was mistaken. It was nothing like our fantasy that day on the Lilos in my Chatsworth backyard. My knees weren't buckling; I wasn't on the verge of passing out. I wasn't ready to explode. This kiss felt soft like Juan Dog's ears. My body felt light, like it was floating. This kiss was as deep as the centre of the Atlantic, as wide as the Pacific. It was shelter in a storm, a cool breeze in the desert, a bonfire in the snow. This kiss felt safe and exciting at the same time. It was hot butterscotch melting over vanilla ice cream; it was a down pillow. This kiss – at long last my serious kiss – felt like arriving, belonging, being loved, loving.

"You," Warren whispered.

He didn't say anything more. He didn't have to. He just kissed me again. And it felt like coming home. That much I'd been right about. A serious kiss feels like *home*. Pulling back the curtains and letting in the light and coming home.

It's complete. It's the beginning. It's the end of emptiness.

It's love. The big it.

It's life, in a desert, if you know where to look.

Nigel Marsh was born in Plymouth. ... years later he was sent to boarding school. He ... the 35 years since thinking of ways of gaining ... on and affirmation of his parents.

Having travelled the world and studied Theology for seven years, Nigel has concluded that Sydney *is* heaven.

The CEO of communications group Leo Burnett Australia, he lives in Bronte with his wife and four children.

Fat, Forty and Fired

Nigel Marsh

BANTAM
SYDNEY AUCKLAND TORONTO NEW YORK LONDON

FAT, FORTY AND FIRED
A BANTAM BOOK

First published in Australia and New Zealand in 2005
by Bantam

National Library of Australia
Cataloguing-in-Publication Entry

Marsh, Nigel, 1964–.
Fat, forty and fired.

ISBN 1 86325 501 X.

1. Marsh, Nigel, 1964–. 2. Fathers – Biography. 3. Househusbands – New South Wales –
Biography. 4. Advertising executives – New South Wales – Biography. I. Title.

306.8742

Transworld Publishers,
a division of Random House Australia Pty Ltd
20 Alfred Street, Milsons Point, NSW 2061
http://www.randomhouse.com.au

Random House New Zealand Limited
18 Poland Road, Glenfield, Auckland

Transworld Publishers,
a division of The Random House Group Ltd
61-63 Uxbridge Road, Ealing, London W5 5SA

Random House Inc
1745 Broadway, New York, New York 10036

Cover design by Darian Causby/Highway 51
Cover candle compliments of Boston Warehouse, Norwood MA, USA
Pages 271–272: 'The Bad Touch' words and music by James Franks. © Songs of
Polygram/Hey Rudy Music/Jimmy Franks Music, Universal Music Publishing P/L. Printed
with permission. All rights reserved.
Page 279: Extract from 'Balance is Bunk!' by Keith Hammonds, © 2005 Gruner & Jahr USA
Publishing. First published in *Fast Company Magazine*. Reprinted with permission.
Typeset by Midland Typesetters, Maryborough, Victoria
Printed and bound by Griffin Press, Netley, South Australia

10 9 8 7

For Kate, Alex, Harry, Grace and Eve
Always have, always will.

Introduction

DO YOU EVER FANTASISE about moving to the country or a beach and downsizing? If so I know how you feel. I've spent the last two decades slogging my guts out in a variety of different jobs, for the most part in a decidedly rainy, urbanised country.

Like most of the population, when I started I had no assets to fall back on or family influence to gain leverage in any particular field for a smooth entry into the workplace. More importantly, I had no money beyond that which I could earn each week. London can be a pretty unforgiving place for a young man with no connections or qualifications beyond being able to read the Bible in Greek and a valid driver's licence.

The early signs after I finished my education and moved to the city to seek my fortune weren't particularly encouraging. But I didn't have a family to look after and sleeping in a mate's car while working on the railway didn't seem all that bad at the time.

As the years passed, I eventually secured a foothold on the bottom rung of a career ladder that seemed to suit my particular talents – the world of marketing beckoned. My progress up the greasy pole was satisfactory and I soon found myself above the poverty line. Indeed, after a few years I even qualified for the dizzy heights of middle management.

My personal responsibilities – four kids and counting – grew, along with my earning power, the former nicely cancelling out the potential benefits of the latter. I began to work harder and harder to stay afloat. I changed jobs, companies – even countries – to further my career. As the years went by, though, I began to be aware of an increasingly persistent voice in my head. *What's it all for, Nige? Your life is slipping away. You need to change your priorities and spend proper time with your family.* The voice wouldn't go away, indeed it just got louder as time passed. Of course for a long time I didn't change my lifestyle or take time off, but that didn't stop me spending the last ten years having escapist daydreams about kicking it all in.

Then, in 2003, I found myself downsized and living in Sydney. The reality didn't quite match the dream. According to a recent headline in the *Financial Times*, 'poor is the new rich and dropping out is the dream'. Bollocks. Poor is poor and dropping out can be a nightmare.

I haven't got a catchy slogan that sums up what I learned

from my year off. I do know, however, that men aren't from Mars and fat isn't a feminist issue. Men are from Earth and fat is fat. I don't claim to have usable wisdom for anyone else. All I can say is that I lived the dream of dropping out for a year and this is how it was for me.

Chapter 1

Paper pants

SANTA DIDN'T COME to Bronte last year. The community nurse came instead. My four kids weren't exactly thrilled with this swap – but then again, neither was I. Having over a kilogram of seaweed gauze repeatedly packed into a freshly cut arse wound does tend to take the edge off one's festive mood. Particularly when your company is about to be merged out of existence and you are stuck halfway around the world, 15,000 or so miles away from family and home back in England.

But worse things have happened at sea, as my Dad always says. How worse things happening at sea is supposed to help, I've bugger-all notion, but it's the sort of useless counsel you seem to get when your life's in the shitter and people are trying to be kind. I was just going to have to put some of the advice I'd gleaned from the covers of those self-help books you see in airports into practice to help me deal with the problem.

The problem had reared its head precisely a week before. A visit to the local GP with what I thought was a boil on my arse resulted in me being told to put a green gown on back to front and sign a lot of forms absolving anyone from blame if I were to die. An anal fistula is the correct medical term for my early Christmas present – Henry V died of one aged 36 – and a fistulectomy is the operation. (The post-operation packing process itself hasn't got an official medical term, as they couldn't translate 'motherfuckingawfulsustained-painandmisery' into Latin.) Twelve hours later I woke up after such an operation in Sydney's Prince of Wales Hospital to groggily tell my wife, Kate, 'That wasn't so bad.'

'The surgery is the easy bit. It's the packing that's the killer,' the doctor rather too cheerfully corrected me. Leaving aside the fact that at that point I didn't know what 'packing' was, all I could think was, 'How bad can that be?' As it turns out, badder than bad. Not just tear-jerkingly, painfully bad but soul-destroyingly, humiliatingly bad. The first nurse who performed this task on me was delightful, empathetic and skilled. She barely batted an eyelid as I screamed like a woman in the final stages of labour.

'There. All done, Mr Marsh,' she said.

'Oh, thanks so much and sorry for all the noise. At least the worst is over now. I don't think I could face ever having to do that again.' It was then that she gently explained that someone would have to do it every day for at least six weeks.

'Every day?' I groaned.

'Every day,' she confirmed.

'Christmas Day?'

'Christmas Day.'

'New Year's Day?'

'New Year's Day.'

Hence me adopting the role of Scrooge, not Santa, and effectively destroying any festive spirit. I soon forgot the airport self-help books and settled into a marriage-wrecking combination of self-pity, anger and helplessness. 'Daddy's cranky,' was how Alex, my gorgeous eight-year-old, put it to all our rejected Christmas well-wishers.

Matters weren't helped by the fact that it was a different nurse who came to perform the packing almost every day. Having a succession of complete strangers (two male) come into your bedroom, move your nuts to one side and fiddle with your arsehole every day takes its toll on your dignity. On Boxing Day, in a bid to arrest my slide into total despair, I announced to my rightly cynical wife that I wouldn't remain bedridden by this minor mishap. 'We're all going to the beach,' I barked. However, my new-found lust for life was short-lived.

'Kate, I've lost it,' I snapped, as I gingerly stepped onto the sand.

'Lost what?' my wife good-naturedly replied.

'My pad. The chuffing panty pad has gone.' Somewhere on the walk between our house and the beach, the panty pad I had to wear over my wound had fallen out of my paper hospital pants.

A radical reappraisal was clearly needed.

Chapter 2

Brainfrog

As luck would have it, the timing was perfect for a reappraisal. A few weeks prior to my arse problems I had received a phone call telling me that our worldwide holding company was to merge with another. No biggie, I thought, it happens all the time. Then my boss went on to explain that one of the end results of this process was that the firm I was running in Australia would have to close – or, more accurately, I would have to close it. Given my partners and I had just spent a year of our lives building it into something of a success, this was less than welcome news. It would inevitably mean many colleagues – none of whom had done anything wrong – would lose their jobs. We had become a very close-knit, ferociously loyal team and this prospect made me enormously sad – as well as guilty. I don't care what they teach you at business school; I view the primary role of any CEO as providing meaningful employment, not taking it away. Any tosser can cut costs, it's building something valuable (in all the senses of that word) that's the real challenge.

As a desperate measure I wrote to the new ultimate boss in Paris, offering to buy the local company from him. To cut a long story short, the answer was '*non*'. In a cynical business such as advertising it is easy to mock when a group of people claim to believe in a common goal beyond naked self-interest but that is precisely what we had at D'Arcy Australia. The company was more than an economic trading unit of an international firm: it was family. Unfortunately, it really did look like the family was coming to an end. And as the head of that family I was ashamed of my failure. I was also exhausted and out of balance. Attempting to look after one family had led me to grievously neglect the other.

The one upside of having to lie on your stomach for a fortnight is it gives you time to think. The more I thought about it, the more I wanted a change. I'd recently read a book called *Manhood*, by a chap called Steven Biddulph, that argued every man should be forced to take his fortieth year off. His theory was that the vast majority of men don't have a life – they pretend to have one. In reality they are lonely, emotionally timid, and miserably, compulsively competitive. One of the main reasons they never get out of this tragic state is that they are enslaved by soulless jobs and careers that lead them to put their lives on hold until retirement. Of course, when this arrives it is too late. While they work they are too busy to think and therefore they have empty lives where they never develop a rich and sustaining inner life. As Biddulph himself puts it, 'Our marriages fail, our kids hate us, we die of stress and on the way we destroy the world.' I wasn't sure if it was the effects of the medication I was on, but his year-off notion struck a real chord. Besides, while I wasn't being forced – I could have looked for a new job – circumstances were rather suited to a pause for reflection and a change of direction.

For a while now I had had the nagging feeling that all my glories were former glories. As my riches had increased, my 'interest factor' had decreased. As a young man I used to have a vibrant social life both inside and outside of work. I don't want to pretend I was a culture vulture but it would be fair to say I had the skill of burning the candle at both ends down to a fine art. Every night was like its own miniature weekend. Live music, stand-up comedy, nightclubs or just plain boozing was the standard fare Monday to Friday. Come the real weekends it got more adventurous as sport, trips away and two-day parties got thrown into the mix. Irrespective of how immature and irresponsible I was, the one thing my life wasn't was one-dimensional. Now I only seemed to work, prepare for work, complain about work or go to sleep – and dream about work.

Also, more worryingly, my 'nice factor' was diminishing. I was sure all parents shouted at their kids but I was less certain they shouted at them quite as often as I did. I'd become a bit player in my family – leaving in the morning before they got up and arriving home after they were in bed (but early enough, unfortunately, to catch Kate and bore the tits off her with yet more dull stories of my work travails). And I was concerned that my four-year-old, Harry, had started to exhibit some bizarre character traits. We only noticed these when one of his pictures came back from kindy signed 'Batbounce'. Kate and I thought little of this until the next artwork came back with 'Brainfrog' written neatly in the corner.

Kate was equally nonplussed by this behaviour, so I decided to take matters into my own hands. I arranged to pick Harry up from his kindy. Rather embarrassingly, this involved getting directions from Kate as it was a task I'd never performed before. Having eventually found the correct street, I parked the car, signed myself in at the kindy door as the 'pick-up parent' and went in search of the person in charge. Pick-up time is mayhem and not the best time to be a worried parent demanding reassurance and attention, but Harry's teacher couldn't have been nicer when I located her.

'Excuse me, I'm Harry's dad. He brought back some pictures with strange names on them last week and I wondered what the purpose of this practice is,' I asked his teacher.

'Oh no, Mr Marsh, it is not a school practice,' she replied. 'It's just that for the last few months Harry has come into kindy each morning and announced his name is not Harry, told us his new name – Spiderpotter, Winnie Ranger, Brain-frog, things like that – and then refused to answer to any other name.'

'Did you say a few months?' I asked.

'Yes, we assumed you were playing along with it at home.'

I tortured myself all week long with increasingly awful scenarios of what this behaviour might actually mean. Maybe it was reflective of deep-seated personality problems that I had given the young mite by being a crap dad? Had my impatience and shouting led him to invent an imaginary set of personalities who enabled him to escape into a nicer world? It was all but impossible to stop this self-flagellating mind

7

chatter – until, of course, the weekend, which I spent shouting at him and his brother and sisters as usual.

Whether or not Harry's name games had anything to do with me, it was clear I had lost perspective. Work had become far too dominant a factor in my life and I was becoming that person I always swore I never would be – an office rat who lived to work, not worked to live. In this case, the problem was compounded by the fact that the work was out of sync with my personal values and motivations. So not only was I spending too little time with my family, but the rare time I was with them was being ruined by my grumpy, conflicted and jaded demeanour.

Advertising is one of those professions that from the outside can often be seen as terribly glamorous. The truth rarely – if ever – lives up to the myth. The industry has long since had its heyday. Advertising agencies no longer pay well or offer an attractive working life full of long lunches and end-of-year bonuses. If you run an agency you not only have to deal on a daily basis with a long list of ever more demanding clients, but you also have to convince an often exhausted and underpaid workforce to work unreasonable hours for precious little reward. Ten or so 14-hour days in a row, a key client defection and a couple of unwanted resignations, topped off nicely by a call from your boss complaining about the firm's lack of double-digit growth, can make you a very irritable and dull boy indeed.

Trouble was, the nastier I became, the nicer my family were. It would have been some comfort if I had a shrew for a wife and revolting, unlikable children, but the reverse was the case. Kate and I had been married for ten years, during which time she had been nothing but supportive and understanding. Along the way she had sacrificed her career and given me four of the most gorgeous children that ever walked the earth. Alex, Harry, and Grace and Eve, our three-year-old twins, created a tidal wave of loving welcome every time I came home after work. The moment they heard my key in the door they would leap up from whatever they were doing (to Kate's understandable irritation if it was dinnertime) and hurtle down the corridor towards the front door, all shouting, 'Daddy! Daddy! Daddy's home!' As they progressed down the hall they would become one interweaved child with eight arms and eight legs. More often than not, they would bang headlong into the door before I had opened it, their combined force making it impossible for me to push it open. Kate would have to peel them away to enable me to squeeze in and receive the breathless daily offering of drawings, paintings and sports results.

A luckier man has never existed, yet increasingly I was responding to this unquestioning barrage of love with a grunt, or worse, a curt flash of anger. On some occasions, having driven home from work I was so spent that I found myself staying in the car listening to the radio rather than going inside. In my more rational moments I would berate myself for this behaviour and sink despairingly into a sea of self-loathing, but mainly I just unthinkingly trampled all over the feelings of those who meant the most to me. And then I had been informed of the forthcoming closure of my firm.

In early December I had taken a long flight to New York to meet Hank, the big cheese of our international company. I had been prepared for the meeting for a number of weeks, ever since it had been announced that all our firm's offices around the world were going to be merged. In these situations, the first person to get the chop is the bloke who runs the firm that is going to be merged – in this case, me – so I was expecting the worst. I'd travelled straight from JFK airport to the skyscraper that housed our corporate headquarterrs. The offices were impressive – all marble and glass. I was ushered to the thirty-third floor and into the ante-room outside Hank's office.

For a man who ran a large global corporation, Hank was pleasantly informal and open.

'Hi, Nigel, good to see you. How was your flight? Can I get Dani to get you a coffee? Water?' he'd asked when I was summoned into his enormous corner office with stunning views over Central Park.

In return I'd asked him how he was and he'd spoken candidly about his year. How difficult it had been. How everyone was out to get him. How disappointing the situation was. Hold on, I'd thought. Aren't you the bloke who has just personally trousered $85 million as a result of the merger deal? Kate and I could handle a disappointment like that. I bit my tongue and said nothing.

He went on.

And on.

And on.

It was 55 minutes into the meeting and he hadn't mentioned Australia, let alone me. We were still on how much travelling he had to do, how hurtful the press were being about his personal earnings from the deal, and how tough it was dealing with the investor community.

I started to doubt if he knew who I was. Perhaps he was playing for time, hoping someone would remind him. I thought I'd help him out.

'Must have been awful for you, I can only imagine,' I said. 'Sounds like you've weathered the storm remarkably well though, Hank. We could do with some of your know-how in *Australia*,' I added, pointedly.

'Ah, Australia,' he replied, visibly perking up. 'Do you still have that harbour?'

'Harbour?'

'Yes, harbour. Sydney Harbour.'

'Yes, we still have it,' I replied. Is it the jet lag or are we actually talking complete and utter bollocks, I found myself wondering. I've flown 14,000 miles to be made redundant and after an hour all we are doing is a slightly retarded geographical trip down memory lane.

I decided to raise the issue myself.

'With the proposed merger, I was wondering what counsel you would give me personally,' I asked.

'My advice to you is to get a seat on the bus – any seat, any bus – just get one and sit on it,' he replied, with surprising and forceful conviction. I couldn't help thinking of that scene in *The Graduate* when Dustin Hoffman is ushered outside at a party to receive some deadly serious career advice, only to be told the single word 'plastics'.

Hank went on to explain laboriously that it was an analogy (no shit, Sherlock) and that in any merger the prime purpose for someone like me was to secure a job at all costs, irrespective of role or location. He didn't mention personal hopes or aspirations. Corporate vision didn't get a look-in either. Remain in employment or else was the simple message. He was eager and seemed genuine in his desire to help towards this end. The meeting ended with him recommending a couple of people he thought I should see who had positions they would like to talk to me about. It seemed picky to point out that both the roles in question were based in the

Northern Hemisphere and I had only twelve months earlier moved my entire family to the Southern Hemisphere. Instead, I thanked him for his time and promised that I would give serious thought to his advice.

Which is exactly what I did. The meeting might have been slightly bizarre but it definitely helped me decide what to do. Hank's viewpoint wasn't unusual and, from a certain perspective, his advice was completely correct. However, from another perspective it's bloody stupid to get on a bus if you don't like where it's going. Not only did I not want to fuck up my own life, I wanted to set the right example for my kids. At the risk of stretching the metaphor to death, I wanted them to know that sometimes it might be better to slow down and walk places instead of being on a bus driven by someone else. You get to choose the route and you could end up learning more. If it all goes wrong, you can always get on another bus.

I couldn't help thinking it was time to take the plunge and take a break from the corporate world. You are a long time dead and I'd always doubted that sitting in an office was the sum of all the world has to offer. Besides, I'd never regretted any previous risk I had taken, be it doing stand-up comedy, moving to Australia, studying Theology, or going for baby number three, which turned out to be twins. In fact, far from being the 'silly' bits of my life, these risks had invariably been the things that made me feel alive and supplied me with the memories I most cherished. Perhaps a year off the hamster wheel was precisely what I, and my family, needed.

The more I thought about it, the more attractive the option appeared. An article in the newspaper gave me added encouragement. It quoted a statistic from a recent survey stating that 88 per cent of Australians are dissatisfied with their work and are looking for a more meaningful and balanced life. Perhaps I wasn't so unusual after all. I began to fantasise in an entirely unrealistic way about all the things I would do if I didn't have to go to the chuffing office. Apparently most people overestimate what they can do in a year and underestimate what they can do in ten. I don't know about the ten-year bit, but I can testify to suffering from chronic self-delusion in the twelve-months part.

My list started with the usual weight-loss and fitness goals. After a couple of beers I'd added learning to speak Russian and drawing regularly. A couple more and I was educating the kids at home and running for mayor. By the time I had finished the sixpack I'd moved on to world peace and a cure for cancer. I only realised I was in la-la land when 'winning Wimbledon for Britain' appeared on the list. After all, there are some things that are never going to happen.

Chapter 3

Lamb or swordfish

SELF-CENTRED THOUGH I may be, I realised that dropping out wasn't a decision I should take lightly – or alone. I clearly needed a proper discussion with Kate before doing anything rash. I took the momentous step of booking a restaurant for dinner for the night after my return. I say momentous because although dinner out in a nice restaurant with Kate is one of the greatest pleasures of my life, it is also one of the most frustrating activities I have ever experienced. Throughout our marriage I have come to dread the never-changing opening scenario involved when Kate and I eat out together. It's not that Kate isn't good company – she is. It's not that we don't like the same places – we do. It is simply that she makes the ordering process mind-numbingly, soul-crushingly painful. In fact, she's made it an art form.

The conversation always starts in the same way. This night was clearly going to be no exception.

'Have you chosen?' she asked, after we'd studied the menus for a couple of minutes.

'Yep,' I replied.

'What are you having?'

'Think I'll go with the swordfish tonight.'

'Are you sure?' she probed.

Oh my God, here we go.

'Yep,' I replied.

'Why?'

'Christ, I don't know. I just fancy it.'

Kate beckoned the waiter over.

'What do you recommend?' she asked him.

'It's all good, madam.'

Oh shit, the worst answer. We're in for the full reduce-me-to-tears version tonight, I thought as Kate replied, 'Yes, but what would *you* have?'

'Er . . . I usually have the lamb or the swordfish, madam.'

'Is the lamb nice?'

'Nice?'

'Yes, nice. Is it good? Do you think I would like it? I'm not sure I'm in the mood for anything heavy.'

'Then I think the swordfish would be perfect for you, madam.'

You think you're clever, mate, but you're out of your depth, I thought. No one gets away that easily.

'No, I can't have the swordfish. Because that would mean we're both having it.'

'That's all right, sweetheart, I don't mind,' I said.

'But that's no fun – both having the same thing.'

'Actually, I've changed my mind. I'll have the lamb,' I said to the waiter, who looked strangely like he wanted to hug me.

'No. You're just saying that. You stick with the fish. I'll have something else,' Kate said.

I was losing the will to live and we were now no nearer a decision than we had been five minutes before.

'What are they having?' Kate enquired, pointing to the next table.

'That's the soup of the day, madam – a very nice light starter,' the waiter replied.

'Could I have it as a main?' Kate asked.

Much more of this and you'll be wearing it as a hat, I thought. I could go on – she did – but I'll spare you. Needless to say, I lost my temper, we had an argument, I forced her into a decision, she sulked and we sat in silence, broken in the traditional way by Kate when our meals arrived.

'Yours looks good. I wish I'd ordered the swordfish,' she said.

That's not to say we didn't have the chat we intended to. In fact it was easier talking about what to do with the rest of our lives than it was ordering the sodding food.

'I think I want to take a year off,' I started.

'You mean they haven't offered you a job you want?' she replied.

'Fair comment. I'm not excited by anything they've offered. But I think it's more than that. I want a life change.'

'To do what?'

'Don't know. Nothing. Not put a tie on. Get to know my kids properly. Be a real part of the family. Find a positive outlet other than a traditional career.'

'But how would we earn money?' Kate asked.

'We wouldn't,' I replied.

'Then how would we live?'

'Off the redundancy payment.' Kate raised her eyebrows quizzically and lit a cigarette before getting to the heart of the matter.

'How long would that last?' she asked.

'If we were sensible, it could last for a year,' I replied.

'What type of sensible?' Kate asked.

'Well, we'd have to move to a smaller house. And sell the Subaru. And the nanny would have to go. Apart from that, not much would have to change.'

'And what would happen at the end of the year?' Damn, exactly the question I'd been hoping she wouldn't ask.

'Honestly?' I replied.

'Honestly.'

'We'd be fucked. All our savings would be gone. I'd be a forgotten, 40-year-old advertising executive who hadn't worked for a year. Unemployable.'

'So I get twice the husband, half the income, and at the end of the year we'll both have to work in Woolworths?'

'Basically.'

Kate thought for a minute. 'If we do this, will you be less of an arsehole?'

'That's the reason I'd be doing it. I can't promise, but I'll try.'

Kate reached over and took a bite of my swordfish. She chewed thoughtfully, then smiled at me.

'Well, I'm up for it if you think it will make you happy.'

If only she was this decisive when choosing a main course.

Chapter 4

Little lunch

AFTER I RETURNED from fistula leave, I still had a month to go
of my old job in which to finally make up my mind about the
future. Merging a company isn't exactly a barrel of laughs but
it was extremely important to me to do it as well as I could,
right up until the very end. Not just out of professional pride,
but because as CEO in many cases my actions would mean the
difference between someone else losing or keeping their job.
Just because I was more than likely going to kick it all in, didn't
mean others had the desire or, more importantly, the means not
to work. Everyone whom I had worked with so far in Australia
had been incredibly fair to me and I wanted to pay them back
by getting as many of them as possible jobs in the new firm or
at least looking after them as generously as I could.

Having said that, winding up a company is a different day-to-day existence from driving a company, so I had more time on my hands. Kate and I were determined that we would use that time to extend my working knowledge of the new life I was thinking of signing up for. Our reasoning was that when it came to the crunch I would be better able to make the final decision to leave the workplace if I had tasted a few of the delights in store for me on the other side. We set upon 31 January as the date when we would finally commit either way.

We started the experiment gently with an easy assignment. I was to take the morning off and do the school run. Not for all the kids, but just for the boys. This would involve taking Alex to school and Harry to kindy. I was terrified of performing this task but wanted to prove to myself that I could do it — after all it was a new, improved, 'balanced' life I was thinking of embarking on. Kate was taking the bus with the girls to something called Kindi Gym and I'd be driving the boys. I set the alarm early. The more time, the better, I thought, as even I knew there is nothing like a deadline and children to get the shouting going. But despite my lack of experience, the kids' truculence and my hangover from dinner, after an hour's feverish activity I was immensely proud to have both the little buggers in the car. Admittedly Alex was wearing Harry's top and Harry had his sister's shoes on, but they were in the car and, more importantly, Alex had a packed lunch made for him entirely by his dad.

It had taken over an hour of tears, shouting and whining to get the right combination of peanut butter, banana, apple juice and crisps sorted out but it was 8.45, the car was running and I had a full 15 minutes to get Alex to school and then another 15 to drive on with Harry to kindy. The traffic, however, was a nightmare. It seemed to take forever as we inched towards the school. Finding a park was just as bad. My already high anxiety levels began to soar. I was still determined we wouldn't be late if at all possible. By then I was liberally cursing under my breath and strangling the steering wheel with a white-knuckled grip. I simply couldn't see anywhere to park the car. In desperation I pulled up illegally right outside the school gates. Three minutes to go. We'd make it if we hurried.

'Open the door, Alex, open the door, Alex, OPEN THE DOOR. Oh for Christ's sake, I'll do it,' I slid the side door open and watched as Alex's school bag fell out of the car on to the pavement and his favourite Clovelly Rugby Club drink bottle dropped out of its top pocket and, in slow motion, rolled into the drain and was washed out of sight.

'Don't cry, sweetheart – Harry open the door – I'll get you another one, Alex. Harry, open the door – come on, Alex, the bell's about to go. Oh for Christ's sake, Harry, I'll do it.'

I ran around to the other side of the car, only to have my progress violently halted by the edge of the 'Don't Park Here, School Children Crossing' sign embedding itself in my left eyebrow.

'Jesus fucking Christ,' I screamed, immediately dropping to my knees. A local mum tutted loudly at my language in front of my – and her – kids. Another more sympathetic mum came over to say, 'You're bleeding, dear. Are you all right?' As she helped me to my feet, she politely asked why Alex had a packed lunch when it was canteen day.

'Canteen day?' I replied weakly. 'What's that?'

'It's the day once a week when parents bring in money for the school canteen and no packed lunches are allowed.'

'Where's the canteen?' I asked.

'Over there, but you better hurry, orders close at nine o'clock.'

I didn't feel well enough to shout at anyone, so I simply dragged my sons to the counter. Amazingly, the $3.30 I had in small change – I hadn't brought any notes – just covered my hurried order for one lunch. Little lunch, however, was a different matter, pushing my budget and my temper over the edge.

'What's little lunch?' I asked the canteen lady.

'It's the favourite part of the day for most kids,' she replied. 'It's when the important bonding happens. All the kids gather outside on the basketball court at 10.20 and have a snack. The ritual swapping of sweets, Tazos and the like is quite fascinating. Most kids would rather go to school with no trousers on than have no little lunch.' This last unhelpful bit of information was said with a pitying glance at Alex.

Five minutes before, I'd never heard of little lunch, let alone known what it was, yet now it was single-handedly ruining my entire life. I felt bad enough for making Alex move schools and countries at the tender age of six, and yet here I was making it impossible for him to fit in because I didn't know the first thing about how his school worked.

I presented my by now miserable little-lunchless son to his class teacher with a muttered, 'Sorry he's late', before driving Harry to kindy while clutching a canteen napkin to my still bleeding eye. We didn't say a word on the journey – so much for quality time with my kids. I'd had visions of a relaxed breakfast, joking together in the car and then larking about in the playground. Instead I had spent the entire time stomping around underneath my own personal storm cloud. I felt guilty, stressed and inadequate. I dropped Harry off at kindy and then took the opportunity to stroll down the hill to the local beach café for a soothing morning coffee.

I sat in the window seat and tried to relax myself by looking at the view of the waves gently rolling onto Bronte beach. It was a pleasant spot and, sure enough, five minutes later I was starting to feel a little better. I ordered a second coffee and had just sat down again when our next door neighbour, who also had a child at the kindy, walked past the window, noticed me and came in to say hello.

'Morning, Nigel, what are you doing here?' she asked.

'I'm having the morning off work. I've just dropped Harry off at kindy,' I replied.

'Oh, isn't he cute. I simply love the way he stands at the Goodbye Window.'

'The Goodbye Window?'

'Yes, the way he stands on his school bag so he can reach the sill to kiss his mum – or obviously today his dad – goodbye before he'll agree to join the others.'

My heart lurched. I excused myself from the conversation and ran as fast as I could back up the hill to the kindy.

'Where's the Goodbye Window?' I panted to a mum who was just leaving.

'Over there. It's the one with the blond boy leaning on the sill,' she said, pointing towards my younger son.

As I approached the window I could see there were tears rolling down Harry's cheeks.

'Daddy, I waited. Where were you?' he asked in a trembling, bewildered voice.

I can't actually find the words to describe how I felt. I hated myself and loved him with equal passion. How could I be such a useless pillock? I only had to do the school run, something Kate managed every day, and I'd completely ballsed it up. I imagined Harry being interviewed in prison in later life, telling a tutting Oprah Winfrey, 'I decided to turn to violent crime after my father left me weeping in front of my classmates so he could get himself a coffee . . .'

This is so hard, I thought as I drove home. Little lunch, Goodbye Windows, what other unknown obstacles were out there waiting to trip me up? I parked outside the house and trudged inside. Kate was sitting in the garden sipping a takeaway latte, looking radiant and relaxed.

'Hi, sweetheart, how were the lads?'

'Fine,' I lied.

'Excellent. Well, now you've done it once, I thought next time you'd like to do it properly and take the girls as well as the boys.'

I couldn't help wondering if the bus still had some seats left on it.

Chapter 5
Kindi Gym

A WEEK AFTER MY disastrous trip with the boys, I took another morning off work to try the school run again. Given my previous experiences I approached this event with some trepidation. Luckily Kate relented on the four-kids-at-once challenge and instead gave me the girls' Kindi Gym trip to do.

Grace and Eve are identical twins. We hadn't planned on having four kids but in retrospect I feel blessed that we were given this particular parenting experience. Half the time they looked like one child with four big trusting eyes and one enormous mop of blonde hair. Until a year before they had actually slept in the same bed with their faces pressed together like two interlocked jigsaw pieces. Both Kate and I still sometimes mistook one for the other and other people did all the time. Harry identified them simply by pointing and saying 'That one hit me' or 'The one with the hat on needs the loo.' Grace has a small mole on the side of her neck and became so used to having people look for it to establish who was who, that now if anyone said, 'What's your name?', she automatically lifted up her hair and pointed to her mole. This was understandably disconcerting when she wasn't actually with Eve and the person asking didn't know she had a twin. On one slightly worrying occasion, a kindly old lady in the local park asked Eve her name. Eve shocked Kate by replying, 'I'm Graceandeve.'

The twins were best friends in a way that made my heart melt, walking around holding hands, hugging each other if one was upset and needed comforting. On top of how they looked, they also sounded cute. Their accents were a unique blend of English, Australian, South African, German, Scottish and Canadian – the nationalities of all the nannies we had been lucky to have over the years.

Although they looked and sounded the same, Grace and Eve had certain distinguishing character traits, food being one of them. Eve could take it or leave it, while Grace had yet to make the link between hunger and food. She simply thought if it was put in front of you you ate it. Whenever Eve offered her plate to Kate, saying, 'Ninished, Mummy,' Grace would invariably say, 'I'll have it, Eve.' After one of their friend's birthday parties, I had had to go to Grace in the middle of the night as she was crying in her sleep.

'Wake up, sweetheart, Daddy's here. You're fine, you were having a bad dream,' I said, rubbing her back.

Grace put both her arms around my neck and sobbed, 'I want lots of cake!' before drifting back off to sleep.

Loving and affectionate, they had the most delightful

natures. One of my happiest memories is when I had finished their bedtime stories one night. Looking and sounding serious, they looked at me and then said in unison, 'Daddy, we want to tell you a secret.'

This was followed by each of them taking one of my ears and whispering, 'We love you, Daddy.'

I had been constantly saddened by the awareness that my work commitments were in essence meaning I was missing them growing up. So although I was trepidatious about this Kindi Gym trip, I was also secretly delighted that I was going to experience a bit of their world. The brutal fact was that I didn't even know where Kindi Gym was and they had been going there for over a year.

It turned out Kindi Gym was housed in an old warehouse a short drive from Bronte. Not much gym goes on there. It's basically an enormous room packed with soft toys and appa-ratus. The combination gave the place a slightly surreal feel. Amongst the serious gym equipment of trampolines, balance beams, pommel horses and rings, there was a riot of brightly coloured plastic slides, huge bouncing balls, crawling tunnels and climbing frames. The floor was covered wall to wall with three layers of blue foam mats. What looked to me like a hundred under-fives were swarming noisily over everything.

I couldn't help thinking of the monkey enclosure at the zoo. Trouble was, unlike the zoo there was no viewing area for humans. Here the parents were in with the chimps – and there wasn't a latte machine or newspaper stand in sight. It may have seemed like hell on earth to me but to Grace and Eve it was clearly heaven. Immediately upon being unleashed they ran off giggling and determinedly proceeded to climb up – and then fall off – each piece of equipment in turn. The padding appeared to be doing its job though, and as they were obviously having a whale of a time I retreated to the side to watch. I had been told there was no structure or guided activity for the first hour to allow the children to indulge in 'freeform aerobicising'. After this, one of the instructors would apparently lead the children in a couple of dances to end the session.

While watching from the sidelines, I couldn't help ruminating on the mix of parents present: apart from me, they were all mothers. Hardly surprising, I know, given that most blokes have to work on a weekday morning, but it just suddenly seemed such a dramatic demarcation of roles. Like some Polynesian island or Shaker community where all the men live in one hut and the women in another. If I wasn't preparing to take a year off, I would never have even known this place existed, let alone be sitting in it. I suppose many boardrooms look the same in reverse – a bunch of men in a room with a solitary woman (if tea is required). I haven't a clue how to make things more balanced, but it struck me we've obviously got a long way to go before roles are genuinely shared. While indulging in this amateur sociological observation, I couldn't help noticing in an entirely unreconstructed manner that the Kindi Gym teacher was actually a real fox. Not a spare ounce of fat on her, lovely smile, brilliant with all the kids and kitted out in the type of sportswear that showed off to dazzling effect her toned gymnast's body.

In fact, was it my imagination or was she paying me special attention? She returned my smile with what I thought was very encouraging prolonged eye contact. Perhaps it was because I was the only man in the entire building. Whatever her reason, I was beginning to quite enjoy Kindi Gym.

After an hour there were three loud claps and 'dance time' was announced. All the children hurriedly made their way to the end of the hall. On my way to join them, the instructor fell in besides me.

'Hi, so you're the dad of the Marsh twins?' she said.

'Yep – they seem to love it here,' I replied.

'Oh they do, they never want to leave at the end.'

'It's nice to see them having such a good time.'

'Well, I do hope we see you here again.' This was said with just a faint twinkle in her eye. I may be fat, forty and fired, I thought, but I've obviously still got some of the old Marsh magic left.

She bounced off into the middle of the melee of children, picked up the tape recorder and asked, 'Right, kids, who wants to pick the first song to dance to?'

Grace's hand immediately tugged at the instructor's arm.

'Yes, Grace, which song shall we have today?'

The assembled crowd of kids, mums and instructors all looked at Grace.

I looked on, positively bursting with pride.

'We don't touch Daddy's willy because it's dirty,' Grace announced.

My buttocks clenched in gut-churning humiliation as 30 pairs of eyes pointedly swung my way.

'Err, it's what I say to stop them putting their hands down the loo when I'm sitting on it.' Oh shit, this is hell, I thought. You're just making things worse trying to explain, you idiot. She didn't fancy you in the first place and now she's probably going to turn you in to the police.

While driving home I consoled myself with the thought that it wasn't the worst thing one of my children had ever said. That honour was reserved for Alex, who excelled himself on a trip to Devon to see Granny Vi – my mother's mother – four years earlier. My mum was an only child and as such had an enormously close bond with her mother. Granny Vi had had another fall and was in intensive care in the North Devon Infirmary. The doctor's message was unequivocal – she was dying and wouldn't make it to the end of the week. She wanted to see her only great-grandson one last time. I drove through the night from London to Somerset to pick up Mum, then continued on to the hospital in Devon.

Granny Vi looked truly awful – shrunken, white, grey around the eyes. The phrase 'at death's door' seemed horribly appropriate. But her eyes brightened when she saw Alex.

'Look, Mummy, Alex and Nigel have come to see you,' my mum said. 'And Alex has done you a picture.'

'Oh that's nice, dear,' Granny Vi croaked, looking at the random bunch of squiggles Alex had handed her. 'What is it?'

'It's the pit of death, Granny,' he sweetly replied.

Come to think of it, having the foxy gym instructor think I have a filthy knob was hardly worth worrying about.

Chapter 6

Missing the bus

AS THE LAST WEEK of my job approached, I started to get cold feet about the whole leaving work and taking a year off thing. I still hadn't finally made my mind up. When it came to the crunch, would I actually go through with it and not look for alternative employment?

There were a number of factors that were wobbling my resolve. The first was the fact that the firm was being incredibly reasonable and had made it clear to me that if I was prepared to be flexible about role and location there were a couple of seats still left on the bus. Second was the fact that it was worryingly clear that whenever I had attempted to sample the 'good life' I was hoping a year off would give me, it had ended in unmitigated disaster. Perhaps it wouldn't be such fun after all. Perhaps I would be bored and depressed once the initial thrill of embarking on a new adventure had waned. What would happen to my self-esteem without a job title or career to fall back on? How would other people react to me? Would I miss the stimulation and affirmation I got from the workplace? What would we actually do if the money ran out? How would Kate cope with having me around the house all day?

The third was the fact that Kate had also put a very real element of doubt in my mind. Her theory was that through-out my life and our marriage I had been a serial spurner of what was expected of me. As she put it, 'You always do the opposite of what people recommend – to prove some point. Trouble is, Nigel, no one – including yourself – actually understands what that point is, or if they did understand, no one would care about it.' I suspected she was largely right. I did tend to react against situations when I felt I was being told to do what everyone else would do in the same situation. My family, in-laws, mates, work colleagues and of course Hank had all been telling me to do nothing rash and continue collecting a pay cheque. Was I just doing the opposite for the hell of it? For what it would look like? Because it would fulfil some laughable need I had to feel I was a rebel? It didn't seem particularly good reasoning upon which to base taking such a life-changing – and potentially life-ruining – step.

Having thrashed these thoughts and worries around for a couple of days, I realised I'd never know if this was the right thing to do or not unless I did it. I would have to take the leap to find out. Most working men who wondered if they should try stepping out of the rat race were caught in a classic catch 22 situation. They'd never know unless they did it if it was the right thing to do, but by the time they could afford to do it their kids had left home and it was too late. It was a sort of enforced inertia that kept men in a tie and at the office. Then again, a number of men I knew used this as an excuse. They had far more money than I would ever have but they kept on raising the bar of what they needed before they would eventually feel comfortable enough to try a change. I'd had a number of conversations over the years with one particular colleague who had two houses, part-share in a light aircraft, and a wife who worked. He passionately maintained he was going to take a year off 'when he had enough money'. He still hasn't done it – and I doubt he ever will.

I felt I had a once-in-a-lifetime opportunity to break the vicious cycle in my own life. If I knew I could feed the family for a year and I still wasn't going to do it, then I really had been emasculated. There would never be a better time. If I didn't do it now then in all honesty I was kidding myself and I would never do it. I didn't want to look back years later and say I wish I had had more courage.

In the end it was a picture I found while clearing out the boxes from my office that made my mind up. It was an archive photo of the firm's original employees in New York. It was dated 1903. It had obviously been taken at some sort of official conference. There were no women in the picture, just 60 or so men, all dressed formally with jackets and ties, sitting neatly in rows on wooden chairs in what looked like the atrium of a large office building. I couldn't help wondering about the content of that conference. Did they talk excitedly about their plans for the company? How they were going to win new clients, expand into different markets, build offices in countries around the world? They would all be dead by now. I wondered if any of them had had any regrets at the end of their lives. If I could talk to them now, what would they say from the grave about the real value of their and the firm's achievements? What would be their definition of what was actually important? Would it be market share, double digit growth and shareholder value, or might their list include such things as meaningful relationships, social connectedness and making a useful contribution? I'd never know about them but I wanted to find out about myself.

There are no guarantees in life. Fear of the uncertain can, and does, hold millions back from pursuing their dreams. I'm not saying I wasn't scared – I was – just that I didn't want the fear to stop me. I determined I was going to look back at the end of my life and know that at least I had tried a different path – however disastrously it turned out. This year the bus would have to continue its journey with an empty seat on it.

Chapter 7

2,800 strokes

THE FIRST DAY OF MY freedom didn't feel particularly momentous. In fact it felt like any other day. Truth was, we hadn't done any planning for our new life. It was a bit like having your first child, where you spend all the time worrying about the birth and none preparing for the next 20 years of being a parent. I had spent all my time either agonising about whether to leave the workplace or constructing entirely unrealistic blue-sky dreams about all the earth-shattering achievements I would rattle off once I'd left the world of office work behind. No time at all had gone into thinking how we were going to live day to day. We hadn't even discussed how we were going to divide the household chores and childcare, let alone reached any agreements. Kate, however, was under no illusions that her life would be getting any easier. She was well aware she was trading a qualified nanny for a useless one. To her enormous credit she didn't immediately load me up with domestic tasks to fill the hours I wasn't spending in the office. I will be forever grateful for the space and support she gave me in my often-ludicrous attempts to better myself and build a new life.

As the reality of my situation set in I began to look around for a tangible goal to focus on – over and above being a better father and husband. I've a characteristic (my wife calls it a weakness, I call it a strength, so here I'll just call it a characteristic) that once I say I'll do something I invariably do it. Be it giving up smoking (25 June 1995, thank you very much) or doing the Sydney Harbour Bridge Run (in a breathtaking one hour and 20 minutes – the winner did it in 29 minutes), once I focus on something I get an enormous pleasure out of logheadedly and systematically following it through to completion. Importantly, I have also found that having a specific purpose gives me sense of purpose generally. I'm all round a nicer and more effective person if I'm working towards something.

The last time I left a job, I decided to do, and did, the coast to coast walk across the north of England. This time, after a week's investigation, I decided I would do the Bondi to Bronte ocean swim. We lived in Bronte, where Kate was training to be a surf-lifesaver. I was already learning to surf at Bondi. The next event was in December – a suitably distant date given my total unpreparedness for such a feat. Swimming between the two oldest surf-lifesaving clubs in the world in the third ever Bondi to Bronte race suddenly gripped me as the perfect challenge with which to throw myself into a different lifestyle and the community. Training in the Pacific every day would certainly make a change from sitting in the bloody office for nine hours at a stretch. Besides, ocean swimmimng was one of the few physical activities the surgeon said I could safely do while I was healing. Apparently sea water does wonders for deep flesh wounds.

The reality of the challenge was, however, mildly daunting to a fat, forty-year-old Englishman who couldn't even do freestyle (the stroke in which you do the race). By all accounts swimming in rough ocean was entirely different and much more difficult than pool swimming. When I asked one of Kate's ocean-swimming friends from the surf club what the difference was between competitive pool swimming and ocean swimming, she had snorted derisively and said, 'Blue-bottles, riptides, shore dumps, seasickness.' I had thought she was joking about the last one until another friend confirmed that it is apparently not uncommon for people to vomit on the longer ocean swims. Lovely. So not only would I have to learn to swim freestyle (or front crawl as it's called where I grew up) and get fit, I'd also have to learn the particular skill of ocean swimming. On top of it all there was also the small matter of sharks. The day of my decision, Bondi beach was closed for three hours because of a shark sighting. When the lifeguards couldn't find the beast, they reopened the beach. And here's the thing – *all the locals simply got back in the water*. Clearly I was going to need a new attitude to our finned friends because ever since I saw *Jaws* when I was ten I'd never been truly relaxed in the sea. I was forever hearing that bloody *dur dum dur dum* music from the film in my mind.

But a goal is a goal, so I started preparations immediately.

The very next morning I walked down to the Bronte beach

pool. This is one of the most remarkable features of living in this part of the world. Many of Sydney's beaches have had beautiful but rugged seawater pools cut into the rocks. Unbelievably, to someone who spent 15 years living in London, these are all immaculately clean and completely free of charge. The experience of a morning swim in one of Bondi, Bronte, Clovelly or Coogee's beach pools, while the sun rises over the horizon and the waves crash against the poolside, is simply breathtaking.

Unfortunately on this day it was slightly more breathtaking than usual. The tide was in and the sea was high. Huge rollers were breaking over the rocks and dumping into the pool, making an enormous frothy whirlpool of the water of the pool. The locals were wisely sitting this one out. Urban legend had it that the year before, a swimmer had been washed out of the pool and out to sea in particularly bad weather and that the year before that a shark had been washed *into* the pool, to the amazement of both the beast itself and the two elderly brothers who were swimming at the time.

Having made my mind up to start today, I was determined at the very least to get in the pool. Immediately upon doing so, a friendly voice yelled, 'Watch out, mate.' I turned in time to see a wall of green above me. Instinctively I dived to the bottom of the pool. It was like being in a giant dishwasher. The wave was quite the biggest one I have ever seen and it buffeted me upside down into the cliff wall with frightening force. In a perverse way, it was actually fun of sorts, but hardly appropriate practice. A change of venue was obviously in order. I got out and walked back up the hill home. I flicked through the *Yellow Pages*' 'Fitness Centre' section, found the number for the Hakoah Club in Bondi and booked a swimming lesson for the next day.

Now, I've been in Irish pubs in Amsterdam, blues clubs in Tokyo, and English Army bases in Cyprus, but never in all my life have I seen such a pure cultural transportation as the Hakoah Club in Sydney. You walk in and you are in Israel. I spent 12 months living in Israel, and the Wailing Wall is less like Jerusalem than the Hakoah Club. Everyone at the Hakoah Club was delightful and friendly but for the first couple of times I visited, I did find myself turning round to look out the front door to check that my mind wasn't playing tricks on me and that I had indeed just walked off a crowded sunny street full of boardshort-wearing surfies and straight into the Golan Heights. The ground floor itself was packed with female coffin dodgers playing the pokies. The lifts were covered in posters that looked like they were designed in the seventies, advertising cut-price rates for the Neil Diamond impersonator night. However, upon alighting at the third floor, another cultural juxtaposition awaited. I walked into a high-tech modern gym and pool complex and booked in with my coach for the session – Zane.

Zane had the stomach definition of Brad Pitt in the bed-jumping scene in *Thelma and Louise*, the physical magnetism of Sean Connery in *Doctor No* and the easygoing charm of Cary Grant at his peak. Maddeningly, on top of all these natural blessings he was genuinely friendly, keen to help and seemed entirely unaware of how intimidatingly perfect he was.

I didn't feel worthy to get in the same pool as him. But then again, I wasn't entirely comfortable standing on the edge of the pool either. I've always thought the male form is a rather pathetic sight unless it is in perfect condition (à la Zane). Dress it in a skimpy pair of budgie smugglers and top the whole effect off with a white paunch, swimming cap and a pair of goggles and it gets downright offensive. Getting in the pool seemed the better option.

I motioned to Zane that I was ready to begin.

'Excellent. Before we start, tell me, do you want to learn tumble turns, bilateral breathing or just some simple stroke correction?' Zane asked.

'Err – it's slightly more basic than that,' I replied. 'I'd like you to teach me front crawl,' I replied.

'You mean freestyle?'

'I think so, you know, overarm.'

'Okay, dive in and show me what you can do.'

I feel I should explain that in England no one does freestyle – unless they are in proper training. Because of the weather, recreational swimming is such a rare thing that the natural default stroke of almost everyone is breaststroke. When freestyle is attempted it is only for short, one-breath-per-stroke bursts and then the universal method is to thrash your arms as fast as possible – the bigger the splash the better. The notion of controlling the stroke or using your legs is yet to catch on.

I took a deep breath and dived in. The pool was over-warm and murky. I could see hairs, Band-aids and broken goggles floating around on the tiles at the bottom of the pool. It felt like I was immersed in a large bowl of pubic soup. Quickly banishing this unpleasant thought, I threw my left arm over my head then immediately followed it with my right. I wasn't sure if my forward motion was because of the dive or the strokes. I threw my left arm over my head again. I could swear I was slowly sinking. This was less swimming and more drowning with attitude. I threw my right arm past my ear and attempted a leg kick at the same time. Now you're showing off, Nigel, I thought to myself. I was running out of breath but I was buggered if I was going to give in. Again I threw my left arm forward, hitting the water with a rather satisfyingly large splash. Summoning all my reserves, I decided to go for another stroke – it was, after all, my first lesson and I was keen to make a good impression. As my right arm hit the water I jerked my head out of the pool and gulped four quick gasps of air. I was bollocksed but actually quite pleased with myself. I'd given it my best and in the process managed to swim a full half-length of the pool. Bronte to Bondi, here I come. I could almost hear Ian Thorpe crapping himself at the prospect of me bursting on to the swimming scene.

Zane was the model of tact.

'Okay, we have some areas we could work on. But first, before we do, did you say you were intending to do the Bondi to Bronte swim?'

'Yep.'

'Do you know how far that is?'

'Nope.'

'3000 metres.'

'So?'

'Well, Nigel – do you mind if I call you Nigel? – this pool is 17 metres long. You can do half a length. That's approximately 9 metres, or six strokes in your case. A good ocean swimmer would do upwards of 2,800 strokes to make it from Bondi to Bronte on a calm day.'

'What exactly is your point?' I said with as much false bravado as I could muster.

Chapter 8

Lower paddock

THE START OF FEBRUARY 2003 was an extremely important time in my life. My first month out of the rat race for 20 years meant so much to me, in fact, that I ripped that page out of our family calendar and had it professionally framed and hung above my desk in the front room. Every morning when I doubted myself or thought up another excuse not to train for the Bondi to Bronte swim or thought about calling the headhunters I'd so rashly knocked back, it would be a tangible reminder of the aspirations for the future I had so clearly at the time of my decision.

February, however, wouldn't be entirely clear of distractions. My parents were arriving from England at the end of the first week to stay for a month. During their stay,

Alex would have his eighth birthday and four-year-old Harry would have his first day at school. This latter rite of passage may not seem such a big deal to some but to me it had enormous importance, rooted in my own peculiar experience of starting school.

My father was working in the Royal Navy at the time and had been posted abroad. This, and other factors to this day unexplained, led my parents to make the extraordinary decision to send me away to a boarding school in the west of England at the tender age of five.

British boarding prep schools are an invention I feel history will not judge kindly. I can't imagine the character of the Australian people or the nature of Australian society allowing such institutions to flourish here to the extent that they did over the last centuries in the United Kingdom. To my mind, a nation's prison and school systems say a lot about the country that devises them. Suffice to say, in this instance Britain obviously got the two slightly confused. Basically these prep schools are fee-paying schools where parents send their kids to live for three 14-week terms a year. The usual stay is from age seven to 12. Just like I'm not sure it is possible for a Londoner to understand or believe how truly idyllic Sydney is unless he comes here, similarly I don't think it is possible for an Australian to fully understand or believe the reality of what the boarding prep school system was like in the UK as recently as the 1970s.

When one of the first mums I met in Australia told me how her eight-year-old boy was 'going away for ten weeks next term', my response was one of sympathy and horror. She had to explain to me that it wasn't a bad thing: it was the annual skiing trip when the entire school relocated to

Thredbo Alpine Village. The kids' lessons were organised for the afternoons and evenings to enable them to ski every morning for two months. I didn't actually believe her until another friend confirmed it was true. It would be fair to say I have more affinity with a culture that sends its children on extended character-building holidays than with one that sends them to soul-destroying quasi-prisons.

My memory of my arrival at prep school is as clear as if it happened yesterday. I got off the (delayed) train at Sherbourne Station and, clutching my green naval-issue suitcase, presented myself to the school office. A stern-looking man with enormous eyebrows informed me I was late and that I was to put on my games kit and report to the Lower Paddock immediately. Matron would show me to my dormitory first. Uttering not a single word more than 'follow me', Matron did just that and I found myself alone in a large room full of beds and wondering what my games kit was. I opened my suitcase to find that my Mum had thoughtfully labelled its contents. To my relief, one such label had 'games kit' on it in Mum's handwriting. Feeling slightly more confident, I put on the clothes and went in search of the Lower Paddock. When I found it, it became apparent that the whole school had received the same instructions, as 180 boys were also in their games kits and were grouped in a huge semi-circle facing the Headmaster. Noticing me joining the group, he looked me up and down. 'What's your name?' he bellowed.

'Marsh.'

'Marsh Minor,' he immediately corrected me. 'Your brother is Marsh Major. You will be called Marsh Minor.'

I didn't know what to say next. A question broke the momentary silence.

'Marsh Minor,' he boomed, 'what's that under your games kit?'

'My school uniform, sir,' I replied.

'Your school uniform?'

'Yes, sir.'

'You put your games kit on *over* your school uniform?'

'Yes, sir, the man told me to put on my games kit.' Tears were welling in my eyes as it dawned on me that none of the other boys had on two pairs of shorts, four socks or two shirts. I was only five, for Christ's sake, and no one had explained to me that you were supposed to take your uniform off before putting your games kit on. Not that that seemed to matter to the Headmaster, who was having a whale of a time publicly humiliating me.

'See this, boys, Marsh Minor obviously feels the cold! Ha ha ha, I wonder what he'll wear when we go swimming?'

This was met with an enthusiastic round of finger-pointing and jeering. I suppose many other children had worse starts at school than me, but it was my intention that Harry wouldn't be one of them. Although Harry was going to the local public school, as opposed to a boarding prison, I was taking time off for precisely such events as his first day of school and I would be with him, come hell or high water. The fact that my own father would be staying with me at this time somehow made it all the more important to me.

This, along with many other childhood episodes, was running through my head as I drove to Sydney airport to pick my parents up. We hadn't seen them since we'd left the UK over a year ago and we were all very much looking forward to seeing them again. It was a long journey for an elderly couple and they had decided to throw some savings at business-class tickets in an attempt to minimise the trauma. I hoped they'd had a better time of it than Kate and I had on our journey out here. But then again our experience was really only traumatic because of the kids.

Our relocation to Australia was basically one catastrophe after another, started in spectacular fashion by Eve, who threw up all over the taxi driver's head before we'd even reached the motorway leading to Heathrow. Forty embarrassing – and extremely smelly – minutes later, he'd pulled up outside the airport. Harry had immediately asked in a loud voice, 'Daddy, is this Australia? Are we there yet?'

'Not yet, sweetheart – a little while still to go,' I'd replied, while helping Kate wipe the dried chunks of half-digested vegetables out of the poor guy's hair with the envelope of my airline ticket.

We made an imposing sight at the boarding gate. Two children, two babies, two car seats, one double buggy and 14 individual pieces of hand luggage (not including the mountain of cuddly toys and brightly-coloured, noisy, plastic Fisher-Price detritus designed to keep babies contented that were falling out of our every pocket). The by now well-matured aroma from Eve's performance in the taxi added nicely to the effect.

You could feel an overpowering sense of 'thank Christ I'm travelling business class' from every besuited male in the queue. When we turned left, not right, into the plane, it almost caused a riot. There was near hand-to-hand combat as the execs fought amongst themselves to present the most compelling case to the flight crew.

'I'm a platinum card holder, damn it – I demand to be *down*graded,' one loudly insisted to a long-suffering flight attendant. Once order was restored, the unfortunates who had to share the business-class cabin with the family from hell settled into a groove of simmering resentment and pointed tutting every time a teddy was thrown or a spoonful of yoghurt was flicked. I have no idea how many of them had originally intended to leave the plane at Singapore but the cabin was significantly emptier for the second leg of the journey. Anyway, Mum and Dad were flying by themselves, I reasoned, so long though the trip was, it couldn't have been as bad as ours.

I parked the car while Kate got a couple of airport baggage trolleys for the kids to sit on. We pushed them to the arrivals gate to wait excitedly for my parents. When they walked through the arrivals gate I was shocked. I say walked, but more accurately my Dad shuffled. They were old. How did that happen? Last time I'd seen them they were just Mum and Dad but now they were bordering on frail. Not that Alex and Harry noticed, of course. They simply hurled themselves – in the way that only kids can – at Granny and Granfie in un-diluted delight.

'You've got fat,' my father greeted me.

'Don't worry, Dad, I'm going to lose it. How was the flight?' I replied.

'Bloody awful, some sodding family was being relocated and they were flying business class . . .'

Chapter 9

Fat

MY DAD'S GREETING may have been untraditional and a tad insensitive, but at least it was factual – I had got fat. Not slightly overweight, but good, old-fashioned 'if I were a woman people would think I was pregnant, trousers having to be done up under the paunch, you need a heavy hammer to drive a long nail' fat. Eighty-four kilograms at my last weigh-in. All my belts were on the first hole and half my shirts would no longer stretch over my belly. In deciding to do the Bondi to Bronte race, I'd vaguely acknowledged that I might need to shed the odd kilogram, but now I realised I had to get serious. I added yet another resolution for my year off: once and for all, I would sort out my size. Not in an unsustainable, one-off way like those wonderfully pointless 'lose weight for the summer and look great in your bikini' diets that women's magazines promote every year. It has always struck me as absurd that people would want to starve themselves for months to look good in their swimsuit for a few weeks and then resort to looking like a sack of crap for the rest of the year. I wanted a permanent, livable-with change, something that would sort it for good and therefore free me from ever having to think, or worse, talk about it again.

I had consulted various books and one of those machines you see in chemists that tell you not just your weight but what you should weigh. Taking a balanced view, I was at least 12 kilograms overweight. I decided to set myself a goal of losing one kilogram a week until I was under 70 kilograms and then remaining under 70 kilograms until, and beyond, the Bondi to Bronte swim in December. If I stuck to the one-kilogram-a-week schedule, I would be under 70 kilograms by July and then have six months to learn how to stay at that weight before the race. My strategy to lose the fat was a simple one: eat less and exercise more. I was relying on willpower for the former and training for the swim for the latter.

I've read a lot of advice in my time about diets and weight loss, and almost without exception it has all been arrant nonsense. It seemed to me that because it was such a simple issue, people couldn't bear having the stark reality of it played back at them, so they willingly went along with all sorts of bollocks that enabled them to ignore the bald truth: that they were overweight because they ate too much and exercised too little. I had long wanted to write a diet book, provisionally entitled *Stop Moaning and Eat Less, You Fat Bastard*, and now seemed a perfect time to test my theory out on myself. If it worked, I seriously intended to write the book – although perhaps with a more sensitive title.

As we waited at the baggage carousel for Mum and Dad's bags, I couldn't help noticing all the overweight people in the crowds around us. I wondered how many of them were unhappy with their body image or were permanently on a variety of ineffectual diets, one after the other. It struck me as a sad and entirely avoidable state of affairs. Life is full of uncertainties. There are no agreed rules on how to be happy or rich or spiritually rewarded. Half the time we work determinedly towards a goal not really knowing whether what we are doing is the right way to get us there. It has always seemed to me that weight loss is the rare exception. Everyone knows what to do. No one disagrees. The issue is totally within each individual's control. It isn't that people don't know what to do, it's just that they are, by and large, incapable of doing it.

The whole weight-loss industry was focused in the wrong direction. New methods of eating differently weren't what was required. In my opinion, what was needed was advice on how to maintain the motivation to sustain the behaviour that would lead to weight loss. Basically, in an increasingly spoilt and soft society, people had lost the ability to delay gratification for any prolonged period of time. The moment they felt hungry, or sad, or in a need of a reward or whatever, their willpower crumbled and they behaved in a way they knew was contradictory to their own desire to be thin. To avoid the feeling of shame that comes with living with this self-knowledge they all conspired with the writers, who gave them the face-saving out of the latest new science or theory about how to lose weight. No one, it seemed, was prepared to stand up and state the truth in a compelling way – if you are fat it's usually because you eat too much.

I, Nigel Marsh, was going to single-handedly transform my own body and then write a bestseller that would forever change the diet industry and help countless millions around the world fulfil their dreams in a way they had never been able to before. With that inspirational thought, I pushed the baggage trolleys into the airport McDonald's, bought the kids a Happy Meal each and an extra large fries and Quarter Pounder with Cheese for myself.

Chapter 10

Applecatchers

MY PARENTS HAD planned their trip months before. Obviously none of us knew then that I would be unemployed and hanging around the house during their visit. Their presence had advantages and disadvantages in equal measure. It was lovely to see them, but the fact that both of them thought I was insane to have left work added to the stress of an already weird situation. Kate and I hadn't quite come to grips with it ourselves yet.

We had a lot of adjusting to do. First up we had to let our delightful nanny, Charmaine, go. This was sad to do – the kids adored her – but we just wouldn't be able to afford her help over the coming months. The day after we told the kids she was leaving, Grace took my hand, led me to the map of the world stuck to her bedroom wall, pointed at it sadly and asked, 'Daddy, where is Nannyworld?'

'Nannyworld, sweetheart?' I said.

'Nannyworld, where Liz, Shannon, Emma, Terry and Laura live?' she trustingly explained.

'Oh, it's here,' I said, pointing vaguely at Canada, all the time wondering if this was going to irreversibly mess her up when she found out there was no such place as Nannyworld. I found it so difficult to know when to play along and when to be factual and accurate. I had visions of her being laughed at in the playground as she insisted to a bunch of geographically-wise classmates that Canada was actually Nannyworld. Perhaps my worries were so acute because of my own similar childhood blunders. I still blush now, 35 years later, when remembering the time at school that I got into a fight with a classmate because he didn't believe me when I said Pete Townsend lived in the North of England in Leeds. A crowd of older boys broke up the fight and then ended up getting involved in the debate themselves. Given my passionate insistence that I *knew* where Pete Townsend lived, I was given the chance to present some evidence to prove my case. Eagerly I rushed off to my older brother's dormitory and moments later returned triumphantly with his copy of the live concert album *The Who Live in Leeds*. Maybe I should have cleared up the whole Nannyworld/Canada thing with Grace after all.

We'd been blessed with the people we'd managed to convince over the years to help us with the demands of four kids and a useless absentee father. It was going to be strange having no one else around in the family, as ever since the twins were born we'd always had someone to help, even if it was only for a few hours a week. It would, I supposed, be nice to have the house totally to ourselves once more. It does rather limit the naked bedroom-to-bathroom walking, shouting arguments and sitting-room sex when you've got a 22-year-old student liable to walk in at any time. Then again, it wasn't just the family who had to put up with the nanny – the nanny had also to put up with the family. On the second morning of my parents' visit I was in the kitchen while the rest of the family were having their breakfast. I wanted to go for a swim and was looking through an overflowing laundry basket for a towel when I came across an enormous pair of underpants.

'Jesus, darling, if you're going to have an affair you might at least have the decency to hide his underwear from me,' I said to Kate.

'Never seen them before – blimey, they are enormous. Perhaps they are your dad's?' she replied.

'Nope, not mine,' said my dad, who had just walked in. 'In the Navy we used to call those Applecatchers.'

Laughing, my mum joined in: 'Granny Knickers is what we used to call circus tents like those.'

I stretched them above my head. 'We could make a shade in the garden out of them – if you're sure your lover won't miss them,' I said to Kate.

'He wouldn't, but I might,' a visibly upset Charmaine whispered as she grabbed them out of my hands and walked up the stairs.

'Bollocksing hell, Kate, why didn't you tell me they were hers?' I demanded.

'I told you, I'd never seen them before,' she replied.

Perhaps a break from Nannyworld wasn't such a bad idea after all.

Chapter 11

Venus

AT THE SAME TIME as we were getting rid of things from our life – asking nannies to leave, selling cars and looking for cheaper houses to move to – I was also trying to add things. For a start I wanted to agree on a swimming schedule with Kate. It was all well and good deciding I was going to train for the race, but with four young kids, and now no nanny, this would inevitably be an extra burden on Kate. On top of the swimming schedule I also wanted to sign up to do things that would force me to engage in the community and experience a different side of life. School canteen duty was the main thing I had in mind at this early stage.

But it wasn't just life outside the office that I wanted to experience – I was after an overall less male existence. Ever since being sent to a single-sex boarding school at the age of five, I felt I had led a particularly male-dominated life. Frankly, women were a mystery to me. They seemed to live in a different world. I had read *Men are from Mars, Women are from Venus* a couple of years back and, leaving aside the easy criticisms that can be made of it, I had found it a powerful eye-opener. Some of women's behaviour was so damn strange.

One of my earliest memories of living with Kate is of her coming home from the office we both worked at, exclaiming, 'I'm dying for the loo.'

'Why didn't you go before you left?' I asked.

'I couldn't. There was someone in there,' she replied.

'You've only got one stall in the ladies' at work?' I asked.

'No, about six.'

'And they were all engaged? Blimey, rush hour down at the old powder room,' I commented.

'They weren't all engaged. One of them was,' Kate said.

'But you said there are six stalls in there,' I queried.

'There are, but I can't go if someone else is in the room,' she explained.

'Why the fucking hell not?'

'Because they might hear.'

'Hear what?'

'Me going to the loo.'

'But it's a toilet, for Christ's sake.'

'You don't understand. I could never go for a poo if someone else was in the room.'

'Bloody hell! In the men's we have conversations with each other over the walls,' I told her.

'That's revolting! While you're going to the loo?' she asked.

'Yep. Some blokes even take their phones in and carry on working.'

'None of my friends would ever do that.'

'You mean it's not just you? Other women think like this as well?' I said.

'Absolutely.'

Clearly a different world – and one I was keen to learn more about as the year progressed. To do so would require not just a change in mindset and some proper empathetic listening, it would also require that I be disciplined in how I spent my time. Already it was clear to me that it would be possible for me to kid myself and spend the year doing the glory bits of parenting – the high-attention, high-reward, interactive, fun bits like taking the kids out, doing the school run and going to sporting occasions with them. While these were all valuable, I was aware they were only the tip of the iceberg. Perverse as it may sound, I actually wanted to do the drudgery bits as well – the cooking, cleaning and shopping stuff. I don't want to attempt to portray myself as a saint – something tells me it would be less than convincing if I did – but it is fair to say I was genuine in my desire to look beyond my one-dimensional male world and be slightly less useless as a partner.

When I mentioned these high ideals to Kate, she naturally had a different perspective. 'I believe you, Nigel. No, no, I do. I'm sure if you get huge amounts of praise and attention for doing so you'll lend your hand to the drudgery.'

I may not have understood her world, but she was clearly fluent in mine.

Chapter 12

Muffia

For as long as my mum and dad were staying, Kate and I agreed that it would be reasonable for me to plan on training for the swim three times a week. We also signed me up to do canteen duty at Alex's school. Truth is, I've always been a bit of a goal junkie and already the list of goals was becoming quite daunting. I wanted to be a better father, better husband, train for an ocean swim, lose 14 kilograms of weight, get involved in the community and attempt to get in touch with my feminine side – or at least a more feminine point of view. All of them, to my mind, worthwhile goals but it didn't really have the look of a very relaxing existence.

At least the swimming was easy to organise. On a good day I could stroll down the hill, have a swim in Bronte ocean pool and be back to wake Kate up with a cup of tea before the kids stirred. But while it may have been easy to organise, I was finding it less easy to *do*. Zane had given me a load of good advice but the simple fact of the matter was I found freestyle awkward and exhausting. After a couple of weeks I was still incapable of doing it for anything but the shortest of times. At the end of February, on the morning of Alex's eighth birthday, I managed three lengths and was pathetically delighted with myself. Then again, it *was* an improvement. I've always been a believer in the philosophy that if you are moving consistently in the right direction it doesn't ultimately matter how slowly you are going. Twenty-five more years like this and and I'd be able to swim the Tasman.

Rather encouragingly, I had stopped putting on weight. The bathroom scales even indicated a minor improvement. I still looked like the Michelin man with my clothes off, but I felt it was the start I needed.

Parenting-wise I was trying my best but overambition, lack of practice and general ignorance was proving my undoing. For Alex's party I thought it would be a good idea to have 16 eight-year-olds to stay for a sleepover. The only place I could fit them all was on the floor of the corridor in sleeping bags. Turns out it was a good idea – way too much of a good idea. They were so excited I couldn't shut the little buggers up. The more excited they got, the louder they became and the worse they behaved. The worse they behaved, the louder I shouted. I felt like that crap science teacher we all knew who couldn't control the children in his lessons. For some reason everyone always pissed around in his class no matter what he did or threatened, while the other teachers could keep perfect control without raising their voices once. I clearly was going to need to learn a different strategy from shouting.

Fortunately, Harry's first day at school went better than Alex's party, and gloriously all my worries proved to be mere projections from my own experience. Granfie, Alex, Harry and I walked to school on the first morning. Harry chatted happily the whole way. Dad and I walked on either side of him, held a hand each and swung him in the air every five steps. When we got to the school gates he ran in to meet his classmates without a backward glance. I, on the other hand, was sick with worry all day, imagining all sorts of bullying and mental torment, but at pick-up time he was the same picture of contentment. In fact, Dad and I both had to hang around for an age while he played 'kick cricket' with a tennis ball on the top grass with his brother and the older boys. (Australians' love of sport doesn't let a simple fact like lack of the proper equipment get in the way of a game.) We walked home via the newsagent so we could treat them both to an ice-cream.

My first school canteen day was also a success. I had been a bit worried going into it as the day before a still-working mate of mine spent the whole evening in the pub telling me what a vicious environment schools were.

'It makes office politics seem like a picnic,' was his opening gambit.

'What does?' I replied.

'The playground.'

'Yeah, kids can be awful, I know,' I agreed.

'No, not the kids, the kids are fine. It's the parents who are the nightmare.'

'You're joking.'

'Deadly serious, mate, there's a pecking order every bit as complex and mean-spirited as at the office.'

'It can't be that bad.'

'Look, mate, once you've been snubbed by the Muffia you'll never forget it.'

'What the fuck's the Muffia?' I asked.

'The handful of mums you get in every school who run things.'

'You mean the heads of the various committees and the like?'

'No, not necessarily. The Muffia don't literally run things, they *really* run things.'

'Oh, I see,' I said, still confused.

'They are the real influencers who work everything out behind the scenes through a hidden unofficial network. Get on the wrong side of them and you're totally rooted. They don't take prisoners,' he said.

Luckily I had a gentle landing as I either didn't meet the Muffia or they were undercover and being nice to me on my first day. The mums I was on canteen duty with were delightful, friendly and helpful. Making and doling out 250 canteen luches was enormously satisfying and fun. It was also a real thrill seeing the look of pleasure in both my sons' eyes when they saw me behind the counter from the lunch queue.

'Hey look, that's my Dad, he's rubbish at surfing. He keeps falling off,' Harry said, nudging the boy in front of him in the queue.

Alex had a more direct but equally random and damning angle.

'Hi Dad, ham pizza. In Indonesia, rather than using the word "very" before a word they just repeat the word. Banana milk, please. So you would be "fat fat" not "very fat". Cool, isn't it? And a cheese stick. Thanks.'

Rather than feel deflated, I felt blessed to have seen and experienced a little bit of their world. I was keen keen, as they say in Indonesia, to go back.

Chapter 13

Lip and Chin

MY NEW LIFE wasn't just packed with self-imposed goals, it was also full of surprises – and learning. For a start, where did all the people come from? I had always imagined when I was in the office that town centres would be empty. But they weren't. They were teeming with people – women and men. Didn't they have jobs to go to? Evidently the entire population didn't spend from nine to five in an office block.

I also began to understand why women were so damn rude when you called them in the late afternoons. It had always irritated me at the end of a hard working day when I would call Kate up for a chat and get short shrift from her.

'Hi, sweetheart, it's me,' I would usually start.

'Yes. What do you want?' she would invariably reply.

'Nothing, just a chat.'

'I can't, I'm busy.'

'Busy? Doing what?'

'Looking after your sodding children.'

'Well, if you can't talk, could you put Alex on?'

'No.'

'Why not?' I'd ask.

'He's in the bath.'

'Harry then?'

'Nigel, I haven't got time for this. They are all in the bath.'

'Jesus, sorry I called,' I would mutter as I hung up.

Thing is, after only a month off I now knew how incredibly irritating it was if anyone called you during the teatime, bathtime, bedtime home straight that made up the end of each day. It is called arsenic hour, and for good reason. You are tired, the kids are getting cranky and you have an amazing amount of stuff to do in a very short space of time. All it needs is a daughter to be difficult during her hair wash or a husband to want to chat on the phone and the whole delicate system collapses and no one gets to bed until ten o'clock. As any mother knows, this is an absolute disaster because it means that the whole day is given over to childcare with no space left for you to be an independent adult before your own bedtime.

Now that I wasn't working, I had never spent more time together with Kate. We would actually meet *during* the day, a welcome development after ten years of living separate lives on weekdays. Previously we had worked hard in different areas towards different ends – her raising the kids, me building a career. Now, for the first time in our marriage, we were engaged in shared endeavours towards one common end

– living successfully together as a family. This was not as easy as it may sound, and it also wasn't always fun. In fact, I found certain aspects of my new life maddening – in particular the way Kate reacted to my efforts to help around the house.

This was entirely new ground for me as previously with our separate roles it was accepted that the household and child-rearing chores fell to Kate. So not only did I now have to conquer my natural laziness, but also my extensive ignorance. I constantly found I didn't know what to do in the simplest of situations. It was one thing being asked to 'dress the girls', but it was quite another knowing what they should wear and where those clothes actually were. Kate didn't exactly help with me with the transition.

'Oh no, not in that!' she exclaimed the first time I emerged from the girls' bedrooms with two dressed twins.

'Why not?'

'Because I never put those tops with those skirts,' she replied.

'Why not?' I asked.

'I prefer it if they wear their green tops with those skirts,' she explained.

'But you asked me to dress them,' I protested.

'Yes, but I like them in a different outfit.'

'Yes, but you asked *me* to dress them – I've dressed them. They look fine.'

'No need to get upset about it – I'll quickly change them.'

'No, you won't,' I replied.

'Why not?' Kate asked.

'Because I want them to wear what they've got on. What I, their father, chose for them to wear. You are always doing this. You ask me to do something and when I do it, the first – the very first – thing you do is criticise. It really pisses me off. How about saying something really radical like, "Thanks for dressing the girls, darling"?' I asked.

'Typical, men always want thanks for doing the simplest of tasks,' she replied. 'When do I get thanked? I dress the girls all the time and you never thank me. Why should I thank you when you do the basic things that you should be doing anyway?'

'Because I would like it and it would encourage me in my efforts to be helpful,' I told her.

'I shouldn't have to say "thank you" to get you to do the chores,' she answered.

'You know what? You're right – you shouldn't. However, I want to be clear with you. It really depresses me that doing such a simple thing as saying "thank you" to your husband causes you such a problem. How difficult is it to say the fucking words "thank you"? What possible harm could it do you? This shouldn't be some sort of point-scoring competition. If it makes me happy and doesn't cost you anything to do, why not do it anyway? Pretend to be grateful, for fuck's sake. What possible outcome are you after by not thanking me and making the first words out of your mouth a criticism? Just imagine for a second that you said thanks and didn't mention that you didn't agree with my choice of clothes. Would it kill you? Or would we have a pleasant morning and the next day I would want to dress the girls again and you could suggest in advance what they should wear and I would agree and I wouldn't think you were a mean-spirited cow who needed her moustache waxed.'

'God, I hate you when you are like this,' Kate replied.

Although I felt I had right on my side (men always do), my

last remark was ever so slightly below the belt. Only the day before, Kate had been into the beauticians' in the high street – the delightfully named Backs, Cracks and Sacs – for a leg wax appointment. The lady who greeted her at the door had taken a lingering look at her face and said, 'So, dear, you're in for a lip and chin?' Kate, the angel, had died on the spot, agreed and come back home with a smooth chin and hairy legs.

Later that night, when I had calmed down, I resolved to get to the bottom of this issue – fairly. I had, after all, promised Kate that if I took time off work I would try to be less of an arsehole. Our conversation was a real education. When she explained it to me – and I was properly listening as opposed to trying to beat her in an argument – I could actually see her point. More than that, I actually found myself agreeing with her. Turns out she wasn't being a mean-spirited bitch – and she hasn't got a moustache either – it's just that she comes at it from a completely different perspective. To her, to have to thank me for doing basic tasks is demeaning. It makes her feel servile, like she is in an inferior role to me. It makes her feel that the childcare is entirely her role and I'm being gracious in condescending to dip in and help her every now and then. I could see how this would piss her off, given I was spending all the family's savings specifically so I could spend a year off properly engaging with the family. We ended up after two bottles of wine agreeing that I would attempt to be less of a needy arse and she would attempt to limit her criticisms to those occasions when my fashion taste was a crime against humanity, as opposed to simply poor.

Besides parenting, the other area where I wasn't progressing as quickly as I'd have liked was in my swimming training.

I had been finding it hard work and unenjoyable. I had been doing it for a month now and, progress or not, it was clear I was crap at it. Then a breakthrough came, courtesy of my friend David Fleeting. David was a parent at the school and a lifeguard at Bronte beach. He swam most days in the ocean, regardless of the weather. He had also done both the previous Bondi to Bronte races and was someone whom I had taken into my confidence regarding my swimming goal. It was too embarrassing and expensive to continue with Zane, so David had taken the role of my unofficial adviser.

'How's the swimming going, Nige?' David asked one day while we were both waiting in the school playground at pick-up time.

'Shithouse,' I said. 'I'm only up to five lengths of the Bronte pool but finding it really hard work.'

'Are you doing bilateral breathing?' he asked.

'Trying,' I replied.

'Using your legs?'

'Trying,' I replied.

'Going fast?'

'Trying.'

'Right, I want you to try this next time. Don't bother with your legs at all.'

'But I'll sink,' I protested.

'Don't be a dill, of course you won't, the legs only give you ten per cent of your power anyway. Forget about them for now.'

'Okay. Is that it?'

'No. I also want you to forget the bilateral breathing, but most importantly, I want you to go as slowly as you can.'

'As slowly?' I asked.

'Yep, as slowly. Don't worry what anyone else thinks, just plod along. You need to find your "jogging" pace.'

The very next morning I put his advice into practice and was stunned by the results. I did ten lengths – easily. I may have still looked like the proverbial rugby player doing ballet but I was totally delighted. Five weeks before I couldn't swim a length. It finally felt like I was getting somewhere.

Chapter 14

Walk on the grass

WITH HARRY SAFELY in school and my swimming schedule started in earnest, I now wanted to dedicate myself to spending some quality time with my parents. Or, more accurately, getting to know my parents. When you go to boarding school when you are five years old, you effectively leave home – with all that entails. It's a simple, if sad, fact that from the tender age of five, I spent considerably more time in the care of teachers at school than with my parents. When I was left on that first day, I didn't see my parents again for 14 weeks. Now, at the time I knew no different, so I simply got on with it. At the age of 40 with four kids of my own, I find the notion utterly barbaric. I couldn't possibly send Harry away at the age he is now, or even Alex, who is three years older than I was then. What were my parents thinking? Harry still asks me to check if his bottom is clean and if I will lie with him after his bedtime story. At Sherbourne Prep I received no love or tenderness. Ever.

My personal space amounted to a bed in a dormitory with 30 other boys, a desk in a classroom with 40 other boys, and a wire mesh locker with two hooks in it in a changing room shared by 180 others. No visits, no privacy, no trips beyond the school grounds, no girls, no weekends off, no hugs, no stories, no tenderness – just the law of the jungle until the end of term. I used to look at the clock in class and every time the minute hand clicked one dash forward I would mentally cheer that I was a minute nearer going home.

On my first night at the school – after the sports kit incident – one boy in my dorm had made the mistake of crying, as he was so homesick. His anguished sobs sounded like the noise a sports car makes as it goes up though the gears. Every night after, for the next 14 weeks, he was taunted until he cried.

'Where's Mummy? Do you think she's missing you? Who's feeding your rabbit? Bet your sister had ice-cream for tea . . .'

If this didn't work, stealing his teddy bear and repeatedly stamping on its head would normally do the trick. Everyone would then lie back and laugh as he went though the gears.

But when I wrote home (we had to write a letter home every Saturday), I was at pains to say how happy I was, because I thought that was what my parents wanted to hear and I didn't want to let them down. I feel this point marked the beginning of an emotional superficiality between us. One boy did make a stab at writing the truth, but the master who read all the letters before they got sent out made him change it.

It makes my blood boil when I hear some Colonel Blimp type talking about how such experiences are character-building. Yeah, right, and what type of character? I know people who never recovered from prep school. I think I would be a therapist's dream. To this day I still crave appreciation, public praise and signs of affection. I also find myself repeatedly and unexpectedly falling into bouts of loneliness and despair, bizarrely usually when I'm in the most jovial and loving company.

Prep school didn't just mean my school days were some sort of *Lord of the Flies* hell. It also ruined what was left of my home life. When I eventually got home after the first 14 weeks, I had changed irreversibly. Moreover, my parents and I had no common ground. It was like the opposite of a good marriage, where you build up shared experiences. From the time I was five we were living separate lives, coming together sporadically as polite strangers who happened to be related.

Anyway, for this and many other reasons, I was determined to try to make up for lost time and genuinely connect with my mother and father before it was too late. This was not as easy as I had hoped. Then again, my strategy probably wasn't very realistic. I decided that I would ask them each out for dinner individually. I reasoned this would give me the time to talk properly to them and go beyond the usual polite chit-chat without distractions. In reality, I think the invitations really spooked them. Kate told me she felt certain that they thought I had booked the dinners to tell them something awful, as they had the look of two people bracing themselves for bad news.

Both dinners turned out to be delightful, but not really what I was after. It rapidly became clear to me on the evening I took my mother out that she thought I was going to tell her over dinner that Kate and I were getting divorced. It took me until dessert to convince her we weren't splitting up. Dad had different suspicions about what our evening together meant.

'Do you need money, Nigel?' he asked as soon as we sat down in the restaurant.

'No, I've got my credit card with me, Dad, tonight's on me.'

'No, not tonight. I mean do you need money? Are you and Kate having trouble?'

'Dad, we're fine. Relax, I just wanted to have you to myself for an evening.'

'Why?' he asked.

'To chat.'

'About what?'

'I don't know, anything,' I replied. 'Career advice?'

'Really?'

'Yeah, it's a start, why not? How did you go about managing your career?'

'Simple. I made a point of doing whatever the Navy asked me. I deliberately set out to get a reputation for being a person they could call on to do the jobs no one else wanted. It didn't matter if I liked the assignment or not, I just wanted to keep my job. Any job. That way I knew I would always have a salary. That's the key thing, Nigel – stay employed. You've got to think of your responsibilities. You've a wife and four kids to look after,' he said, sounding strangely like Hank.

I didn't really need another 'seat on the bus' chat, so I changed the subject to more comfortable and superficial topics.

* * *

The next day Kate and I agreed that maybe a group occasion was more appropriate than the one-on-one approach. Perhaps if we could combine a family dynamic with a special event it would help prompt the intimacy I was after. Luckily, we had just such an event up our sleeves. The year before, my brother Jon had visited Sydney and gone to a restaurant in a national park north of the city that you access by seaplane. It's called the Cottage Point Inn and he had raved about it so much that Mum had called up from England and as a surprise thank-you gift, booked us all on the same flight on the strength of Jon's recommendation.

I was delighted, not just because it was another opportunity to bond with my folks, but also because for me the Australian attitude to air travel was yet another wonderful aspect of the life here. It may make me a geek to admit it but I actually *like* Sydney airport: well designed, welcoming and with lots of space, it is the precise opposite of Heathrow. Sydney airport wasn't what I liked best, however, it was the smaller airports – and airplanes – that had grabbed me. The smaller the better.

I had come to completely revise my opinion of plane trips. When I lived in the UK, a plane journey rarely lasted less than six hours, and always involved at least a 150-seater aircraft and a visit to either of the appalling Heathrow or Gatwick airports. Since coming to Australia I had experienced a whole succession of stress-free, exciting and short flights from airports with terminals no bigger than the average house. Flying was simply no big deal – it was how you got around. It was no more special than train travel used to be in England; in fact there were many similarities. On one flight from Hervey Bay to Brisbane, the pilot announced, 'Our flight time to Maryborough will be five minutes.' I remember thinking I must have misheard him, but sure enough, five minutes later we were pulling up outside Maryborough 'airport', which looked more like the village shop in 'Postman Pat' – complete with white picket fence out front – than an airport.

I started to keep a personal record of airports visited – Newcastle, Gladstone, Uluru, Hervey Bay, Bankstown, Lord Howe, Albury. Each was wonderful in its own way. My favourite to date was Jindabyne. I had been on a holiday when an emergency call had come through. I had to get back to the office pronto. I couldn't take the car and leave the family stranded, so one of those short-hop flights was booked. When the cab dropped me off, I was convinced there had been a mistake. Not only was there no terminal or taxi rank, *there was no runway*. In fact, there was nothing beyond a hand-written sign on the gate to the field that rather grandly stated 'Jindabyne Aerodrome'. I searched the countryside for any other sign of air transportation. I couldn't see any of the traditional clues, not even a windsock – nothing. But I was in the right place. After a short wait, Avant Air Flight Number 2 appeared on the horizon, buzzed the field once, before bumpily landing on the rutted grass and taxiing up to my side. In the UK taking your own four-seater plane is the behaviour of an oil magnate or multi-millionaire. In this case it was costing the firm considerably less than the price of a taxi from Gatwick to the centre of London.

On the day Mum had booked for the flight to Cottage Point, we drove the couple of kilometres to Rose Bay, the site of Sydney's old water airport. I was doubly excited as I'd never flown in a seaplane before. The water airport had once been a thriving concern – now it consisted solely of a hut the size of a phone box on a wooden jetty jutting into the harbour opposite Shark Island. The plane was also tiny – so small, in fact, that I had to sit in the co-pilot's seat, with Kate and my parents crammed in behind me. The pilot was typical of the people we had met since our arrival in Australia; cheerful, helpful and humorous. His in-flight safety announcement was a classic.

'In the event of an emergency you'll find the emergency door located on your right,' he said, pointing at the very door we had all just climbed in. There wasn't any other door. It was *the* door.

The in-flight service was equally wonderful.

'Would you care for a light refreshment?' he asked us as we taxied away from the jetty.

'Yes thanks, that would be nice,' my mum replied.

'Excuse me, mate, would you mind passing me that bag?' the pilot asked me, pointing to a rucksack at my feet. I lifted the bag across my lap and gave it to him, whereupon he reached inside, took out a plastic bottle of water, opened it and passed it to Mum. BA Club Class eat your heart out.

He was clearly an excellent pilot. The journey was short but breathtaking, swooping first over the harbour, then the national park, before coming in to land on the Hawkesbury River and pulling up alongside the restaurant terrace. A four-course lunch followed which could only be described as bliss. Mum and Dad were on sparkling form and Kate looked radiant, beautiful and relaxed. After years of trying to engineer an open and engaged relationship with my parents, here I was drinking and laughing with them while our own private plane waited to fly us home whenever we so desired. If this was what not working was like, it definitely got my vote. Then again, to be fair, not working back home in England wouldn't probably have been so idyllic. This day trip was the type of thing that you can only do in Sydney. The city is full of so many unexpected delights that Kate and I had fallen totally in love with the place.

The love affair started on our very first visit to the country, when we came to look for a house before my job started. We were walking in the Botanical Gardens behind the Opera House when we came across a sign: 'Please do walk on the grass'. I did a double-take and looked closer. Sure enough, the council had erected a sign saying, 'Please do walk on the grass'. Underneath, in smaller letters, the writing continued: 'And talk to the plants and hug the trees. It's your park, it's here for you to enjoy. Have fun.' I was stunned and have never really been the same since.

Barely a week has gone by in the last three years when I haven't had a 'Sydney moment'. Whether it's the outdoor cinemas, the New Year's Eve fireworks, an unexpected view of the Harbour Bridge, the ocean pools, the harbour, the beaches or gay Mardi Gras, the city never ceases to amaze and delight me. I am utterly biased and find it impossible to imagine a nicer, happier city on the entire planet. On their own, the harbour or the surf beaches or Centennial Park would be enough to make a city. Sydneysiders have to put up with having all three. With stunning ocean and harbour coast within 25 kilometres of the Opera House, you can't drive for more than ten minutes without falling across yet another natural wonder. Unlike London, where you feel that unless you win the lottery you'll never get a slice of the action, in Sydney 'ordinary' people really can surf before work or swim at the end of the day.

While I had been working I constantly felt like I was missing out on the best that Sydney had to offer. I resolved to make the most of the city now I had the chance. My birthday gave me another excuse to do just that. I left nothing to chance and planned it myself and, fortunately, it went gorgeously to plan. Kids woke me up with presents (I didn't shout once), then I went for an early morning run along the Bondi to Bronte coast path before having breakfast with my parents. Then Kate and I did the short drive to Lady Bay Beach to do our traditional birthday skinny dip (have I mentioned before Sydney is an incredible place? It even has a nudist beach *in* the city), before lunch with pals at Watsons Bay, looking across at the Bridge and Opera House. This was followed by an afternoon of surfing at Bondi, tea with the kids at home, before then ending the day by going to a film in the Botanical Gardens open air cinema with Kate and my parents. It was *Gangs of New York* – total unmitigated bollocks despite all the fawning reviews. But by that stage of the day I was so happy I didn't care. For me it really was the perfect birthday and it served as a fitting end to my parents' visit, for in the morning they were flying home.

But the next day, while driving back home from the airport having waved Mum and Dad off, I couldn't stop my mind wandering to the darker side of my situation. It had only been a few weeks. Of course I was having a good time *now*. But what about when the initial excitement wore off? With my parents and Charmaine gone we now had no one extra to help with the kids, so there would inevitably be less free time than before. What about when the money started to run out? All my projects and goals were fine and honourable, but losing weight and doing an ocean swim wouldn't pay the bills. I had four young children and neither my wife nor I currently had a job. We had no income whatsoever. The situation, looked at in a coolly rational way, was actually rather serious. I've always taken my family responsibilities seriously. Something needed to be done. I made a decision to do something that was at least proactive – if not entirely what the situation called for. I booked a holiday for myself away from Sydney, the family and, I hoped, my worries.

Chapter 15

Leaded petrol

TASMANIA IS IN MANY ways the perfect place to run away to. If I couldn't escape from my worries buried deep within a World Heritage listed wilderness at the edge of the earth, then where could I? It would be easy to paint the trip as self-indulgent. In fact it was self-indulgent, and enormously inconvenient for Kate. But at the same time it was only a week away and it was precisely what I needed. I was supposed to be embarking on a new, more considered life away from work, but instead the operation and recovery process, my parents' visit, the final details of actually leaving the job, the demands of the kids and coming to grips with the whole new world of being a proper part of running a household, plus my absurdly ambitious swimming goal, meant I was caught up in what seemed like a constant blur of activity and noise.

I hadn't stopped and reflected properly on what I wanted – really wanted. Running around like a headless chook, filling every waking second with activity, was not what I originally had in mind when I was lying on my stomach at Christmas dreaming of a career break. If I carried on the way I was going I might as well have stayed at work.

My first day off work had been a false start. I, or the world, hadn't changed. One day had just run into another, then another. I wanted to make this trip a watershed – the week when I sorted some fundamentals out in my mind so that when I got back home I could make a fresh start and continue the way I meant to go on. I also wanted to get pissed and walk up a few mountains with my good mate Jon.

Jon is one of my friends from college. I've known him for over 20 years. I was an usher at his wedding and he was an usher at mine. I am godfather to one of his gorgeous children and he is godfather to one of mine. By a bizarre coincidence, he had moved to Melbourne a few months after Kate and I had moved to Sydney. Yet another of my problems with the conventional world of work for male executives is it's all too easy to neglect your non-work mates. Between the twin demands of office and family, there just doesn't seem to be the time to keep up any significant relationship with them. For most men this is a real loss. The people I know who have managed to maintain a meaningful connection with friends outside of their work are without exception noticeably happier and more relaxed than those who haven't been able to.

There is a growing body of opinion among certain academics that 'social capital' is as important a measure of genuine success as 'financial capital' and the next big battle for developed economies will be to recognise and adapt to this reality. Irrespective of the truth of this theory, Jon was the friend I did the coast to coast walk with eight years ago, the last time I had a major career change, and now that I was embarking on another one I was delighted he was joining me again.

Apart from the fact that we get on and he is great company, he was also the perfect companion for this particular trip as he was ideally suited for enabling me to confirm my prejudices about the life choice I had made. Jon was in a different industry from the one I'd just left but his role was every bit as high-pressured. Each day I'd goad him about how crap his job was and then smugly listen as he poured out his woes about how out of balance his life was. I'd use these sessions to retrospectively justify my supposedly heroic stance against the machine when in reality Jon's woes were the normal tales of any working man. I was grasping at straws to assuage the guilt of not having immediately jumped back on the hamster wheel as so many of my friends, ex-colleagues and family were urging. The irony of me talking about wanting a more balanced life as I gently strolled around the Apple Isle with no job or family to bother me, having left my wife alone to fend for herself with four young kids, was something I didn't dwell on.

Given my situation, we had set – and agreed to stick to – a tight budget. Air miles had covered my return flight so transport within Tasmania was the next big item to take care of. We hired the cheapest car we could find from the cheapest firm we could find. No offence to Toyota, but I have never before or since been in a worse vehicle than the hundred-year-old Corolla we were presented with at the airport. The

Crapolla, as we affectionately dubbed it, had no wing mirrors, no fifth gear, no central locking, no power steering, no heating and no air-conditioning – basically it was an engine with wheels. And what an engine. Top speed of approximately 90 kilometres an hour, at which the noise was unbearable – a high-pitched whine like a jumbo jet about to take off while stuck in first gear. Conversation was all but impossible above 25 kilometres an hour.

But it was cheap. We worked out on the way to the first petrol station past the airport that, on a daily basis, it was actually less than the cost of a Sydney latte for each of us. This was the fact we constantly mentioned in order to justify our clearly ridiculous decision to hire such an inappropriate car for a holiday that would involve a major drive on all but one of the days.

As I got out of the Crapolla at the petrol station I asked Jon 'Leaded or unleaded?'

'Don't know,' he replied.

I turned and asked the strangely smiling attendant who was approaching us across the forecourt.

'That will be leaded petrol you'll want for that,' he said, nodding at the Crapolla.

'Excellent,' I replied. 'Fill her up with leaded, please.'

'We don't sell leaded petrol.'

'What do you mean you don't sell leaded petrol?'

'No one on the island does – no money in it anymore.'

'But I've just hired a car that only takes leaded petrol.'

'Bet it was cheap,' was his unnecessary retort.

There are in fact some stations that sell leaded petrol on Tasmania, but it did mean we had to take some pretty bizarre routes to get to even the most popular places. Still, the island is so stunningly and consistently beautiful that neither of us minded going on winding routes. After all, it was all good thinking time.

The week was everything I had hoped for and more. On one hand I was sad when it came to an end but on the other I was itching to get back to Kate and the family. It's all well and good running away from your responsibilities every now and then, but, for me anyway, it is not a healthy long-term strategy. I didn't want to be happy by constructing a life *away* from my family; I wanted to be happy with the day-to-day reality of my lot – warts and all. The trip had not only been brilliant in its own right, it had also served to remind me once again how lucky I was to have such a gorgeous brood. I missed them and wanted to get back to properly start my new life with them.

Before I flew home to do so I had a few hours on my own in Hobart – Jon had flown to Melbourne in the morning and my flight to Sydney wasn't until the evening. Aware that I had taken a week off my training for the Bondi to Bronte ocean swim I took the opportunity to visit the Hobart Aquatic Centre. It's incredible to a Londoner that a small city like Hobart has such an amazing facility: huge, clean changing rooms, Olympic-sized pool, separate kiddie pool and play area, pleasant café – the works. I ground out 20 minutes of continuous freestyle and although it half-killed me to do it, and my style was non-existent, I was actually quite pleased with my progress. So pleased, in fact, that I felt it might even be time for me to start doing some of my training in the rough water, as opposed to pools, when I got back to Sydney.

I was also starting to lose weight. The walking and swimming were taking effect. My trousers were sufficiently looser that I had to tighten my belts and my face was notice-ably changing shape. It was becoming less of a face within a face and more of just a face. Still a pudgy one, but not a total porker. I was encouraged and as I tucked into a full English fry-up to reward myself, I took stock.

I hadn't been off work long enough to actually achieve anything but I was in good spirits and keener than ever on the experiment ahead. I had done a lot of thinking – self-indulgent, pompous and pretentious thinking – but thinking none the less. I had started on a number of projects that were important to me – over and above the swimming. I was drawing and writing, I was genuinely starting to bond with my children (when I wasn't going on holidays without them), the surfing was improving in leaps and bounds and I'd even started reading again – a passion that work pressures had long since squashed.

A feeling of enthusiasm and optimism swept over me. I was incredibly lucky. I had so much to be grateful for and so much to look forward to, so much I wanted to do and ex-perience. At that moment I felt so alive I never wanted to waste another second of my life. I wasn't just going to be all right. I was going to be fantastic. A world-beater.

There was only one problem. I was an alcoholic.

Chapter 16

Tomorrow I'll be different

I HAD BEGUN TO suspect I had a drinking problem about 20 years earlier. Ten years later, on 23 January 1993, I decided to do something about it. As is usually the case with me, this meant buying a book. I was living in London at the time and I took the Tube into Covent Garden specifically to buy it on the first day of its release. It was called *Tomorrow I'll be Different* and it was written by a man called Beauchamp Colclough. I'd never heard of him, it was the subtitle – 'The effective way to stop drinking' – that drew me to it. Clutching the book like a guilty secret, I travelled home to our flat in Queens Park (Kate and I hadn't yet been married a year – this was before the onslaught of all our kids). I remember that day as if it were yesterday. I was already two chapters in before I got off the Tube. When I got home, I immediately sat down, carried on reading and didn't get up or pause for anything until I had finished. It was exactly 6 pm. Time for a drink. Except this time (probably the first time in over five years) I didn't get myself a drink. I vowed I wouldn't touch a drop for the next four weeks. I've always been a determined type so I saw the month out. It was, of course, an entirely pointless exercise as within a matter of days I was back to my old ways and on it with a vengeance.

However, my life had permanently changed. Up until that day, I had drunk with considerable enthusiasm and gay abandon every day. From this point on I continued to drink with considerable enthusiasm every day but 'worry' replaced 'gay abandon'. Five years later, Harry was born and I decided to give it another shot. Again I chose to give up for a month (May 1998). Again I succeeded with ease. And again it was utterly pointless as an exercise, proving nothing apart from the already-known fact that I can be single-minded and deter-mined when I want to. Hours after the month was up (after a friend's wedding), I was off my tits, singing 'Flower of Scotland' to a bunch of bemused strangers in an Ipswich pub after closing time.

Four more years, and a lot of beer, later I was in Australia with a high-pressure job and four young kids. My drinking was still at an enthusiastic level. Not 'get uproariously pissed with your mates and hotwire a car' pissed but 'come back from work every night and grimly drink six beers' pissed. I was constantly struggling with my drinking and once again made the monumental (to me anyway) decision to give up for a month – from 11 October 2002.

Again this was precisely what I did. Again I went back on

it afterwards as if nothing had happened. Clearly the month off thing wasn't working. I was still in denial. I was still pretending to myself after ten years of trying and failing, that I could drink in moderation. I would constantly justify my behaviour to myself and others with ludicrous logic: 'Well, I may have said I was only going to have one, but six isn't that many, and it's not like I've got a problem. Of course I shouted at the kids, but anyone would do the same, they were being annoying,' was the type of cock Kate had to listen to every morning as yet again she shouldered the burden of looking after the kids and running the house alone with no help from her husband.

This time my epiphany wasn't long in coming. It came in the form of a rugby match shortly after my return from Tasmania. The Waratahs were playing the Crusaders in the Super 12 tournament. It was *the* match for the Waratahs. Although the Crusaders were runaway favourites, the Waratahs could save their season if they could pull off an against-the-odds victory. Something in me sensed they would do it (like when I knew that England would beat the All Blacks in 1993). To cut a long story short, they did do it, and in famously memorable fashion – a replacement kicker (take a bow, Shaun Berne) striking a beauty from 50 metres out in the last second of extra time to steal it at the death. Amazing, wonderful stuff. None of which is the point. Although it was one of the most dramatic games I have ever been to (and I've been to a lot), it is not the rugby or the result that I remember, but my drinking.

You see, I had made a promise to myself while on a run that morning that I wasn't going to drink that night. Not for a month but just for that night. I was taking my older son, Alex (as I do to every game – Saracens when we're in England, Waratahs when we're in Australia), and I had a slight hangover from dinner the night before, so I had plenty of reasons to stay off it. Besides, I wanted to stay off to prove I could stay off. I needed to show myself that I didn't have to drink.

As I approached the bar in the stadium to buy Alex a Coke and some popcorn, the voice started in my head. *One won't hurt, don't be a killjoy, what's life for if you can't enjoy a beer now and again? You're such a fucking baby, you're no fun anymore, you're so bloody extreme. Why on earth would you choose tonight of all nights not to drink? No one's going to notice, it's not as if anyone else has asked you to not drink, it's just some silly resolution you made while hungover on a run. You've got to learn to be flexible, give yourself a break, you've earned it, start tomorrow, tomorrow you'll be different . . .*

'I'll have one Coke, some popcorn and a couple of beers, please.'

Hold on, I'm only with Alex, why am I buying two? Well I suppose it will save me having to queue at half time. Ten minutes later I heard myself asking, 'Would you like another Coke, sweetheart?'

'No thanks, Dad, I haven't started this one yet.'

'OK, you just wait here, Daddy's going to the loo.'

'I'll have a VB,' I said, on my way back from the loo.

Hold on, I've now had three beers. Enough is enough, Nigel. If you stop now then you haven't got a problem.

'Dad, can I have that Coke now, please?'

'Sure, back in a minute.'

The voice was back again. *There you go, spoiling a great night with all your self-help bollocks. You're having the time of your life, it looks like the Waratahs might actually do it and you're whining* on about having a drink problem. *Your problem is you should relax, give yourself some credit every now and then, you're a good bloke, great dad, it's Saturday night for fuck's sake, have a beer . . .*

'I'll have a Coke and a beer please.'

Berne sent his kick over, the home crowd of 30,000 went wild, I went to the bar for a celebratory beer. *Not because I need to, of course, but it will pass some time to let the carpark empty and Alex wants to see the team do their lap of honour. Did I say 'carpark'? Shit, I drove. Now how much have I had . . . let's see . . . that's five beers . . . but it was spread out over the match so maybe I'm not over the limit. Definitely shouldn't have any more, but then again I did have a big supper . . . be a shame to waste this one now I've bought it.*

Alex and I were in fine form when we got home. Alex wanted to tell Kate all about the game. I thought I might as well have a beer while he was reliving the match. Then Alex was in bed and Kate was asking me to come up. 'In a minute, darling, I just want to check our hotmail,' I said as I thought about the other cold beer I saw in the fridge door. Kate retired to bed; I sank the beer. *What I need to round off the perfect night is a nightcap. Damn, out of beer . . . but there is a bottle of my favourite wine, Pipers Brook Dalrymple Sauvignon Blanc . . . probably shouldn't open it just for one glass . . . oh bugger it – I fancy a glass – I can always put the cork back in.*

Our hotmails are all old. *Should probably go to bed now . . . but then again, seems a shame to leave the last glass in this bottle . . . I wonder if there are any porn emails in the junk folder . . . I could just have a quick look while I finish this bottle . . . Big Dicks in Small Holes . . . what's that about then? It's incredible what people will do for money, all these links are amazing. I probably shouldn't actually go in to this site . . . then again, what*

*harm will it do? Blimey, they really do fuck animals . . . Shit, I'm
out of wine . . . fucking house . . . there's never any booze in . . .
you'd think Kate would make sure there was at least a couple in
the fridge . . . she knows I like a cold beer . . . it's not too much to
ask . . . it's not as if I've got a drink problem . . .*

The next morning I decided that I would stop drinking. Not
give up for a month, or a year. Stop. Never touch another
drop for as long as I lived.

It was a deeply personal decision and because of that I
didn't feel the need to change the externals. I didn't walk
around the house throwing bottles or glasses out. I didn't ask
Kate to stop drinking in front of me. I didn't stop going to
the bottle-o to buy her wine. I didn't even change my social
lifestyle – if people wanted to meet me in a pub, fine. I just
wasn't drinking. A couple of friends mentioned it must have
been a relief that I wasn't working as my previous job had
entailed a lot of entertaining, inevitably involving booze. In
reality this made no difference whatsoever. The *decision* was
the key thing. Once I made my mind up it wouldn't have
mattered if I had been in a teetotal monastery or a German
beer festival. It wasn't harder or easier depending on the situation I was in. *It just was.* It was similar to the weight loss
deal. Once I'd made my mind up to stop eating badly, the
amount of visible temptation became irrelevant. I believed
that if my resolve weakened I wasn't going to be saved by not
having beer or chocolate in the house – I was either going to
stick to my guns or not. In some ways it actually helped
to be exposed to temptation. Call me picky, but to my mind
not drinking because you can't find a drink is hardly sorting

the problem. This most definitely isn't to say it was easy. It wasn't.

The voice didn't go away. But I started to tell it to fuck off rather than attempt to reason with it. I've re-read Colclough's book and feel I have an understanding of my, and I suspect a lot of others', problem. The world can be divided into two camps: those who don't have a drink problem and those who do. For those who don't, Kate for example, I heartily recommend they drink as often and as much as they like. I want them to enjoy it. Not just when I'm not around but even in front of me – in fact, especially in front of me. I have no problem with others drinking, I have a problem with me drinking, because it's not about amounts or frequency, it's about your mental relationship with alcohol.

There was a simple question in Colclough's book that got to the heart of this. He asked the reader to imagine a simple scenario: your best male friend is introduced by you to your best female friend. They get on famously. You really want them to be a couple. They become a couple. You couldn't be happier. They couldn't be happier. You really hope they get engaged. They get engaged. You couldn't be happier. They couldn't be happier. They set a date and invite you to the wedding. At the bottom of the invitation it mentions that it will be a dry wedding. The question is, what would your immediate mental reaction to the invitation be? Be honest with yourself, you need never tell anyone the answer. If, as it was for me, it's 'oh fucking hell, I don't want to go to Alan and Mary's bloody wedding,' I humbly suggest you seek help (there are some contact details at the back of this book).

I didn't want to tell people about my decision – I just wanted to do it. I had obviously confided in Kate, who was amazing about it. For some bizarre reason, I thought she would be angry or dismissive. In reality she was gentle, understanding and supportive – on top of being absolutely delighted. Despite wanting to keep it quiet until I had some success under my belt, I was determined to take all the advice and help available rather than simply butch it out on my own with willpower, like I usually did with major challenges. Rather than seeking help from friends who knew nothing about the issue, I sought the counsel of strangers who were experts.

My first trip to Alcoholics Anonymous helped me enormously. I was reluctant, and not a little embarrassed, to go. But immediately upon arriving I felt a huge sense of belonging. Apparently, I was a yeti, basically meaning I was one of the rare problem drinkers who was yet to totally fuck up his life, but who had recognised his problem and given up. Normally, alcoholics have to be 'beaten teachable' as the first speaker explained it. It's a double-edged sword, being a yeti. On the one hand it means you possess a certain level of self-awareness and have an iron will. On the other, there is the ever-present danger that you will fall – and when yetis fall, they fall far further than the place they were at before they stopped drinking. For the first time since I had bought Colclough's book ten years earlier, I was meeting people who genuinely understood what I was going through and not only wanted to help, but had the life experience to offer useful advice. It made me doubly determined never to pick up a drink again.

In fact, the whole AA experience was a revelation. I found it had benefit and relevance far beyond the narrow confines of the specific issue of drink. Although I am not a regular attendee, I find the meetings I have gone to as spiritually rewarding as any religious service I have attended. They seem to me to be one of the few occasions in modern life where people – especially men – are open, honest and caring with each other, with all the bullshit stripped away. I have to confess to feeling slightly ashamed of the ignorant pisstaking I used to do of AA in my drinking days. But then again, as my Dad always says, 'there is none so virtuous as a reformed whore' and I don't want to go and completely lose my sense of humour. Suffice to say it worked for me. So far.

Chapter 17

Pingu

BY THE END OF MARCH the office was becoming a distant memory. My parents had left the country. Tasmania, medical problems, drink and eight kilograms of excess weight were behind me. I was swimming up to 20 minutes of continuous freestyle (in a pool, I'd still not started training in the open ocean). I was more committed than ever to the ideal of using this, my fortieth year, in a special and life-changing way. However, a surprising discovery was nagging away at the back of my mind – I was yet to get into a routine. Since my last day in the office I've never been busier. Many friends told me after a couple of weeks I'd be going out of my mind with boredom, and having never taken time off before I had no idea whether they were right or not. Well, they couldn't have been more wrong. I would have loved the chance to get bored. The idea of waking up and thinking, 'Oh bloody hell, what am I going to do with the next 12 hours?' was yet to become a reality. In fact the last time I could remember that feeling was during the long summer holidays when I was at home from prep school and the only thing on the telly was horse racing (thank Christ for masturbation).

So now that my parents were gone and my holiday was over, Kate and I sat down to discuss how best to organise our regular, day-to-day family routine. Now, I like to believe Kate and I aren't pushy parents. We never set out to do more or 'hothouse' our kids' development. We just wanted to do the basics that were expected of a normal family that was part of the local scene. Despite this attitude, there seemed to me to be an enormous number of fixed events around which we had to plan. On both Monday and Tuesday the boys went to school and the girls went to kindy. On Wednesday, Alex had band practice in the morning before school, Grace and Eve had swimming at midday, Harry had football after school and Alex had cricket (in a different location). On Thursday, the girls had Kindi Gym in the mornings and Kate had Pilates in the afternoon. On Friday, Alex had rugby league after school. Saturday mornings were match day (cricket) for Alex; Saturday lunchtime was swimming for the boys. Sunday morning both the boys had Little Nippers at the beach and there was touch footy in the afternoon.

And that wasn't the half of it. It was the preparation for these activities which would test the patience of a saint. To go to school they had to have clean uniforms and a packed lunch. To go swimming they had to have dry towels and costumes, to play rugby the sodding mouthguard needed to be found, being in the school band meant having to practise the saxophone at home (when?). That's not to mention the homework they needed to be cajoled into doing, the two washing loads that had to be put on every day, dried, then folded away, the shopping that needed to be done and the meals that had to be cooked. Oh, and the twins were growing like weeds so needed new clothes and shoes constantly.

It was all a little daunting. How on earth does anyone find time to have a job, I found myself thinking. When the hell was I going to write, or train for the ocean swim or have a social life or surf?

A few weeks into my new life, I discovered that I was utterly shagged. Completely drained in a way that work never affected me. Work pressure usually energised me; the relentless domestic grind simply took my lifeforce, crushed it and spat it out. At 5 pm, just when my energy levels were at their lowest, the 'teatime, bathtime, homework, bedtime' quadruple whammy would kick in. By 7.30, when most of them were in bed, I'd sometimes need to physically lie down. Nothing a good night's sleep wouldn't go a long way to sorting, I initially thought, but with four kids under nine, the actual number of nights when none of them woke up, or needed a nappy change or were ill, was currently running at 1:4. I was so frustrated I actually worked it out.

I say this not to be a bleeding-heart, liberal, new-age SNAG, but because it's true: most men who have a traditional office career haven't a clue how hard their partners work. I know I certainly didn't. A self-help author I know maintains he always says to any man who comes to him with his 'I'm going to take a year off to be with the family' story, 'Come back in six months when the novelty has worn off and then we'll talk.' I was beginning to see his point. Childrearing is not *easier* than office work, it is simply *different* from office work.

Any notion that not having to put on a suit and go to work would mean I was going to have time on my hands was by now completely dispelled. It was a hand-to-hand fight to cut out the space to do anything other than wipe arses or read *Pingu*.

Not that I was complaining. This situation was precisely what I had wanted. If I hadn't taken this year off I would have more than likely worked through continuously until after the kids had left home and never actually experienced the family at this feral level. It scared me that so much life had been going on around me that I wasn't even a bit player in – I was simply unconnected to it. This year was giving me a chance, that most men never get, to throw myself at a different lifestyle. I wanted to immerse myself in it, warts and all. Not just to see how I would cope and what I would learn, but also to grow as a person and be more present in the family I had chosen to be a part of. These self-indulgent musings led me to volunteer for even more trouble. On top of the school canteen roster I put myself down to take a reading group on Thursdays. A small step in the life of Bronte Primary School, but a huge leap forward for Nigel Marsh.

Chapter 18

Accidental encrustations

AT THE SAME TIME as all this 'new man' malarky was occurring, I was also getting back in touch with another side of my life – religion. Now, before you put the book down or skip this chapter, please let me briefly explain. This wasn't a new affectation. It was simply a side of my life I had recently let slip. Religion is a subject I have always been fascinated by. So much so that not only did I choose to do an A level in it, I actually spent three years studying it at university. This led to some interesting job interviews – a degree in Theology and an ability to read the Bible in Greek not being top of the list of most companies' criteria for their graduate intake. I like to think this goes some way to explaining why I spent the first month after I moved to London sleeping in the back of a car.

Then again, the drink might also have had something to do with it. But religion just seems too important to ignore. Enough people have gone on about it for long enough for it to warrant at least some investigation. Besides, if any of it is true, then it's far too important to leave to the 'experts' (at the time of writing it seems that I can't open a newspaper without reading about yet another clergyman up for child abuse or some such).

Put simply – what's the point? Or less simply – are we the centrepiece of creation or are we merely accidental encrustations on a tiny planet, helplessly hurtling around within an enormous meaningless universe? I don't want to get too heavy here, but it seems a shame if life's all just about upgrading your car to the latest model or paying off your mortgage.

The perplexing riddle of the purpose of life is perfectly encapsulated by the contrast of two of my favourite quotes.

The first is by the remarkable George Bernard Shaw: 'The true joy in life is being used for a purpose recognised by yourself as a mighty one, that being a force of nature instead of a feverish little clod of ailments and grievances complaining that the world will not devote itself to making you happy. I am of the opinion that my life belongs to the community, and as long as I live it is my privilege to do for it whatever I can. I want to be thoroughly used up when I die, for the harder I work the more I live. I rejoice in life for its own sake. Life is no brief candle to me. It is a sort of splendid torch which I have got hold of for the moment and I want to make it burn as brightly as possible before handing it on to future generations.'

Danny DeVito, in his role as Larry the Liquidator in the film *Other People's Money*, was slightly more succinct: 'The person with the most money when he dies, wins.'

My vote goes with Bernard. But unlike people of genuine unshakable faith, I don't 'know' what my purpose is. It has always irritated me that I can't simply sign up to a religion and be done with it. The internal questions don't go away. I've never been able to pretend to believe in order to access the nice comfortable bits of a tradition. I'm fine with 'love thy neighbour' but can't for the life of me believe in the virgin birth or water into wine. I deeply admire some Buddhist traditions but can't get my head around reincarnation. Come to think of it, the whole God thing is a bit of a stretch for me as well.

The problem isn't so much God himself, but the people who talk about Him. They always seem to want to claim that they, and they alone, have the answer and everyone else is wrong. It seems self-evident to me that if you were born in Bombay you are unlikely to be a Welsh Methodist and if you were born in Upper Tumble it is similarly unlikely you'll be Greek Orthodox. It seems obvious that location and era have a huge part to play in one's belief patterns. My natural suspicions regarding anyone or any church claiming an absolute monopoly on the truth, combined with my desire to understand the point of life, left me no alternative but to study it for myself. I haven't yet found the answer but I have got the solution to those Jehovah's Witnesses who come to your door at the most inconvenient moments – just fetch a copy of the Bible in the original Greek and they run a mile.

My search for a religious tradition I could honestly align myself to bore fruit about eight years ago while in conversation with a couple we met on holiday. She was from an orthodox Jewish family; he was a Quaker. Over a drunken dinner he recounted the tale of their wedding. Apparently his family had 'won' and it was therefore a Quaker ceremony, not a Jewish one. Now most people, including me at the time, wouldn't know anything about Quakers apart maybe from a vague awareness that they make oatmeal. He had to explain their method of worship to get the full flavour of the occasion across. I wasn't sure if he was exaggerating or not but he claimed that all Quakers did in church was sit in a circle and say nothing for an hour. No sermons, no prayers, no hymns – nothing. In fact, no church, even. Quakers call it 'meeting' and insist it is always held in a plain room or hall with absolutely no finery. He painted a wonderfully funny scene of one half of the congregation, his wife's family, waiting eagerly for the wedding to start and being perplexed and then horrified when before they'd even noticed anything had happened it was all over and people started filing out of the hall.

I don't know whether it was the drink or the way he told it but I laughed so hard my jaw ached. Beyond the humour, though, my interest had been aroused. Surely Quakers didn't actually sit around in a circle doing nothing? I was so intrigued that I made a promise to myself that when I got back to London I would find out more about them. Eight years later and I'm still attending Quaker meetings.

The Quakers have no desire whatsoever to prove they are right and others are wrong. They simply state that it is their belief that 'there is a little bit of God in everyone and therefore everyone is equally worthy of respect and love.' People who properly sign up are called Friends; those who just go to meetings are called Attendees. I think of myself more as a Pretender than an Attender. I've still got too many unresolved questions. However, I find their way of being and thinking has enormous value. The people I've met through the

Quakers almost invariably seem to live up to the aspiration of George Fox, one of the founders of the tradition when he said (350 years ago), 'True Godliness does not turn men out of the world but enables them to live better in it and excite their endeavours to mend it.'

Quakers actually *do* something about their beliefs. Wherever I've attended meetings there has always been some announcement or other at the end where details of a demonstration against some social injustice are given or volunteers are asked to staff the soup van for the homeless. This, combined with their philosophy that 'a simple lifestyle freely chosen is a source of strength', made them, in my eyes, a remarkable group of people. If the truth be known, they humbled me. Despite the fact that my lifestyle was neither freely chosen nor simple, I found them such a welcome change from the other churches I had experienced that I resolved to keep 'Pretending' until I discovered something better.

Anyway, I'm not sure whether it was the sobriety or the religion, but as I got further and further away from my office-slave routine I was starting to gain glimpses of how a family could exist happily as one. The school run ceased to be hell. The relentless grind got steadily less exhausting. I even started to look forward to bits of it – five in a bath doesn't get you very clean but it's a shedload of fun if you're not on a deadline and you don't mind water up the walls. When I was working, Kate often used to talk long into the night about me putting in so many hours and her worry that I was turning into a largely absent father. And while that was a completely legitimate concern, to my mind it goes beyond simple time spent with the kids – if you spend so long away from them and so long at work it can actually corrupt your emotional radar. American author Arlie Russell Hochschild argues that 'owing to the religion of capitalism and the emotional draw of a work culture, what many professionals find is it's easier to love work.' She quotes a nursery school director to chilling effect: 'This may be odd to say but the teacher's aides we hire from Mexico and Guatemala know how to love a child better than the middle-class parents. They are more relaxed, patient and joyful. They enjoy the kids more.' I truly believe this time off work was mending my emotional radar. Work had been turning into my major source of security and engagement. It had got to the stage where I'd put more love and care into reviewing a business presentation than I would into reading my own sons' school reports. Now it was my family who were providing the joy and intensity.

Chapter 19

Knock knock

OF COURSE THE CHANGES I was going through affected Kate as much as me. Luckily, Kate said she was delighted with the change. To have me fully engaged with the kids was a joy not just for them but also for her. We'd been married for ten years and through that time had gone through a number of life stages together, spanning the spectrum all the way from 'young, double-income, no-kids couple' to 'four-kids, no-income, middle-aged marrieds'.

Throughout these ten years the one thing that never changed was my unshakable belief that marrying Kate was the best thing I had ever done, indeed will ever do. Kate, you see, is the kindest, strongest, most intelligent and beautiful woman that ever strode this planet. Her sisters call her

'Perfect Katie' – praise indeed from the biggest bunch of overachievers you're ever likely to meet. People consistently express amazement that she is with me. My dad's speech at our wedding started with the words, 'Nigel, I don't know what you've done to deserve her, she's far too good for you. Treat her badly and she'll leave you.' Um, thanks, Dad.

Kate also used to work in advertising, and she was far better at my job than me until I got her pregnant three times and forced her from the workplace. She's a far better parent than me and now here I was encroaching on her space again. And this time, as with the last, she was being loving and supportive every step of the way.

I don't like talking about it as it makes me sound like a Bible-Belt fundamentalist, but for me our marriage *is* my life. But it hasn't always been perfect. We have had what you could refer to as a couple of rocky episodes. The first was in the very early days of our courting. I was smashed in the company bar, larking around with the boys from the media department after a long day's work, when Kate appeared and joined our group. Ignoring her, I proceeded to tell a joke.

'Knock knock,' I started.

'Who's there?' the group replied.

'Kate.'

'Kate who?' they asked in unison.

'That's casual sex for you,' I replied.

Charming.

It took us a while to get over that one, but when we had I couldn't help but press the self-destruct button again. We were in Florida on holiday when I spied a bungee-jumping site. This was so long ago that bungee jumping was still a very new phenomenon. This venue was on the roadside with a big, hand-painted sign saying 'Gatorjump'. Essentially, someone had filled a small pond with writhing, hungry alligators and placed a large industrial crane beside it. For $200 you could buy the pleasure of jumping off the top of the crane and hurtling – almost – into the pond. I was hooked and immediately knew I was going to do it. Kate, on the other hand, was equally certain that she wasn't going to. No problem – if I'd left it there, but for some inexplicable reason I felt the need to persuade her to join me. To prove it wasn't fatal, I went first.

'Kate, it's brilliant, you've got to do it,' I enthused when I got my breath back.

'Sweetheart, I really don't want to do it. I hate heights and, unlike you, it's not another goal I want to tick "achieved".'

'Come on, darling, you'll love it.'

'No I won't, I'll hate it.'

This mindless argument went on for about half an hour until, unfortunately, I successfully wore her down. Shaking and white, Kate was strapped into the cage and lifted to the top of the crane. Eleven storeys up on a small metal platform above a pit full of alligators and a crowd of cheering onlookers is a pretty intimidating place to be, even if you wanted to do it in the first place. I had been terrified. Kate, however, was frozen. The instructor evidently knew exactly how to deal with such a situation

'Don't worry,' he reassured her. 'You needn't go face-first like your boyfriend. You needn't go at all. Just turn around and face me. Hold my hands and lean back. Get the feel of it. If you are comfortable with this you can then do it backwards. If not, I'll take you down in the basket.'

Kate, trusting soul that she is, moved to the edge and did

as he asked. But then, rather than ask her how she felt, he simply let go. It's a moment I've long since tried and failed to forget. Kate screamed and desperately tried to grab the edge of the platform. The Californian hippie next to me yelled, 'Fly! Fly like a bird!'

I was silent until the bouncing of the rope stopped and the crane lowered Kate onto the mattress beside the Gatorpond. To my profound relief, Kate was laughing.

'Look,' I shouted to the crowd who had witnessed my moment of heartless cruelty in forcing her up there in the first place. 'She loved it, she's laughing.'

I rushed over to help unclip Kate from the harness. Her whole body was shaking as she emitted sobs – not of laughter, but of abject terror and misery. She was hysterical.

As courting went, I clearly had a bit to learn.

Chapter 20

Single

I LIKE TO THINK I've improved my act a little over the decade or so since that particular incident. Either way, I was loving the time off work not simply because I was learning to enjoy the kids, but also because it gave me the opportunity to spend proper time with my best friend, lover and partner. And this time I was determined not to balls it up. In fact, more than not ballsing it up I actually wanted to do something special. The perfect opportunity was staring me in the face. By a bizarre coincidence, my good mate Giles was getting married in France in April, precisely a week before Kate's youngest sister, Jane, was getting married in Italy. Giles had asked me to be his best man and Jane had asked Kate to be her maid of honour. Normally if I had been working these would have been just the types of occasions we wouldn't have been able to attend together – if at all. At best we would have taken it in turns to stay behind in Australia to look after the kids while the other one flew in and out in a mad dash.

In this instance, however, I had a cunning plan. I booked a table at our favourite spot for dinner to do the sales pitch. I got the usual sinking feeling as the menus arrived. But a remarkable thing happened. As expected, Kate agonised over her choice of food. What was unexpected was my reaction – I didn't get irritated and therefore we didn't get into an argument. This was an entirely new but welcome way for us to start an evening out. Kate was on sparkling form, I was chilled, and we were getting on better than ever.

'Look over there, Nigel,' Kate said.

'Where?' I replied.

'The table on your left by the window. The blonde,' Kate challenged me.

'What about her?' I queried.

'She's obviously single.'

'No she's not, she's with her partner,' I said.

'They're not together,' Kate replied.

'What are you talking about? They are holding hands,' I pointed out.

'Doesn't matter. I know they aren't married,' Kate insisted.

'You're talking rubbish. Besides, you've never met them,' I countered.

'Don't need to – I can always tell.'

'Okay, clever clogs, you've got me. How can you tell?'

'Simple, she's at pains to look interested – really interested – when he's talking.'

'That's it?'

'Yep.'

'Is it that obvious?'

'Always. Women never give their *husbands* that type of attention.'

'Blimey, that's so depressing.'

'Harsh but fair, sweetheart, harsh but fair.'

'Well, I need you to pretend to be interested in what I'm about to say.'

'Can't promise. I've heard it all before.'

'Not this, you ungrateful cow. I think we should go to the weddings. Both of them. Together. '

'Love to. Two slight problems, however: we can't afford it and we've got no one to look after the children.'

'Wrong on both counts. I've called British Airways and we can get to London and back on the last of my airmiles. And Liz and May will look after the kids,' I proudly announced. I had it all worked out.

'Liz lives in Scotland, you dufus. Who the hell is May?' Kate asked.

'May is Liz's sister. They have been planning a trip to Australia for over ten years. They've agreed to time their holiday over our trip and take the kids to school and baby-sit in return for use of the house and car. It's the perfect arrangement.'

Liz was one of the first nannies we'd had in London. Kate and I adored her, and, more importantly, so did the kids.

Kate looked genuinely stunned. She was silent for what felt like an age before announcing, 'Nigel, you've excelled yourself – anyone looking at me now would think I was single.'

I spent the rest of the evening filling her in on the details. Not only would we leave the kids behind, we would make an extra adventure of it by driving, rather than flying, across France and Italy between the ceremonies. We had the time we may never get again. This was going to be our first trip back to the Northern Hemisphere since our move to Australia. We both resolved to make it a second honeymoon.

Rather than getting upset at being left behind, the kids were ecstatic when we told them our plan. Liz had become part of the family and it had been a real wrench for Alex, Harry, Grace and Eve when they had to say goodbye to her at Heathrow. Truth is, they weren't bothered about missing us as they were far too excited at the prospect of seeing and spending time with Liz again.

In fact, if anyone was worried about the trip, it was me. Was I just running away from my responsibilities again like I had with the Tasmania holiday? How would I keep up with my training for the ocean race? How would three weeks away from the kids affect my newly formed closer relationship with them? And perhaps most worrying of all, how the fuck was I going to get through two wedding ceremonies sober? Then again I wasn't *that* worried.

Three weeks later, as we got into the taxi to the airport at the start of our trip, I couldn't help but ponder the upsides of being put out of work. Clearly this lifestyle wasn't sustainable for the long term but in the short term it sure as hell beat the crap out of going to the office.

Chapter 21

BA?

As we were flying on airmiles, we were, of course, seated next to the lavatories at the very back of the plane. Kate was in heaven. I'd never seen her look so relaxed. To just sit down and be left alone without a child tugging or whining at her had sent her into a serene state of bliss. 'We must do this more often,' she dreamily said to me as the plane taxied along the runway before takeoff.

I, however, was in shock. In my previous life, I'd been lucky enough to do a lot of longhaul travel – all of it at the front of the plane. I've never understood the people who whinge about business travel. In my experience, it's simply fantastic. All you could possibly want to eat and drink, sleeper beds, films on demand from an enormous library and, perhaps most seductive, an army of pleasant staff paid to make you feel like you are very special, and deserve to be treated like an overgrown baby who obviously couldn't be expected to get up to do anything and must have his every wish anticipated and fulfilled for the entire duration of the journey. 'Would you like cheese and port after the meal, Mr Marsh, or shall I simply pull the fluff out of your belly button with my tongue while you're enjoying the film?' was the type of hostess attention I had come to expect. I'd been on this plane for at least half an hour and I hadn't even seen a flight attendant, let alone been offered a massage by one. Quite apart from that, the seat was breathtakingly small. I was so tightly wedged in that I had to struggle to move my arm to press the recline button. The response when I did so made me give an involuntary snort.

'What's wrong, sweetheart?' Kate inquired.

'Not only is my seat clearly designed for a midget, it's chuffing well broken as well,' I informed her.

'Don't worry, just speak to the attendant.'

'I don't think there are any attendants.'

'Don't be silly, there are lots of them up there, I'll call one.' I hadn't realised that the gruff, scruffy bloke who had been taking the piss with his gruff, scruffy mate during the safety video was the crew for this part of the plane.

'Yeah?' he enquired as he reached the very back of the plane where we were wedged.

'Oh yes, hi – sorry to bother you, but my seat is broken. When I press the recline button it simply hiccups back an inch or so.' I told him.

'Are you trying to be funny?'

'No,' I said, with a sinking feeling that I hadn't felt since

I was a young man and had been given my own number by directory enquiries. (I'd just answered the questions they'd asked me. Name? Address? It was only when they said 'the number is . . .' and spelt out the home number I was calling from, that I realised they didn't mean *my* name and address. Anyway, I digress.) As he returned to his mate in the galley, I thought I heard him muttering something about an anchor or banker. Whatever else the flight was, it was obviously also going to be 'an opportunity for personal growth', as the Americans say.

But my physical discomfort was soon forgotten. One of my all-time favourite experiences is the view from any plane that is either taking off or landing at Sydney. It actually would be impossible to oversell it. Sydney airport is in Botany Bay. Literally in it. The two runways jut into the water so you have the impression of landing or taxiing on the sea. In its way I find it far more impressive than the old Hong Kong airport experience that every seasoned business traveller talks about. But that's not the best part. After the plane has taken off it is impossible not to get a picture postcard view, whichever way the plane is flying. On this occasion we took off facing inland and the heart of the city. Within a couple of minutes we were over the harbour, the bridge and the Opera House. Because of the proximity of the airport to the centre of the city, you are always at the perfect height at precisely the right time. At the height we had gained by then we could see the entire harbour, both Heads and the northern beaches all the way to Palm Beach. We were high enough to get a majestic sense of scale and perspective but low enough to pick out almost every detail. Individual cars, surfers, boats – all were clearly identifiable. The plane then banked sharply to start the long

180-degree turn to get it facing towards London. This process affords the best view of all, involving a coastline tour of the eastern suburbs' beaches, near where Kate and I live. The plane does a gentle arc that takes you from Bondi Beach all the way past Tamarama, then Bronte (was I really going to be able to swim that far?), Clovelly, Coogee and Maroubra, before retracing its path back over Botany Bay. There is a communication tower in Bondi that has an almost religious significance for me. It's sort of my own private Eiffel Tower or Bow Bells. If I can see it, I feel I'm 'home'. This, along with our house, the boys' school, the girls' kindy and all the various sports fields they play at had all been clearly visible for over ten minutes. As they slowly receded into the distance as we climbed to our cruising height above yet another breathtaking sight (the national park below Botany), I found myself matching Kate for serenity.

Chapter 22

35 pounds

THE FLIGHT TO THE UK is one of the longest you can do on this planet – and on airmiles it feels it. It takes hours to even leave the Australian land mass. When Kate's mum first came out to visit, the pilot announced, 'We are now crossing the Australian coastline' as the plane flew over Darwin. She put her coat on and got her passport ready. Five hours later, they touched down in Sydney. I remember when we first came out my kids refused to believe when we did the stopover that Hong Kong wasn't Australia. 'How can it be possible to have flown for so long and not be where you are going?' my older son reasonably asked. It *is* slightly perverse; you do one long-haul flight, get off for an hour and then do another.

This time the stopover itself provided more than the usual

interest as it was the height of the SARS epidemic. As Kate and I strolled around Hong Kong airport, we casually wondered if it was totally sensible being the only people who weren't wearing face masks. My slightly woolly theory was that it had all been over-hyped by the media and that if everyone else was wearing masks then by definition we needn't bother. Kate thought this would be of little comfort to the poor unfortunates who would have to look after our four young children if we were to cark it, but before the argument could really get nasty we were back on the plane for the long leg to London.

I don't really want to relive the flight – once was too much. Boring sustained discomfort probably best sums it up. All capped off nicely by the descent to Heathrow. A more depressing approach I cannot imagine. Miles upon miles of featureless urban sprawl. The flights from Sydney all arrive very early in the morning and the grey dawn light does London no favours. You're always tired by this stage and the vista does nothing to lighten the mood. I'd lived in London for all of my adult life and had wondered what feelings returning would evoke. At this stage I thought it best to put my current emotions down to jetlag and homesickness for the sun and surf of Sydney.

Matters weren't helped by the fact that when we got to the hotel I opened my bag and I discovered everything in it had been soaked through with dirty brown water. Although we were on a three-week trip, I only had one set of smart clothes with me, and I needed to wear them that evening when we were meeting Kate's sister's fiancé and family for the first time at a swanky dinner, given partly in our honour. There was no chance I could get my suit and shirt cleaned in time. Even if

I did, I suspected they would still be stained brown and look ridiculous. There was nothing for it – I decided to call British Airways.

Now, I've never had a problem with BA. They've always done what I think is a good job in a difficult industry. Besides, I was a platinum cardholder with a truckload of airmiles, so I usually got treated with an element of respect. I called the number on the back of my Frequent Flyer card and explained my story and circumstances. They listened politely until I had finished and then told me I needed to speak to Customer Services. They couldn't put me through. I called Customer Services and again explained my story and circumstances. They too listened politely, waited until I had finished and then told me I needed to talk to Baggage Claims at Terminal 4 in Heathrow. Again, they couldn't put me through. The jetlag was starting to set in and this process was beginning to piss me off. I called Baggage Claims at Terminal 4 and explained my story and circumstances. They also listened politely. However, this time when I finished they said, 'How awful, Mr Marsh. You're a valued customer. You quite clearly need to buy a new set of clothes for tonight. Take down this reference number and quote it when you send us the receipts for a full refund of your purchases.' Now this is more like it, I thought.

'Kate,' I yelled, 'I'm going shopping. You get some kip. BA has come up trumps. I needed a new suit anyway. Cheers.'

I've never liked shopping, but when someone else is paying it tends to give proceedings a certain extra injection of fun. I shop fast and within two hours I was the proud owner of an entire head to toe ensemble. I was particularly proud of the Todds' shoes, and felt however posh this new set of in-laws were, I would be more than well enough dressed for the occasion.

I called BA back. 'Hi, it's Mr Marsh again. I've purchased my clothes and have all the receipts and a reference number. Where do I send them, please?'

The nice man told me the address and then added, 'As a matter of interest, Mr Marsh, how much did you spend in total?'

'Let me see, that would be . . . 870 pounds and 50 pence.'

'870 pounds?'

'870 pounds and 50 pence, yes.'

'Mr Marsh, there's a 35-pound limit.'

'Limit on what?'

'Limit on refunds for ruined clothes.'

'You've got to be kidding! What type of clothes do you think I could get for 35 quid and why the fuck are you telling me this now, you arsing moron . . .' I'm not proud of the rest so will spare you the details, bar saying that waking Kate up with a cup of tea didn't really cut it when it came to telling her I'd blown three-quarters of the holiday budget before we'd even spent one night away.

Chapter 23

Gloves

WE DECIDED TO GO our separate ways until the function that evening. Not just because Kate was angry with me for wasting all our money and didn't really want to be in the same room as me for a while – she wanted to spend some time with her elder sister, Sarah. This suited my purposes as I had a swimming routine to keep up. I knew I would be busy catching up with old friends and family over the next three weeks and that there would be a lot of eating, drinking and party-going involved, but I didn't want the socialising to get in the way of my training.

Swimming in London doesn't exactly compare to the ocean pools of Sydney. As a matter of fact, it doesn't even come close to the municipal pool experience of Hobart. The council pool in Crouch End I ended up in made the Hakoah Club look like the Homebush Olympic pool. Having said that, I had an excellent swimming session. Just before we left Sydney I had bought a book in an attempt to help me improve my technique in the water. I never knew there was so much skill involved in swimming well. I just thought it was a matter of strength, will to win and getting fit. The book was a revelation. Technique was everything. Apparently all the Olympic swimming winners since records began had taken fewer strokes than their opponents in their races. I had to read it twice. Fewer strokes. I would have sworn blind the opposite would have had to have been the case. But there it was in black and white. Fewer strokes. It was all about efficiency of stroke, economy of energy expended and minimum of resistance to the water.

Just as David's advice about slowing down had radically improved my endurance, the book was transforming my technique. I started to try to 'swim downhill', chin on my chest, leading with the top of my skull, not my forehead. I no longer splashed my arms into the water but instead imagined I was threading my hand into the sleeve of a suit jacket being held in front of me on each stroke. (Given my experience earlier that day I tried not to think how much that suit jacket had cost while I was doing this.) I wouldn't claim I was pretty to watch, but the improvement was extremely satisfying.

I got back to our hotel in high spirits. Kate was also in fine form, having had an excellent, if jetlagged, day shopping with her sister. I didn't feel it was my place to point out the lack of logic in reacting to losing lots of money by spending even more. As I've already admitted, I don't really understand women – and anyway I was just happy that she appeared to have forgiven me. I thought of it as a sort of absolution by credit card. Suffice to say, we had now both recovered from the experience of BA9 and were enormously looking forward to our evening out with Kate's family and soon-to-be-in-laws.

I've always had a fond spot for Jane, Kate's youngest sister. And indeed the whole Turner (Kate's maiden name) family. Jane was the last of the sisters to get married, Kate was to be matron of honour and I was to make a speech at the wedding. All very exciting, but as we'd moved to Australia two years before, we had never even met her intended, Max, or his family. Tonight was the night. Kate looked stunning in a dress that thankfully hadn't been packed in the bag that some baggage handler had left sitting in a puddle at Hong Kong airport. I also thought I looked great – it would be difficult not to given the amount of dough I'd unwittingly thrown at my wardrobe for the occasion.

As luck would have it, Max and his folks were, and are, delightful. Jane looked the picture of happiness and, best of all, Kate immediately hit it off with Max. The setting was divine and it is here that I need to add a bit of background colour. We were having dinner in Max's parents' polo club. Not the polo club where they play (although they do that as well) but the polo club they *own*. You see, it would be fair to say that they aren't short of a penny.

'Blimey, she's done well,' I said as we arrived and took in the gorgeous surroundings.

'Oilwell, more like,' Kate replied.

The sisters are a competitive bunch. They would all deny it but they each have a deep latent need to prove themselves to each other and to their parents. I couldn't help feeling sorry for Kate as I was clearly a bit of a disaster in the 'validation through your partner' stakes. Her other two sisters, Sarah and Claudia, had also both married hugely successful and nice men. It was Kate's lot in life to have few bragging rights in the husband department. I somehow thought 'Nigel has given up drinking and can now do bilateral breathing' might not cut it amongst tonight's crowd – or indeed with her mother.

Beyond crippling envy, however, I've never had a problem with the super-rich. In my – admittedly limited – experience, they've always been humble, thoughtful and generous. It's the averagely-rich who are the nightmares. But then you'd expect me to say that given I've some new super-rich in-laws to suck up to.

The hospitality was expertly thought through and delivered. They'd clearly done this sort of thing before – nothing over the top or too intrusive, just a number of perfect touches to create the right ambience. Both sides of the family appeared to like each other. The wine was going down quickly (down everyone but me, of course) and before long the room had that wonderful noisy hubbub to it which signifies a crowd of happy people in a shared mood of energised gregariousness. Sort of like a Quaker meeting in reverse. Everyone talking – rather than listening – at the same time, leading to a heightened group mood. Only peals of laughter and screams of welcome occasionally broke the loud background hum of good-natured banter. When the time came for food it took an age to get everyone seated.

The meal was in keeping with the rest of the evening – elegantly understated but somehow just exactly how you would have wanted it. After the main course a glass was tapped and the place fell silent as Jane and Max stood to say a few words. Max went first. He spoke movingly about his parents and other family members, giving each a present in turn. When he finished, Jane took over the proceedings. She began by thanking each of her sisters. I couldn't see the presents that Sarah and Claudia got but from the look on Kate's face the sparkling thing in the little blue Tiffany box she'd been handed met with her approval.

Jane however had clearly saved the best for last. She made a delightful speech about her Mum, Mary, at the end of which she handed her a small envelope. Mary opened it to find a return ticket on the Orient Express, a trip she had harboured a life-long ambition to make. She followed this show stopper up with another touching speech, this time for her Dad, John. Again a small envelope was given. John opened it to discover the keys to a classic white Porsche which was parked outside. It was the very car he had always dreamed of driving – now he actually owned one. I was oohhing and aahhing with the rest of the guests when to my astonishment yet another speech was started.

I couldn't believe it. This time I was the subject in question. Jane was clearly touched that I had made the effort to fly all the way from the Southern Hemisphere for their wedding. I could only imagine how they were going to show their appreciation. My luck had clearly changed. Perhaps it wasn't so stupid to have bought those clothes after all. The talking stopped and I was handed a small package. My hands were actually trembling as I opened the parcel. I pulled away the tissue to see . . . running gloves. A pair of black cotton Nike running gloves, available in all good sports stores at 25 dollars a pop.

I frantically looked inside each of the fingers for a lottery ticket or a set of car keys or a diamond – anything to elevate my gift to previous just-seen levels. My search was in vain. The gloves didn't come with any hidden extras. I don't want you to think I'm ungrateful, they are nice gloves. In fact I love them. Besides, I've always felt Porsches are overrated.

Chapter 24

Kulfi ice-cream

WE WEREN'T JUST keen to see family. We'd been away from the UK for 22 months and we had a number of friends that we were dying to see face to face, as opposed to the phone and email methods of communication that we had had to rely on to keep in touch from Oz. The face-to-face option involved numerous trips around the city. A congestion charge had just been introduced, making the traffic even worse than I remembered. The weather was also shit. To cap it all off, there wasn't a beach in sight. In fact, gazing out of the window of the car on one of these journeys, I couldn't help noticing that everyone looked miserable. It was strangely instructive seeing London through the eyes of a visitor. I had thought the city would evoke a homing-pigeon response in me, but the reverse was the case.

I could absolutely see why tourists and super-rich residents loved the place. It is, after all, an amazing city. However, it is the reality of what it means for 'ordinary' people to live in London that spoils the deal. If you live on the edges of Hyde Park in a house with a garden, a roof terrace and a nanny, have your own garage, drive a short distance to work where you have a parking space under your office and earn north of £600K, then it is a pretty agreeable place to spend some time. If, however, you live in one of the suburbs in a terraced veal crate and have to take the Underground to work every day, it is a different proposition altogether.

I began to wonder what my year off would have been like if I had been in London instead of Sydney. Would I have even decided to do it? How much of my decision was really me proactively deciding to take control of my life and how much of it was a lucky accident that I happened to be in the world's most livable city at the moment I lost my job? Walking the kids to school through the leafy streets of beachside Sydney is quite removed from having to drive them through peak-hour London traffic – congestion charge or no congestion charge. What on earth would my big goal for the year have been? There weren't many ocean swims in North London. I obviously could have chosen another goal – I was, after all, a master at making them up – but I somehow doubt that the London marathon, or whatever, would have exerted the same romantic and motivating influence on me as attempting to swim between the two oldest surf clubs in the world (Bondi surf club and Bronte surf club to this day fight over the honour of which one of them is the world's original surf club).

Regardless of how much I love Sydney, though, there is one thing it doesn't do nearly as well as London: curry. Of all the curries I've eaten in Australia – and there have been a lot – not one of them has come even close to the foothills of a decent London curry. I was reminded of this essential cultural distinction when we spent an evening with our good friends Simon and Becky in their local curry house. It was great to catch up with them. The setting was in its own way every bit as perfect as the setting at the polo club had been. Bright white sign outside the restaurant, laminated menus, awful music, greasy pappadums, surly, uninterested staff and suspiciously crusted pickles served in a little metal lazy susan thing. The evening was topped off perfectly by the uniquely English ritual of the London Curry House Pudding Offer.

Every country has a number of its own entirely pointless traditions. In academic circles they are called 'standing waves'. Things that once used to have a point but which have continued long since that point has passed. The QWERTY keypad is probably the best example. It was actually designed to slow typists down when typewriter technology couldn't keep up with the speed of secretaries of the day. Now computers can go faster than any human hand can type but we still have the QWERTY configuration.

I can't possibly think what the original point behind kulfi ice-cream was but now no one – and I mean *no one* – eats it. Ever. Unless of course they are so completely shitfaced that they have no control over their critical faculties. I've long maintained that the London Police could do away with the breath test in their bid to catch drunken drivers. Instead of asking drivers to blow into a bag, a simple 'Would you like some kulfi ice-cream, sir?' would do the trick. Anyone who showed the slightest interest could be arrested on the spot with absolute confidence. But despite overwhelming evidence to the contrary, nothing has ever convinced London curry houses to stop determinedly attempting to sell the stuff. A bit like you've got to admire the Chinese for resolutely hanging in there with the whole chopstick thing, you've got to admire the tenacity of these guys with their kulfi ice-cream sell.

Strange though it may seem, nothing in our whole stay in London made me more homesick than being offered some revolting ice-cream that I have never had any intention of eating.

But later that night Kate and I agreed it wasn't quite a good enough reason to move back home just yet.

Chapter 25

Cleaning the oven

DISAPPOINTING THOUGH London may have been, I was actually pleased we had a few days left in the city as I had a number of things I wanted to do before we flew to France.

One of these was to go to the Quakers. The nineteenth-century historian George Bancroft maintained that 'the rise of the people called Quakers is one of the memorable events in the history of man. It marks the moment when intellectual freedom was claimed unconditionally by the people as an inalienable birthright.' I'm not sure I would go as far as George, but for the last eight years whenever I had travelled to a new city I had always sought out the local Quaker meeting house if my trip fell over a Sunday. London was hardly a new city for me, but I hadn't been back for a while and I was determined to keep up the tradition on this visit.

The Quaker form of worship is called the Ministry of Silence. Basically, a group of you sits in a spartan room on wooden chairs for an hour. No hymns, no prayers, no sermons – nothing. At any time anyone can stand up and say anything. You can't go with a prepared speech, you can't interrupt, and you can't respond to what anyone says. Half the time no one says anything and you just sit there for an hour in silence. Utterly ridiculous. But, thing is, I love it. It gives me time to think, to still the mind. An amazing thing happens when you've been quiet for half an hour and someone next to you stands up and says something. You listen to them. Really listen. You don't judge them. You just listen. And when they've finished talking you don't waste energy trying to come up with a response that will make you look good or prove them wrong, you simply think about what has just been said. Maybe for a whole 30 minutes if no one else speaks. It can be a remarkably powerful and enriching experience. Then again, I'm not saying it's easy to do well – stilling the mind can be a real challenge.

The next morning when I went to the Quaker meeting house in Euston Road, I was all but useless at it. You're supposed to sit there in silent contemplation and welcome the Lord in. Instead, my mind wouldn't stop racing, thinking about the holiday and weddings ahead. I mean, Jesus, without the kids around I might even get my leg over. Sex in marriage is one of the few great uncharted territories left – a bit like the deep oceans. It's not that people don't talk about it. They do. It's just that they almost always lie. Kate and I are obviously at it day and night but a *friend* of mine has a wonderful story that illustrates a key truth beautifully. His sexual frustration got so bad that he decided to do that most un-manly of things – he decided to communicate his feelings. In a loving and sensitive way, of course. He didn't think it was right or fair that he should be made to feel bad about wanting sex. It was, after all, natural and supposed to be fun. He was monogamous. He loved his wife. He was in good shape (even if I say so myself, although this is a friend I'm talking about, you understand). His belief was that he needed to first ascertain where sex ranked in his wife's priorities.

'Sweetheart, is sex as important to you, say, as a holiday away?' he started.

'No? Okay, how about a weekend away?' he continued.

'No? That's fine, that's fine. A good meal?' he suggested.

'No? No problem, it's important you're honest. Does it rank above a glass of wine?' he asked.

This line of questioning went on until – and I'm not making this up – he got down to 'cleaning the oven'. At this stage, he got into a serious debate with his wife about whether sex was something she looked forward to more or less than cleaning the oven. She eventually settled on an equal ranking.

Another friend of mine once told me in a deep depression that his marriage was 'like running a kindy with a roommate you used to date'. Nice.

I brought the subject up with Kate on a number of occasions but it always seemed to end in tears.

'Sweetheart, how often would you say we have sex?' I once asked.

'Do you mean make love?' she replied.

'Yeah, whatever, make love, sex.'

'Well, definitions are important or else I can't answer the

question properly. I mean, do you want me to count "assisted wanks" among the number?'

'Er . . . what's an "assisted wank"?'

'You know, when I'm there but not there, if you know what I mean.'

'No, I sodding don't know what you mean.' It descended from there as the gap between 'making love' and 'assisted wank' became ever more apparent and hurtful to both sides.

There seemed to be such a fundamental difference between women and men when it came to sex. Men, especially married men with kids, weren't so much pussy-whipped as pussy-neglected. Time upon time I would hear stories from friends who'd bemoan the fact that sex was the cause of tension and stress in their marriage rather than a source of fun, excitement and togetherness.

When I was working, one of my clients had once opened up after a few drinks. 'It's always a wearing-down process, Nigel. I make a move and she rejects me. I wait a few days then suggest it again. She rejects me again. I feel resentful and hurt. She feels guilty and pressured. I wait a few more days. Women in the street, newsreaders on TV and gargoyles on the top of buildings start to look strangely appealing. We argue. I shout. She cries. We make up and she says something like, "Oh go on then, you big bear, I'll let you." Trouble is, I don't want to be "let". I'd like her to want to. I don't want it to be a reward for good behaviour or Olympic patience. It makes me feel dirty and ashamed that I want to get my end away. I'd like to be surprised and delighted by my sex life, not depressed and bored.'

'Reminds me of what Jimmy Carter, of all people, said,' I'd replied, slightly lost for words.

'What was that ?' He asked

'He said that his wife was more understanding and accommodating of his sexual needs in their seventies than she had ever been in their thirties.'

'Reminds me of a recent article in a men's magazine,' he said. He was clearly warming to his theme and increasingly worse for drink. 'In it they asked women and men what were the three words they most wanted to hear. The overwhelming answer from the women was "I Love You."'

'What about the men?' I asked.

'Pick Any Hole,' he replied.

On the evidence of this Sunday morning's hour of 'quiet contemplation', I felt there was a way to go before I made the grade as a Quaker.

Chapter 26

Headphones

THE OTHER THING I wanted to do before we left London was to spend some time with my brother. I've only got one brother – no sisters. Jon is older by two years and had the joy of having the same schooling experience as me except without an older brother to look after him. He's always had the burden of being 'the first' and having to watch out for his younger brother.

During our school days, at the end of each term we would have to travel home unaccompanied to wherever the navy had located our family that year. In some cases – when we were living in America or Belgium, for example – this would mean quite a significant journey. Jon would have to be the responsible one while I could piss around and be cute to the stewardesses. When we got home I would invariably kick a football through a window (or commit some such wickedness) and he would get beaten for it, not me, even when I owned up to the crime. On one famous occasion, he scratched my new metal pea shooter, so I took his new pea shooter, went into the garage, got a hammer out of Dad's toolbox, completely flattened his pea shooter from one end to the other, took a spade out of the garden shed and buried his now ruined pea shooter as deep as I could in the back yard. Cute yuh? It's a miracle really that he didn't continually beat the shit out of me, but he never did. Instead he looked after me. All in all, the best brother a man could hope for.

He also happened to be one of the most naturally funny men I've ever met. It didn't matter what topic we were discussing, he would never fail to come up with a brilliant line or story that I would then use for the next year and get all the kudos for being a natural wit – 'He's funny, that Nigel.'

As always we met in a pub.

'You've lost weight,' he said, as I gave him a hug.

'You've gone grey,' I replied.

Jon's in the army and has been for over 20 years. It keeps him trim and he looked fantastic. But grey. Fuck, I thought, surely I'm not old enough to have a greying brother.

Meeting in a pub was an interesting choice for an alcoholic. I was still off the booze but couldn't help thinking of myself as a drinker who was abstaining rather than a nondrinker. It's an important mental distinction and I wasn't there yet. It was easier to abstain with strangers or people whom I had never drunk with, but my brother and I had been drinking together since we were twelve-year-olds necking cider in the local woods. I had come to realise that, despite my initial belief that it was only my decision to stop drinking that mattered, not the external influences, I needed to be more careful with the social situations I placed myself in. We could just as easily have met in a restaurant or his flat but instead I'd chosen the one location where all I could do was 'not drink'. Talk about making it hard for yourself. To his huge credit, Jon didn't make a fuss or pressure me. I still found it a challenge. I started to wonder how on earth I was going to cope with the weddings that were coming up. All my mates would be at one, all Kate's family at the other. On top of that, I had the pressure of having to make a speech at both occasions.

Despite the inappropriate environment, we still managed to have a great night. Over five pints of beer for him and 14 glasses of apple juice for me (I tended to drink more liquid now I was off the booze), we covered every topic under the sun – Jon keeping me in stitches for most of the night. He saved the best for last. Given the train of thought I'd had at the Quakers the day before, our conversation naturally swung to sex. Despite my being out of work, Jon and I were at similar life stages, both married with kids. We had a lot of common ground (although of course it goes without saying that he and his wife, like Kate and I, were also at it like rabbits every day of the week). He patiently listened to my description of one of my particularly badly pussy-neglected friends.

'Know what you mean, Nige, but that's nothing compared to Mike,' he said.

'Do you mean Mike as in Claire and Mike?' I asked.

'Yeah. They've recently moved to Milton Keynes. She's

working hard, the baby's not sleeping, and he claims he hasn't had it for over a year.'

'Jesus, he's a reclassified virgin.'

'Yep, just qualified last month.'

'Poor fucker,' I said.

'Or not, in this case.'

'But that's not much of a story, Jon. I know a couple of men who have recently reclassified,' I said.

'No, that's not the story. Because of his lack of action in the sack he had to take matters into his *own hands* – so to speak,' he explained.

'Know what you mean, Jon, know what you mean. But I still feel this story doesn't live up to your usual standard,' I complained.

'I haven't finished. Last week Claire was entertaining three of her top clients. Basically taking them to a show and then dinner.'

'So?'

'Well, thing is the show was cancelled.'

'So?'

'So she took them for an early dinner and then home for a nightcap. Mike hadn't been expecting them for at least another three hours.'

'So?'

'Wait, wait. Be patient. Claire showed them into the house, told them to make themselves at home in the sitting room while she fixed the drinks in the kitchen. She had hardly got the ice out of the freezer when they all came into the kitchen. The head client explained there was a problem in the sitting room. Claire told him not to worry and that she would see to it when she'd done the drinks. None of the clients would move. The head client had a strange look on his face and simply repeated, "There's a *problem* in the sitting room." Claire went into the sitting room to find Mike in his favourite chair, watching a porn movie, trousers round his ankles, having one off the wrist.'

'But surely he would have heard them coming in the door?' I protested.

'Nope, turns out Mike likes doing it while listening to his favourite rock album through the hi-fi headphones. He couldn't hear a thing. She had to tap him on the shoulder to get him to stop. Apparently it made the introductions interesting.'

I made a mental note to lock the door in future.

Chapter 27

Beyblades

SEX OR NOT, THE UK part of the trip was over. It was time for us to leave London. Giles' wedding was the first up. He was marrying a French lass from Provence. The wedding itself was in the village of Trets, just east of Aix-en-Provence, so we were having to fly to Nice. Given our financial situation we decided to put the huge price differentials between the different airlines to the test and fly CrapAirline.com. It was the no-frills deal taken to the extreme. To our surprise, we were both genuinely impressed. There was no pretence about the whole deal. When you fly BA economy you are paying a premium but for what? When you fly CrapAirline.com there is no pretence and you actually get pleasant staff. Your expectations are exceeded. On BA you can't help hoping that perhaps the seats will be slightly bigger or the service slightly nicer when in reality the reverse is usually the case. Unless you're flying business class, my vote is with the Whizaways and CrapAirline.coms.

The flight may have been a pleasant surprise but the destination was a different matter. Nice was anything but. I've always found the coastline of the south of France to be a massive disappointment. This is not because of unfavourable comparison with Sydney, I've thought this ever since I went there backpacking as a teenager years ago. It's either horribly spoilt or horribly pretentious. There doesn't seem to be a middle ground. Because of my career I usually spent a week each year in Cannes and I never ceased to be amazed at how such a dive could manage to attract major film, advertising, and porn festivals. Then again, come to think of it, the porn festival is probably the perfect partner for the town. I wouldn't care if I never had to spend another minute of my life on the Riviera. Which makes the juxtaposition of the gorgeous inland countryside all the more surprising and delightful. It is a wonder to behold – all you have to do is drive for ten minutes inland and the landscape is transformed. It reminds me of those city harbours where the water that laps against the port wall is filthy and full of crud yet a couple of metres out the sea is clean and you can see all the way to the bottom. Thankfully Trets is inland. Not just inland but positioned at the foothill of Cézanne's favourite mountain, Sainte-Victoire.

We had learnt the lesson from my Tasmanian car hire experience and had hired ourselves a car from the current century. The drive was delightful. We stopped off in a small medieval village for lunch. Just Kate and I sitting on a wall by a stream, eating baguettes and cheese. It was the first time we had been away from our children for over eight years. We were alone, no one was tugging at us asking for sweets, no one needed their nappy changed, no one was crying because their brother had changed the TV channel, and best of all we knew that when we got to Trets that evening we wouldn't have to make kids' tea and survive arsenic hour. Only one thing was wrong – we missed the kids.

I know this sounds contradictory, but we were alone and relaxed for the first time in almost a decade and we both just sat there on that wall and talked about our children non-stop. I couldn't get the way they get into bed out of my head. They don't get in at the right place like adults. Wearing their little pyjamas with rockets on, they leap upside down on to the bottom of the bed and then roll all the way up to the top and then get under the duvet head-first, before turning the right way round under the bedding and then re-emerging the right way up. It's pretty inefficient but at that precise moment the memory was so cute it was breaking my heart.

I started to laugh, remembering the time I was walking downstairs with Harry when without notice he dropped to his stomach and slid down the entire flight of stairs head-first before getting up at the bottom and holding my hand again, as if it was an entirely natural thing to do. Kate brought up the time we were having lunch and, as if in a Steve Martin comedy, the mop bucket appeared upside down on the twins' heads with only their ankles and feet showing. It then proceeded to walk across the room with the accompanying soundtrack of muffled two-year-old giggles.

Finally we could take it no longer and decided to call home to speak to them. Harry answered the phone.

'Hello, Harry, sweetheart, it's your Dad.'

'I'm not Harry, I'm Beyblades,' Harry replied before handing the phone to Grace.

'Go away, Daddy, I don't love you,' Grace said.

'I love you, Daddy,' I could hear Eve shouting in the background.

'Well I don't. You're a poo-poo head,' Grace added, rather unnecessarily.

Alex grabbed the phone. 'Have you got me a present yet, Dad?'

Despite the abuse it was lovely to speak to them. When the phone was finally passed to Liz, she confirmed what we had been hoping – they were having a whale of a time. As we left the phone box we decided we could allow ourselves to look forward to the wedding itself without feeling guilty about deciding to do the trip without the children.

Chapter 28

Cézanne

WE ARRIVED AT OUR hotel, a restored chateau, in the late afternoon. We checked in at reception, went straight to our room and opened the shutters that led on to the balcony. The view was breathtaking. An uninterrupted vista of Mont Sainte-Victoire. Giles had arranged for me to have this room not just because I was his best man at the wedding, but also because he knew how much it would mean to me. One of my favourite places in the world is the huge converted railway station in Paris that is the Musée d'Orsay. Kate and I went to Paris the year after Alex was born and I had spent a day there, awestruck by the sheer amount and quality of Impressionist paintings on show in such a unique setting. Cézanne has many works on show in the Musée d'Orsay, among them a number of the more than 60 paintings he did of Mont Sainte-Victoire in his lifetime. And here I was, looking not at the paintings but at the subject itself.

One more thing I had resolved to do in my time off was to teach myself to draw. As part of this process I had bought and studied an incredible book by a woman called Betty Edwards about accessing the right side of your brain when drawing. It's actually quite sad. Its central thesis is that most of us halt our artistic development at nine years old. Up until that time, when we draw, it's all in symbolic icons: houses all have doorknobs, and people all have ten fingers. Then one day, at around the age of nine, we realise what we're drawing doesn't look like things in the real world. So we try to draw them realistically and of course when we do they look nothing like real life, *so we give up*.

Betty Edwards has a theory which is not only dramatic, but which works. I know because it's worked for me and I was the world's worst, most hopeless case. Put simply, she says when we try to draw realistically, the left, logical, side of the brain keeps piping up and telling us, 'Don't be stupid, it's a house you're drawing. Houses have doorknobs so put in a doorknob.' Never mind if you can't actually *see* a doorknob. This happens over and over again with everything we attempt to draw: 'It's a car, put in four wheels', 'It's a person, show both her eyes'. But the secret to drawing realistically is as simple as drawing what you see.

Ignoring what the left side of your brain tells you you know is there – as opposed to what you can actually see – is the hard part. If we ignore the left side of our brain it becomes almost easy. Edwards has devised a number of exercises that force you to ignore the left side of your brain. Things like copying upside-down pictures, and drawing without looking at the page. I copied one picture that was the right way up and it was awful and childlike. I then copied another that was upside-down. To me it just was a bunch of meaningless random squiggles so I simply concentrated on getting down what I saw. When I'd finished and turned it round, I was stunned to see it was a 100 per cent accurate and incredibly lifelike and detailed picture of Stravinsky sitting in a chair. It's one of my prized possessions – I can't believe I did it. If I'd known what it was before I started drawing, the left side of my brain would have messed it up for me by saying 'where is his other knee?' and 'what about his fingers?' It's one of those exercises that once you've done, you'll never forget or go back to how you thought beforehand.

Anyway, the reason I mention this is because in preparation for this trip I had bought a book on Cézanne and while sitting on my balcony I read the following quote from the great man: 'We must not paint what we think we see, but what we see. Sometimes it may go against the grain, but this is what our craft demands.' It can't have been the drink because I was still off the booze, but the profundity of these simple words spoken over a hundred years ago made me want to weep. Cézanne and the other Impressionists had to endure all manner of ridicule and humiliation for their craft before they were eventually vindicated (in many cases after their death). The whole situation just yelled at me – we are only here once, don't toe the line and be a timid, whimpering clerk who doesn't follow a dream because he's too busy doing what he feels other people expect him to do.

Then again, perhaps I should take up drinking again if this is what it makes me like when I look at a mountain sober.

Chapter 29

Lucky bastard

I WOKE EARLY THE next morning. I was excited about the imminent arrival of my Bristol friends. One of the upsides of not having to go to an office five days a week is that it gives you more time to appreciate those around you – or indeed those friends who are on the other side of the world. Most of my longstanding non-work friends come from my time at university. For one reason or another I had lost touch with everyone I'd ever been to school with but had successfully kept in touch with everyone from college. They were an incredibly important part of my life and one I worked hard at nurturing.

For the eleven years before Kate and I departed for Australia, we had spent every New Year's holiday with this group of friends in a variety of holiday cottages in Devon and Cornwall. Apart from being enormous fun, it was an amazing reality check regarding the passage of time. When we first started going, we were all young, slim, not married and almost permanently addled with drink and drugs. Then, as each successive year passed, the signs of the inevitable rites of passage became apparent. Someone got engaged, then another married. Incredibly to us at the time, someone actually brought a child one year. And, here's the thing: it was theirs. The last year we went, when we saw in the new millennium, half of us were sober and there were more kids than adults in the cottage. It was all rather uncomfortably like a popular TV series of the time called *Cold Feet*. Although, touch wood, none of the six couples involved had yet divorced. They were all coming to Giles and Sophie's wedding. He was the last of the group to get married. Indeed, it had been ages since the last wedding and this was a wonderful opportunity for us all to get together for the first time since Kate and I had moved to Oz.

Something else that had slowly become apparent was that the magnetic effect London had had on us all at the start of our careers had reversed and in the last two years we had nearly all scattered to different parts of the world. Whereas we once all lived within an eight-kilometre radius of each other in North London, we were now all located in vastly different places: Sydney (Kate and I), Provence (Giles and Sophie), Belfast (Ian and Christine), Melbourne (Jon and Jane), and Brighton (Paul and Janine). Only Simon and Becky (Kentish Town) flew the flag for good old London. Irrespective of the distances involved, everyone had made the pilgrimage to see Giles' big day.

I was sharing the best man duties with another of Giles' close friends, Richard, and I'm pleased to say (although I can't claim any credit as, with me being in the Southern Hemisphere, Richard did all the work) that the day went off as smooth as glass. The service was in the ancient church in the middle of Trets. It would be hard to imagine a more romantic setting. The duties of a 'bestie' in France are slightly different from those in the UK, but the one duty that was the same was the fact that we each had to give a speech.

I'm sure it must be down to gross vanity on my part, but I have always loved giving speeches. Not so much the preparation, but the physical act of delivering one. I think it might go back to my stand-up comedy days. The thrill involved when it goes well is something I find delicious. Making people laugh and then, best of all, riding those laughs, for me is right up there as one of the best experiences life has to offer. The only slight hitch in this case was that over three-quarters of the audience couldn't speak a word of English, so at least some of my speech would have to be in French. It would be fair to say I speak more Klingon than French, so this presented something of a challenge. However, remarkably, once I'd started I found the performing drug kicked in irrespective of language or lack of alcohol and I had a fine old time bollocksing on in an accent that would make my old French schoolteacher weep.

The speech, even though I say it myself, was well received and that being the last of my official duties I could well and truly relax and enjoy the rest of the occasion. First I quickly nipped off to find a telly that was showing the Heineken European Cup semi-final. Munster had got through and was playing Toulouse. I badly wanted Munster to win. Unlike in religion where I couldn't find a particular brand that ticked all the boxes, in sport I had no such problem – rugby union had grabbed me at an early age and it has been my passion ever since. The sight of a centre breaking through the line with only the fullback to beat is my favourite of any sport. Brian O'Driscoll's performance in the first Lions test against the Wallabies in 2001 still thrills me even though I must have watched the game 30 times. The film made of the Lions tour of South Africa in 1997 is my favourite film of all time. Not just my favourite sport film, but my favourite of all films. Anyway, I found a set and was rewarded by a nail-biter. Munster led all the way until the seventy-fourth minute, only to be cruelly denied by Toulouse with a late try, scored in extra time.

When I returned, the wedding festivities were in full joyful swing. As I expected, it was an even bigger test of my resolve not to drink than meeting up with my brother had been. Over and above finding it strange to be at such a happy occasion surrounded by my friends and not pissed, there was the added pressure of my peculiar decision to take a year off. Although I don't like to think of myself as a 'keeping up with the Joneses' type of person, I was worried about my old friends' reaction to my unemployment. After 20 years in an office career it wasn't a simple task to divorce my self-worth from my job – however much I had convinced myself I was no longer going to define myself by my work I was still concerned about what other people might think. Especially my friends. I know this admission makes me shallow but I wanted to appear to them like I'd got it all together. (Even though the truth was I was making it up as I went along and in my quieter moments I was scared shitless of the future.) It was just too confronting for me to dwell on the reality with my friends and risk being thought of as a sad loser. Just a few months ago, this worry was precisely the sort of thing I would have used drink to help me get over. Now that social crutch had gone.

Although everyone seemed incredibly supportive of my choice not to go back to work, I couldn't help suspecting that many of them (especially the women) were simply being polite and had already translated 'decided to take a year off' into 'poor bastard can't find a job'. Some of the men were clearly envious and oversimplified the bright side.

'Christ, you're a lucky bastard, Nige. I'd love to be made redundant. Must be wonderful,' was a typical response. I spared them the stories of arsenic hour, Goodbye Windows, and crippling worry about the future. Playing along with the 'Nige is spending a year having a laugh and surfing' story was easier – and it made me look good. Or so I thought.

I'm pleased to say my resolve held and I didn't touch a drop. You are not supposed to rely solely on willpower to beat the booze. Whether it is working the twelve steps, having a mentor, using a support network – or in many cases combining all three – you are always advised never to attempt to do it alone. Kate maintains this is the one area of my life where my hideously black and white and determined character doesn't make me a 'selfish, intransigent pain in the backside' (as she sweetly put it a few days ago) but instead actually helps me and the family. I take issue with the intransigent pain bit but I feel she may have a point about this finally being a useful outlet for my stubbornness. Whatever, at this stage of my recovery it was all I had.

Being sober actually gave me a different and richer take on

the evening. In previous years I would have got stuck into the refreshments and tried to be the funny guy all night long. This would inevitably mean a certain tunnel vision and me unwittingly upsetting a number of people along the way. This time I spent the night truly aware of my surroundings and what the people in them meant to me. I felt extremely fortunate and blessed. Kate looked stunning. Watching her dance and laugh with Becky, Christine and Jane, I realised again how lucky I was to be with her. We'd been married for ten years. Wonderful years. I made a silent resolution to strive to make the next ten even better. Giles and Sophie were in that blissful state that only newlyweds can be in. I couldn't help but be deeply moved by it all. I had known these people for over 20 years. So much had happened in that time. I said a prayer for Giles and Sophie and for the future happiness of all in the room. I couldn't help wondering where we would be in another 20 years' time.

Chapter 30

Chicken

SEEING AS I WAS the only guest not sporting a hangover the next morning, I got up early and went for a walk by myself around the foothills of Mont Sainte-Victoire. I took my sketchbook and did a number of shamefully poor pictures of the mountain in Cézanne's honour. Today was the start of the second half of our Northern Hemisphere tour. After lunch in Aix with all the Bristol crew, Kate and I planned to drive to the Italian lakes for a few days before continuing on to Venice for Jane's wedding (and another speech). Neither Kate nor I had been to the lakes and everyone we knew who had been raved about them. The real point of the trip, however, was to have some time alone together. Bizarre as it may sound, even though we had left the kids behind we still hadn't had much time alone. We were so busy and pleased to be catching up with our friends and family that the subplot of the trip (a second honeymoon) was in danger of being overlooked. We both knew Venice would be as full-on as Provence, so this week was our chance to 'take a chill pill', as Alex had put it on the phone to me the night before when I'd called him to let him know the Munster result.

Returning to the chateau mid-morning, I found the group slowly gathering for the trip to Aix and lunch. It felt slightly like preparing for the Last Supper. We all realised it might be a very long time before we were together again as a group. Rather than spoiling the occasion, it lent proceedings an interesting poignancy. I found myself saying the things I wanted to as opposed to wasting the event with mindless chit-chat. As Kate and I drove away at the end of the lunch and our French adventure, we both agreed the trip had already been a huge success regardless of how the Italian adventure went – and indeed the 35-pound refund disaster.

To get to the Italian lakes we headed north up the motorway towards Gap. It was going to take us two days to get to the lakes, so we put a pin in the map in the vague area of what looked like halfway to decide where we'd stop for the night. Le Monêtier-les-Bains, the pin told us, so Le Monêtier-les-Bains it was. The drive was fantastic – no kids squabbling in the back, no 'Wheels on the Bus' on the tape player. Just lovely scenery and no pressured deadlines. After Gap the motorway ran out as we climbed into the mountains. The last town before Le Monêtier-les-Bains was Briançon, which proudly and repeatedly announced itself on gaudy road signs as 'the highest town in Europe'. Briançon appeared to have little else to recommend it. A grubby urban blot on the otherwise gorgeous surroundings, it even had its own Burger King and KFC for good measure.

As our chosen village was only 14 kilometres further up a side road, we began to doubt the wisdom of the 'pin method' of accommodation selection. We couldn't have been more wrong. Le Monêtier-les-Bains was a delightful Alpine village. We couldn't believe our luck. I've no idea why it is so unspoilt, but everything from the church to the High Street to the chocolate-box perfection of the little auberge we had booked made us immediately fall in love with the place. The village was surrounded on all sides by the most breathtaking mountain range. It seemed a shame we were only going to be there one night. Having quickly unpacked the car of our overnight kit, we went for a walk to get the most out of the place before night fell. Back in the auberge afterwards, against the pleadings of Kate, I went to reception and called the kids.

The call was a game of two halves, as the sports commentators say. Alex came to the phone first and was full of excitement about that weekend's rugby match. His team – the Clovelly Eagles – had won and Alex had scored a try and got two conversions over. I tried to control my fatherly pride and while congratulating him also talked about how it was a team game and tackles were more important than tries. No pretending, however, I was fairly bursting with joy at his pleasure in the whole day. Did it matter that I wasn't there to watch him? I tried to justify our choice by remembering that I hadn't missed any of Alex's previous matches and that in a rugby-playing career spanning 14 years, my own dad had watched me just once, and then his only comment after the game had been, 'You dropped the ball twice.' Having finished with Alex, I asked him to pass the phone to Harry.

'Hi, Harry, it's your Dad.'

'I'm not Harry, I'm Punch Buggy Green.'

'Oh, okay, sweetheart, what did you do today?'

'Nothing,' he replied. 'Dad?' he enquired, in that cute way kids do with just the inflection at the end of your name.

'Yes, Harry.'

'I'm not Harry, I'm Punch Buggy Green.'

'Oh, sorry. Yes, Punch Buggy Green?'

'Isn't it funny how they have one word for two things?'

'What do you mean, sweetheart?'

'You know, one word for *two* things.'

'I don't understand, darling.'

'You know. Like "chicken". "Chicken" meaning an animal and "chicken" meaning a sandwich.'

'That's not two things, darling, chicken is the animal that we eat in sandwiches.'

Now at the time that felt like a perfectly normal, and indeed helpful, fatherly thing to say. Writing this now, months later, having the hindsight of the reaction I caused, it just seems bloody stupid. If I could take it back I would. But then again, one more vegetarian won't hurt, either. Harry, or Punch Buggy Green as he was at the time, went silent, then started crying quietly, then walked away from the phone. It's difficult to accurately describe how much of a shit you feel when you've just made your five-year-old son cry and you are 14,000 miles away from him and he won't come back to the phone.

'How was that?' Kate asked as I returned to our room.

'Oh, fine,' I lied. 'Harry is Punch Buggy Green today. He sends his love.'

Chapter 31

Bored

WE SET OUT EARLY the next morning and were rewarded by the most beautiful drive either of us can remember. The route across the mountains and over the French–Italian border was spectacular but not for the fainthearted – lots of unfeasibly narrow roads with hairpin bends overhanging sheer drops into seemingly bottomless ravines. Not for the first time, I congratulated myself on having learnt the lesson from Tassie – I wouldn't have fancied the drive in the Crapolla.

But things changed abruptly once we came down the other side of the mountains. The drive from Turin to Milan was a real eye-opener. Just because it was Italy, I had naïvely assumed it would be all vineyards and history-soaked landscapes. The disappointing reality was that it was a cross between Parramatta Road and the Hume Highway. We stuck to the motorway and made as fast a time as we could. Our destination was a place called Bellagio.

Bellagio is on Lake Como and it is world famous for two things: George Clooney has chosen it as the location of his get-away-from-it-all holiday home, and it is the location of the Villa Serbelloni hotel. The Villa Serbelloni is one of those fabulous hotels that is a destination in its own right. Unfortunately, Kate and I neither knew George Clooney nor had a budget that could accommodate the Serbelloni's buttock-clenchingly expensive rates. Instead, we stayed in the hotel next door – *looking* at the Serbelloni.

Despite the lack of a hotel swimming pool, I was determined to maintain my swimming training – especially in the light of my recent progress – so that afternoon I decided to try my luck, stroll across the road and pretend to be a guest at the Serbelloni. Heart pounding, I walked with as much outward confidence as I could muster through the reception area and followed the signs to the health spa, a splendid, ornate affair in the basement of the main hotel building. Rather worryingly, there was an officious-looking uniformed lady behind an oak counter just inside the door to the spa. I decided selective truth was the best policy.

'Hi, I've come to use the pool,' I said, looking her straight in the eye.

'Certainly, sir. Welcome to the Serbelloni Health Spa. We haven't seen you at the hotel before, have we? Are you a new guest?' she asked.

'First time in Bellagio. My wife and I just arrived this afternoon.'

'And you are staying . . . ?'

'For four days,' I interrupted, before she could ask which room I was in, as my policy didn't extend to telling a direct lie. 'We've a wedding to go to.'

'Oh, how exciting. The marquee is being erected as we speak. Do you know the bride or the groom?' she asked.

Hold on, I thought, I had no idea there was a wedding at the hotel. This clearly was my chance.

'It's my sister-in-law who's getting married. I'm a little nervous about the speech I have to make,' I replied truthfully but entirely misleadingly. 'I was rather hoping to fit a swim in every morning we're in Bellagio. What time do you open?'

'Six in the morning, sir,' she replied, handing me a luxuriously fluffy embroidered towel.

From that moment on she clearly believed I was a wedding guest at her hotel, and every morning she greeted me with as much enthusiasm and warmth as the Kindi Gym instructress had before Grace ruined my chances. I rationalised my behaviour with the excuse that I wasn't doing anyone any harm and I hadn't actually told a lie – I was indeed staying four days and going to a wedding. Just not at their hotel, or in Bellagio. Besides, it wasn't the worst case of bluffing I had been guilty of. My Serbelloni confidence trick was positively insignificant compared to the sports instructor 'career' I manufactured when I was working in London.

There was a sports club just around the corner from the office where I worked and I got it into my head that if I played my cards right I could earn some extra money as a squash coach. Bizarrely, the fact that I had never coached anyone in my life, been coached myself or indeed even played for a team didn't deter me. I drew up a couple of ads to stick in the sports club reception and went to find the manager.

'Hi, I'd like to speak to the manager, please,' I said to the tracksuited hunk at reception.

'You're speaking to him.'

'Oh, great. You've got three squash courts here and I was wondering if I could use them to give a few lessons,' I said, passing my ad across the counter.

'What've you got in mind?'

'Just sticking these ads up on your noticeboard and splitting any business I get with you 60:40. If I get too many clients and start jamming up the courts I'll stop any time you like.'

'Can't see why not,' he said.

And that was it.

Taking the lessons, however, proved slightly more problematic than getting the gig. My ad had rather ill-advisedly read: 'Call Nigel Marsh for one-on-one squash sessions, relaxed, friendly. Flexible times to suit any schedule. All standards welcome.' Again, no word of a lie but entirely misleading. The last sentence was the biggest problem. I started to get calls. A lot of calls. The children and beginners were no trouble. I actually think I helped a few. It was the people who were clearly better than me that were the challenge. A couple of them were in line for national trials – I hadn't even made the school team. It would be obvious by the warm-up if I was in trouble. Whack, whack, whack – they would smash the ball with a flawless swing and inch-perfect precision down the wall.

'Okay, couple of things we can work on there,' I would say in my best Zane impersonation.

'Excellent – what?' my client would ask eagerly.

'I think we need to work on your swing and precision,' I'd reply.

I'd then spend 30 Monty-Pythonesque minutes getting them to go through a variety of routines that I had devised precisely for clients such as these. Amongst other things these involved them trying to hit the ball back to themselves ten times in a row while blindfolded or playing left-handed or standing on one leg. On one occasion I even made someone play with a table tennis bat. Anything but play *me*. All the time I would nod thoughtfully and wisely, but vaguely, commenting, 'Interesting, let's try that on your backhand,' or 'I want you to relax more at the moment of contact.'

Luckily for the future of English squash, after a couple of months the stress of constantly fearing that I would be rumbled led me to 'resign' from the post and concentrate on my office job. I was a few hundred pounds richer but, more importantly, I had learnt first-hand the truth of the cliché that if you wear a doctor's coat with enough confidence you can walk around a hospital for a surprisingly long time before anyone will ask you who you are or what you are doing. My bluffing ability was hardly at the level of that bloke DiCaprio plays in *Catch Me if You Can*, but I was rather glad of the opportunity it was giving me now, ten years later in Bellagio, to continue my swimming training. Kate had a slightly different attitude towards my blagging, maintaining that perhaps it wasn't such a bad thing that I hadn't spent all that much time with my kids over the previous years, as who knows what kind of scams they'd be running now if I had.

The swimming itself continued to go well. Now I had found my 'jogging pace', as David called it, it was more a matter of practice than learning. I found I could now easily swim for 20 minutes or more without stopping. I was relaxing and concentrating on my style. I was even starting to get comfortable with bilateral breathing. Once or twice I actually enjoyed it. I was starting to feel confident about making the move to ocean swimming when we returned to Australia.

Doing Bellagio – and indeed the whole holiday – 'on the cheap' had reopened my eyes to an entirely different way of living and consuming. I realised I had practically been pouring money down the drain on a weekly basis during my recent working life. If I had been working when I'd gone to Tasmania I would have spent three times the amount I ended up spending, yet I very much doubt we would have enjoyed the week any more. Similarly, if I had been working during this European jaunt we wouldn't have been staying at the Hotel Florence blagging someone else's pool but I genuinely believe we wouldn't have enjoyed Bellagio any more by staying somewhere more expensive. Then again, wondering where we would have been staying on this trip if I had still beeeen working was kind of academic, given that I wouldn't have had time for such a holiday with Kate if I had still been working.

It was as if I'd been living in a yuppie zone where I bought what was expected of someone in my position without pausing to question whether it represented good value. Looking back, I realised I had got into the habit of having 90-dollar haircuts and drinking 35-dollar bottles of wine. While I no longer drank, I had just had my haircut for ten bucks and I'd been very pleased with it when I walked out of the barber's. I suspected if I was still on the booze I'd be drinking cheaper wine and enjoying it just as much. This is not some pathetic 'isn't poverty great' mantra. It isn't: poverty is shithouse – it ruins lives, breaks up families, causes wars and generally squashes the human spirit. I'm not talking about poverty. I'm talking about overprivileged people losing their sense of perspective. A few months before I had finished work, I had gone to a drinks party in a gorgeous house overlooking Bronte Beach. Within five minutes the host had started complaining about the house. Not 'I'm a lucky fucker who has a house 60 seconds' walk from one of the nicest beaches in the world', but 'we're finding the noise at the weekends distracting'. Even at the time I remember thinking, *Get a grip, you tosser.*

Looking back, I could recall hundreds of dinner parties where we all sat around and bemoaned the fact that we probably couldn't afford to send our kids to private school. So what? Send them to a state school like everyone else. The problem, it seems to me, is that some people have never, literally never, had to struggle. Be it because they have always worked in the city or have rich parents or made a fortune on a house – whatever. After a few years of not having to agonise about money they cross an unseen line where they come to subconsciously believe that they deserve and are owed the good life by right. Then, when something happens that means they can't automatically have exactly what they want, they talk about it as if it is a tragedy and other people should care. I've lost count of the number of conversations I've been in where people who work in the City of London have complained about the size of their bonuses since the recession. The fact that even these pared-down bonuses were four times the size of the annual wage of a GP, or the fact that they had enjoyed ten years of 'really good' bonuses, didn't seem to register. It was too long since they'd crossed the invisible line of 'I've a right to this lifestyle'.

Similarly, having to move to a less nice house because you suddenly haven't got as much money is not a tragedy. It's not even a shame. It's life. Count yourself lucky you had a nice one in the first place. This may sound harsh, but I mean it. Although it hardly ranked in terms of real hardship, Kate and I were going to have to move to a cheaper, smaller place down the hill when we got back to Oz. We would have moved earlier, before this trip, but we had a fixed-term lease that we couldn't get out of until the end of May. A number of friends were appalled at the fate that was befalling us and were genuinely sympathetic. All I could think was, 'Clovelly, brilliant, another wonderful Sydney beachside suburb. Our rent would be double to live in a place half as nice in London. We didn't really need the spare bedroom. Anyway, it'll do the children good to share.' Kate thought this attitude was simply an obvious case of retrospective justification, given my situation. I prefer to believe it was a brilliant flash of insight and a searing indictment on the professional classes in the developed world. But then again, I still tuck my vest into my pants if she's not watching.

Our stay in Bellagio was everything I hoped it would be – I got bored. Properly bored. It happened on the second morning. To start with, I got up when I woke up, not when a twin smashed me in the nose with a Teletubbie. When I came back from my swim I found a note from Kate saying she was going shopping and would meet me for lunch. I had a bath, a very long bath. After that I ordered a latte and freshly squeezed orange juice, sat on the balcony and read the newspaper in that way which I never thought I'd ever do again – cover to cover without interruptions or rush. Then I did a drawing. Then another. Then – and it is difficult to adequately describe how wonderful this felt – I actually found myself thinking, what on earth shall I do now? I didn't want to go back to bed. I didn't want another bath or to read another paper. I couldn't surf, I wasn't drinking, I didn't have a job to go to, there were no kids to look after, Kate was out, there were no friends to socialise with, no family to accommodate, no one had our telephone number and my mobile had been off for days. It was such a totally alien experience – pure bliss, in fact. I sat on the balcony in a state of semi-shock, watching the ferries arrive and depart from the terminal below. So this is what it was like to be properly chilled out. It occurred to me I was finally doing what everyone probably thought I'd been doing the whole time – sitting on my fat, beautifully healed arse, doing bugger-all. It wasn't a lifestyle I could afford in the long term – or even the medium term, come to think of it – but as a short-term strategy it definitely got my vote. Besides, it wouldn't last long anyway, as we were soon to set off for Venice, but I damn sure was going to revel in it for as long as I could.

Chapter 32

Veniceworld

SURE ENOUGH, BEFORE I had time to slide from bored to comatose (a state I had been eagerly looking forward to), we were packing to leave Bellagio. But the disappointment of leaving was more than compensated for by the prospect of Kate's sister's wedding and our first-ever trip to Venice. It was a surprisingly easy drive and upon arrival we immediately made our way to the airport to return our hire car. We had hardly put our bags onto a trolley when a handsome bloke in a suit came up to us and introduced himself in impeccable English.

'Are you with the wedding party?' he asked.

'Er, yes. I'm Nigel and this is Kate,' I told him.

'Excellent, we've been expecting you. Please leave your bags with my colleague and follow me.'

Rather uncertainly we followed him to his car as a porter loaded our luggage onto a trolley.

'Please,' he gestured to the back seat as he held open the door, 'it is less than two minutes' drive to the boat that has been arranged to take you to your villa.'

'Villa?'

'Yes, it is one of my favourites. You're on the Grand Canal right opposite the Guggenheim museum. Both St Mark's Square and the Accademia Bridge are within five minutes' walk if you want to see any of the sights before the wedding.'

Obviously the wealth of Jane's soon-to-be-in-laws was matched only by their generosity. Now, I consider myself to be fairly widely travelled but in the last 40 years nowhere has had such a dramatic effect on me as Venice. I don't know whether it was because we were experiencing it first class or because I was totally chilled after Bellagio or simply because of the uniquely wonderful place it is, but Venice stunned me. Just the boat ride from the airport would have been enough. I found the whole thing difficult to take in. I spent a year living in Little Venice in London and all I can say is the person who came up with the name for that particular piece of north London deserves a marketing medal. Located between a number of London's busiest roads, Little Venice is not even a proper suburb – it's basically the few streets that border the intersection of two narrow, polluted canals. More 'Open Sewer' than 'Little Venice', those canals are railed off from the general public so you couldn't access them even if you wanted to. Little Venice is *nothing* like Venice.

Venice is one of those globally iconic destinations that doesn't disappoint. I remember, in contrast, my utter astonishment when I saw the Egyptian pyramids in person.

'Oh look,' Kate had said, 'it's a pretend Sphinx.'

'Madam, that *is* the Sphinx,' our guide rather huffily corrected her.

We couldn't believe that the minuscule cat at the bottom of the pyramid was the Sphinx. It is amazing to me that every postcard ever taken of the Sphinx and the pyramids has deliberately used perspective in such a way as to give the entirely misleading impression that the Sphinx is almost as big as the pyramids themselves.

Venice, on the other hand, was *better* than the postcards. It really is a city in the middle of a lagoon, with canals instead of roads. If that isn't enough, it also has the most incredible collection of art and historically significant architecture anywhere on the planet.

The only downside I experienced in the whole week we were there was on the second day, when I got stuck, literally stuck, in the middle of a guided group of American tourists on a crowded, narrow walkway. Within minutes, the awe-inspiring city I had fallen in love with took on a 'Veniceworld' feel. I became a member of a herd. A rather overweight, bored-looking herd that was being systematically shepherded from one 'attraction' to the next. At times I half-expected them to complain that it wasn't a very good theme park and ask where the rides were. This short blot apart, it turned into one of the most fabulous weeks of my life. Kate was largely busy with arrangements for her sister's wedding, so during the days I was free to wander the city by myself.

Apparently Venice has over 400 bridges – I swear I must have walked over all of them. Though the fact of the matter is I could have stayed for another week and done it all over again. I constantly felt guilty giving such a short bit of my time to each of the wonders I came across. I could have spent a week in the Scuola Grande Di San Rocco alone, which the rather right-on guidebook I had bought told me I could never be prepared for until I saw it. And it was right. Basically one man – Tintoretto – spent 23 years of his life creating works of art to adorn the walls and ceilings of the famous building. Every painting is a masterpiece in its own right – and he did over 50 of them. I had mixed emotions. On the one hand it was wonderful and awe-inspiring, and on the other utterly depressing. My own efforts were lame by any standards, but by Tintoretto's they were pathetic, tragic and pointless.

I consoled myself with the memory of Harry's response every time he saw one of my sketches. 'Daddy, you're an artist!' he would shout enthusiastically while pointing in wonder at my latest scribble – irrespective of how appalling the particular drawing in question was. He was genuinely delighted and amazed at my output. Kate might roll her eyes whenever I showed her my most recent picture of her (invariably looking like an 80-year-old witch done by Picasso on an off day) but to Harry, for the time being, anyway, I was Tintoretto in board shorts.

This memory served not only to make me smile but also to ache for Harry and his brother and sisters.

'God, I miss the kids,' I said to Kate.

'Me too,' she replied.

'Wouldn't it be fabulous to bring them here and show them all this?'

'Fabulous – and entirely unrealistic,' she remarked. 'Unless you go back to work we won't be able to afford to take the kids anywhere but the local park.'

Much as I hated her for spoiling the moment, I had to admit she had a point.

Chapter 33

Back by Ten

HOWEVER, I WASN'T in Venice to sightsee – I was there for a wedding. My wife has three sisters, or the Macbeth witches, as I prefer to think of them. It was the youngest one who was getting spliced this time. At our own wedding, Kate's dad, John, started his speech by saying that the only time in his life when he wasn't interrupted was when he was giving a speech at one of his daughters' weddings. I wondered what his emotions were now he was finally to be rid of them all.

To have four grown-up daughters is an achievement to rival Tintoretto's in my book. I only had two daughters who were barely three and I could hardly cope with the *thought* of the years ahead. What on earth I was going to do when they actually started maturing, God alone knows. It's a man's worst nightmare – when your darling baby girls start to have boyfriends. Every father knows from their own shameful personal experience that these little bastards will have one, and only one, thing on their minds, no matter how nice and polite they are to the crusty parents. It's just human nature. At the tender age of nine, my father promised me one hundred pounds if I didn't smoke one cigarette before I was 20. I had seriously toyed with the idea of offering Grace and Eve 10,000 dollars each if they didn't have sex until after I was dead. Then again, the day after my father made his offer I went out and smoked my first cigarette, so perhaps it wasn't the most effective policy.

One of my Australian friends has two grown-up daughters, and one day, after a glass or two, he told me how he would swap all his wealth and success for the chance to bring up his daughters again – differently. He got steadily more depressed as he filled me in on the details.

'I thought I could manage them like I managed my business,' he told me. 'I had it all mapped out. Whenever my elder daughter had a boyfriend visit the house to take her out, I would make sure my wife delayed her so I could be alone with the lad in question.'

'Why?' I enquired.

'So I could fill him in on the ground rules,' he replied.

'What were the ground rules?'

'Well it was more *a* rule than rules. I simply told each one of them that if he didn't have my daughter back home by ten o'clock that night then I would have him killed.'

'Fucking hell, that's ridiculous. How old were these poor bastards?'

'Oh, anywhere from 15 to 19.'

'And that's all you said?'

'No, I also said I'd have them shot if they told my daughter about our little chat.'

'So what happened?' I asked.

'Well,' and here his voice got quiet and mournful, 'they all brought her back by ten o'clock.'

'A result of sorts, I suppose.'

'No, it was a total disaster. I didn't realise it at the time, but it fucked her up for life. She couldn't work out why no one liked her enough to spend any time with her and always cut her dates short. Unbeknownst to me she tried everything – and I mean everything – to make them like her. None of it worked, of course, and they all brought her back by ten. She's never actually got over it. Twenty years later and she still hasn't a clue how to relate to men. And it's all my fault.'

'But what about your other daughter?' I asked.

'Worse,' he said.

'Worse? Fucking hell, how could it be worse?'

'I did the same drill on her. Panned out slightly differently, however.'

'How differently?'

'It was her first boyfriend. I got him in my study and gave him my speech. Half an hour later my daughter was yelling in my face, calling me a fascist pig, Stalinist sexist and a whole bunch of other politically confused and extremely unpleasant stuff. Turns out the ballsy little bastard had gone right out and told my daughter what I said to him. She left home and went to live with him to spite me. Had two kids out of wedlock, then left him. But even worse was that she told my elder daughter, who then worked out why none of her relationships had worked. She challenged me on it and I admitted what I'd done. She hasn't spoken to me since.'

Tragic though his story was, I was glad to have heard it. Ever since, the thought of unwittingly ruining Grace and Eve's lives by being a loving but utterly useless father has been even more painful than the thought of them being pawed by a succession of horny teenagers. Hopefully when dating time comes for my own daughters it will mean I've at least *some* balance and sensitivity. Or, more truthfully, that I'll have the sense to ignore my instincts and listen to Kate instead.

Chapter 34

Offshore

As FAR AS I COULD tell, John had made a slightly better fist of parenting than my Australian friend, but nevertheless I'm sure his fatherly duties had brought with them a certain amount of stress. The ending of this particular era was clearly a huge rite of passage for him and the occasion, especially given the location, was filled with significance. Jane and Max had really pushed the boat out with the arrangements. The night before the wedding there was to be a white-tie dinner for 150 guests in a private palace on the Grand Canal.

It had been a while since we'd had the polo club experience in London so both Kate and I had forgotten the type of company the happy couple mixed with. Perfectly nice and all that, but just so totally alien to our normal frame of reference.

Models, bankers and rock stars seemed to be the main categories. I was told *Tatler* magazine had solemnly pronounced that this was the third-most-important social occasion of 2003. Then again, Elton John's birthday party was apparently number one in the same article, so it was a peculiar ranking system, to say the least.

The evening was a white-tie affair. Before this trip I hadn't even realised white tie existed. Now I knew it was one stage beyond black tie. Definitely not a board shorts and thongs occasion.

The combination of the marvellously ornate palace with the hundred or so immaculately and formally dressed guests was quite breathtaking. Getting off our gondola at the entrance was ever so slightly like arriving at the Oscars – it felt grand and somehow important. I, on the other hand, felt ill at ease and awkward. It wasn't just the prospect of yet another social engagement without drink, but the fact that it was all but impossible to find any common ground. The first person I was introduced to, when she heard I was from Australia, said, 'I simply love Australia. In fact, so much so that I wanted to move there, but my accountant tells me they don't do offshore.' The second person, for some reason assuming I was a banker working in New York, told me she wasn't going to the Hamptons that year because it was getting too downmarket. The third person told me her husband hadn't seen the inside of a commercial plane until he was 21. Excellent, I thought, at last something I can engage with. 'What a shame,' I said. 'It must have been wonderful when he finally got the chance to travel.' She looked at me as if I was speaking Klingon before replying. 'A *commercial* plane. Jimmy visited over 70 countries on his father's jet before he was 18.' And so it went on.

It was these people – and a whole lot more like them – to whom I had to give a speech after dinner. We were clearly from parallel universes. They probably won't even understand me, let alone find me funny, I thought as I sat down to dinner. The guests on my table only increased my sense of 'otherness'. On either side of me were models. One of the 'super' variety, the other of the 'lingerie' variety. Kate was sitting at the head table in her capacity as matron of honour so I was left alone to tapdance through the thoroughly alien (to me, anyway) *Tatler* crowd.

The first course arrived and the model on my left (lingerie) took one extremely small bite from it, wrinkled her nose and then immediately put her knife and fork down and pushed the plate away from her. I resisted the temptation to do a Grace and say 'I'll have it', instead observing that 'caviar wasn't my favourite either'. She looked at me as if I were ET. It was only when she did exactly the same thing with all six courses that I realised it wasn't that *this* food wasn't to her taste, it was that *food* wasn't to her taste. She obviously didn't eat. At all. Over the course of the evening I swear she couldn't have had more than a dessertspoon of food. In total. Then again, I bet she looked pretty acceptable in her lingerie. Bizarrely, the model (super) on my right ate like a horse the whole night. Thoroughly confusing.

The time for speeches came around all too quickly. Three of the groom's friends spoke before me and their speeches were genuinely touching. Rather than a mindless rich kid on the international playboy circuit, Max clearly was a rather special bloke who had earned the respect of everyone who had dealt with him through his hard work, humility and decency. Finally the microphone was handed to me. I was crapping myself as I stood up and the sea of beautiful faces turned my way. I'd not had so much attention focused on me since Kindi Gym. Except this time I was dying of nerves, not embarrassment. I couldn't have read my notes if I'd wanted to as I was half-blinded by the bling from all their jewellery, so I did what any self-respecting envious Brit does when he is out of his depth – I took the piss out of Max. To my astonishment, they loved it, so I laid it on as thick as I could to ever-greater applause. Max took it in good spirit. The whole thing reminded me of the bloke whom Burt Lancaster hires in *Local Hero* to tell him he's an arse once a week, just to keep him honest.

With the speech out of the way I could relax, but unlike at the wedding in France, there wasn't a rugby match to sneak off to. Instead I made my way to the balcony with Kate and gazed at the incredible view. The dinner was being held in the Palazzo Pisani Moretta and the scene below of the Grand Canal and all its evening traffic was almost as good as the view of Cézanne's mountain from our room in Trets the week before. I suddenly felt enormously fortunate. And then guilty about having had so many ungenerous and mean-spirited thoughts about the guests. Who the fuck was I to be so censorious? The people back inside were human like the rest of us. It was a tribe thing. We all like to belong and I didn't belong in their tribe. That doesn't make them any worse or me any better. Just because they didn't have money worries didn't mean they didn't have problems to deal with like everyone else. Just because I didn't have any common ground with them didn't make them in any way silly or superficial. I may not have had their specific financial or social advantages but in a different way I was every bit as spoilt as them. I resolved to go back inside and mingle 'without prejudice', as George Michael almost said.

I turned to Kate. 'You know, sweetheart, just because they've got money it doesn't mean that they are any happier,' I told her.

'Course it does, you dozy prick,' she replied. 'Have you been drinking?'

Chapter 35

Mummy's painting

THE DAY OF THE wedding started in glorious fashion. I was still determined to keep up my training for the ocean swim. Luckily, the rest of the wedding party had taken over the Hotel Cipriani and as a wedding guest I had carte blanche to use all the hotel's facilities – including its enormous heated outdoor pool.

I took the private launch to the island opposite St Mark's where the Cipriani is rather splendidly located, and made my way to the pool area. Immediately upon arriving poolside, there was a yell of 'Nigel, Nigel, over here!' I looked around for the source of such an embarrassingly loud and public invitation. On the other side of the pool were three drop-dead gorgeous models I'd met at dinner the night before. In their designer swimsuits, they were frantically motioning to me while patting an empty sun lounge next to them. I waved a pleasant hello to them and got on with my training as intended.

Actually that last sentence is a complete lie. What I really did was suck in my stomach as far as I could and swagger smugly across the terrace, hoping as many people as possible were noticing this demonstration of my physical magnetism to the opposite sex. The speech the night before had proved a minor hit and for one glorious hour I was an honorary member of their tribe. Talk about beauty and the beast. I was wearing my board shorts and Saracens Rugby Club t-shirt. All three of them were in the smallest bikinis imaginable, had full make-up on and were sporting elaborate hairdos. When I could hold my stomach in no longer, I got in the pool and showed off by doing a full 30 minutes of continuous front crawl. I was delighted with my swimming progress. The only downside of the training session was that by the time I got out I was once again a mere mortal. I obviously didn't look as good in the pool as I was starting to feel – the bevy of lovelies had long since left the poolside.

I got dressed quickly and hailed the private launch. I wanted to speak to the kids before the wedding ceremony. I called home immediately on my return to our villa.

'Hi, Liz, how are the kids doing?' I asked.

'They're fine. I'm sure they'd like to speak to you,' she replied, passing the phone to Alex.

'Hi, Dad, was the Bismarck a warship?' he said.

'Yes, sweetheart. What've you been doing today?' I asked.

'Nothing. I've got a lolly and I'm not afraid to use it.'

'Er . . .'

'Dad, are weddings embarrassing?' he asked.

'Embarrassing, sweetheart?'

'Yeah. Liz told me you have to kiss someone in front of everyone,' he explained.

Before I could think of a suitable reply, Eve grabbed the phone,

'Sorry, Daddy, it wasn't on purpose. It was an accident, I was changing my mind up,' she said.

'Don't explode, Dad, don't explode,' Alex shouted in the background.

'Explode about what?' I asked. However, Eve had already passed the phone to Harry.

'Dad, I can count to a hundred,' he said.

'Can you, darling? That is wonderful,' I said, marvelling at Liz's educational prowess, since he could barely count to ten when we left.

'Yeah, I'll show you. One, two, skip a few, three, four, skip some more, ninety-nine, one hundred. Eve drew on Mummy's painting,' he added.

'Could I speak to Liz?' I asked. But the phone had been grabbed by Grace.

'Jingle bells, Batman smells. Where's Mummy? I want to talk to Mummy,' she demanded.

'Mummy's not here at the moment, sweetheart, it's Daddy,' I replied.

'Don't want to talk to you, I want Mummy,' she answered.

My mind was reeling. Apart from the abuse and the confusion of this four-way conversation, I couldn't get 'Mummy's painting' out of my mind. They were talking about one of our most prized possessions, a painting I had bought for Kate for our previous wedding anniversary. More accurately, I had commissioned it. I had given the brief to a friend of ours, Mark Collis. My brief to Mark had been twofold and very specific. 'There are only two rules,' I had told him. 'One: it can't be of the bloody Opera House. Two: I do not want to know what it is until you are completely finished. You can paint a one-inch picture of a dog turd or a 25-square-foot oil of Kate at the altar. The subject, medium, and size are entirely up to you. Regardless of whether we like it or not, I will buy it on the condition that neither of us finds out in advance what it is.' After nine weeks' painting, he unveiled it to us. Kate and I were both dumbstruck. He had painted an enormous exact copy of the two pages of the street map showing where we lived in Sydney. It covered the boys' school, the girls' kindy, the beach, the route of the ocean swim I was to do, the field where Alex plays rugby, the pitch where Harry plays football – everything. In one fell swoop he had captured our lives and provided us with a symbol of our Australian adventure. We absolutely adored it and now I had visions of it covered with scribbles.

Eventually I got Grace to stop telling me she loved Mummy more than me and she passed the phone to Liz, who confirmed that Eve had indeed shown great initiative, stood on a chair and defaced our favourite painting.

'It was with washable paint, though, so I'm sure a good scrub will get it off,' she optimistically informed me.

I was sure Mark hadn't painted with future Ajax scrubbings in mind, so I resigned myself to the fact that our favourite piece was ruined. How the hell was I going to break the news to Kate? With no job, commissioning artworks was going to be out of our reach for the foreseeable future, so I could hardly tell her I'd replace it as a sweetener. Beyond the painting itself, what on earth did this behaviour say about how the kids were coping with our absence? A feeling of guilt and doubt came over me – regardless of what fun we were having, perhaps it hadn't been such a bright idea after all to go off jaunting around Europe without the kids.

In the circumstances I thought my 'Serbelloni selective honesty' policy was the best approach when I met up with Kate later that afternoon and she asked me how her angels were.

'Wonderful. They're all fine. Grace especially sends all her love. And Eve is learning to paint,' I replied.

Chapter 36

Hearing aid

RUINED FAMILY HEIRLOOM or not, it was now time to focus on the main event. We had the bride and her family staying with us, so there was a considerable amount of preparation involved. The villa was soon in a frenzy of well-ordered chaos. The place was crawling, not just with people getting dressed but also with yet more people *helping* those people get dressed. A handsome bloke in jeans and t-shirt whom I'd never seen before approached me.

'Are you all right if I do your hair now?' he enquired.

'What do you want to do with it?' I replied.

'Just to do it,' he answered confusingly.

'Er, all right then.'

I'd never had my hair 'done' before. I haven't got that

much of it to do. I keep it short and a swift left-hand run through it in the morning has always seemed to do the trick. That said, it was strangely enjoyable to have someone fussing over it with such obvious concentration and seriousness. Fifteen minutes later, he held a mirror in front of me. I looked like a cross between Elvis Presley and Johnny Suede-head. I went in search of Kate to ask how best to change it without causing offence. But within two minutes enough people had spontaneously commented on how great it looked for me to leave it how it was. Maybe the left-hand-through-the-hair strategy wasn't 'leveraging the full potential of my best natural asset', as the hairdresser put it. Talk about different world.

The wedding service was held in one of Venice's landmark churches – the Basilica di San Giovanni e Paolo. The guests arrived in a flotilla of old wooden water taxis. It is against Venetian law to close such an icon for a private service, so the happy couple were wed in front of 200 family and friends – and 200 German, Japanese and American tourists. To their credit none of them heckled or started the Mexican wave and it actually lent a slightly regal air to proceedings. The trip to the reception intensified this feeling. As the flotilla of boats made its way down the Grand Canal and under the Rialto Bridge, the crowds that are ever-present in Venice started applauding, cheering and waving. I felt like David Beckham must most days of his life. As in the pool earlier in the day, I gave in to my hidden shallows and rather than meekly blushing I started waving back. The adulation might have been unearned and totally misdirected but damn, it felt good.

The reception was in the Cipriani Hotel. No expense or

effort had been spared and it was a wonderful evening. My enjoyment of events was further enhanced by the attentions of a gorgeous-looking middle-aged lady. By 'attentions' I mean the full hand-on-forearm-leaning-right-into-my-personal-space-hanging-off-my-every-word-full-eye-contact type of attentions. I've always thought that the older Helen Mirrens and Isabella Rossellinis of this world give the younger Kate Mosses and Cindy Crawfords a damn good run for their money. Now I had one sitting next to me and she was making it painfully clear she was mine for the asking. If Kate had been looking she most definitely would have been able to tell that this woman was single. She wasn't so much interested as swooning.

I started to suspect that my luck might be in when the first thing she did was – without any shame or embarrassment – move her chair unusually close to mine. My suspicions were further alerted when she announced 'My name's Sam. It's a lovely treat at my age to be sitting next to such a handsome younger man.' She said this while all the time looking directly into my eyes and holding my hand and – I swear I'm not making this up – pulling me even closer. On several occasions she asked me to retell a story and laughed uproariously each time. Throughout the evening, when I was talking to her she would often mouth the words along with me as if I was some sort of guru imparting spriritual wisdom. On one bizarre occasion she even went so far as to ask me what men of my age found attractive in women. On another she made me repeat the name of the villa where we were staying three times. I don't want to brag, but it was clearly game, set and match to the not-so-fat anymore, fired forty-year-old.

As Kate and I got ready for bed later that evening I couldn't resist retelling the story.

'I pulled tonight, sweetheart,' I graciously kicked off the conversation.

'Really,' Kate replied, 'and who was that with?'

'That good-looking middle-aged posh bird, Sam something.'

'And what precisely made you think she fancied you?'

'God, it was so obvious, it was embarrassing. She was clearly gagging for it. Whenever I was talking she would sort of lean in and look me in the face really intensely.'

'Did she also cock her head slightly to one side at the same time?'

'Now you mention it – yes, she did. Quite endearing, really.'

'And you say she leaned in when you were talking?'

'Yes – for God's sake woman, enough of this background context. I'm just trying to inform you that your husband is so magnetically attractive that he has to beat women off with a stick and tonight in particular I had a babe positively throwing herself at me.'

'Okay, but one question. What does the fact that she leaned in closely when you were talking, and looked . . .'

'Gazed,' I interrupted.

'Okay, *gazed* intensely at your face, say to you?'

'I've already told you – that she fancied me like mad. What the bloody hell does it say to you?'

'That she is Sam McClusker, one of my mother's oldest friends, who is completely deaf in one ear and extremely hard of hearing in the other. She lip reads on formal occasions so she doesn't have to wear her hearing aid.'

'Er . . . but she put her hand on my arm.'

'Nigel, she has lived with her same-sex partner for eleven years. It's more likely that you'll get a job in the next month than that she would fancy you.'

Women can be so unnecessarily cruel.

Chapter 37

Beaten teachable

WE HAD PLANNED TO stay on in Venice for a few days after the wedding party left. This seemed like a good idea when we were booking the holidays, but in reality, with me not having a job and Venice being one of the most expensive cities in Europe, it meant moving to a small, over-expensive chicken coop of a tourist hotel. The free pass to the Cipriani's pool was no longer valid, either, so the swimming training was going to have to be put on hold until our return to Australia. It all served to heighten the vast chasm between the worlds of the ultra-rich and the average tourist. There literally is no relation. You can be in the same city, in the same street and still inhabit entirely parallel universes. There is nothing inherently wrong with either universe, it's just not perhaps such a good idea to juxtapose them as dramatically as we did.

Our new hotel room reminded me of one of those bottles with ships in them. I had no idea how they had got the tiny double bed into the room. You couldn't open the door more than a couple of feet before it hit the mattress. You then had to close the door before you could walk into the rest of the room. I say 'walk into' but 'edge around' is a more accurate description as there were no more than ten inches between the bed and the wall. And that was it. No bathroom, no minibar, one cupboard that you couldn't open properly because of the bed, and a TV that didn't work fixed to the wall. It did for hotel accommodation what travelling on airmiles does for airline travel. The location, however, was fantastic. We put our luggage on the bed (there was no other place for it) and headed out for a cheap dinner.

Venice doesn't really do 'cheap dinner', so we ended up in a pizzeria. You'd be forgiven – but wrong – for thinking that a pizzeria so narrowed Kate's options that the ordering process was painless. If anything, it made it worse. After our traditional argument and sulk we settled down to one of those gorgeous evenings you sometimes have at the end of a successful and eventful holiday. We started by talking about the trip that we were on and relived every memorable moment. I 'fessed up to the real nature of my telephone conversations with the kids and we laughed until the people sitting next to us started to give us pointed looks. We then moved on to *every* holiday we had been on together. We'd never actually taken this particular trip down memory lane before. Kate asked the waiter for a pen and we wrote them all down, first randomly, then again in chronological order. It was a strangely moving, intimate and enjoyable process to go through. It had been an incredible ten years. I was amazingly lucky. I was happy. I was relaxed. I fancied a drink.

'I think I'll have a glass of wine tonight, darling,' I said.

'Don't be an idiot, Nigel,' Kate said.

'No, seriously. Just one. I really fancy it. No beer or cock-tails or anything like that. Just a single glass of an earthy, heavy red,' I replied.

'What could possibly make you want to do something so ridiculously stupid?' Kate asked.

'Calm down, sweetheart. I'm only talking about one. I'm determined not to touch a drop when we get back to Australia. I just really fancy a glass tonight. We haven't got to get up early tomorrow. I'm feeling really happy. I'd like to drink something other than sodding mineral water tonight. Besides, all those holiday stories remind me of how much fun we used to have when we'd get on it together. It's been a great holiday, a real second honeymoon, and it seems a shame not to have at least one drink with you,' I reasoned.

'So you've stayed dry in London, on the road trip and at the two weddings, but now you want to "crown a moment" in a crappy pizzeria? I don't know what they talk about in AA but it sounds to me like you're in denial.'

'Jesus, I'm only talking about one. I feel I've earned it,' I replied.

'Darling, you know it won't *be* one. You always say that but then one inevitably means another and then another.'

'Well, all right, but it wouldn't really do any harm if we shared a bottle between us. Like we always used to do in the old days, just once more?' I suggested as I motioned to the waiter.

'Nigel, you've done so well,' Kate said. 'I'm really proud of you. Really proud. You've been a different man to live with. You're helpful. You're good with the kids. I can't believe you'd throw it all away. This is how it always starts. You feel you've proved you can control it by abstaining for a number of weeks, then you think you can go back to it in a moderate way. You can't. You spent ten years trying. You always failed. You'll be fine tonight. You'll probably be fine for a week, but I know in a month you'll be drinking more than you want to and then you'll be back to square one.'

I felt my contradictory nature start to assert itself. Who the hell was she to tell me what to do? I didn't try and stop her enjoying herself, so what gave her the right to try and stop me? She was such a fucking killjoy. It was all right for her, sitting there with a fag and a cocktail, but what about me? Normally at this stage I would say something horrible to her and then to prove a point do exactly the opposite of what she wanted me to. The waiter approached.

'I'll have a latte, please,' I heard myself say.

'I thought you wanted a drink,' Kate said.

'I know. I did. But I don't. Well, I do but I don't – not when I think about it. You're right. I love you. I'm a fucking idiot. The whole point is never to pick up the first drink. Ever. I'm sorry.' I said.

'Don't be. It's an amazing thing you've done. I just don't want you to go back. Not just for my and the kids' sakes, but for you. Having said that, if this was all some sort of elaborate ruse to say nice things to me to get my knickers off, you'll have to do better than that.'

On reflection, it was one of the most important evenings of our entire marriage. I genuinely think Kate saved my life in that conversation. Or at the least saved me and the family from another ten years of failed moderate drinking. But it wasn't just an important evening in my life, it was also a revealing one.

After my moment of weakness had passed, Kate and I settled into a rather lovely flirty cosiness during which I quizzed her on her seemingly natural ability to control her drinking.

'You never get wrecked or even drink more than you want to. You're always leaving drinks unfinished. I suppose we're just made up differently,' I said.

'Maybe. But then again, what was that phrase they use in AA – "beaten teachable"?'

'Yep, that's it.'

'Well, I think I wasn't so much beaten teachable as "embarrassed sensible",' she said.

'What do you mean?'

'Really want to know?'

'What do you think? Of course. Tell me.'

'I've never told anyone this story before,' she said.

'Get on with it – you're driving me to drink,' I replied.

'You know the first job I had?'

'With the bank?'

'That's the one. It was all rather overwhelming. I was young . . .'

'Yeah, yeah. Enough of the excuses. Get on with it,' I interrupted.

'Well, at the end of my first week one of the traders invited me to lunch. I was very flattered. I was just a secretary and he was one of the "Masters of the Universe", as Tom Wolfe called them.'

'I get the picture: he wanted to nail you.'

'Nigel.'

'Sorry.'

'Anyway, lunch was in a wine bar – this was the eighties, after all. I thought it was going to be just the two of us but there was a group of them. Men and women. They were all drinking champagne. Like it was water. They kept filling my glass. I was nervous, but enjoying it. It seemed so glamorous. The blokes were all good-looking and every single one of them was flirting with me. Trouble was, I wasn't used to drinking so much – definitely not at lunchtime and definitely not champagne. After an hour we still hadn't ordered any food and I suddenly began to feel incredibly ill. I slipped off to the Ladies and was violently sick.'

'Silly, but nothing special,' I said, unimpressed.

'Thing was, I didn't quite make the toilet. I got to the Ladies but not to the cubicle. The moment I opened the door I was sick over the sink, floor, mirrors – the lot. It was like that scene from *The Exorcist*,' Kate continued.

'What did you do?' I asked, horrified.

'It was hideous. The place was a real mess. I was desperate to impress my new colleagues so I tidied myself up as best I could and went back to the table they were all standing around.'

'Leaving the loo as it was?'

'Didn't really have much choice, I wasn't carrying a bucket and mop with me. I obviously needed to cover my tracks as I didn't want anyone to know it was me, so on my return I said in a loud voice, "People can be so revolting: it's disgusting in the Ladies, someone has been sick all over the room and just left it there." I had all their attention and was going to continue but I was overcome with a second wave of nausea. Before I could even put my hand over my mouth I projectile-vomited onto the chest-high table we were gathered around. Christ, Nigel, it went everywhere. I don't think there was a person who wasn't hit. It was awful. Like when Eve was sick on the taxi driver on the way to Heathrow – times ten.'

'I grant you, that is bad. What happened?'

'Everyone left to get cleaned up – it's not much fun eating lunch smelling of puke. I went home alone. Worst weekend of my life.'

'And on Monday?' I asked.

'Everyone was really nice. Which bizarrely made it worse. The guy who had invited me called me to say it didn't matter at all,' Kate said.

'And did you see him again?'

'Course not. Neither he, nor indeed any of them, ever spoke to me again. The next Monday my boss called me in and let me go.'

Chapter 38

Poo-poo head

WHEN IT WAS FINALLY time to leave Venice there was no nice man to shepherd us to his boat to take us to the airport. We lugged our bags on public transport to the check-in desk of CrapAirlines.com and bid farewell to Venice from the microscopically small seats of our hundred-year-old 767. We were flying to London first, as the only flight to Sydney we could get was from Heathrow. We stayed in the country just long enough to drive from Stansted Airport to Heathrow, but it was still long enough for me to pick up the worst bout of hayfever that I'd had in years. I have always been a chronic sufferer and yet another of the benefits of Australia was that I hadn't had any symptoms at all since my arrival. I've long since learnt to live with the effects of my allergy but this time my continual sneezing brought with it a whole new set of challenges. We were still in the height of the SARS scare and, as you can imagine, my sneezing made it a barrel of laughs disembarking and boarding during our stopover in Hong Kong. I had more fun with the community nurse.

When the plane started its descent into Sydney I was surprised at my emotions. I'd thought a three-week dose of the Northern Hemisphere would have made me homesick for Blighty when in fact the reverse was the case. Sydney felt like home even though we hadn't even lived there for two years yet. Even something as simple as the surfboard bags on the baggage carousel made me smile and feel welcome.

However, although I love the city and was overjoyed to be 'home', it doesn't mean that I was blind to its less-good sides. For a start, we landed in driving rain. A bit like people not letting on that childbirth is actually extremely unpleasant, there is a myth perpetuated about Sydney's weather. Take it from me: it does rain and it does get cold. It's entirely possible to have London weather for weeks at a time. When my parents first visited a year earlier it rained every day for a month.

This time, as soon as we passed through Customs we were reminded of another of the less appealing aspects of the city. The taxis are without doubt the worst I've experienced anywhere in the world. It's not that they are dirty or danger-ous or even unfriendly, it's just that the drivers haven't got a clue where they are going. Call me a stuffy old traditionalist, but I reckon that's a pretty core skill for a taxi driver. These blokes don't even pretend.

'Bronte, please,' I said as we climbed into the back seat.

'Where?'

'Bronte.'

'Whereabouts?'

'Oh, about halfway down Macpherson Street, please.'

'No, not whereabouts in Bronte. Where is Bronte?'

Now Bronte is possibly the second-most-well-known beach in Sydney. It's just a couple of kilometres south of Bondi and barely 6 kilometres from the airport. It's a bit like a London cabbie not knowing where Hyde Park is, or Trafalgar Square.

'If you head towards Bondi, we'll show you the way,' we offered.

'How do you get to Bondi?'

'Just head to the city centre.'

'Which way?'

I ended up getting out of the car and into the front passenger seat and directing him street by street. The thing is, this wasn't the first time this had happened to me. When I was working I had often been asked to direct cabbies for journeys *within* the city centre.

But not even a crap Sydney taxi ride could spoil my mood as we approached the house. I was almost ill with excitement. I hadn't seen our kids for three whole weeks – the longest time ever. Alex was first to the door.

'Daddy, Daddy, Saracens have signed Taine Randell!'

Harry was close behind. 'Daddy, how does hair grow?'

Eve appeared. 'Daddy, you've got grass on your face.' (I'd grown a beard on the trip.)

Grace finally presented herself. As I opened my arms to give her a hug she walked up, looked me in the eye and announced, 'You're not my father, poo-poo head,' before walking off.

Not sure whether the poo-poo head or doubted parentage jibe hurt more, but as I lugged our bags inside I couldn't help saying a silent prayer in hope that it was only Eve who had taken up painting in our absence.

Chapter 39

Pinch and a punch

OUR EUROPE TRIP PROVED to be a real watershed. Slipping back into domestic life felt good, comfortable. I got stuck into the kids' lives as never before. School canteen became a regular duty; I even coached the under-six football team on occasions. The latter is more difficult than it sounds. The phrase 'shepherding cats' springs to mind. The angelic little bastards just wouldn't listen. As I was talking, they'd all be gazing off into the distance or scratching their nuts or fighting. I found it a totally draining experience. The next week I watched the regular coach do it with none of the problems I had encountered. Afterwards I asked him how he did it.

'The secret is to keep them moving,' he explained. 'If you

get them to do things, they are fine. The moment you ask them to stand still and listen to you, it's carnage.'

I thought back to the week before. He was right. Amazing how something so simple could make such a difference. I realised that over the months off I had been picking up tips like this one on a weekly basis. All of them were making me a more capable father – not to mention a happier one. These tips regularly made the difference between me having a shit day or a wonderful one. I had, for example, come to hate school pick-up. Every day I had an argument with Alex – me wanting him to come home straight away, him wanting to stay and play footy. It was ruining the end of each day for the family. I would arrive home furious and Alex would be in a sulk. This in turn would make Kate upset. Not the ideal combination for arsenic hour. Then one day I asked a friend how he seemed to manage it so well.

'You really want to know?' he enquired.

'Yes.'

'Okay. Why are you so keen to take him home straight after the bell has gone?'

The question threw me a bit. I had no idea, it was just what you did, wasn't it? School pick-up was a task that I was volunteering to do, and in a typically male fashion I had decided that like all tasks it needed to be done quickly and efficiently. I explained this to my adviser.

'Okay, I understand, but if you let him play for 15 minutes and then took him home what would happen?'

'What do you mean, "happen"?'

'I mean, what would be bad about it?'

I thought for a moment. 'Nothing,' I replied.

'Okay. What would happen it you let him play for half an hour and then took him home?'

'Nothing.'

'Okay then. What would happen if you let him know in advance that you were always going to let him have 30 minutes of playing after school before you took him home?'

'We'd never have an argument, he'd have more time with his friends playing outdoors as opposed to watching TV, I wouldn't lose my temper and the evenings at home would be infinitely more pleasant.'

'I'd recommend you try it then,' he suggested.

I pondered his advice. 'There's a flaw,' I eventually said.

'What?'

'Well, what if I don't want to spend half an hour each day hanging around a kids' playground?' I asked.

'Then you don't. You're thinking about this all wrong. It's not supposed to be a military operation with a medal for who can do things quickest. Watch your son, get to know his friends, chat to the other dads and mums. If you don't want to do that, then use the time to make the calls you need to on your mobile. Lastly, if you really can't spare the time, turn up at three twenty-five, not three o'clock.'

'Is that allowed?'

'Of course it is.'

'Do you do it?'

'All the time. As long as you let him know, he'll be fine with it. My lad prefers it.'

After this conversation I actually looked forward to school pick-up as one of my favourite bits of the day. There were countless examples like this. None of them were splitting the atom – indeed some of them were as simple as leaving the butter out of the fridge overnight so making packed lunches in the morning was easier – but they all contributed to transforming my days. It made me think back to when I was working and how on many occasions I was too busy doing things badly to ask for, and then listen to, advice. I resolved that if I ever went back to work, I would remember this simple lesson: if you are regularly struggling with a task, try asking the counsel of someone who excels at the thing you are struggling with. The worst that can happen is that they refuse – although this has never happened in my time off and I somehow think it wouldn't in the workplace either. People on the whole are delighted to be asked about things they're good at.

Rather astonishingly, given the outcomes of my first attempts, I even started to enjoy taking the kids to school in the mornings. I actually preferred it when I could take all four of them in the car together – dropping the girls off at kindy first, then driving on to school with the lads. Seeing the girls with their pink and blue lunch bags on their backs walk hand in hand into the kindy was as cute as the conversation in the car with the boys was funny.

'Lads, that's a revolting smell. Which one of you monsters has cracked his cheeks?' I asked one morning as I got back into the car having kissed the twins goodbye.

'Not me, Dad, it was Alex,' Harry said.

'He who denied it supplied it: it was Harry,' Alex countered.

'He who smelt it dealt it: it was you, Dad,' Harry changed tack.

'He who rhymed it crimed it: you're both guilty. Besides, you know Dad doesn't fart,' I replied.

'Daaaad,' they both chorused.

It was puerile but fun. I was finding that I could get the most enormous amounts of joy out of the simplest of things. Harry would stand next to me in the mornings and mimic me shaving. The girls would lie either side of me when I was doing sit-ups and raise their arms and legs while shouting, 'Look at us, Mummy. We're exercising.' Alex and I would sit on the same armchair together and watch *The Simpsons* most evenings – all the time with him impersonating the characters and making unflattering comparisons between Homer and me. The beginning of each month was a particular favourite. Far too early in the morning, all four of them would burst into our bedroom and pummel me with a traditional 'pinch and a punch for first of the month'. I would just lie there moaning 'white rabbits', while Kate would egg them on by saying, 'Ignore him, too late'. When I moved into the 'slap and kick for being so quick' mode of defence, Kate would simply change the rules, scream 'get Daddy!' and join in on the kids' side. Women.

Chapter 40

Nelson Bay

IT WASN'T JUST THE family routine that I was increasingly happy with – I was also starting to get on top of my personal game. For the first time since I was 19, I was now at my ideal weight. It hadn't been easy but I had stumbled on a workable weight loss regime (maybe I'll write that diet book after all) and I loved how it made me feel. The swimming training was also well on track. The week after our return from Europe I stuck to my plan of starting to train in the ocean.

To begin with, Clovelly was my choice of beach as it has a long, thin stretch of water protected on three sides from the elements. The training had clearly paid off. I had expected it to be a bit of a shock when I switched from the pool to the sea but after the first few tries I found I wasn't bad at it – and, more importantly, I loved doing it. Within a couple of weeks I was a regular at Clovelly and a convert to the whole ocean swimming experience. Being indoors, swimming between ropes in flat chlorinated water or outside in the confines of an ocean pool no longer seemed to be the real thing. I started to really look forward to each session. I found it impossible to be tired or miserable after even the shortest of swims in the sea, and the sights, sounds and smells of the ocean soon became to be as important to me as the exercise itself. After a few more weeks I was confident enough to start training with friends, mainly at the weekends. These friends were all qualified lifeguards and had done shedloads of proper ocean races. Swimming with them meant I could broaden my horizons from Clovelly and before too long I was swimming at all the beaches from Bondi down to Maroubra. I was touched that they could spare the time to piss around with such a novice as me.

It was with real pride that I did my first beach-to-beach swim. It was a rough day. I had decided to attempt the short distance across Nelson Bay from Tamarama around the headland to Bronte. For a local, this swim would seem like stepping over a small puddle; for me it was like swimming across the Pacific. I deliberately chose a rougher day as I wanted to experience a bigger swell, because an important part of the challenge of ocean races is the getting-in and getting-out bit. The year before, 15 people had had to be rescued at Bondi during the Bondi to Bronte race, because getting out beyond the wave break was too demanding. Swimming in a pool is tiring, but getting out through substantial breaking waves is a different challenge altogether. As a beginner, if you get it wrong then the chances of you being able to swim another 3 kilometres in open sea are dramatically reduced.

As with the school run, I decided to ask for advice. My friend David, who had given me the slow-and-steady swimming tip earlier in the year, kindly agreed to help. He was an excellent coach.

'The important thing is to dive well before the wave reaches you,' he said. 'Swim deep, grab sand if you can. Stay down and swim at least a couple of strokes after you feel the wave pass over you before you come up. You don't want to come up in the backwash froth, as that is seriously debilitating if you do it a couple of times. When you come up, be prepared to immediately dive again. It is tiring but under no circumstances stop until you are out back. If you do, you'll just end up being caught in the washing machine where all the waves dump. That's a dangerous place to be – even for a good swimmer.'

It was clear from the way David said this that in his eyes I didn't qualify for that particular description. It was all a little bit daunting as I stood there watching the waves roll in. I thought to myself, what on earth am I playing at? I'm a pudgy, unfit businessman who doesn't really have the right to be in swimming trunks, let alone to be on this beach about to do this swim. But then again, bugger it. That is why I'm here – precisely because I don't want to *be* a pudgy, unfit, businessman.

Clinging to this last motivational thought, I walked into the water and promptly got knocked off my feet. David helped me up and shouted in my ear, '*After* the last wave of this set, I want you to follow me.' Two more waves broke before he made his move. I followed him as if my life depended on it. Come to think of it, it probably did. I can well imagine how rooted you would be if you got caught in the middle of the breaking waves and had expended all your energy – there is only so much a lifeguard can do. I now properly understood how there could still be so many fatalities each year. I followed David's instructions to the letter and within a few exhausting minutes I was successfully beyond the breakers. It was wonderful. I loved the feeling of the swell as it repeatedly picked me up and brought me down again. It was the first time I had ever been properly 'in the ocean', as opposed to 'at the beach'. I floated on my back for a while looking at Tamarama beach in front of me, Mackenzies Point to my right and Shark Point to my left. For some reason I couldn't help laughing.

At the risk of getting religious, it was as near to a numinous experience as any I'd had recently – and that includes in the Quaker house. We had to swim further out to avoid the rip off the north Bronte head. The further the better, as far as I was concerned – I didn't want the swim to end. A surprise, and a real bonus, was that even though we were what seemed like miles off the shore, I could see the bottom, and all the glorious sea life in between, the whole way round. As we made our way towards the south end of Bronte beach we passed behind the group of surfers that the big conditions had attracted. A year earlier, if I had been standing on this beach on a day like this I wouldn't have been able to imagine being in the sea, let alone being as far out as the surfers. Now I was passing behind them. Despite the few mouthfuls of water I had inadvertently swallowed on the journey, I felt like a cross between Jacques Cousteau and Johnny Weissmuller when I climbed onto dry land at the Bronte beach pool.

For David it had been a quick dip in the sea; for me it was a huge milestone, a real rite of passage. As we stood chatting, I became aware of another remarkable aspect of what we'd just done. Not the swim itself, but the fact that it was winter and we'd both just swum across Nelson Bay without the need for wetsuits or caps. Have I mentioned that I love Australia?

Chapter 41

Blue line

IT WAS AS IF THE benefits of being off the hamster wheel were not only cumulative but exponential as well. Five months into my year off, it all seemed to be coming together. I'd never been happier. Another source of joy was that on top of all the swimming I was doing I had also made a successful return to my running career.

I first took up running on 1 January 1996 and have kept a diary of every run I have done ever since. To date I've filled three books cover to cover with small, densely packed writing. Reviewing them gives a sort of arm's-length commentary on my life. All my travels are detailed, as wherever I go I always take my running kit. I don't believe I've really experienced a city unless I've run in it. I 'collect' cities and look forward to each new one so I can tick it off on the map.

Sometimes my runs are what I remember most fondly of a visit. A run around the Imperial Palace was the highlight of a trip to Tokyo; same with a jog around Central Park last time I was in New York. In 1997, I went to Athens on a horrendous business trip where I was expected to visit nightclubs and brothels with a client – 'eating and drinking for other people's pleasure', as the famous business commentator Sir Harvey Jones so wonderfully described business entertaining. The run I did up Lykavittos Hill made the trip for me, although refusing to partake of the delights on offer in the Moscow Queens strip-club did nothing for my reputation with the client. I don't just collect cities on my runs, I collect people too – friends, work colleagues, family, strangers; anyone and everyone I've run with has in some way enriched me, and they get recorded in the diary. Running is a fantastic leveller and an excellent way to get to know someone a little more deeply than you normally would. Gender, seniority and age become somehow irrelevant when you're three kilometres into a jog around Sydney Harbour. (I find surfing, or indeed anything that involves taking your shirt off, can potentially have the same beneficial effect.)

Most importantly, in the past running had transformed my relationships with my children. When my elder son turned one, I reviewed my parental performance and concluded I was a crap dad. Nothing too bad, just not really properly involved. I went out that day and bought one of those baby jogger prams. I then told Kate that on Saturday mornings she was banned from doing anything with Alex. From that day on I got up every Saturday and took Alex for a run to somewhere he found interesting – usually a train station, for the first 18 months. We'd sit there chatting and when he got bored I'd run back. He got out of the house, Kate got a break and I got a bonding opportunity with my son as well as some exercise. It worked so well that I did the same with Harry, and when Grace and Eve were born I went out and bought a double buggy and did the same with them. When they are older they will probably tell their friends that the worst bit of their childhood was the bloody runs they had to do with their dad, but for me they're some of my most special memories.

For the years until we came to Australia, I was running three times a week, on average, but since the move, the pressures of the job and four kids had taken their toll to such an extent that whole months had passed without me so much as lacing a training shoe. To most people, that would be no great loss but for me it bordered on the tragic. I loved running. It had become a central part of my life and was responsible for many of its high spots. I'm well aware that my relationship with the 'sport' is alternative to say the least. The difference being that I don't view it as a physical activity: I view as a spiritual one. Many casual joggers speak of how they feel their running not only keeps them fit but also gives them self-confidence and heightens their appreciation of the world they live in. I too can attest to these feelings – but for me running does more than that. In many ways I credit it with saving my life. I genuinely believe my running has made me not just a better father and husband, but a better person full stop. One of my cornerstone philosophies is that with sustained, focused effort, you can achieve almost anything. Now, as a theory on its own this can come across as a bit Pollyanna-ish, but every time I run, I can re-invent myself how I want to be. Every race I finish, every person I connect with, and every city I discover proves my life philosophy back to me.

Running also keeps me honest. In 1996 I resolved to run at least one race a year. The clock doesn't lie or listen to excuses – if the newspaper says you did the 10 kilometres in 70 minutes, then you did. It doesn't mention that you were really stressed at work and couldn't find the time away from the family to train. It just says you ran the 10 kilometres in 70 minutes. It's truth stripped down to its barest form. Whether you think running 10 kilometres in 70 minutes is pathetic or heroic is your business. It just is. It provides you with a rock of certainty in an otherwise rather confusing world. What you do with that truth is up to you. The glorious thing is if you do decide to improve it, the results of your efforts are laid bare in the same manner. Unlike with so much in life, you can't fake it: you either improved or you didn't.

When I was in London my regular race was the Crouch End 10k. I did the first one alone. I was starting out and running was personal, almost a guilty secret. However, each year after, I made a point of running with friends and family and having a party in our house afterwards. In 1998 I ran it with my brother, my sister-in-law, my brother-in-law, my sister-in-law's boyfriend, Giles and three work colleagues. Both my and Kate's parents, plus an assortment of friends from the area, came to the post-race lunch in our kitchen. I've a picture taken in the garden on that day. When they are writing my obituary I'd be very happy for it to be the one they use. If only every family or social occasion was so stress-free and joyful. Think large family Christmas without the bickering. I've still got my finisher's t-shirt from each of the six Crouch End 10ks I've done, and nerdy as it is, they would be the first clothes I'd rescue if the house caught fire.

To avoid injury after such a long layoff I had deliberately

got back in to my running slowly. I actually started with a series of short walks, gradually extending the route each time. When I got up to a full 30 minutes I tentatively added in short bursts of jogging between random markers that I would set on the spur of the moment. 'Right, you fat tub of lard, let's see if you can jog to that bus stop from here,' I'd challenge myself before running to this self-imposed finish line and continuing to walk again.

To my slight surprise and delight, within a couple of months I was injury-free and back to a regular running schedule. In fact my running was going well (and by 'well' I most definitely don't mean fast or long – I mean enjoyable). A surfing instructor once said to me the best surfer is the one who is smiling the most. By applying that criterion to running, I was comfortably more successful than Carl Lewis and Linford Christie put together, so I signed up for the City to Surf race with my friend Sally.

This is an amazing event. It starts in the centre of the city, in Hyde Park, and as the name suggests makes its way to the surfing beach at Bondi. Fourteen kilometres in all. It is the world's biggest timed running event with over 60,000 runners participating each year. Sydney seems to have a knack of doing these types of occasions incredibly well. Throughout the year there are numerous community events – not just sporting festivals, but everything across a spectrum as diverse as Gay Mardi Gras, the New Year's Eve fireworks and Sculpture by the Sea. People turn up to these happenings in their thousands and the events always seem to be immaculately run and trouble-free. No wonder the Sydney Olympics were such a success.

On the sunny morning in August, it was wonderful just waiting in the crowd at the start line. Sixty thousand people, all in a good mood, gathered for a common purpose. My strongest memory of the day is the surreal image of the sky filled with flying clothes as people threw their pre-race sweat-shirts into the trees just before the starter's gun. It was like those scenes in *Lord of the Rings* when the archers all fire their crossbows into the air at once, except here it was shirts, not arrows. By the time the gun went, every tree was dressed like an alternative Christmas tree. This being Sydney, the organis-ers of course had a plan for this annual tradition and collected up all the discarded tops for charity.

The race itself was a joy. I was determined not to get caught up in the macho 'reach for the sky' bollocks that can sometimes overtake you on race day. My race plan was to start out slow, get slower, then taper off towards the end. I wanted to savour every minute. A bit like my Nelson Bay swim, the longer I took the better, as far as I was concerned. I'm pleased to report I excelled myself in this regard, coming in 33,748th place behind an assortment of runners dressed as nuns, elephants and one nutter who I swear was wearing a full diving suit and hood. Despite not troubling the leader board, this race ranks up there as one of my all-time favourites. The t-shirt I've got from the event has pride of place in my wardrobe along with all the Crouch End 10k ones.

I was so enthused by the City to Surf, and encouraged by how the family was getting on with each other, that I decided to take the plunge and enter a race with both Alex and Kate for the first time. Luckily another of the finest fun runs on the planet – The Bridge Run – was only a month or so away. This route starts at the North Sydney Oval, winds its way gently across the Harbour Bridge (which is specially closed for the occasion) and ends at the Opera House. Oh, and the whole way you are running on the blue line that is still on the roads from the marathon course of the 2000 Olympic Games. Talk about collecting a city. We sent off our entry forms and started the process of preparing for our first race together. Neither Alex nor Kate being runners, this was more of an operation than it might sound. At times coaxing them out the door in their training kits reminded me of the persuasion I had to engage in to get Kate to do her bungy jump, but on the whole our jogs together were even-tempered affairs. Besides, however hard I may sometimes have had to push, at least there were never any 'gators involved.

Chapter 42

Jaws

ALL IN ALL IT WAS A pretty dramatic turnaround from the fat, lethargic executive I had been just a few months before. I loved being active and slim. I found myself in a virtuous circle of energy: the fitter I got, the more I wanted to do and so the fitter I got. I reached another swimming milestone – again with David. This time it was swimming from head to head, not beach to beach. We dived off the edge of the famous Icebergs pool on the south head of Bondi Bay, swam to the north head and back again – a decent distance even for a good swimmer. This may sound incredibly sad but I was so excited by the prospect of this challenge that I actually counted every single stroke I took. 2,200 exactly. As I climbed out of the ocean onto the edge of the Icebergs pool, I couldn't help thinking that Zane would have been impressed – even if I was still 600 strokes short.

With this feat successfully behind me, I felt sufficiently in shape to apply for the Bondi to Bronte race. Up until now I hadn't felt I'd earned the right to even fill out the entry form. Reading the form, however, was an intimidating experience in its own right. One particular bit stood out from the rest, and I quote: 'Please note the Bondi to Bronte ocean swim is a demanding event. Possible risks include drowning, being hit by a boat, shark attack or blue bottle sting. Swimmers enter at their own risk and are responsible for their own physical condition.' Sell it to me, why don't you.

One of the many benefits of my new state of fitness was that my surfing had gradually begun to improve. I'd been hooked from the very first lesson I'd taken on Christmas Day 2001, at Bondi, but my progress had been frustratingly slow. Unless you've grown up near the water, surfing is actually an incredibly difficult thing to do. To a beginner surfer, those videos of the guys riding monster waves in Hawaii are as relevant as videos of Tiger Woods winning the Open are to a novice golfer. It gives you no idea how difficult it is. To start with I'd found it a stretch to even carry the sodding board along the beach, let alone to then paddle the thing in the ocean.

For a beginner, paddling out is exhausting. Just as you think you've got the hang of being on the board, a wave hits you, knocks you off and sweeps you back towards the beach. There is no respite. The waves are relentless. You simply have to keep getting back on the board and paddling for all you're worth. The goal is to get out back where you can sit up, have a rest and read the ocean for the best place to catch the breaks. On many days it is impossible for novice surfers to make it out back. There is an unofficial safety code that says that if you can't get out back quickly then the conditions are too big for your standard and that you should get the hell out of the water.

Like many things in life, surfing is completely unfair for the beginner. Just as banks only lend money to the people who don't need it, surfing becomes easier and less effort the better you get. Paddling a surfboard uses muscles you don't use when sitting at a desk working on a computer. After my first lesson I ached for a week and winced every time I had to move my shoulders back to get a shirt or jacket on. The first time I made it out back I was so shattered that rather than sitting up and looking around, I lay face down on the board like a beached whale and gently moaned.

But getting out back isn't the half of it. You then have to learn how to catch a wave. And leap to your feet. And ride a wave. This takes not only skill but also strength and agility. Regular surfers have bodies that defy the normal rules of human evolution. Forget the ludicrous bodybuilder physique – these guys and gals have perfect sculpted forms. Not an ounce of fat on them. Rock-hard muscle honed purely around the specific actions needed while on a surfboard. Broad shoulders, V-shaped backs and entirely flat stomachs are the norm. Throw in the sun-bleached hair and year-round tans and you can see why surfer culture is seized upon by marketers as diverse as Coke and FCUK and even used in countries that haven't actually got beaches. Kate and I saw many such posters while in Venice and the French Alps. I suppose the skiing link could explain the posters in the Alps – but Venice? Unlike many supposedly-inspirational looks that are obviously artificial and manufactured, the surfer dude has a certain rugged credibility about him that yells authentic. It certainly appealed to me – but then again, as Kate regularly reminded me, I was clearly going through a mid-life crisis.

I was now capable of getting out back in moderate conditions. Reading the ocean was my new problem – that and the surf code. A city beach such as Bondi is often crowded. Breaking the surf rules is a definite no-no and being a beginner is no excuse. The main principle is you never, ever, 'drop in', which basically means that the person who catches the wave first has right of way. If you catch it later and drop in on a surfer who is already riding the wave, you piss them off mightily. Given the size of them, this is not something I recommend.

Getting out back brings with it another problem. Sharks. I've never been sure precisely where the shark net is at Bondi. On days when the tide is out and the surf is big you can find yourself a way out to sea. It's only natural to start wondering. And rural beaches don't even have shark nets. Locals readily admit there are sharks in the ocean. They have a refreshingly simple, two-pronged safety policy: 'If you are worried about sharks, either get out of the ocean or get over it.' To be fair to them, 'getting over it' involves slightly more than just not worrying. There are certain basic rules that you are advised to follow to avoid being taken by a Noah. One of them is not to surf at dusk or dawn, another never to surf alone. In my newfound enthusiasm I idiotically ignored both on a weekend trip to the aptly named Boomerang Beach, a few hours north of Sydney.

I had woken early. The kids and Kate were still asleep. My surfboard was on the roof of the car from the journey the day before. It was calling to me. I could have a surf, buy breakfast for the family and be back before they woke up, I self-servingly reasoned. I leapt out of bed, flung my kit on and drove the 3 kilometres to Boomerang Beach. After a while you tend to get blasé about beaches in Australia. It's a bit like going snowblind while on a skiing holiday. There are so many nice beaches that you come to expect miles of white sand, clear water and gorgeous views. Even by Australian standards, however, this one was a pretty nice beach and, wonderfully, it was completely deserted. Not a soul in sight. It was still semi-darkness, the sun just starting to appear on the horizon. The waves were a decent size, but I got out back without any bother. I sat up on the board and soaked in the moment. I was on holiday, in the ocean before breakfast. This was every-thing I had dreamed Australia would be. At times like these I ignored the fact that I was a 40-year-old unemployed ad exec-utive and that I had no idea how the family was going to support itself. I couldn't be luckier, I thought to myself.

No sooner had I finished counting my blessings than a slate-grey flash in the water to my left caught my eye. Or was I imagining it? I had, after all, just been daydreaming. No, there it was again. I wondered what it was. I looked around. The beach was still deserted. Although it was foolhardy to be out here alone, I felt comfortable. The conditions were well within my capability. If I got tired I could easily paddle in within a few minutes. The only thing that could possibly go wrong was a shark attack, and how likely was that, for Christ's sake? I mean, they were incredibly rare, weren't they? There hadn't been a shark-related fatality since we'd moved to Oz. Well, there had been that diver that was killed, and that German tourist, but they were the exceptions.

Suddenly the *Jaws* panic gripped me. For fuck's sake, Nigel, I thought. What are you playing at? I'm alone in the ocean before the break of dawn. If anything happened I'd be screwed. It wouldn't even need to eat me. Just a leg or an arm, a hand even, would do it. I'd never make it to shore – there's no one here to even *try* to rescue me. I'll just drown pathetically. Kate doesn't even know where I am. Snap out of it, calm down, take a few breaths, look around, get your bearings, then gently paddle to shore. I'm getting a bit chilly anyway.

I felt better. A bit silly, in fact. I was always having these *Jaws* fantasies. Best to save the drama for when I was actually in one. I started paddling to shore. And stopped again as a fin, no further than ten feet away, glided across the front of my board, between me and the beach.

That was a fin, it is a shark, I am fucked, I thought in quick succession.

I attempted to sit up with my feet on the board, and promptly fell off. You normally use your legs in the water for balance when you sit on a surfboard. I hadn't developed the skill of sitting on the board without them. Then again, I thought, I won't have any fucking legs if I don't get them out of the water pronto. I hauled myself onto my board and lay flat on it. One of the few advantages of being a beginner is that you have a bigger board. Mine was over 8 feet long. I could lie on it with no part of me touching the water. The fin appeared again, this time to my right. Jesus, it's sizing me up for breakfast. Surely if I just lie here it will go away. I mean to shark's eyes, I must just look like an 8-foot bit of wood. It was then I remembered an article in the weekend's paper about how sharks can detect human urine from over 100 metres away. A marvellous memory, given I'd only recently indulged in one of the delights of an early morning surf – a warm piss into a cold wetsuit.

This is quite serious, I thought. I'm actually going to die. Talk about irony. I was just putting it all together and I'm bloody well going to be eaten by a fucking fish before I can enjoy it all. I wonder if Kate will remarry? Alex will probably captain the British Lions and I'll miss it because I'll be an unfound skeleton at the bottom of the sea off the New South Wales coast. At least I won't have to watch boys with all the wrong intentions taking my twins out. How will the family support itself? The life insurance will go some way to easing the first year, I suppose. Hang on – what life insurance? You're unemployed, you idiot, you haven't got any life insurance. Oh billy bollocks, I've really screwed it up this time.

The fin appeared again, this time followed by another one and another. Oh, fuck me sideways in Bourke Street, they are hunting in a pack. I gingerly got my car key out of the water-proof pocket in my ankle strap. Great, I'm going to ward off three sharks with a Toyota Tarago key.

It would be fair to say it was one of the low points of my year. Lying on a surfboard, surrounded by circling sharks, shivering with fear and clutching a car key in self-defence. I looked to the beach. PEOPLE! I could definitely see people. Two of them. Carrying surfboards. Hold on, it looks like they are getting *in*. Shit, I should warn them. Can sharks hear? Fuck, if I shout it could annoy them. Then again, maybe they will eat the other surfers, not me. Christ, they're paddling out this way. Jesus, they're coming to say hello. The fins were clearly visible, this time to my left again.

'How're you going,' they said as they got out back next to me. 'Isn't it great this morning?'

'BeachgotobeachgetoutofthewaterfinsthreefinsItriedto warnyou,' I whispered incoherently.

'What's that, mate? Yeah, three of them. Bloody wonderful – surfing with dolphins before breakfast. Sets you up for the day, doesn't it? Is that a car key in your hand? You can get a pocket for those if you buy the right ankle strap,' one said, before turning round to study the ocean swell.

Don't know about setting me up for the day, but the breakfast I took back to Kate and the kids sure as hell tasted good.

Chapter 43

Show and Tell

AS WELL AS A chance to make permanent life changes like kicking the booze and getting fit, I also viewed my time off the corporate wheel as a once-in-a-lifetime opportunity to do some of the more minor, one-off things on my personal wish list. The sort of things people say they'd like to do but never get round to for whatever reason. One of these things was a Lads and Dads trip. Well, Lads and Dad, to be precise, as I wanted to do it alone.

Pressures of work and the realities of having four kids meant it was extremely rare for me to spend proper time just with my sons. Because Harry was still only five, I was forever going off with just Alex. Whether it is for this or other reasons, Alex and I had developed an incredibly strong bond.

I desperately wanted to do things with both of them, but below a certain age it is difficult. I had tried taking Harry with us to the rugby on a couple of occasions but he was too young and I ended up feeling guilty that I was forcing him to do something he clearly wasn't enjoying. I adored Harry with a passion and didn't want him to think there was any favouritism. My suspicions that he wasn't convinced of this weren't so much aroused as rammed through my heart with a stake when I awoke one morning to find Harry standing by my side of our bed. As usual he had his pyjamas on inside out and his hair was sticking up like a mad professor. I could have eaten him, he was so cute.

'Morning, Bonkers,' I said.

'Morning, Daddy,' he replied. 'Daddy? Who do you love best? Alex or me?'

'Sweetheart! I love you all equally – you know I do,' I exclaimed.

'Okay, Dad. Daddy, I can spell market. M-a-k-i-t,' he said before wandering off.

Leaving the issue of his spelling aside, I was determined to use this little exchange as the spur to make me seize the moment and actually go on, as opposed to talk about, a Lads and Dad adventure.

As keen as I was to do a trip, I was equally keen not to replicate some of the mistakes my own parents made on similar outings. I've extremely strong memories of well-intentioned but disastrous family holidays where our parents assumed my brother and I would like the same things as they would. A car trip around the New England forests particularly sticks in my mind. Four days spent driving through trees. Trees. Not girls. Not rugby. But trees. Mum and Dad were busily oohhing and aahhing at the 'lovely views', while my brother and I were not so quietly going insane with the point-lessness of it all. After two hours, we ended up sitting on the floor of the car playing cards while Mum and Dad looked at the scenery for the next three and a half days. Sightseeing just isn't an activity for anyone under 20. Especially 'landscape sightseeing'. Talking to my friends, I discovered all of them, without exception, have their own horror stories of holidays spent stuck in the backs of cars having to look at scenery.

My idea was to drive the lads to Canberra, stay a night and drive back the next day. The location wasn't important to me. I just wanted to do a boys' trip. None of us had been to Canberra and it was the right type of distance away. Alex and Harry were ecstatic when I suggested it to them.

'Will we have KFC, Daddy?' Harry said.

'Does the hotel have a TV?' Alex asked.

'Yes and yes,' I replied. I was determined not to force them to look at or do anything on this trip. I don't know if this qualifies me as a crap dad, but given that we spent every other waking hour forcing them to do or not do stuff, I figured a day and a half off wouldn't do them any harm. They could spend the entire time eating KFC in the hotel room while watching TV as far as I was concerned, as long as we had a laugh together.

It was a blast from the moment we got in the car. At the first station, I stopped for petrol and treats. I also bought a disposable camera. Alex had been sent a *Harry Potter* tape by his grandmother so they spent the two hours before our lunch stop munching wine gums, listening to Harry, Ron and Hermione getting in and out of trouble, and never once looking out the window at the view. As it happens, the view is rather nice so I had a decent time as well. Lunch was a dietician's nightmare – hamburgers, chips, ice-cream and a lolly for after. I read the *Goulburn Gazette* and nursed a latte. I was still off the drink and I couldn't help musing that I wouldn't have been doing this trip if I weren't. Or worse: I would be doing it but looking for every opportunity for a cleansing ale and finding the kids irritating in the meantime. Goulburn's news was hardly earth-shattering, but I found it strangely comforting reading about the proposed pavement-widening scheme that had local residents up in arms. We strolled back to the car. As we were doing so, I felt a little hand creep into mine. I glanced down and said 'Hi, Harry.' For once he didn't correct me on his name. Then, more surprisingly, I felt another hand creep into my other hand. This time it was Alex. This didn't happen much anymore, now that he was eight and there were usually schoolmates around who might see. I deliberately took the long way back to the car so I could prolong the walk with all three of us holding hands.

Another two hours of *Harry Potter* and we were approaching the outskirts of Canberra. We drove past a big roadside poster for Virgin Blue airline, simply headed: 'Next time take the plane. Sydney to Canberra $69 return.' It was obviously aimed at the business audience, not the Lads and Dads target market. However, for the first time in months it made me think about the advertising business and how I alternately loved and hated it. Sometimes the combination of idea, execution and media placement is so perfect that it is one of the most powerful weapons a company can wield. I can't imagine a weary businessman who had just driven four hours to a meeting passing that poster and *not* thinking, 'Sod it, next time I *will* take the plane.' As I wondered if I would ever return to the advertising agency scene, we ground to a halt at the back of a long traffic jam. Canberra doesn't usually have traffic jams but roadworks had temporarily brought the phenomenon to the capital city. We crawled at a snail's pace into the centre. I gazed out the window at the city and drove straight into the car in front of me. It was completely my fault – no two ways about it.

The driver of the car I had run into was already out of her vehicle and walking hurriedly towards me. I braced myself.

'Thank you, thank you, thank you,' she said.

'Umm, what for?' I replied.

'Running into us. My kids have been driving me up the wall the whole way from Sydney. I'd told them if they continued to muck about then we'd have an accident. My son – the cheeky bugger – had just said, "Yeah right, Mum," when you hit us.'

I looked into the backseat of her car and sure enough, there were two children sitting bolt upright, being very, very, well-behaved.

'It's a pleasure to be of service,' I said.

Half an hour after our 'accident', we pulled up outside the hotel I had booked over the Internet. Harry and Alex were beside themselves with excitement. I, on the other hand, was in a state of shock. The hotel had come recommended as 'one of the premier establishments in Canberra'. In reality, however, it was like a downmarket motel that had been stuck in a 1970s time warp. It made me sad just standing in its foyer. By the lifts there was a glass case labelled 'Some of our famous guests'. Inside – and I swear I'm not making this up – were black and white photocopied pictures of four people. Not four hundred, or forty-four – but four. I can only assume they were famous in a different era as I'd never heard of any of them.

The room was appalling.

'Cool, this is great, Dad,' said Harry, jumping up and down on the micro-sized double bed.

'Yeah. Mega brill, Dad,' added Alex. 'Can I switch the TV on?'

I let them veg in front of the box while I ordered a cup of tea and some ice-cream for the lads.

'I'll have a pot of tea please, with skim milk, and two bowls of ice-cream. What flavours do you have?' I asked.

'Vanilla. We haven't got skim milk,' I was told.

'What other flavours have you?'

'None.'

'Okay, I'll have vanilla. Full cream milk is fine. How long will that be?'

'I'll be up in about 45 minutes.'

I refrained from asking how it could possibly take anyone 45 minutes to make a pot of tea and put two scoops of ice cream into a couple of bowls. Instead I resolved to spend as little time as possible in the place.

I unpacked and got the guidebook out to plan our afternoon's activities. Once I'd got that sorted, I called Kate to let her know we had arrived, that everyone was fine and that the lads had eaten lots of vegetables. Halfway through our conversation the doorbell rang so I handed the phone to the nearest boy – Harry – and went to open the door. The lads looked on wide-eyed in amazement as the man who clearly staffed both reception and room service brought in a tray with two bowls of ice-cream on it. As I signed the receipt, Harry was filling his mum in on all the details in his best loud telephone voice: 'Mum, our room is well nice, the bed is humungous, there's a TV and best of all, we've got a servant!'

The 'servant' gave me a look which reminded me of the flight attendant on our recent flight to London.

'Harry, sweetheart, he's not a servant,' I corrected.

'He's a slave?' Harry interrupted. This time the 'slave' shot me a look that reminded me of the type I'd got at Kindi Gym after Grace's helpful announcement. For a moment I was tempted to say, 'No, darling, he's a humourless prick with the style and elegance of a car crash.' But I refrained, simply muttering, 'He hasn't stayed in a hotel before. It's all very exciting for a five-year-old. Thanks for the tea.'

As I escorted the slave to the door, I could hear Alex on the phone behind me. 'Vegetables? No we haven't had any – or fruit. Dad's been brilliant. We had sweets in the car. Burgers for lunch. Then ice-cream and a lolly. And we've just got some more ice-cream delivered to the room. And Dad says we can have KFC for dinner.'

After calming Kate down, we made our way into Canberra proper. Or tried to. Because Canberra is a new, purpose-built city, it was designed rather than evolving naturally. Unfortunately the town planners made the mistake of confusing 'large, open and green' with 'good to live in'. The city is well spaced out but precisely for that reason it lacks a centre and therefore a heart. Apparently Prince Philip once upset Canberrans when he remarked on an official visit to the city that Canberra had no soul. The travel writer Bill Bryson went one step further and suggested Canberra's official slogan should be 'Canberra – why wait for death?' While I wouldn't go as far as either Bill or Phil, I could see where they were coming from. Canberra is – how can I put this? – rather open plan and suburban.

You would be wrong, however, to strike it off your list of places to visit. The city itself may be on the dull side of vibrant but the attractions within it are world-class – and numerous. I couldn't get the kids out of the interactive Science Museum, or the Telstra Tower that looks over the entire city and countryside beyond. They even enjoyed the National Gallery. Not half as much as me though. I couldn't believe the quality and sheer quantity of art they had on show. It was like someone had relocated the Musée d'Orsay to the outback. They even had Pollock's 'Blue Poles' on show – one of my favourites of any painter.

We then did the National Portrait Gallery, where Alex was delighted to find a full-length portrait of David Campese. I've said it before and I'll say it again – I sodding love Australia. In an English portrait gallery you'd expect to have to wade through hundreds of pictures of blokes on horses, looking like they were just off to subdue a few natives, or royalty with their noses in the air. In Oz you get a real mix: politicians, rugby players, businessmen, writers. An unaffected, interesting mix that felt truly reflective of the country as a whole. It's a matter of perspective, I suppose. I naturally see the good bits of Australia and actively look for the positive side of things. If, however, you come at it from an ex-colony/prison point of view, as many English people do, I can imagine there is enough wrong with it to keep you happy. My mother-in-law once memorably remarked, 'I can't understand the point of Australia.' Inadvertently or not, I think she hit the nail on the head. You either see the point, and it is the most remarkable place on earth, or you don't, and it is forever letting you down as it's never quite the same as New York or London. I'm sure none of this was going through Alex and Harry's heads as they stuffed themselves on KFC while we toured Canberra stadium before we retired – as late as I could possibly arrange it – to the hotel.

I'd like to pretend that sleeping with your two young sons in a small double bed is fun but it isn't. They had nine hours of deep, uninterrupted sleep while I lay awake all night. It reminded me of the time I slept in the garden shed of our house in London with Alex as 'an adventure'. He loved it. I, on the other hand, still have the small scar on my back which sleeping all night squashed against a hedge trimmer gives you. After our slave – as I was now happy to think of him – brought us breakfast, we checked out and made for the Parliament buildings and war memorial. I was determined not to make the kids stay longer at any attraction than their natural attention span dictated. This may have meant we ended up doing whistlestop tours of places where normally I would have loved to stay longer, but I like to think it also meant the kids enjoyed the trip rather than suffered it.

When we got back to Sydney that afternoon, I got the roll of film from the disposable camera developed and gave a set each to Alex and Harry as I tucked them up in bed that evening. Because of a lack of parental approval or affirmation when I was a young boy, I am forever overcompensating and telling my lads how wonderful they are and how proud I am of them. This night was very special to me. I'd just spent a heavenly couple of days with my sons and I felt enormously protective of them as I began my evening pep talk. 'You're both smashing lads. Daddy is very . . .'

'Yeah, yeah, we know: very proud of us. Dad, you've said that so often it's lost all meaning,' Alex interrupted.

The next day when I picked them up from school, one of Harry's classmates saw me across the playground that was, as ever at pick-up time, crowded with parents and teachers. 'Have you got a job yet, Mr Marsh?' he yelled. 'Harry says you have had to move house because you have no money.'

On top of Alex's comment the night before, I couldn't help remembering how a friend of mine recently told me how in trendy tree-hugging circles embarrassing or crushing comments made to a child by an adult are described as 'soul murder'. I wondered if I could report my sons to the police for a reverse case of it.

With my self-esteem in shreds, I made my way to Harry's classroom. Before I could vent my annoyance, his teacher rushed up to me.

'Oh, Nigel, your boys did so enjoy the trip. Harry brought all his pictures and took the class through them at show and tell. Mr Jansen tells me Alex did the same. They are lucky boys to spend so much time with their dad.'

Glad someone thinks so.

Chapter 44

Folds flat

THE PLAYGROUND MIGHT not have been the forum I would have chosen to discuss it, but Harry's mate had a point. We had had to move to somewhere cheaper. I don't want to pretend here – I'm well aware my situation was far more fortunate than most. But as much fun as I was having and as undoubtedly fortunate as we were, it didn't mean our finances were a laughing matter. We had a small lump sum that was eroding rapidly. The nanny, second car and big house were only just affordable when I had a job; without one they had all had to go. I didn't mind moving to a cheaper place but it wasn't actually that easy to find somewhere that was both near enough for the kids not to have to move schools and big enough – and within our new price range. Having four kids does tend to limit your options.

We eventually found a place and to my mind it was perfect. Kate suspects I would have said this about any house in Sydney because I am so biased. Given it was near the school and beaches, I just couldn't see any justifiable reason to complain. But it was much smaller, so we had to get rid of a lot of stuff. I actually found this incredibly enjoyable. I hate clutter and it was a wonderful excuse to do what I'd wanted to do anyway. It's amazing how much crap you end up carting around as a family unless you are rigorous about it. We currently pay hundreds of pounds a year to keep two crates of storage in a lock-up facility in London. For the life of us, Kate and I can no longer remember what is in them, although at the time it must have seemed important for us to have wanted to pay to keep it. I was determined not to make the same mistake this time. 'If in doubt, chuck it out' had been our motto for the move. The local Vinnies didn't know whether it was Christmas or Easter.

A side benefit of the move was that it gave me a chance to indulge a private fantasy I'd been nursing ever since I read about a movement that had sprung up in San Francisco a few years earlier. To cut a long story short, this group dedicate themselves to committing frequent and regular random acts of 'kindness'. They started with the simple act of paying for the car behind them at the bridge tollbooths. It struck me as a wonderful way of increasing the overall pot of happiness and I'd long since secretly wanted to give it a go.

My chance came the day before the move. I was taking Grace and Eve for one last run in the double baby jogger. They were now three and getting too big for it, and there was nowhere to store it in the new house. As I approached Clovelly beach, I ran past a young woman struggling to get a pram out of the back of her car. Inside the car were two babies. I stopped running and enquired in a voice as far as possible removed from that of a stalker, 'Excuse me, are they twins?'

'Yes,' she said.

'Gorgeous. How old?'

'Eleven months,' she replied.

'Hope you don't mind me asking, but would you by any chance want a double jogger?' I felt more than a little stupid at this point.

'What do you mean?'

'A double jogger. This double jogger.'

'Er . . . I'd love it. I used to run before these two were born but I haven't been able to find the time to do it since. This pram is bloody useless as well. I can hardly get it out of the car, let alone run and push it. I've always wondered if those jogger things were as good as they looked. Can you take it on the beach?'

'Yep.'

'And you can actually *run* behind it?'

'Yep – I've done races with it.'

'Does it fold flat?'

'In about 15 seconds, once you've got the hang of it.'

'How much would you want for it? Don't they cost 600 bucks? I haven't got that sort of money.'

'Nothing.'

'Nothing?'

'Nothing.'

'Are you sure?'

'Sure.'

'When could I pick it up?'

'I'll help you get your girls in it now if you like.'

'Really?'

'Really.'

I got Grace and Eve out of the jogger and showed her how to strap her girls in the seats.

The whole conversation took less than five minutes. As I walked my twins up the hill towards home, I realised I hadn't even got the lady's name or number. As random acts go, it was pretty random. I suppose I was lucky, as I could have got a smack in the mouth or a hearty 'piss off, you patronising git'. But I didn't, and without wanting to sound like I've got a Messiah complex, it felt bloody wonderful.

Chapter 45
Lenny Bruce

WITH OUR HOUSE MOVE over and no further trips planned, we settled into a routine of enjoyable domesticity. The world of work seemed several light years away. Kate and I started not just going out again but planning to go out. There is a big difference. Previously a suggestion of an evening out was almost always met by me with a 'Going out with whom? Tonight? Jesus, when were you going to tell me? I can't stay out late, I've got a meeting in the morning.' Blah blah blah, you know the sort of thing. Not so much 'soul murder' as 'relationship murder'. These days we spent time actually planning a social life in advance. It's remarkable how much free entertainment is on offer in Sydney if you seek it out. It is equally surprising how far a limited budget can stretch if you're smart about it. We were seeing so many concerts and plays on the cheap that I was half considering applying for a job as a paupers' art critic with the *Herald*.

Importantly, this newfound lust for a varied and stimulating social life enabled me to get back in touch with another lapsed passion – stand-up comedy. My love affair with comedy predates even my love affair with running. In London I used to go see stand-up at least twice a week, yet I hadn't been once since arriving in Australia. We arranged to go to a show one weekend.

The evening had a strange effect on me. I'm a harsh judge of comedians and two of the three acts on offer were distinctly ho-hum. Lots of swearing and jokes about student days, shagging and pot smoking. Embarrassing, frankly. Just as I was beginning to think I had outgrown stand-up comedy or that Australia just had crap acts, the last comedian came on. From his first words – a freewheeling rant about how boy bands should be called boy choirs as they don't play instruments – it was clear he was on fire. He slayed the audience. For 20 minutes straight everyone in the pub was roaring and yelling. He just took the laughs, rode them and flung back yet more ammo to keep the hilarity on the boil. He was in total control of a room full of people who five minutes ago had never heard of him. It was quite a performance, yet all I could think was how much I pitied his girlfriend.

My own stint as a stand-up comic started shortly after my career as a squash coach ended. And when I was doing stand-up, I was impossible to live with. I was lucky enough to be doing well at it but this luck didn't extend to Kate. For some bizarre reason, I banned her from attending any of my gigs.

Instead of the performance itself she got the after-show: a thoroughly unfair swap. I'm not sure it's possible to properly describe what it's like to go down a storm as a comedian to someone who hasn't done it. It's like sex, winning the lottery and scoring the winning try in the World Cup final all rolled into one. It gets even better if you wrote all your own material and you suffer from unresolved childhood issues that give you an unhealthy need for public shows of affection and praise.

On one particular night, I was having such a result that I actually ended my set, 'My name is Nigel Marsh, watch out for my show on Channel Four this October. Thank you for being such a good audience, good night.' They cheered all the more in the knowledge that they were witnessing an up-and-coming TV star. The thing is, it was complete bollocks. I made it up. An out-and-out lie. There was no TV series. There was more chance of me playing for England than me ever appearing on TV. But at the time it was real. *I* believed it. I was Lenny Bruce. I was so in character at that particular moment that if I'd been offered a TV series of my own I wouldn't even have been surprised.

And that is where the problems started, for Kate, anyway. I would get home to our bedsit and be mildly surprised to find that the world's media wasn't camped on my doorstep and downright outraged that Kate hadn't put up bunting and hired a brass band for the return of the conquering hero. The coming down from my Lenny Bruce complex was not a good spectator sport and unfortunately for Kate she was always the only one in that particular audience. Add in some Olympic-standard drinking and it all gets pretty ugly.

My mood was made worse by the fact that I knew I was living a lie. You see, I didn't just lie at the end of my act – I

Marsh

lied to get the gigs as well. I hadn't set out to lie, but the first time I called up to arrange a spot hadn't been a success.

'Hi, I'd like to do a gig at your stand-up night,' I said down the phone to the owner of a famous North London pub.

'Okay, mate, three weeks Wednesday we've got one slot left. How many gigs have you done?' he replied.

' Er . . . none. This will be my first time.'

'First time? You never done this before?'

'Er . . . no.'

'Don't know about your act, mate, but you certainly sound like a fucking comedian to me,' he said before hanging up.

Clearly a bit of bluffing was going to be needed. Reminding myself of my squash coaching experience, I looked through the paper for another pub that had comedy nights. I called one at random – an inner-city bar just off Oxford Street.

'Hi, I'm calling to book a spot at one of your comedy nights.'

'Good timing, I've just had a wanker cancel on me. Are you free Thursday week?'

'Yes.'

'Rightio. Hold on, you're not one of those first-time tossers, are you? We don't do those anymore since the last one had to do a runner off stage when my punters started throwing bottles at him. Poor prick got hit by a couple and started crying on stage. Pathetic.'

'Sounds tragic all right,' I said, thinking of both myself and the poor prick.

'How many have you done?' he asked,

I felt my Lenny Bruce complex take over. 'Don't know.

Stopped counting at a hundred. Probably two hundred or so by now,' I lied.

'Excellent, in that case I'll bump you up the bill a bit. Are you all right going on second?'

'Yes,' I lied again.

'Can you give me fifteen minutes?'

'I'll have to cut some good stuff out, but sure, if that's the time you want,' I lied yet again. Listen to me, I'm a bloody schizophrenic. I haven't got five minutes of material, let alone fifteen. Next thing I know I'll be telling him I'm Lenny Bruce.

'What did you say your name was?' he asked.

'Lenny Bruce,' I replied.

'Very funny. Your real one.'

'Oh, Nigel Marsh,' I confessed.

Bizarrely, on the night itself I avoided any bottle-throwing. In fact I even got a couple of big laughs and a half-decent round of applause at the end. From then on whenever I called to book a spot somewhere, I would lie about my experience. It meant I rarely got turned down but it played havoc with my nerves. I wasn't just petrified about dying on stage, I was petrified that the lies I told in each booking conversation would be revealed in some hideously humiliating way. But I never did die on stage, or get found out. Every week I thought that was going to be the week, but it never was. The pressure built to unbearable proportions so I decided to quit while I was ahead. 'Bottled it' was how Kate supportively phrased it.

Cowardice or not, the weird thing was I found I enjoyed *telling* people I used to do stand-up more than I enjoyed *doing* stand-up. It was a damn sight easier as well. Remembering these stories brought me to my senses. After a brief moment of reflection I realised that there is no sense in trying to re-live absolutely everything good about your past – some things belong there. Comedy performing, like drinking, is probably one of them. I decided to stick to running instead.

Chapter 46

One-legged faker

I CAN PINPOINT THE precise moment when I realised my transformation from 'Executive Dad' to 'Bloke Who Doesn't Work' was complete. It happened one morning when I was in our bathroom. I couldn't find any toothpaste.

'Kate, where's the toothpaste?' I yelled.

'We've run out. Could you please buy some for us today?'

'We can't have run out. I've got about a hundred of those small ones from BA and Qantas somewhere.'

''Fraid not, I finished the last one yesterday.'

Blimey, I thought, I'm actually going to have to buy some toothpaste. Owing to my previous job involving a lot of travel, I hadn't paid for any toothpaste – or shampoo, come to think of it – for over a year. Hotels and airlines were so wonderfully generous with stuff like that – especially when you were travelling in business class. It may seem a trivial event, but to me it set in train a whole series of thoughts. I hadn't worn a tie or jacket in the last nine months. Eve had drawn all over my just-completed sketchbook the week before and I hadn't lost my temper. Harry had taken to creeping out of his bunk bed in the middle of the night and sleeping under Kate's and my bed. Rather than shouting at the little lad, the third time it happened I lay down on the floor next to him and asked him why he did it. 'Because I don't like rectangles, Daddy,' was his reply. At least he was still using his real name. Grace was warming to me and on the weekend had even hugged me and said, 'Daddy, I'm not a vile children, really.' I – and the family – really, genuinely had changed.

This is in no way to suggest I was even remotely approaching the foothills of being perfect. The kids' nickname for me was still 'Shirker Tensing'. The house would ring out with the cries of 'Shirker! Shirker! Mum wants you!' whenever I was dodging my parental chores. My most regular shirk was to offer to 'put the bath on' whenever teatime got just a little too hideous. I would then slip off to the bathroom, turn the taps on and then watch the bath fill as if this act was in some way helping. It drove Kate up the wall. I knew when I was in real trouble because she used my name at the end of an expletive. 'Fucking hell, what have you been doing all this time?' is a million miles of anger away from 'Fucking hell, what have you been doing all this time, *Nigel*?'

It wasn't just my shirking that caused tension. My goal-focused nature had its downsides as well. This was no more apparent than when the time came for Kate, Alex and I to do the Bridge Run. It was the first race we were to do together and I was enormously excited. Unfortunately, it is likely to remain the only race we have done together. The race itself was heavenly. I love Alex beyond words and warming up with him on the North Sydney Oval before the starter's gun is still one of my all-time favourite memories. It was precisely the type of occasion that makes me adore Sydney – thousands of happy people sharing an experience together in the most wonderful of settings in the most gorgeous of weather. I found running on the actual blue line of the 2000 Olympics an amazing and fantasy-inducing event. Half the time I wasn't Nigel Marsh, or even Lenny Bruce, but a cross between Daley Thompson and Seb Coe. And therein lay the problem. While the race itself may have been fabulous, the ending was sub-optimal.

To my utter shame, I feel my happiness, enthusiasm and private fantasies may have led me to 'encourage' my running partners just a little bit too much. As we crossed the finishing line together at the steps of the Opera House, Alex's legs started to buckle and his face turned deathly white. A race marshal rushed to his aid.

'This boy has been pushed far too hard, he's badly de-hydrated. We need to get him to the medical tent. Where's his father?' he said.

'I think he's over there,' I said, pointing in as vague a way as possible. 'He said he would be gone for a while. I'll look after the lad until he returns if you like. Bloody irresponsible if you ask me.' Kate, God bless her, didn't blow my cover and a cup of water and a handful of jellybeans later, Alex was released from the medical tent in rude health and in high spirits at having completed the course. I, on the other hand, rightly got the tongue-lashing of my life, hence my suspicion that it may be a while until we do a family event like that again.

I wouldn't want you to think Kate was perfect herself, though. For the 12 years I have lived with her, she has taken the tea bag out of her cup and rather than put it in the bin, she has placed it on the kitchen countertop *next* to the bin. It is beyond my quite considerable powers of comprehension to understand what could possibly make someone do something so moronic, so often, for so long. Especially after the rows we have had about it. Then again, it is entirely possible that with some sort of twisted logic she does it *because* it irritates the crap out of me. As I've said before, women can be so cruel.

These imperfections apart, however, the Marsh family had found a very nice balance indeed, thank you very much. I was swimming, surfing, running, sketching, and writing as much as I wanted, while at the same time being an involved and improving husband and father. I was keeping the weight off and, most important of all, I was still off the booze. This was an enormously significant change – and in all probability the factor that had enabled and continued to enable the other changes to take place in my life.

Giving up drinking is a difficult subject to talk about, let alone write about. People's reactions are so completely polarising. One group is enormously supportive – thank you to all those concerned, especially Kate – while another group is actively destructive.

This latter group devotes considerable energy to trying every conceivable way possible to make you drink. 'Go on, just have one. How can one hurt?' they say. This may seem slightly fantastical, but it is true. What makes it all the more strange is that amongst their numbers are people who are supposedly close to you and care for you the most. I'm not blaming these people. It is a complex issue. Part of it, I'm sure, stems from the discomfort in having someone so close change so fundamentally. It can be a bit unnerving if all you've ever done together is get drunk in pubs to then have to find something else to do or face the awkward reality that the friendship was only drink-deep, so to speak.

There is, however, a group who are far worse. These are the people who are seemingly tormented with a compulsion to prove that you didn't have a drinking problem in the first place. Initially it took a while for me to spot them, but as the months went by I was able see them coming a mile off. They'd usually start off slow and then build into it.

'I hear you stopped drinking, Nige,' they'd say to me.

'Er, yeah,' I'd reply.

'Why's that, then?'

'Just had enough of it, mate.'

'Really? I thought you loved a drop.'

'Truth is, I did, but I've got a bit of an issue with it, so I've decided my drinking days are over.'

'Bit of an issue? What's that, then?'

'Well, I don't want to go on about it, but I just started to find it was becoming too important in my life so I decided to stop before it got totally out of hand.'

'You're not saying you're an alcoholic, are you?'

'Actually, now you mention it, yes. But I . . .'

'You're not an alcoholic. My brother, now he was a *real* alcoholic. Ran someone over on his way back pissed from work one day, spent a year in jail. Bottle of whisky before lunch for 20 years before he finally kicked it.'

'Er, well, I'm glad he's sorted it now.'

'Yeah, and my mate Simon – he had a real problem. He'd wet himself at night, sleep with prostitutes, get into fights, go on benders that lasted for five days!' This last bit would be emphasised with the type of pride and pleasure normally associated with telling someone you'd just become a father or won gold at the Olympics.

'How awful. Is he all right now?'

'Dunno, haven't seen him in a while, but take my other friend, Jane. She's a scream, right nutter. Her husband doesn't know it, but she's added a "pick-me-up" to her morning tea for years. Last Christmas he noticed her hands shaking and she had to go through this whole charade of pretending to go to the doctor and then making up some story about a potentially-life-threatening hereditary shaking disease. Silly bastard believes her and he's devastated. Now *that's* a real drinking problem! I've never even seen you be sick. You don't even drink before lunch. You're a lightweight, mate. Take the bloke I worked with last year . . .' And so it would go on.

The stories differed, but the intent didn't. I was somehow offending these people's sense of what a 'real' drunk's story should be. I wasn't a premier league drunk – I was merely third division. Pathetic. My life hadn't gone off the rails enough for them. If only I could have an affair, lose my job or maim someone in a car accident, I'd be a brilliant bloke. It just got right up these people's noses that I stopped before a dramatic disaster befell me. It was all slightly sinister. Like touring a hospital ward and haranguing amputees with stories about people who'd lost two legs. Two! Not one like you, you one-legged faker.

The vocal insistence of this group is almost worse than their breathtaking disregard for your well-being. I'm relaxed about my failure to qualify in their eyes as a real drunk. Delighted, in fact. I couldn't be happier that the story of my addiction is boringly tame. On one level I'm pleased to tell it — if it helps one person recognise they have a problem earlier than they would have if they believed that they had to be a tramp on the streets before they qualified as having an issue, then I'll actually have done some good. The point is, I don't actually like talking about it. But these people are like a dog with a bone and feel the need to publicly go on and on and on about it.

Of course in the end the problem isn't how other people react: it is the internal battle that is the key. I was finding it easier and easier as the months passed, but it was still a subject I thought about most days. Unlike many alcoholics, I find the 'never again' notion helpful, not off-putting. The classic syndrome is taking 'one day at a time' because the thought of not drinking ever again is deemed just too overwhelming an idea to cope with. Whatever works for the individual, I say.

Without wanting to tempt fate by making any grand pronouncements, I'm increasingly comfortable in potentially difficult drinking situations and am enjoying the sober life in general. That isn't to say that there aren't regular challenges. Only a few weeks ago, as I was walking across the car park of a local school to the AA meeting held in its basement, I bumped into an old business colleague. He wasn't fat, hadn't yet reached forty and, far from being fired, ran the largest and most successful advertising agency in Sydney.

'Hi, Jim,' I said. 'What are you doing here?'

'Oh, I'm here every Saturday morning. This is where Olivia comes for her ballet classes. They're held in the hall on the first floor. What are you doing here, Nigel? Are Grace and Eve taking up ballet?'

'Er, no . . . I'm going to the AA meeting in the basement.'

Embarrassing moments like this aside, I was actually loving my new life. It may have taken nine months, but all in all I had eventually found (or created) a set of circumstances I was totally happy with and had no desire to change.

Almost immediately upon coming to this realisation, disaster struck.

In September I was offered a job.

Chapter 47

Anaïs Nin

AT LEAST I COULDN'T complain about not having enough time to think the job offer through. For the next week, every swim, run or dinnertime was spent laboriously weighing up the merits or otherwise of a return to the hamster wheel. The job being offered was fantastic and one which in my former life I would have leapt at. It involved running a well-known and successful communications company. Of that type of job it didn't really get better. What's more, I had friends in the company. One of my partners would be Todd, an ex-colleague from my previous role whom I admired both professionally and personally. He had a certain something about him that suggested he hadn't yet given up and become a total corporate squirrel. A couple of years before, he'd taken three months off work and climbed to the summit of Mount Everest. Solo.

I also loved how he took his personal values to work. On one memorable occasion a client of ours had been attempting to excuse her appalling behaviour with the explanation that she wasn't like that at home, only at work. Todd replied, 'Susan, if you are an arsehole at work it doesn't mean you are an arsehole *at work* – it means you are an arsehole.'

It would be good to hook up with him again. Beyond old friends, however, was the fact that the job was a proper leadership role. It offered me a real chance to make a difference. I've always remembered a story I read in a biography of the British Prime Minister Gladstone. He kept a diary recording how he used each 15 minutes of his life so when he was called to account at the Pearly Gates he would have the evidence that he hadn't wasted the divine gift of a life. I'm not quite as rigorous as Gladstone, but I do want to look back and feel I've used my four score and ten well – if I get that long.

Also, much as I was loving time off work in my new-found 'man around the playground' persona, the money was running out and the kids were still a bit young to shove up chimneys. I was coming round to the idea of going back to work. I had made some dramatic improvements in my life – but not yet in the biggest issue facing me.

Work/life balance.

I had found that, unlike many men, I could enjoy not working. But on the balance front all I'd really found out was that I was good at juggling life and work when I didn't have any work to juggle. But I knew I had to go back to work soon. The bigger question, therefore, was could I go back to work and retain the changed parts of my life and the attitude that I had come to value deeply over the last few months? This seemed to be the biggest challenge of all.

If I were to limit myself to only the easier challenges (swimming, losing a bit of weight), my time off might just turn out to have been a period where I made a few minor adjustments, ones that did a bit of good here and there, but which ultimately had no dramatic bearing on my and my family's longer term welfare. Fundamentally an excellent, very long holiday, rather than the permanently life-changing event I wanted it to be. But I'd tackled some harder issues this year too, and surely if I could crack the drink issue, I could crack the balance one. I was, after all, good at resolutions. My time off had shown me beyond any doubt that if I really set my mind to something I could usually do it. Whatever it was.

Deep down I wanted to take the job. I decided that I would only take it if at the same time I made a resolution to attempt to control the impact it would have on my broader life. This would be no small step. For me a resolution should not be an exercise in wishful thinking. If I'm not prepared to devote a year's worth of dedicated and persistent time and energy to a particular goal then to my mind I haven't actually made a resolution.

And yet I couldn't get rid of the nagging doubts. What about the effect it might really have on the family? I didn't want to revert to being the dad in a suit who grumpily dropped his kids off at school in the morning without so much as a preoccupied glance backwards. Would Grace start calling me 'poo-poo head' again? Would Harry's pictures start coming back from school with different names on them? Would I stay off the booze? Get fat? Would I manage to complete the Bondi to Bronte ocean race? What about the lifeguard course and exam I'd signed up to take in October? Or the Rugby World Cup games I'd arranged to go to with Alex? We had plane tickets and hotel reservations to follow the England team around the country on an extended Lad and Dad trip in November. Would we still go to the games? Would this mean I would have no time to write? Or draw? Or surf?

Irrespective of how good the new firm itself was, did I really want to get back into an industry that so often polluted the ether with a steady steam of mindless shite? Just that morning I'd caught an ad on TV that made me groan and hold my head. 'Have we gone mad? It's carpet madness at Carpet Universe! You'd be insane not to check out our crazy, crazy prices. Yes, we've gone mental. You'd be nutty if you didn't take advantage of our loopy deals!' All delivered by a bloke shouting at the top of his lungs. The week before I'd seen two other ads, both of which I couldn't for the life of me work out. Not just what they were on about, but what they were selling *or* who they were for. For the last few months I had been reading the paper from cover to cover every day, yet on most days I hadn't read, or even noticed, one single ad. There seems to be an almost paranoid fear on the parts of companies or their advertising agencies of being honest with people about their products and the real role they play in people's lives. On the rare occasions when a company does speak honestly and with a bit of charm and empathy, it leaps out at you. And here's the rub – the more I hated the business, the more I wanted to get back into it. We could do it better. I wanted to do it better. Not just the end product bit, the ads, but also the bit that produced the end product bit. People.

At the start of my previous job I'd given an interview to the press where I was asked what I thought the primary role of a CEO was. I replied that I viewed my primary role as 'providing meaning'. They then did a piece about the whacky theologian CEO. Trouble was, I meant it then and I mean it now. I believe a CEO's role is to provide meaningful employment. That doesn't mean he or she doesn't have to make the numbers or take difficult decisions. It means he or she has to provide a point for the employees. And for me this point has to be something a little bit more involving than 'I'd like you all to work very hard at a job you don't like much to make some shareholders you'll never meet richer.' (I'd understand if you didn't believe me, but I have been in that very presentation. I think the man who delivered the speech was actually disappointed when, at the end of his piece, the audience – all of whom, including me, weren't shareholders – didn't stand up and cheer.) I had loved my previous CEO role and was excited about another one. I believed I had something to offer in this field and found it difficult imagining passing up this chance to potentially make a difference.

Anaïs Nin once remarked that life expands or contracts in direct proportion to one's courage. If I had learnt only one thing from my time off, it was that I vehemently agree with her sentiment. I didn't want to settle for a life of regret and disappointment. I passionately believe that if you eradicate your limiting assumptions, raise your expectations and work damn hard at your goals, it's remarkable what you can achieve. If you have the right attitude you can have a damn good laugh while you're at it as well. I wanted to expand my footprint on the world, not shrink it. You are, after all, dead a long time. The more I thought about it, the closer I came to deciding to take the leap and go back onto the hamster wheel to see if I could actually crack the work/life dilemma and be a success both in my job and at home.

In the middle of these self-indulgent deliberations, however, real disaster struck.

Chapter 48
Granfie

MY MUM CALLED ME from England to inform me that my dad had fallen desperately ill. He had been diagnosed with Parkinson's disease over 10 years earlier and until now, a strictly monitored drug regime had kept the condition to a frustrating but manageable state. Apparently things had dramatically declined overnight to such an extent that he'd had to be moved to hospital. Mum, understandably, sounded dreadfully upset. I made the snap decision that I would go and see them immediately. Mum was overwhelmed when I told her. The moment I put the phone down I made another decision – I would take Alex with me. Granfie, as my kids called him, had always adored Alex and lavished him with the type of attention and praise I rarely, if ever, received. In this case, the cliché of a grandparent being able to express love more easily to a grandchild than to their own child was spot on. Mum and Dad had invited Alex down to where they lived in Somerset, in the English west country, for a number of weekends by himself. On each occasion he was looked after like a king, taken fishing, played endless draughts games, fed treats – basically spoilt rotten. He returned after each trip with a book done by his granny, detailing each day's activities including photos stuck to the pages at all the critical moments. A real bond existed between them and I couldn't bear the thought of Alex not seeing his granddad again. Besides, part of me thought that seeing Alex might actually help my Dad.

Deciding to go was one thing. Arranging the trip was another thing entirely. The only flight that left the next day went via Singapore *and* Rome, with a combined travel time of a little over 30 hours. Once that was booked, I had Alex's headmistress to negotiate. To be fair to her, she was brilliant. Our flights had Alex returning the day before the school play and so we struck a deal: I could take him out of school for the week as long as I guaranteed I would make him practise his lines every day.

After some hasty packing we jumped in a taxi and barely hours after the initial phone conversation we were checking in for the first leg of the marathon journey to Somerset, England. We may have been flying economy, but I still had a shiny airline frequent flyer card that was yet to be downgraded. To the computer, I was still super exec, not super dad. Having said that, I think the system picked up that my circumstances had changed slightly after I spent two hours in the first class lounge wearing shorts and a t-shirt and playing magnetic battleships with Alex.

The journey was uncomfortable, long and made longer still by delays at every stopover. The time spent with Alex, though, was simply magical. I was so proud of him. He was a wonderful companion. It didn't matter to me if we were stuck in Rome airport for a week, it was just so much fun being with my elder son. The irony wasn't lost on me. We, father and son, were travelling arm in arm to see my own father whom I had never been close to. We were going to spend the type of week together, one-on-one, that I had never had with my father as an adult, let alone as a child.

Money was getting tight, so at Heathrow we reverted to 'Tasmanian Rules' and hired the cheapest vehicle in the entire airport. It is actually quite difficult to hire the cheapest car. Whether it is because they work on commission or because they simply can't believe you don't want comfort, the Eurocar and Budget salespeople of this world challenge themselves to rent you their best vehicle. In Ford's defence, the Ka we ended up with may have had the power and comfort of a lawn-mower, but it didn't break down once and boy was it cheap.

When we arrived in Somerset, it was midnight. Mum was delighted to see us and smothered Alex in hugs. It was too late to visit the hospital, so we put Alex to bed and Mum and I shared a pot of tea while she filled me in with the details. Dad was in Frenchay Hospital, Bristol, about 40 miles away. He was extremely confused and had lost all mobility. He was also having enormous difficulty talking beyond the simplest of remarks. The specialist was attempting to find a new drug regime that would arrest the decline and bring some improvement. It was acknowledged that recovery would not be complete, if there was any improvement at all.

But none of the descriptions adequately prepared me for

the reality. Seeing my Dad the next day was simply heartrending. With respect to the NHS, the ward was like a Crimean War hospital tent. No privacy, no comforts, just two rows of iron beds with ill people in them. Alex was a lifesaver.

'Is it good in here, Granfie?' he asked cheerfully.

No answer.

'When are you going to get your knowledge back, Granfie?' he went on.

No answer.

'I'll chat to the doctor and get you a TV, Granfie. There's a *Simpsons* special on this weekend.'

No answer.

And so on. For half an hour. Apart from taking Dad to the loo twice, I was a bit player in the visit.

Walking to the car later, Alex took my hand. 'Don't be sad Daddy, Granfie's getting old.'

Beyond the sadness, it just felt so unfair. Dad had had an extremely humble upbringing. His early life was far from easy and frequently marked with tragedy. His own father died young after a long illness. Both his sisters also died young in tragic circumstances and Dad was left an only child with a mum who never recovered from the hand that life had dealt her. Dad had to spend every hour he wasn't at school or sleeping working in the pub where Nanna was a barmaid. When National Service came, Dad found it a step up, as opposed to almost all his contemporaries, who had experienced a drop in their living standards. Dad was a man with a strong sense of duty; he stayed in the Royal Navy for 32 years. Then he took a role in the United Nations. Just seven more years until he could allow himself to relax and enjoy a well earned retirement with his wife. Then, bang – this.

Kate had always clicked with Dad, saying he had such a glint in his eye and an ever-present, dry, gentle humour. He may have been light on the huggy kissy stuff to his sons, but he was a good man who had strived all his life to do the right thing, irrespective of how hard he had personally found it. Latter-day notions of chasing personal happiness would have made Dad laugh. You had to do your duty. If that made you happy, fine. If that made you miserable, fine. While this could lend him a hard edge, I had an enormous amount to thank him for. At every step of the way he was there doing his best for me. He may not have been telling me, but he was doing it, making the sacrifices, putting in the hard yards, spurning easy popularity and religiously sticking to his guns. He brought my brother and me up well. I loved him. I was miserable. It was only day one of the visit and I was all over the shop. Snap out of it, Nigel, I thought.

Chapter 49

Mrs Sargeant

THE WEEK WAS emotionally rewarding, though, as well as draining. Apart from time with Alex, I was also having the type of quality time with Mum that I'd never had before. Nine months before, I'd thought I could create this type of experience by taking her out to a fancy dinner. I realised now that most of the time important moments happen when they will, not when you decide you want them to. I cringe at all the times in the past I must have forced matters in the hope of an emotionally rewarding exchange. Then again, if you hardly spend any time with someone you haven't really got much choice but to hothouse those rare moments when you're together. Or, as the American self-help gurus say, 'You need quantity time for quality time.' On the second day, I drove

Alex over to stay with his cousins, so it was just Mum and I in the house. Time with her was as happy as visits to Dad were sad. Most days I drove Mum with me to Bristol. We'd spend the journeys reminiscing, retelling favourite family stories even though we'd told them hundreds of times before.

Mum surprised me on one trip with a story she had never told before. The story wasn't the surprise – indeed, I starred in it – it was the fact that she was telling it. You see, we'd never mentioned it once in the 30 or so years since it happened.

The setting was the terraced house in Yeovil where we lived when I was a kid. My bedroom was at the back of the house and looked over the yard between our row of houses and the row behind us. In fact, my bedroom window looked directly into the bedroom window of the couple who lived at number 17, the Sargeants. I'd been given a pair of binoculars for Christmas and, in my defence, I didn't have many things to look at. It seemed natural to rest my elbows on the window sill and look through them at Mrs Sargeant as she got dressed in the mornings.

One such morning, she looked my way and paused. She peered intently in my direction. She moved closer to her window to get a better look. She was obviously going to spot me if I didn't move soon. Problem was, I'd been brought up in a military family and one of my childhood lessons learnt at Dad's knee was that when a flare went up in the jungle you never dived for cover, as the movement would give you away. It was the people who stayed completely still even though they were momentarily bathed in light who weren't spotted. They were simply mistaken for a bush or a tree.

With this theory as my guide, I stayed still. Mrs Sargeant was now right at her window and she was looking directly at me with an outraged expression on her face. I stayed as still as a statue, hoping to be mistaken for something other than a perving adolescent. Mrs Sargeant called over her shoulder to her husband, who came running into the room. Mrs Sargeant pointed at me. Mr Sargeant recoiled in horror as he saw his neighbour's ten-year-old son staring at his naked wife through a pair of binoculars. He made a rather rude sign and mouthed something even ruder. I clung to my military theory and didn't move a muscle. Mr Sargeant left the room. I heard the phone ring and Mum pick it up. I could hear one side of the conversation

'How dare you, Mr Sargeant. My son would never do such a thing. If your wife has ugly fantasies about my boy, that's her problem, not Nigel's. I know for a fact he's upstairs doing his homework. If I were you I'd spend more time getting Brenda to stop parading naked by her window than slandering your neighbours.'

And I still didn't move. I didn't move when Mum came into my room. Or even when she stood next to me looking out the window at both Mr and Mrs Sargeant pointing back at me as I remained frozen, with my elbows resting on the sill and my eyes glued to the binoculars. So much for the bloody military. Perhaps it's not surprising I'm the only Marsh for a couple of generations who hasn't signed up.

As Mum told this story, I was surprised by my reaction. I found myself laughing. Really laughing, as if I were hearing a mate tell a funny story, not cringing while a parent revealed a shameful secret. The fact that we both knew the story in question didn't matter. It was wonderful: the harder I laughed, the harder Mum did. By the time she had finished with Mrs Sargeant, we were both giggling like teenagers. To this day I feel that moment was a permanent breakthrough in our relationship. Strange how unexpected benefits come from the least likely of events — it's almost enough to give leching a good name.

On the last day of our UK stay, I wanted to visit Dad alone, without having to worry about either Alex or Mum. Although the doctors told me his condition wasn't life-threatening, I had an awful feeling that this was going to be our last goodbye. After my usual forced cheery comments dried up, this time I didn't fall silent. Instead, I started mumbling about how much I loved him, admired him, had always looked up to him, wanted him to get better and would be thinking of him every day in Australia.

To my surprise, Dad stopped me. He raised his arm and placed a shaking hand on my wrist. He was looking me directly in the eye. He found it difficult to speak and his words were slow and faint. I leaned forward to listen.

'. . . Means so much to me that you came, Nigel . . . and that you brought that fine lad of yours . . . I'm so very proud of you . . . I always have been . . . Your mother and I adore Kate and the kids . . . It makes us so happy to hear of your progress in Australia.'

It was like a different man was talking. Dad never spoke like this. When I had told him I was getting married to Kate, he berated me for not having a good enough job. When I'd told him we were having twins, he'd asked me how on earth I thought I could afford to have so many kids. When I was promoted to my last job, he asked me if it would be in *The Times*. Having to admit it wouldn't even be in *Campaign* magazine nicely made sure I didn't get above myself.

I didn't know how to react. Or rather I did. I cried. Not

just then, but walking to the car. And in the car park. On the drive home, I had to pull over because I couldn't stop crying. Just when I'd stopped, I started all over again when I got home and Mum asked me how it went. I'm loath to admit it, but I'm crying writing this now. You look bloody silly at the traffic lights in a Ford Ka blubbing like a baby or writing in a Bronte beach café with tears pouring down your face – perhaps emotional repression isn't such a bad thing after all.

On the journey home to Australia I reflected again on the choice facing me. Whether it was this job or another, I would have to start earning again soon. If I were to go back to running an advertising agency I could think of few better than the one where this job was. They prided themselves on their integrity and thoughtfulness and besides, the founder – Leo Burnett – seemed a man after my own heart, one of his more famous quotes being, 'Advertising is somewhat less than the main purpose of human existence.' Precisely.

After six hours thrashing around in yet another hideously uncomfortable BA seat, I struck a deal with myself. I blame all those self-help books I've read. The deal was that I would write down on paper a detailed description of the type of person and boss I wanted to be. Also the type of family and company I would be proud to be a part of. I would then use this tangible commitment as a way to help me ensure that the positive changes I had undergone over the last nine months were permanent, not just forgotten as soon as I returned to the office.

Before I dealt with setting foot back in an office, I had to cope with the reactions of those around me to my *decision* to go back. For a woman who'd only months ago been made to get rid of the nanny and pack up the family and move house to a smaller place, Kate was remarkably understanding about being left to deal with it all on her own. While she didn't complain about her lot – my mother rather charmingly suggested she probably couldn't wait to get me out of the house – she did express serious concern that my life changes would prove temporary once I got properly back to work.

However, Kate's worries about my return to the workplace were easy to deal with in comparison to the reactions of others. They divided into a number of camps, the two worst being what I call the Patronisers and the Jealousites. The first group's reaction was characterised by a 'I see the boy has finally come to his senses, I told you it was just a short-term affectation' type of sentiment, while the latter group's was more along the lines of, 'You've had a year off that we never had so we secretly hope you have a really bad time now to make up for the months of freedom that we resent you for.'

Amongst such mean-spirited and gossipy reactions the response of my swimming chums was wonderfully refreshing. 'Just because you've wimped out of your sea change experiment doesn't mean you've got an excuse to wimp out of the sea,' was how one of them supportively put it as she expressed their common fear that I would stop my swimming training and, worst of all, not complete the ocean race.

Having absorbed the gamut of reactions, I wrote my 'personal contract' the day before I was to return to the office. Then I showed it to Kate. No one else has seen it. No one else will. We were both rather pleased with it.

Writing it was one thing – living it was a different matter entirely.

Chapter 50

House of pain

IT WOULD BE FAIR to say my return to the hamster wheel wasn't exactly smooth. I prepared for my first day with excitement. We hadn't had time to replace the car we'd sold and as I was still to work out how to get from Clovelly to McMahons Point, on the north shore of Sydney Harbour, by public transport in less than two hours, I had ordered a taxi. The idea was that a relaxing cab ride would give me the perfect opportunity to get my thoughts in order, as the very first thing I was to do in my new role was to address the entire company, at nine o'clock sharp.

In hindsight, and given my knowledge of Sydney taxis, I can't believe I was so stupid. The problem turned out to be different from the usual 'How do you get there?' variety. This time, the issue was a cabbie who wanted to talk. And boy could he talk. He was totally impervious to any hint I gave him that I wanted to ride in silence.

'That's fascinating. I don't like Thatcher either, but if you don't mind I've got to prepare a speech, so please don't think I'm rude if I do some work now,' I said after my fourth attempt to shut him up had failed.

'Oh. No worries, mate. I understand. Sometimes I get so busy myself that I just can't focus on anything else. Drives my missus crazy. Ha ha. Take tax return time. Do you fill out your own tax return?'

'Er yes, but I've really got . . .'

'Me too. I hate it. Always leave it to the last moment and then have to lock myself away without any distractions . . .'

And so he went on. Eventually I had to spell out that it wasn't that I didn't like him but that I didn't want to have a conversation and could he please not disturb me. Miraculously, he actually stopped talking, but instead – and here's where it all went wrong – he turned the radio on.

Now I am one of those people who can't get the last song they've heard on the radio in the morning out of their head all day. For this very reason, when I'm working I only ever listen to news radio – never music – in the mornings on a weekday. This guy clearly didn't have the same philosophy – Puerile FM started blasting out at deafening volume. My big mistake was hesitating before asking him to turn it off. I had, after all, just said I didn't want to talk to him, so I felt a bit uncomfortable telling him he couldn't listen to the radio in his own car, either. By the time this thought process had come and gone the song had already caught hold of my brain.

'You and me, baby, we ain't nothing but mammals, so let's do it like they do on the Discovery Channel. You and me, baby, we ain't nothing but mammals, so let's do it like they do on the Discovery Channel. You and me, baby, we ain't nothing but mammals, so let's do it like they do on the Discovery Channel,' blasted out of the radio.

It might have been repetitive, but it sure as hell was catchy. When I arrived at my new office I was a lost cause.

'Good morning, Mr Marsh. Welcome to Leo Burnett,' the friendly and professional receptionist said.

I heard my mouth say 'Morning' while my brain sang, 'You and me, baby, we ain't nothing but mammals, so let's do it like they do on the Discovery Channel.'

Todd was the second person to greet me. 'Hi, Nige. They are all in the boardroom waiting for you,' he said.

'You and me, baby, we ain't nothing but mammals, so let's do it like they do on the Discovery Channel,' I replied.

'What?'

'Oh, nothing – have you heard that song?'

'Yeah – catchy, isn't it?'

'I'll say.'

'Nige?'

'Yeah?'

'They are *still* all in the boardroom waiting for you,' he repeated.

'Oh. Of course. I'll be right there,' I replied. Walking up the stairs to the boardroom, I tried to focus myself, while all the while having to listen to the internal soundtrack of the mammal anthem.

It was all a bit surreal but I managed to get through the speech and the day satisfactorily. Unfortunately the rest of the week most definitely wasn't satisfactory. Think Dunkirk without the boats. In my first meeting with the firm's second-largest client, they politely informed me that they were moving to a different agency. Visions of being fit, forty-one and fired again flashed through my brain when they told me. It was my fourth day in the office and I was unprepared, to say the least. So unprepared, in fact, that I was wearing an England rugby shirt as it was the day of the opening ceremony of the Rugby World Cup, which I was attending later. (At least the Rugby went to plan – God bless you, Jonny Wilkinson.)

The moment they told me of their decision I knew it meant I would have to make redundancies. I know some executives who lose no sleep over doing this – indeed they positively relish the chance it gives them to prove their steeliness and seniority. Personally, taking away the livelihoods of colleagues is something that makes me ill. I can never quite rid myself of the notion that those who least deserve the bullet tend to get it, however hard you try to arrange matters more fairly.

Rather than a 'steady as she goes' fact-finding start, my first month was spent telling people I was retrenching them. I hate the word 'retrenching', it's almost as bad as the 'I'm going to have to involuntarily separate you from the payroll system' euphemism apparently used in certain American firms. My brother tells me the army has a slightly more robust approach to such matters, 'All those with a job take one pace forwards . . . not so fast, Dickens,' being an example he claims to have witnessed personally.

I tried to steer a middle course between British Army gallows humour and confusing American double-speak as I delivered the bad news in a series of back-to-back meetings. But certain industry commentators were more blunt. One of the better headlines from my early days back at work was 'Bloodbath at house of pain as new CEO rips guts out of once-proud agency'.

Catchy though the song in the taxi had been, I felt more like an earthworm than a mammal by the end of my first month.

Chapter 51

Low frequency

WORK WASN'T THE only cause for concern. My personal life started to fall to pieces.

For a start I didn't do the Bondi to Bronte swim. For me this was devastating, not just because it was a goal I had been working towards for nine months, but more because my attempts to reinvent myself throughout the year had somehow come to be embodied by the race. Whenever I went for a training swim or even thought of the race, it reminded me of the broader goals I was working towards beyond completing the event itself. To not even enter the race therefore made me feel that I had failed completely.

It's not that I didn't want to do the race – I desperately did. My training had gone well and after completing a few cross-Bondi-Bay swims (there and back) I knew I was ready to do it. The trouble was work. My new firm's headquarters were in America and I had to attend a conference there on the weekend of the race. Sitting in Chicago on the morning the event was taking place in Sydney, it was difficult to put things into the proper perspective. To add insult to injury, at my next doctor's check-up, she told me all my training for the race had given me 'swimmer's ear'.

'What's that?' I asked.

'It's a common condition in Australia. It means there's a build-up – like the furring of a lead pipe – in your ear canal.'

'And what does that mean?' I asked.

'Well, it impairs your hearing, I'm afraid. But luckily in your case it's only low-frequency sound that will be affected,' she reassured me.

'Oh. Good. What's included in low-frequency sound?' I asked.

'Human speech, mainly,' she replied.

Wonderful.

Beyond the race, many other areas of failure seemed to appear. A key part of my written personal contract was an agreement with Kate that every Wednesday night would be 'date night'. This was to be the evening where, irrespective of work and career pressures, I would drop everything and go out with Kate. This commitment was devised not just as an end in itself (i.e. a good night out), but it was an important means to an end as well. It would be a way of helping me keep tabs on my work/life balance, the reasoning being if I couldn't take one night a week off, then I would know I was losing the plot. Twelve weeks into the job and I hadn't been able to get away once. Not once. Twelve dates cancelled in a row. Lovely.

On top of the cancelled personal time I was soon bringing my work home and tormenting Kate with the travails of my job. Déjà vu with knobs on. I was also starting to shout at the kids again. One morning during my second week back, I actually managed to make all four of them cry before Kate woke up – a bizarre personal achievement for someone who was supposed to have changed his outlook on life in general and family in particular.

I was struggling. To top things off nicely, just when I thought things couldn't get worse I read an article in *The Sydney Morning Herald* that quoted the former CEO of Microsoft in Australia. I'd never met Daniel Petre but it was like he was warning me personally when I read his opinion on the life CEOs lead: 'They have no friends other than work; they have no relationships with their spouse; their kids don't care about them; they have no hobbies. They lead very insular, single-dimension lives and they don't have the courage to admit it.'

Sugar the pill, why don't you.

Chapter 52

Winegums

A WHOLE GENERATION OF women has long since realised that the 'you can have it all' dream was just that – a dream. This is a lesson that seems to have been lost on men so we're still trying to achieve it. There is a mountain of literature advising men on how to achieve work/life balance, and I believe that not only is this advice misguided, it is also part of the problem. Stressed executives all over the developed world now have the added stress of trying to do it all. All our striving for balance is making us less balanced, not more. The bar has been set at a completely unrealistic level. Many men try desperately hard to do it all – and then beat themselves up when they aren't home for their kids' tea. When they do finally get home, they feel like failures and deal with their frustration by being morose and shouting at the wife and kids. (Well, that's what I was doing.)

For a while in the 1990s, it was like a collective madness had taken hold. No one had the sense or guts to ask, 'If it didn't work for women in the 1980s, why on earth do we think it will work for men?' Instead, a whole host of commentators gave the message that with a few compromises, men *could* have it all. If you think some of the old *Cosmo* articles advising women to have the best of both worlds by staying in the office all night and faxing their orgasms to their husbands are funny, you should read some of the bollocks written by so-called experts about fathers. Most display a complete lack of understanding about the economic, family and business realities that 99 per cent of us have to live with. No one will admit it, but just like employers avoid employing women who seem like they might just get pregnant soon, they also don't want men who genuinely have a balanced life. They want the job done well and they know that doing something important well demands a person's full investment – when it comes down to shareholders, your marriage and the school canteen can go fuck themselves.

There are signs, however, that although the situation isn't necessarily improving, at least a more honest debate about it is starting to happen. The business magazine *Fast Company* led with a front cover splash 'Balance is Bunk!' in its October 2004 issue, with an article inside calling the idea of work/life balance fatally flawed and discussing the central myth of the modern workplace: 'The truth is, balance is bunk. It is an unattainable pipe dream, a vain artifice that offers mostly rhetorical solutions to problems of logistics and economics. The quest for balance between work and life, as we've come to think of it, isn't just a losing proposition; it's a hurtful, destructive one,' read the article.

However, the debate has also got to be honest on an individual level. There's no point me boffing on about comfortable generalities if when it comes down to it I then kid myself about my own real feelings towards the office. I have a confession – looking after four young children *isn't* always as rewarding as performing well in a business meeting. It *is* sometimes fantastic to be able to leave the domestic chores behind and go on a business trip. I *do* get a large part of my identity from my role at work. I find it enormously satisfying and motivating to be part of a group of people that is engaged in common endeavour towards a shared goal. Even when that goal is business success. No, that last sentence is dishonest: *especially* when that goal is business success. I like hard work. Nothing worthwhile is ever easy. I'm competitive and find winning a thrill – not at all costs, but I am prepared to make personal sacrifices to achieve commercial victory. I mean look at me: I didn't even last a year before I traded in arsenic hour for the business lounge.

So am I recommending all men just give up trying to lead more balanced lives? No. I'm not recommending anything. I haven't got any answers. I do, however, look at things in a different way now. I have stopped looking for perfection. Having spent my life so far seeing only black and white, I am now more comfortable with grey. Life is hard, and as far as I can see it will always be hard. The vast majority of us will *always* have to struggle – whatever lifestyle choices we make. Admitting this to myself was liberating in its own right. I then started to put my focus on trying to enjoy the struggle rather than attempting to create a mythical stress-free nirvana. I've started to praise myself for the small victories rather than beat myself up for the bigger failure of not having a perfect life.

Now every time one of the kids does or says something gorgeous, instead of descending into a pit of despair that I'm missing all the *other* gorgeous moments, I count myself lucky that I was present for that one. I'm grateful for every time I manage to drive the kids to school rather than resentful for those times that I can't. I'm basically working on the habit of counting my blessings, not whining about the challenges.

I may be struggling but the struggle is slightly more enjoyable and less damaging to those around me than it was a year ago. The contrast between the two Christmas holidays either side of my almost-year off couldn't be more dramatic. Admittedly, I didn't have to wear paper pants for the latter one but I was working just as hard, if not harder. Yet despite the work pressures I had the most magical family time.

Harry was full of surprises, as usual: on top of his list for Santa he wrote 'a big warm blankit'. When Kate asked him about this request he said he had been cold all year. Along with the problem of it being rectangular in shape, no wonder he didn't like his bed.

Eve was unbelievably proud that people kept on talking about 'Christmas Eve' which meant Grace walked around telling everyone who would listen that she was 'Christmas Grace'. One of their presents was a video of *The Sound of Music* so I spent half the time being made to whistle and then watch as the girls stood to attention shoulder to shoulder before marching around the house. (Unfortunately this didn't last.) When I asked Alex if he had had a nice Christmas he looked at me and replied, 'Dad, it was great. I'm only eight and I've already got so many good memories.' There were arguments, of course, but even they were wonderful in their own special way.

On Boxing Day, Grace came running into our bedroom in floods of tears. When we asked her what was wrong she held up her right hand so the palm was facing us and sobbed, 'I showed Eve the stop sign but she kept doing it!' She said this in a tone of stunned amazement that the 'stop sign' hadn't worked. Apparently kindy had just the other week taught them to use this technique. I bow to their superior child-rearing skills, but they are going to have to come up with something slightly more effective to stop Eve hitting her sister. When I sternly told Eve off for this 'unacceptable behaviour' her bottom lip started to quiver and she ran into our bedroom to tell Kate, 'Mummy, Daddy's hurt my feelings!' Peace was resumed a few minutes later and without warning Eve came up behind me, put her arms around my neck and whispered into my ear, 'Daddy, I love you all round the Harbour Bridge much.' Not quite sure what it meant, but it will do for me.

Encouragingly, the successes weren't just confined to Christmas. I'm still sober, not having touched a drop since April 2003. I am trim – no sixpack yet but definitely still trim. The bond with my children has been permanently improved. Harry continues to use his real name, Grace has ceased to torment me in public. I not only took Alex to a number of the rugby World Cup games, but I have also done another Lads and Dad trip – this time camping in the bush for a weekend with him and his brother. I entered and completed not one but three ocean races in 2004. I've kept up my running and even started to go for runs with Alex in the morning before work. I no longer sit in the car outside the house after work. Most importantly of all, Kate continues to put up with me.

I of course continue to be a deeply flawed executive, father and husband but I have no doubt that my year off was more than just an extended holiday – it started me on a personal journey. I have no illusions of ever arriving at a final destination but I am deeply committed to sticking with it, wherever it may lead. This may be to completely surprising places, as almost every week teaches me something wholly unexpected. A recent revelation seems a fitting point on which to bring this story to an end.

It happened while I was on a hike with my brother, Jon, and cousin Clive at a recent family reunion in the UK. We were going to be walking all day and had each agreed to bring some sweets and chocolate to keep us going. On the way to meet them I stopped at a garage to fill the car up with petrol. When I went into the shop to pay, I was delighted to notice that some bright marketing genius had finally got round to releasing red and black winegums.

Winegums were my favourite childhood sweet and to this day I still buy them when going on long car journeys or walks. Trouble was, for every packet I bought, I always had to eat ten or so sodding green, orange and yellow ones just to get to the one or two red or black ones. Now everyone knows that the best winegums are the red or black ones. No one prefers the orange, green or yellow ones. At best they are tolerated – never looked forward to or savoured. A whole pack of *just* red and black ones was almost too good to be true. It's the confectionary equivalent of your wife saying, 'I thought tonight I'd surprise you with the nurse's uniform and suspenders. Don't worry about me, I just want to do all those things you mention when you're drunk that we've not got round to doing yet.' I was so delighted with my discovery that I bought the entire stock – 17 packets, to be precise. We were definitely going to have enough energy on the walk.

Jon and Clive shared my excitement when I showed them my confectionary goldmine. But the weirdest thing happened on the walk. To start with, we munched our way through the packets with gusto. Then, after a couple of miles hiking, we all simply stopped eating them. We ate some chocolate instead or drank water. I still had 12 packets of red and black winegums in my rucksack at the end of the day, despite running out of all other snacks. The truth hit me on the drive home. The reason I used to like red and black winegums so much was *because* of the orange, green and yellow ones.

Which, I suppose, is the point. You've got to be careful what you wish for in life. It may not turn out to be as wonderful as the fantasy. With the right attitude, the bad bits aren't always that bad and indeed most of the time they are the very reason you actually enjoy the good bits. I may be struggling being back at work but I'm happy with the struggle, I'm happy with the year off and I'm happy with the year ahead. Struggle and all.

Which is not to say I wouldn't appreciate a bit more involvement on the suspenders and nurse's uniform front . . .

Acknowledgments

A NUMBER OF PEOPLE were enormously encouraging and helpful during the process of writing and publishing this book. I would like to thank:

Tara Wynne, Jude McGee, Jessica Dettmann, Benython Oldfield, Cheryl Akle, Kate Rumble, Carol Davidson, Margie Seale, Claudia and Jonathon Crow, Vickie and Miles, Paul Wilson, Bill Ford, Katie and James, Charlie Lawrence, Hugh Mackay, Justin and Jacqi, David Rollins, Miche Holdsworth, David Holtham, Ilona Levchenko, Peter Guitronich, Tom Loewy, Margaret Marsh and, of course, the tea bag beacher herself, my darling wife, Kate.

I would also like to thank everyone who worked at D'Arcy Australia and all of my colleagues at Leo Burnett Australia –

two very special groups of individuals. I feel privileged to have been a part of each team.

Lastly, my gratitude to everyone who has gone out of their way to make us feel welcome in this wonderful country. You know who you are. Your kindness has been genuinely touching.

Alcoholics Anonymous Australia can be contacted via its website, www.aa.org.au, or by looking in your local phone book for your nearest meeting.